MISSING IN
Rangoon

Also by Christopher G. Moore

Novels in the Vincent Calvino crime fiction series

Spirit House o *Asia Hand* o *Zero Hour in Phnom Penh*
Comfort Zone o *The Big Weird* o *Cold Hit*
Minor Wife o *Pattaya 24/7* o *The Risk of Infidelity Index*
Paying Back Jack o *The Corruptionist* o *9 Gold Bullets*

Other novels

A Killing Smile o *A Bewitching Smile* o *A Haunting Smile*
His Lordship's Arsenal o *Tokyo Joe* o *Red Sky Falling*
God of Darkness o *Chairs* o *Waiting for the Lady*
Gambling on Magic o *The Wisdom of Beer*

Non-fiction

Heart Talk o *The Vincent Calvino Reader's Guide*
The Cultural Detective o *Faking It in Bangkok*

Anthologies

Bangkok Noir o *Phnom Penh Noir*
The Orwell Brigade

MISSING IN

Rangoon

A VINCENT CALVINO P.I. NOVEL

CHRISTOPHER G. MOORE

Heaven Lake Press

Distributed in Thailand by:
Asia Document Bureau Ltd.
P.O. Box 1029
Nana Post Office
Bangkok 10112 Thailand
Fax: (662) 260-4578
Web site: http://www.heavenlakepress.com
email: editorial@heavenlakepress.com

Heaven Lake Press paperback edition 2013

Jacket design: K. Jiamsomboon
Author's photograph: Ralf Tooten © 2012

ISBN 978-616-7503-17-2

For Busakorn Suriyasarn

In the nightmare of the dark

All the dogs of Europe bark,

And the living nations wait,

Each sequestered in its hate;

Intellectual disgrace

Stares from every human face,

And the seas of pity lie

Locked and frozen in each eye.

In Memory of W.B. Yeats 1939

W.H. Auden

ONE

The Definition of "Spit"

EVERY TIME ALAN Osborne telephoned Calvino's office, Ratana imagined a dark, dense mass of bats, excited, purposeful in their hunger, flying like a solid black cloud from the mouth of an ancient cave. She lifted the handset, preparing herself to hear his voice as she placed a plastic lotus to mark her place in the detective novel on her desk. She hadn't decided whether to get up and go around the partition to Vincent Calvino's desk with the news. Or she could tell Osborne what he didn't want to hear.

"I will tell Vincent that you phoned, Mr. Osborne."

She waited half a beat.

"Did I ask you to tell Vincent that I phoned? I asked you to put him on the fucking phone."

"I will take your message, Mr. Osborne."

"Is he going to look for my son in Rangoon? Yes or no?"

"I will ask him to phone you."

"Tell Calvino that I want a fucking answer."

That was Osborne. Fucking phone. Fucking answer. Fucking this, fucking that—an auto-add adjective to every noun he wanted to emphasize. It was an error that Georgette Heyer would not allow in one of her detective novels, and certainly never in one of her regency romances.

Ratana hung up the phone and read a couple of pages from *Death in the Stocks*. There was something in the personality of Osborne that resembled the murder victim named Andrew Vereker. Solving the murder of a nasty, unsympathetic character required truly extraordinary writing ability.

Osborne hadn't been murdered—yet—but she did wonder how he had escaped such a fate in Thailand with his temper, cursing, disrespect and disagreeable aggressiveness. In Thai culture, Ratana knew, any transgression is ranked as a possible capital offense, depending on who is offended.

Ratana hadn't waited long before her boss summoned her.

"I need help with a Thai word!" Calvino shouted from his side of the office.

She sighed and walked around the partition.

"Osborne phoned again."

"I don't want to go to Burma," he said. "Everyone's piling in. It'll be a zoo."

"Phone him and tell him."

Calvino shrugged and repeated, "I need help with a Thai word."

"The same one?"

He nodded. She'd helped him earlier. He'd forgotten what he'd learnt.

Calvino focused on Ratana's face as she slowly rounded her lips and tongue to pronounce the correct sound for the Thai word "*thouy*." A foreign sound, he'd read, has to have lodged in a person's brain by the age of five. Otherwise, even when hearing it in slow motion, the adult brain resists. As far as Calvino could tell, Thai tones happen inside a musical registry where every note sounds the same. He marveled at the capacity of a toddler to get the tones right while sucking on an ice cube. *Thouy.* Life isn't fair, he thought. Brains age, tongues stiffen. Tonal ignorance, like all ignorance, expands over time, leaving adults in a shrinking world.

Vinny Calvino was not one to give up. He told himself he wouldn't leave the office until he'd learnt how to say "*thouy.*"

Calvino's mouth and jaws froze into the mask of a snakebite victim as he looked to his secretary for confirmation that he'd mastered the right combination of tongue, lips and jaw.

She shook her head and emitted a long sigh.

"Your lips…"

"What about my lips?"

Ratana stared at Calvino's lips before moving to his eyes.

"Your lips end a little… I don't know. Like a shuttle landing platform upside down on a space station."

John John, her boy, had a particular affection for video games. Mothers borrow their metaphors from their children's toys—or at least, this was Calvino's theory, as he tried the Thai word once again. He had picked up the Thai habit of producing a proverb or some sort of saying for just about everything that happened in life. To him it seemed that the Thais fell back on old proverbs the way that Cockney gangsters used their own slang to talk to each other around the police.

On Calvino's desk were a couple of photographs. One showed a Thai man in his mid-twenties with a puffy right eye and a swollen upper lip. Another showed a distinguished looking Thai in an official white ceremonial uniform with gold braiding and epaulets. Putting the photographs side by side, as Colonel Pratt had done, created a geometry that went by a number of non-mathematical names: yin and yang, chalk and cheese, insider and outsider.

The language difficulty that had stalled Calvino and kept him at his desk—and given Ratana, arms folded, her stern schoolteacher's face—had come in the wake of Colonel

Pratt's unannounced visit. He'd burst into the office a couple of hours earlier, sat down across from Calvino and asked if he knew the Thai expression "*thouy*," and Calvino had said with a smile, "It means to spit."

Pratt rolled his eyes. "'*Thouy*' is also slang."

Calvino shot him a hard glance. "Police lingo, you mean? Spit and polish to keep the boots mirror-like?"

"As in snitch."

Colonel Pratt removed several photographs from an envelope and laid them on Calvino's desk.

"They look happy," Calvino said.

Masterminds like these embodied well that joyful you-can't-touch-or-mess-with-me look.

"Not for long," Pratt said. "The *thouy* told us their story."

The "spit" in this case referred to the collar left alone in the interrogation room with several cops. At some point, the Spit had decided that the time had come to drop the dime on another crook. The best Thai slang, it occurred to Calvino, often hinted at a deeper story about how powerful people got the job done.

No native English speaker would ever think of the full range of metaphorical possibilities of good old spit—like using it to suggest fear, the kind of fear that overcomes a man after he spits out his own teeth and clots of blood on an interrogation room floor. This spit had mass. It made a mess on the table and the floor, but there were always cleaners for that, whereas cleaning up a mystery often proved more difficult for everyone. It usually happened only when the Spit finally coughed up the name, the identity of the mastermind, and spat it out like a bluebottle fly that had flown into his mouth.

Although that would be very important information anywhere in the world, in places like Thailand extracting the mastermind's name is always the endgame. He is the pot of gold at the end of the investigator's rainbow. Get that motherfucker, and the world will be a better place, lions will sleep with lambs, people will hug each other in the streets and sing "Kumbaya" around the campfire because the *khaya sangkom*—garbage of society—has been dumped in the gutter and flushed into the deep, dark sea.

However, before taking out the broom and shovel and getting their singing voices ready, the Thai cops always found it a good idea to run a background check on the piece of garbage. His family, where he came from, the name of his patron—the layers of insulation that might protect him from the heat when the gamma rays of the police investigation rained down. These specks of information were examined in the spit, and, like tea leaves or chicken gizzards, they told a story. The Thai variety of spit had brought Colonel Pratt to Calvino's office to tell him and his secretary, Ratana, that the following week he'd be flying to Rangoon.

Pratt pulled out the photographs of the two yin-and-yang Thai men and a third man, dressed in white shirt and longyi—one of those wraparound half-kilt, half-skirts the Burmese wore. Whatever the three were up to, it was unlikely they'd been singing "Kumbaya" around a campfire. Pratt had a drawn a bead on the criminal enterprise they ran, but he hadn't yet pulled the trigger.

The pictures the Colonel showed to Calvino told a story, one that had emerged during an interrogation. The showdown between the Spit and the cops had happened in a small room—a table and a couple of chairs and nothing else except the actual pain and fear of the interrogation, which gnawed away the Spit's fear of what his boss would do to him and his family. Pain crosses a threshold in every man. Beyond that point is pure terror, a space that closes in on him as he's caught between two tigers, one near and one far, and nowhere to jump free. The tiger in the room is always more frightening than the one outside.

The Spit fingered the three tigers in the photographs. These men carried on a business across an international border. When a man cracks, everything spills out at once—names, dates, places. The smallest details. He actually wants to talk, to cleanse himself by spitting out the bad taste along with the blood. Break the bonds that hold him together, and the man is reborn, and no one can shut him up.

"You're going to Rangoon to look for these men?" Calvino asked.

Pratt smiled. "I am going to play the saxophone. See some people. Look around. If I run into these men, well, I might have a question or two."

"Ratana said you have some kind of jazz festival."

The Colonel shook his head. "Not a festival. There's a band, and they asked if I might like to sit in with them."

"Given that you're a famous jazz saxophone player."

The Colonel ignored the jab and changed the subject.

"You told me you had a client who wanted to send you to Rangoon."

"And you thought we might go together," Calvino said.

"It crossed my mind. It's up to you."

"I haven't decided to take the case."

Calvino studied the photograph of the Burmese man.

"You'll need a few days to arrange a visa."

Pratt had it all worked out. He pulled out the Burmese visa application form, which was completed except for Calvino's signature, and put it on top of the photographs.

"Just in case you decide to go. The paperwork's under control."

"I'll let you know."

Calvino locked eyes with the Colonel, who smiled. One of those knowing silences expanded. They both knew that each time they'd traveled outside Thailand together, things had turned out in ways no one described in tourist brochures.

Ratana came into the room carrying incense sticks, yellow candles and orchids.

"You're late to meet Khun Ed," she had said to Calvino. "You'll need these."

Colonel Pratt nodded as he examined the items for a ritual to appease the spirits.

"You should help your boss with this Thai word, '*thouy*.' It's a difficult one for foreigners."

The Colonel omitted that it was even more difficult for the Thais—not to pronounce, but to think about the story behind the word. It caused a shiver and a prayer that the Lord Buddha would protect them from ever finding themselves in that situation.

The Square had never been a pretty place. Originally designed in the shape of a large horseshoe, it consisted of rows of Chinese four-story shop buildings—squat rectangular structures built for function and not designed to win awards. At last the redevelopers had found their sweet-spot price and slowly bought the horseshoe, piece by piece. The Lomesome Hawk Bar had been part of the shoe. It had been Calvino's home away from home, his makeshift office, the crossroads café where men drifted in from the oil fields, foreign wars and domestic firefights to shelter, heal up and decide on Plan B.

Calvino stepped around a pile of concrete debris and garbage as he turned toward the Lonesome Hawk—or the shell that once had been the bar. Inside he found Ed McPhail sitting at his favorite booth. The cushions were gone, the walls were bare, and the floor was cluttered with scraps of wood.

"Hey, buddy. I thought you weren't coming."

Calvino eased into the booth.

"Colonel Pratt showed up at the office."

McPhail smoked a cigarette, his eyes looking around the bar. He wasn't listening to Calvino.

"The place is a wreck," McPhail said.

"I'm thinking of going to Rangoon."

"Most of the regulars are dead. They never lived long enough to see this."

"Why don't you come along?"

"Rangoon?"

Calvino nodded. "It's opening up."

"This place is closing down."

He flicked a long ash on the floor.

"George used to sit over there and shout at the girls, 'Turn down that goddamn music!' If he'd seen the place looking like this, it would have killed him."

Calvino pulled out the candles and incense sticks.

"Give me your lighter."

"That's a good idea. A remembrance. That's what I said we should do."

Calvino walked over to the bar counter. The stools had been stripped, and the bar broken in places. Lighting the bottom of each of three candles, he stuck them on the top and then lit the wicks. He found a glass behind the bar and put the incense sticks in and lit them. He placed the orchids in front of the glass.

A moment passed.

"That's it?" asked McPhail.

The bar had been fading away for a long time. Like a terminal patient, it had grown weaker, smaller and less friendly, more foreign. George had died. Most of the regulars had died too, or drifted away. Its time had passed. No one was surprised at the end that it had rolled over and died with the rest of the Square.

"You die and then what?" asked McPhail.

Death, Calvino thought, looked a lot like one more missing person case where there's no evidence.

"I figure it's like one of those dashes," Calvino said finally, "that mark you find in a sentence linking one part with an explanation. Life on one side, and it stretches through the dash into an empty void. Remember when everyone came back after George's funeral and sat around the bar, arguing and bullshitting about death?"

"What if death isn't a dash but a period?"

"You know what I think, Ed?"

A silence fell between them as McPhail stared at the makeshift altar.

"The whole universe is connected to the end of that dash."

Rituals with candles, incense and flowers, Calvino thought, are supposed to allow people to make their peace with the destruction and the absence. But the ache of the loss is never easily appeased.

"It's time, Ed. I've got to get back to my office."

McPhail nodded, exhaling a cloud of smoke. He opened a bottle of rum and took a long drink before screwing the cap back on.

"Rangoon," he said.

"Think about it."

"You think the Lonesome Hawk might have been reincarnated in Rangoon?" said McPhail, taking another hit from the rum bottle.

Calvino laughed. "A new bar," he said, "filled with all of the old regulars, reborn in Rangoon, asking George, 'What's the special?' And Baby Cook coming out of the kitchen with her blouse hiked up over her belly, sweating and smoking a cigarette."

McPhail slid out from the booth. He walked to the bar and placed the palm of his hand over each candle, extinguishing the flames one at a time.

"I don't want to say goodbye more than once. You go to Rangoon. You find that bar. And you tell George and Gator and Bill and the rest of them that McPhail loved them. I did. You know that, Vinny."

Calvino watched him walk to the door and look back one last time.

"You've got to get back to your office," said McPhail.

They'd done what they'd come to do—perform one last small gesture. Rituals last an instant, memories a lifetime. The two things may be out of proportion, but however a man measures the difference, Calvino figured, in the grand scheme of things they aren't all that far apart. Rituals and memories have never been meant to last forever.

It was time to go. They pushed through the door with the crumbling poster for free food. They walked around the piles of rubble and into the old parking area. Calvino stopped and took a final look. McPhail kept walking.

The flow of time carries all men and all things. It had swept away the Lonesome Hawk, and the river of time would always move through the minds of men, drowning them in the past or sweeping them downstream into the future. There was a choice.

"McPhail, wait up. You really should come to Rangoon."

McPhail swung around on his heels.

"Next life, Vinny."

TWO

Pseudoephedrine Is Not an Illicit Drug

RATANA SMILED AS Calvino came back into the office. He returned the smile.

"How did it go with McPhail?" she asked.

"He doesn't want to go to Burma."

"I meant with paying respect to George and the others at the Lonesome Hawk Bar."

"They haven't got back to me."

Her eyes smiling, she said, "They will let you know."

"Any calls while I was out?"

She shrugged.

He walked into his office, removed his jacket and sat at his desk. Ratana had placed his passport, two photos and the Burmese visa form beside the keyboard. The documents were surrounded by the mouse on the left and on the right, his favorite pen for signing documents.

It was up to him. Of course it was. He sat at his desk and woke up his screen from sleep mode. There was a note in Ratana's handwriting on top of the passport: "Brad Morrisey, RIP."

She'd smiled when he'd come in, and there are layers to a Thai smile. Stacked one upon another, with no instructions on how to unpack. The note, the papers, like a jazz solo, had been in Ratana's smile. Calvino understood. She knew that he would.

Brad Morrisey had disappeared upcountry to a small village, retreating to a small room in a house on stilts, pigs and chickens and dogs running in the dirt pathways. But Brad had holed up there with a bar girl who bought him "ice," lit his pipe, watched him smoke and then asked for more money. After three days without food or sleep in his self-imposed exile from reality, he found an ATM and withdrew more money. Brad, an ex-firefighter from London, Ontario, had once put out other people's fires for a living, until he came to Thailand and used ice to torch his own life. Set the whole thing ablaze. His family had hired Calvino to bring him to Bangkok and send him back to Canada. Brad hadn't wanted to leave the village, but Calvino persuaded him to return to Bangkok for a medical checkup.

The tragedy was, Brad didn't want help. He told Calvino he wouldn't be going home to Canada. The day of his flight, Brad jumped from a sixth floor hotel on Soi 22, Sukhumvit Road. It was his third morning in Bangkok. Calvino went to the scene of the suicide that morning and saw the man he'd coaxed back from the village in Surin Province lying dead on the sidewalk in that strangely awkward sprawl of broken limbs, blood pooling.

The death of his client had happened six months ago. The family hadn't blamed Calvino. They didn't have to; he blamed himself. There hadn't been a day when he hadn't asked himself what he could have done differently. He vetted the death like a pathologist trying to unravel the mystery of cause and effect in a corpse, only to find that for a private investigator, studying the death of a client was like watching life advance by staring into the rearview mirror. The scene behind never changed. It belonged to the past, and the road ahead never allowed for a U-turn.

"Ice," Calvino learned, is a designer drug that alters the alpha waves of the mind, bringing supercharged delusions of power, confidence and strength of purpose. Brad hadn't wanted to kill himself. He'd thought he could fly. The police found one last blue pill in his jeans.

Warp-speed mind travel, tearing through the fabric of time and space before the free fall—for Brad ice created an ache of hunger to stay forever inside that headspace. The visions there changed faster than sheets in a short-time hotel. Sooner or later someone had to pay the laundry bill.

Colonel Pratt beat him to the suicide scene by twenty minutes. Ratana had phoned the Colonel to tell him what had happened. When Calvino showed up, he found Pratt near the body, talking to a uniformed police officer.

"There were half a dozen witnesses," said Colonel Pratt.

They all told the same story. Brad standing on the balcony, arms spread out, head to one side, saying he was flying home.

Six months later, there was Brad's name again on Calvino's desk, attached to his travel documents, the neatly prepared papers for a trip to Burma, in recent years officially known as Myanmar. All he had to do was sign the visa application form. When the Thais want something, Calvino thought, they are all efficiency. The Colonel clearly wanted something.

Calvino also understood that Colonel Pratt's visit wasn't an invitation to explore the psychological state of drug users. That was someone else's business. Breaking a nationwide distribution network that stretched into Burma was the goal. And getting in the way of important people's money had a high probability of blowback.

The Colonel hadn't said so, but Calvino understood why the Colonel had come to his office with the travel forms already filled out. Colonel Pratt needed someone he trusted to watch his back, but being Thai, he couldn't come out and ask directly. It was, as the Thais always say, up to him.

They had left the decision hanging in the air. The Colonel had left Calvino's office, and neither man had mentioned the downside, or whether there even was a bridge from there to a possible upside. Cases like Brad's come in pairs, Calvino thought. Rob Osborne, who had gone missing in Rangoon, was about the same age as Brad, and like Rob he was confused and fully mortgaged to ideas that owned him. People like Brad craved the experience of a rewired, hyper-stimulated brain. Brad's girlfriend saw the benefit. Enablers always did.

When Calvino had returned to the shell of the Lonesome Hawk Bar, not far from where Brad had died, he'd realized with new certainty that life is about the living. The dead are to be remembered, but the living have a larger claim on our minds and hearts. He wouldn't go to Burma because Brad had died on his watch; he'd go because the thing that had killed Brad was still circulating among the living.

It become public knowledge that, just as pseudoephedrine is embedded in ice, ice was embedded deep in underground rivers of commerce. The source of that river had become a big, ever-widening story in the *Bangkok Post* and the *New York Times*, and surfaced as dozens of blogs joined the discussion about how pillars of the establishment had networked to supply the essential ingredient found in remedies for the common cold to the hard men who ran the illegal cross-border drug cartel. Cold pills had a fleeting fifteen minutes of fame. Though the problem festered like an untreated wound, it had been one of those stories that quickly vanished from the collective mind. As quickly as the pavements dried after an afternoon monsoon rain, the news cycle returned to reporting political infighting and celebrity gossip.

This wasn't the usual drug network case. Colonel Pratt had a roster of unusual suspects—doctors, hospital administrators, pharmacists and government officials. Pretty much everyone in the chain of the health profession had been implicated. Cold pills that had been delivered to the front door of a hospital or clinic went out the back door, loaded into pickups by the people who delivered the pills to those who had set up shop across the Thai-Burmese border.

With that number of players involved, it was only a matter of time before someone noticed a game was in progress. A secret game, with the players moving huge quantities of cold pills to an end zone that had nothing to do with treating a cold. They had a nice little business, turning over a large profit.

"On February 16th," Calvino read on the screen, "a contingent of Burmese police discovered an estimated 8.7 million amphetamine tablets and guns when they raided some houses in Tachilek Township." The writer even characterized the Burmese village as being "pointed like an arrow at Thailand." Someone had missed a payment to the Burmese cops, he thought. The problem with greed, whatever the enterprise, was that it tended to show up once the accounting was done, the audit conducted, the traffic checked to see no one was cheating. Cheaters ruined things for illegal businesses as much as the legal ones. It was only a matter of time until someone noticed they'd been cheated, and if they wore a uniform and carried a gun, they had a way to do something about the cheater—as the events of February 16th had proved.

As the fallout over the cold pill scandal spread, a number of important people scrambled for shelter. The time had come to seek out a warlord for protection. The distribution network as reported had been confusing, opaque, complex, blurring the line between legal and illegal. Pseudoephedrine had left a trail through Thai hospitals, health agencies and clinics, like breadcrumbs leading to the nest of hawks. It was time to find out who had powerful friends and who didn't. Calvino's Law for operations like this: Get inside the pipeline to witness the flow of money; find out who runs the pumps and where the pipeline leads.

For years in Thailand, whenever he'd had a cold or sinus problem, Calvino had run down to the local drugstore and bought a packet of Actifed, popped out a couple of the pills, swallowed them with a glass of water, beer or whiskey, and soon he could breathe again. Then the authorities banned them from over-the-counter sales and the black market found a new money-maker.

Calvino picked up his passport and flipped through the pages filled with visa stamps. He thought of the Colonel sitting in front of him earlier that morning.

"You volunteered for the Burma assignment?" Calvino had asked.

Colonel Pratt had half-smiled. "The police department isn't a volunteer organization, Vincent."

"So I've heard."

"With what happened to Morrisey a few months ago, I thought you might be interested."

Calvino had stood up from his desk, paced behind it, looked out the window, paced again.

"What's the problem?"

"Every time we've traveled together, I recall being shot at. Phnom Penh, Saigon, New York. Sooner or later, you get unlucky."

"We had that trip to Singapore a couple of years ago. No one fired a shot."

"Singapore isn't Burma."

Colonel Pratt had smiled and nodded. "So I've heard. All I am saying is I want you to know that I'm going to

Rangoon. You mentioned a case that might take you there. I thought we might do some sightseeing."

A new case had been the second arrow to the Colonel's bow. First Brad, the dead ice junkie, and then it was only a matter of time before Pratt would mention Alan Osborne and his missing son, Rob. Calvino wasn't so much a private investigator as a triage expert brought in by families of expats to save broken hearts.

Calvino had leaned forward on his desk. "Sightseeing in a cold pill factory isn't my idea of a holiday." He'd paused and sat back in his chair. "Did the department say why they're sending you to Burma alone?"

"A delegation would be noticed. It would require official approval."

"You're going to Burma off the record."

Colonel Pratt had smiled. "The country is opening up. Everyone is going in off the record these days. It's called fact finding."

"Facts? Like beachcombing for seashells on Koh Samui?" Calvino had said. "They're kinda hard to find in this part of the world. All the facts and shells have been picked over till there are none left."

"One day when I become a famous saxophone player, you'll be glad to have gone to Rangoon with me."

"I'll be glad to be alive on that day."

Pratt had left the Burma visa application along with a UN report from its anti-narc agency. Calvino read through it. In 2009, it said, Thai authorities pulled 15.8 tons of methamphetamine pills out of circulation. It was only the tip of the iceberg. The report fingered Burma as the main source of the pills crossing borders in Southeast Asia. What it didn't say was how much was still finding its way over the border and who on the Thai side of the border was making the operation profitable for all concerned.

Calvino put the UN report down and picked up the visa application.

Ratana came into his office as he was signing the visa form. She waited until he looked up, shaking his head.

"I'm crazy to do this," he said.

"I knew you wouldn't let Colonel Pratt go to Rangoon alone," she said.

"I get to play one-man entourage to a sax player."

"Manee was worried about her husband going to Burma alone," she said.

The truth was coming out. Colonel Pratt's wife had already co-opted his secretary in the campaign to get him on the plane to Rangoon.

"And you're not worried about me?"

She shook her head, taking his passport and papers from his desk.

"Not really. You have luck. Manee said the same thing."

"What does that mean? Am I some kind of human amulet? Maybe I should buy a gold chain and hang myself around Pratt's neck."

Calvino lost any chance of resisting. He doodled on his notepad. Brad Morrisey. Rob Osborne. *And the high probability of getting shot.* There was that old ghost pain, the memory of a bullet hitting hard. Saigon and Phnom Penh. Colonel Pratt had been there. And Manee—she knew this history—still thought that Calvino came down on the side of having luck. He couldn't figure it out. After being shot a couple of times, he found it impossible to think clearly about his odds the next time around. Up to now he'd either underestimated or overweighed the chances of something bad happening, and he had no reason to think he was getting any better at assessing the odds with experience.

It was too late in life to take up playing a musical instrument. He'd have to go into Burma as a businessman. Enough of them were streaming across the border to make it easy to join the parade and disappear into the crowd of faces.

"Bring me the Osborne file," he said.

He watched her leave his office. Turning back to his computer, he clicked on iTunes and then on Colonel Pratt's debut album, the one he'd made after the Java Jazz Festival a few years earlier. He'd reinvented himself.

Ratana returned with the file. Rob, the son, was still missing in Rangoon.

"I love Colonel Pratt's saxophone," she said. "He's so talented."

As with many reinventions, the original platform remained functional underneath. The Colonel was still a cop who played the saxophone and not a saxophonist who played at being a cop.

"He's had some good audiences," said Calvino. "Burma's a tough one. Like New York, they're edgy, streetwise, hard to impress, harder to fool."

Colonel Pratt had his saxophone as shield and sword. It made going into Burma unofficially easier to pull off. And jazz and ice, like rum and coke, go together, Calvino thought. Siamese twins. Heading to Rangoon as a cop would look like an official investigation, and that would mean going through channels. There was no straight-ahead way to cold call into the hospital cold pills smuggling operation without some powerful sleeping giants sitting up, rubbing their eyes and gazing around to see who was causing all the commotion.

Pratt would play the saxophone and, between sets, sit back at a table as the flow of information—facts, names, ranks, connections and a timeline—washed through the late-night conversations. He had a back channel. That's what Calvino heard him saying between the words. All the Colonel had to do was tune in. Locating a secure back channel sometimes came from a spit. Once it was found, law enforcement would drop a saxophone player, or the equivalent, into the action to report back whether the Spit had lied to them.

Burma had a history of men who stood immune to laws. The way to bypass such an immune system was to find where these men played and relaxed. Colonel Pratt knew their game—its rules, rituals, referees, players and audience. What the Thai history books failed to teach was that there were men on the Thai side of the border playing on the same operating system. Together, they were an audience of immunity brothers, and the Colonel had a mission to hack the system. He'd have to conquer them one jazz improvisation at a time.

When a saxophone player dies and an autopsy is performed, the pathologist won't find any musical notes inside, just blood and bones and gore. But somehow these are all the things that once made the music, causing people to move their bodies and dance.

The time had come to go dancing.

THREE

Sticking Chicken Shit on a Monkey's Nose

OSBOME'S NUMBER FLASHED on Calvino's cell phone. He stared at the screen. He'd made it a practice not to give his private number to potential clients.

He had a reason or two. Actually he had a long list of reasons to keep his number private in a place like Bangkok, where clients lost track of the hour and were often hit by a sudden surge of paranoia. Calvino had felt that surge himself.

"Somebody's gonna die." Vincent Calvino, private investigator, tried to remember ever hearing this declaration pour from the sweet lying lips of a prospective client as he explained how he was asking Calvino to handle a routine assignment. The pitch was always the same—a simple missing person case that any moron could solve.

Clients seemed never to understand that when a person goes missing, there are reasons for it, and that finding those reasons is as difficult as finding a silence in a drunk's telling of his life story. Alan Osborne was no different.

When Osborne had walked through the door, pulled up a chair and asked him to take a case, Calvino remembered him looking him in the eyes and saying not, "The person I want you to get information on would as soon shoot you as look at you," but something more like, "You'll turn up my son in the first Rangoon bar you walk into." Staring back as Osborne continued, Calvino heard less comforting words inside his head: "Your presence in Rangoon will unleash a psychological firestorm like a nuke blast, and you'll feel the heat and radiation peel the skin from every square inch of your body."

Paranoia could make a listener substitute one set of words for another. Osborne's words had that effect on Calvino. Maybe Osborne's visit had come too soon after Brad Morrisey's leap from the hotel balcony. He'd been a missing person case, too.

When it came to missing-person clients, almost always a *farang* found Calvino through an Internet search (as Brad's parents in Ontario had) or else through a buddy who'd said Calvino was the best private eye in Bangkok. This more flattering route was Osborne's claim.

Calvino could remember the face of each client who'd leaned forward and with complete sincerity said, basically, "What I have in mind is so simple I'm embarrassed to ask you to take it on. Deliver a birthday card to an old flame of mine." Or, "Go through this contract and let my Thai partner know if you have any problems." Or, "My friend is coming to town and wants a bodyguard. It's just a status thing. He doesn't need protection; he needs someone who knows the ropes that he can pal around with."

Yeah, sure. Not one of those cases ever came close to being simple.

Calvino had heard all the top ten client pitches. Any other pitch was just a variation of one of them. There were no new tunes, just new people singing old tunes, not knowing they'd been sung by other *farangs* in similar situations.

The way Calvino saw it, those tunes were the background music to a movie script that played inside the *farang* mind. They thought they had it all figured out—beginning, middle and end—like a butcher with a cleaver, starting at the head of the cow and working toward the tail. Whatever the client told him at their first meeting, he'd write it down, but when he looked at it after he'd wrapped up the case, that script never looked anything like the final cut of the movie. If he'd been a film producer, he could have reduced those first meetings and assignment pitches to one line: "People— some good, some not so good—are gonna get killed, and Plan B rolls over and dies in the same muddy, diseased ditch as Plan A."

And pitch-makers always left something else out—some variation of, "Instead of seeing any money at the end of the case, you'll get treated to coffee and donuts."

Instinct whispered into Calvino's ear to remember that there was a difference between what you could expect from an old hand, as opposed to the *farang* fresh off the boat. Old hands were the most dangerous clients, he found, because it was all too easy to let his guard down. They forgot they were client and investigator and fell into an easy conversation of friends, asking about people from the old days. Those who'd died. Those who'd had moved back to wherever they'd come from. The ones in hospital, in prison or on the run. Or disappeared in some upcountry village like Brad Morrisey, going native, living like a savage, held hostage by desire and fear, head buzzing with drugs or booze. Their names sounded from an old hand's roll call of acquaintances from the past. An English writer once said the past is a foreign country. It's something else, too: a foreign cemetery, with bodies and memories and secrets buried in a common grave.

The morning Colonel Pratt strolled into his office wearing civilian clothes, Calvino had spent close to a week avoiding a decision on taking the assignment to find Alan Osborne's son, Rob.

Alan Osborne had built one of the most memorable wonders of Bangkok's nighttime entertainment scene—

the Mermaidium, a bar with a glass-walled swimming pool—and filled it with naked girls. On its opening night years ago, Sukhumvit Road had flooded with rain, which hadn't stopped Calvino, his trousers rolled up to the knees, from sloshing into the bar. By ten o'clock a dozen *yings* were diving to the bottom of the pool to retrieve coins thrown by customers from the bar. Now, except for the old hands, most *farangs* hadn't heard how the water world of the Mermaidium had revolutionized the bar scene in Nana Plaza by fashioning a Houdini, Flipper and Caligula trifecta. Osborne had gone on to commercialize the Garden of Eden as sexual fantasy into a highly successful business empire.

Osborne had been a stern, demanding father who had made his fortune in a tough business and a tough, corrupt neighborhood. Living up to such an example was never easy for a son, especially one who wanted to carve out his place in the music business. Rob played in a local jazz band, and no band was ever going to match the revenue of pimping on a mammoth scale.

"I am a pimp," said Osborne. "It's a good, solid business model with a long history of success. My son had me as a role model. I spent a small fortune on his education. I wanted him to join my business. And instead, what does he decide to do? Join a band. He's nothing more than a glorified street entertainer. No better than a busker panhandling in someone else's bar. He makes less than a bar girl during her period. People throw coins in a small box he passes around. How is it any different from throwing coins to the girls in the Mermaidium pool?"

Osborne didn't expect an answer, and Calvino didn't disappoint him.

Ratana brought him a glass of water.

"You have a little something in your desk drawer to put in this?"

Calvino leaned over, opened his bottom drawer and pulled out a bottle of Johnnie Walker Black. He opened the bottle and poured. Osborne stretched his arm forward and pressed a finger on the neck of the bottle.

"Don't be a Cheap Charlie, Calvino."

No one ever stopped mentioning to Osborne the health consequences of years of trading food and sleep for cigarettes and single-malt whiskey. It wasn't that he didn't know or hadn't been warned. He didn't care about life itself as much as he cared about good whiskey, women and cigarettes. Osborne knew that he was dying. If he found a bartender had cheated on the nightly take, he'd shrug and fire her, but with death, what was available except a shrug? She—of course death was a she—could steal his life, rob him blind as he watched her stealing, and there was nothing he could do but rail against the death goddess and finally submit to the thief no man could defeat. Osborne took a long drink from the glass of Johnnie Walker and water.

"My father was born in Burma. His family owned property in Rangoon. He knew George Orwell. The country was under British rule then. Have you read Kipling? Of course, you're an American. Americans don't read Kipling. If they did, they'd know that this 'opening up' business is all rubbish."

Sitting his glass down, he pulled out a pack of cigarettes and lit one. Calvino hadn't known about Osborne's father having a birth connection to Burma.

"My grandfather was a senior official in the colonial administration. I may be a pimp, but I come from a long line of colonial plunderers."

"He hasn't phoned? Emailed?"

Osborne shook his head and took another drink.

"The little bastard's hiding out in the old family lair. Rob has always caused me fucking problems. While you're in Rangoon, I want you to check if I still have any claim on the old family property. You were a lawyer. You can find that out, certainly."

Osborne sat across from Calvino's desk, smoking. His face was sallow, lined, the skin loose and in puddles like melted wax. Calvino had been waiting for him to raise the real reason he was interested in Burma.

"Hire a Burmese lawyer, Alan."

His eyes rolled so far as to leave, for a brief moment, two full yellowish moons in his eye sockets.

"Come on, Calvino. They're useless. No, I need you to investigate. Find him and bring him home. And find out how my father's house can be returned."

The only thing more difficult than a missing person case, Calvino thought, was an ex-colonial claim against property confiscated half a century ago. Calvino figured that Osborne knew the score, but knowing the score and accepting it were different things.

"Forget about the property."

"My son hit me. Did I tell you?"

"You told me."

"I am an old man. I never hit my father. And he could be a bastard."

"There's usually a reason," said Calvino.

"Money," said Osborne. "For his band, Monkey Nose. What kind of fucking name is that, I asked him. He hit me."

The Thais have a saying about the moment when they can no longer avoid butting heads in the same physical space. It is *khii-kai ji dang wok*, which means sticking chicken shit on a monkey's nose. The monkey is bound to take offense. It's a primate thing.

Calvino visualized father and son circling each other, each man's eyes narrowed to slits, jaws clenched, fists clutched into lobster claws as they sized each other up, waiting for

26

the one other to utter a single word—the shit on the nose—that would ignite violence.

Rob wanted his father to front the money so that he could make a video of his band. The problem with naming a band after only half of a proverb is the message may get lost along the way. And Monkey Nose had wandered for years in obscurity, playing in dives before fifty people, most of them talking and drinking, checking their email on cell phones. Obscurity was the shit on the end of an artist's nose. Alan Osborne had no problem pointing it out to his son.

Rob never got the money. He took a swing at his old man, caught him with a right hook that knocked him back in his chair. A trickle of blood ran down Osborne's mouth onto his shirt. Rob had hit a man who was dying. Osborne smiled. The punch in the face hadn't surprised him.

Calvino thought the father might have baited his son, daring him to hit him.

Osborne touched his mouth with the back of his hand, examined the smear of blood, looked up at his son and said, "Piss off. And don't bother to come around again. My funeral will be invitation only. You're not on the list. And you're cut out of my will."

Osborne had changed his will so many times as to establish prima evidence of mental incapacity to make a will.

The next day, Rob took off with the band's Burmese lead singer, who had a sexy, smoky voice and wore black stockings, high heels and velvet dresses as she belted out "Mad About the Boy." Mya Kyaw Thein was twenty-something, with a voice as hot as a boiling cauldron of honey, and a past as murky as a Bangkok *klong*. Unstable, talented, impulsive and theatrical, after the first song she owned the audience just as she owned Rob Osborne.

After the blowout with the old man, Rob and Mya Kyaw Thein had left Bangkok. No one had heard from them in six days. They'd disappeared into Rangoon. Enough time had now passed that Alan Osborne decided he wanted his son accounted for, and Vincent Calvino was the man for the job.

"It's more like an audit exercise than any demonstration of paternal affection," Osborne said.

Roughly translated, the words seemed to mean that having a loose end like Rob, his only son, his flesh and blood, disappear under the carpet in Burma, without his lifting a fatherly finger to find him, wasn't any good for his reputation. If a man didn't look after the welfare of his son, how could he be expected to look after his shareholders? These public-relations ramifications hadn't escaped the old man. Even if the father did nothing, the kid would still cost him money. Osborne wanted to cut his losses. Getting his son back had become a personal fiscal policy.

"Have you tried contacting the girlfriend?" asked Calvino.

Osborne smiled, lit a cigarette, inhaled and took a sip from his whiskey water.

"She's in Rangoon. If I had a phone number or contact, why would I be sitting here drinking your whiskey and wasting my time?"

"Hire someone in Rangoon. I wouldn't know where to start looking for him."

"If I knew someone I trusted in Rangoon, would I be sitting here drinking—"

"Okay, I get your point. Have you talked to anyone in Rob's band?"

"They're useless. They can barely find their way home at night. A bunch of cheap drunks who take drugs and live in dreamland. Just like my son."

"You don't know anything about the girl's family in Rangoon?"

"Mya Kyaw Thein. I mean, what kind of name is that for a singer? It sounds vaguely Jewish."

"I'm half-Jewish."

"Your name doesn't sound half-Jewish."

"The girl, Alan. You know someone who can give you some information?"

Osborne drained the glass.

"I know someone in Bangkok who might be able to help. Will you take the case?"

"I'll think it over and get back to you."

Osborne sighed and dragged himself out of the chair.

"What the fuck does that mean? I don't see a line of clients waiting outside your door. Take a few minutes, then tell me you'll take the case, and I'll see you receive a retainer."

Calvino watched him finish the last sip of whiskey and put the glass down a little too hard on the desk.

"We'll talk later."

Osborne wasn't the kind of man who liked to be kept waiting for an answer. The mention of money hadn't done the usual trick of accelerating the decision in his favor. It was like pulling the pin on a grenade, throwing it and then waiting as nothing happens. Calvino hadn't moved an inch. The money grenade landed like a dud.

After Osborne left in a state of advanced annoyance, Ratana waited a couple of minutes before going into Calvino's office. She found her boss behind his desk, his fingers pressed together in the form of a *wai* as he watched a gecko crawling on the wall. She could see he was deep in thought. As she came in, the lizard uttered a tiny bark of menace. She looked up at the gecko, staring at its large bright eyes that stared directly back.

"*Jingjok tak*," Ratana said.

The office lizard had squawked his verdict on Alan Osborne.

"It is a warning, Khun Winee," she said.

He'd heard the squawk, too. He studied his secretary. She had graduated with a law degree from Ramkhamhaeng University. She'd lived in England. Travel broadens some minds; others, it closes down a lane. In Ratana's case he felt it wasn't possible to slip a piece of paper between her beliefs and those of a rice farmer's daughter from Issan. Messages from house lizards weren't something she'd picked up in school or abroad.

"Since when does a *jingjok* decide who I take on as a client?"

Ratana was ready with her answer when the lizard on the opposite side of the partition hit another two-chord melody. If someone had sworn to have heard the name "Alan" in that noise, Calvino wouldn't have lifted an eyebrow.

"If you don't believe, you can't say there wasn't a warning," she said.

He had long ago accepted that his business model as a private investigator in Bangkok needed to incorporate spirit house offerings, lizard and gecko yammering, fortune tellers' predictions of auspicious days and times, and Chinese readings of faces and head shapes before any decision could be made. Adapting to crazy beliefs wasn't that difficult, Calvino had found; the day soon came when they no longer seemed crazy. That was the day Calvino started worrying about how you could ever climb back up that cliff once you'd fallen over it.

At the bottom of that cliff was a house lizard. He talked to you. The Thais have an expression: *Jingjok tak.* The house lizard has a voice, and his advice is a factor not to be ignored. It comes from an old superstition that if a person comes to the house suggesting a plan or project, and the lizard talks, the wise man understands that the cosmos is using the lizard to tell him to avoid the plan. Like the chicken shit on the monkey's nose routine, Calvino had found that house lizard yammering was a cultural message people took seriously. He'd learned that in Thailand, to survive, you needed to have a guidebook to animals and their shit.

Calvino had spent the better part of week avoiding a decision on taking Osborne's case. Osborne had been in Thailand a long time, and that Thai lizard may have known something about him that was worth considering. But now that Colonel Pratt had come around with his plans for a trip to Rangoon, Ratana was singing a different tune.

"The *jingjok* changed its mind about Khun Alan," she said. "He remained quiet after the Colonel left. It's his way of saying you should take Alan's case."

The best thing about superstitions, Calvino thought, is their vast adaptability to the changing moods of the people who believe them.

"Let me get this straight. The *jingjok* barks. Don't go to Rangoon. He doesn't bark, it means go to Rangoon."

A radiant smile crossed her face.

"That's what I tell my mother I love about you. Khun Winee understands Thai culture just like a Thai."

He'd received worse insults but couldn't think of one at that moment.

Later that afternoon a messenger arrived with a package from Alan Osborne. Calvino opened it. Inside were two books—a volume of collected essays by George Orwell and another volume containing the collected poetry of Rudyard Kipling—along with a handwritten note from Osborne. Calvino read the note: Forget about the guidebooks on Burma. Read Orwell and Kipling, and you'll understand something about Burma. It was Osborne's way of apologizing without ever saying he was sorry.

FOUR

Le Chat Noir

WITH A MISSING person case, the place to start is his friends. When someone goes off the grid, they often talk about it long before they act on it. Musicians in a band have a tight bond. It was as good a place as any to start.

Calvino stood at the entrance to a bar, studying a poster of the Monkey Nose band taped to the sliding glass door. Some design had gone into making it, drawing on Théophile Steinlen's poster for Le Chat Noir circa 1896. Around a large black cat, five members of the band smiled into the camera: Rob Osborne, Mya Kyaw Thein, and three others—two Thais and a *farang*—whom he'd come to pump for information about the missing lead singer and electric bass guitar player. The portraits were all back lighting and attitude. Mya Kyaw Thein, lips parted a few inches from a handheld mike, wore a black vest over a white T-shirt and cargo pants, her long dark hair falling to her shoulders. The men members wore T-shirts and jeans. Frozen in that youthful posture where attitude mattered as much as music, they held their instruments in the play position.

Le Chat Noir was the place where drunks, drifters, the lost, crackheads, prostitutes, smugglers, bums, poets, musicians, singers and voyeurs from the straight world went out for a night of walking on the wild side. The non-voyeurs actually lived on the wild side and slept while the other world went to their offices, desks, factories and shops.

Calvino moved through the long room. The remaining members of Monkey Nose, between sets, were in relaxation mode except for an intense, wired-up *farang* named Alf, a blues alto sax player. Alf came from Texas and hated America with the passion that only an ex-lover could nurse and sustain in its full fury year after year after the relationship had died.

"Rob had enough shit from his old man. He split. And Mya, she had the brother problem. What Asian chick doesn't have a brain-dead brother who drains the family resources?"

"What's the problem with the brother?" asked Calvino.

"Got his ass arrested in Burma for smuggling teak."

"Teak?"

"Stupid, yeah. Not opium or pills. He got caught with a truck of fucking wood. What kind of country throws people in jail for transporting wood? Burma. The whole world is clapping that the generals have seen the light. Not according to Mya and her brother. It's a jungle. One with a few less teak trees. Go figure."

"Is that why she went back to Rangoon?"

Alf nodded his head, took a long drag on his cigarette. Smoke poured out of his mouth as he answered.

"Family pressure. Rob said he tried to hit his old man up for money to pay whoever you have to pay to get out of a wood smuggling charge in Burma. But he got turned down. Rob and his old man don't get along."

"His father told me Rob wanted money to shoot a video of the band."

"Whatever."

"You're saying that really it was Mya's family problem?"

"When you play in a band with a guy and his woman all night, week after week, you pick up on things. Like who wears the pants."

"Mya calls the shots."

"Did I say that? I was talking about pants. And you know what, she has a voice that can drive a man to do and say things, promise things he couldn't imagine himself doing."

The owner of the bar walked over as the band was about to go back on stage. Alf called him over and introduced the big man to Calvino. Gung, whose name was the Thai word for shrimp, shook hands with Calvino. In his time Calvino had bought a boatload of shrimp on his tab, not to mention a trawler's worth of fish and one or two drinks. It was private eye fishing bait. This Gung drank rum and coke. A few rum and cokes would crack open the shell of most people named Shrimp. Patience was all that was needed.

"Gung," said Alf, "I was just explaining about Rob and Mya. This fella is working for Rob's old man, who wants him to drag our boy's ass back to Bangkok."

"I'm all for that. You guys sound like shit without him."

"Go blow yourself, slumdog breath."

Gung smiled.

"What is it you want to know?" he asked Calvino.

"Rob's address in Rangoon. Assuming you don't have it, then can you help me narrow down where I might find him? My first question is what made Rob and Mya take off for Rangoon? They have work here. Rob wanted to make a video of the band. Doesn't sound like a situation he'd want to leave. Second question, why haven't they contacted anyone in the band in over a week? That doesn't seem normal. They're friends. Why haven't these friends got his address and phone number in Rangoon? That's about it," said Calvino.

"You talk like someone from New York."

"I am from New York."

"Intense, man. Like a machine gun on rapid fire."

"Tell you what, after you answer my questions, you can tell me why you named the bar Le Chat Noir."

Gung scratched the reddish stubble on his chin. His rum and coke arrived in an oversized glass. He took a sip.

"I'll start with your last question since that's one I can answer without any bullshit. When you die, that's it. There is no afterlife. Zip, zero, a blank screen without snow. 'Le Chat Noir' really means to me the big blackout. Gone baby, gone," said Gung, the *luk kreung*—mixed race—owner/ manager. He was a big man with a large head who looked half-Viking, half-mongoose, born into a coiled cobra of a world. The mongoose DNA came from his Thai mother.

"Le Chat Noir was actually my second choice to name the bar."

Calvino watched Gung size him up, as if he had shrimp antenna whipping through the air around his face.

"And your first choice?" asked Calvino, who was doing his own assessment.

"Fuck Everybody," said Gung.

His eyes narrowed as he sucked on a cigarette.

"But the assholes who run 'The Big Show' wouldn't let me register it. They said you can't use 'fuck' in the name of a company. And I said, 'Truth. Isn't that a good enough reason?' But the Big Show runners, man, they just don't get it. Rob did. So did Mya Kyaw Thein."

Alf butted in: "'The Big Show' was Rob's expression. He wrote a song called 'The Big Show.'"

"Mya Kyaw Thein came up with the name," Gung added.

Alf rolled his eyes and said, "Man, in Texas, you'd be thrown on the barbecue, Gung, for telling such lies."

"Ain't a lie. She's the one who taught him what she called the Lesson. The Burmese know a thing or two about the Big Show. They get it. Only they got a different cast in Burma. But nothing's changed. It's still the uniforms who run the country on one big policy—Fuck Everybody. Now the rest of the world thinks that Burma's opening up and everything's gonna change. Bullshit. Same Big Show, different actors."

"That's what Mya said?"

Alf's Texas drawl had a little contempt in the tone.

"But she's not here, is she? This man wants information about her. I am answering his questions."

The price was a giant rum and coke.

"Yeah, you're just talking, Gung. A noise just a couple of decibels above your farting frequency. And I can't ever tell one from the other."

"Back to work, Monkey Nose."

Alf pushed off. Gung suggested that, while he took care of some owner's business, Calvino wait for him at one of the tables and chairs on the street in front of the bar, where they could hear each other better. Soon, in his new, more ear-friendly location, Calvino could hear the sound of guitars and drums blasting from the stage and through the sliding door. Then Alf's voice, singing the lyrics to "The Big Show," drifted through the Bangkok night. After a few songs, Gung joined him again.

"So... I'm looking for Alan Osborne's son."

"Rob the missing person," said Gung. "I knew he was crazy over that girl, so I'm not all that surprised he's gone MIA. She's the one who kept at him, telling him to stand up to his dad. When you work a bar for years, you know what you find out about women? They hate weakness in a man. It terrifies them, and finally it disgusts them. Burma is place of strong-willed women. Aung San Suu Kyi under lock and key for fifteen fucking years. Not a lot of men have the balls to do what she did. Mya's cut from the same sarong. She kept at Rob until he went to his old man for money. I

36

heard he hit the old fucker after he turned him down. But he might have said that just to get Mya off his back."

"Rob did punch him."

Gung smiled. He held up his glass, signaling the waitress for a refill.

"I'm a practical guy," said Calvino. "I'm looking for leads. Save the political analysis for someone who has the interest. 'The Big Show,' 'the Lesson'... I have no idea what those things mean or the time to find out. I want information that will help me find him. Nothing more complicated. Am I making myself clear?"

Gung smiled and shook his head.

"Most people don't understand," Gung said. "To find Rob, you've got to get inside his head, and that means inside Mya's head, and understand how they think. What motivated them to run off to Burma. That's the point. The Lesson for Mya meant one day she opened her eyes and realized that all her life she'd been programmed to obey and not question. Those who ran the show wrote the script, and that was what the Lesson was: stick to the script. Don't change a fucking thing."

"And she changed something?"

Gung nodded, his lower lip sticking out for a moment.

"She started posting articles on websites that were critical of the regime. She'd write shit in between sets and post it. Next thing, her brother's arrested."

"Any idea where in Rangoon I can find her?" asked Calvino. "Maybe she said something about family or friends?"

Gung had the expression of a longshoreman who'd found out that his request for overtime had been turned down.

"Mya said you gotta find the escape hatch, climb out and make a run for it," Gung said. "Otherwise you stay locked inside the incubator. You get it? Inside a cramped machine that processes the raw material of your life into money for the show runners."

Alf, palming a joint while the band was on a break, sat down at the table.

"Her brother's in jail," said Alf, "because she couldn't shut up about corruption, and that offended some people in the government. Don't know how that could ever happen. It's a huge mystery."

He took a long hit off his spliff.

"You got that right, Alf. I told her that she was too public and political," said Gung. "The generals don't like big mouths making trouble about loot and treasure."

By the end of the second liter of rum and coke, Gung had laid out Mya's creed about how the Big Show ran its global operation by selling ideas about progress, commerce and capitalism. She'd blogged using the name La Chatte Noire and given interviews naming names. A blogger whose handle referred to the name of the club where she worked was asking to be exposed. Mya was fearless, dedicated and determined. She fit the profile of a person who doomed their relatives to persecution and suffering, the Black Cat who watched from the riverbank as her kittens were drowned. Calvino had a feeling the brother never knew what had hit him or why when he'd been thrown into prison. An activist sister ran up the odds of a brother finding himself in all kinds of trouble. Boyfriend, brother, friends, family—the list of vulnerabilities that a government might use to target the pain most effectively, until the true believer questioned her faith.

A man doing ordinary things in an ordinary life made do. It rarely occurred to such people that they should revolt and refuse to live like domesticated animals, bred generation after generation, docile suckers competing for meaningless jobs, believing they could somehow slip inside the Big Show. They just wanted money to buy smokes and beer.

Gung had been right about one thing. Getting inside Mya's head was giving Calvino a better idea of Rob's behavior.

"Was the band planning a video production?"

Alf laughed. "We have half a dozen videos on YouTube."

Rob had lied to his old man about the money. It was for Mya and her brother's problem. The kind of problem that an old hand like Osborne would have dismissed out of hand as the usual scam by a family to milk money.

"Mya asked Rob to help her raise money for her brother," said Calvino.

It wasn't a question. Alf and Gung looked at each other and nodded.

"That pretty much nails it," said Alf.

Calvino smiled and took a long drink.

"She sounds like the kind of woman who gets under a man's skin."

He was getting an image of Mya Kyaw Thein as someone who'd volunteered to set fire to the big tent, and Rob had been detailed to buy the matches.

Alf sucked hard on the spliff, the tip burning hot, ashes spilling.

"You can say that again. She's a woman a man would do anything for. Take my word for it."

Gung took the spliff from Alf, inhaled, eyes hooded, and said as the smoke rolled from his lips: "She wanted Rob to be Henry Miller walking the earth—fucking whores, hungry at midnight with no money but with a fire in his belly, and figuring out how to stop the world from stepping on his shadow and capturing his soul, selling it to the devil for a weekly paycheck."

"Fuck that," Mya Kyaw Thein had said, according to Gung.

Alf had returned to the stage along with the other band members.

Over the roar of the electric guitar, Calvino leaned forward and shouted, "Does her mother live in Rangoon?"

"Man, I'd love to meet her mother. If you find her, tell her she can drink at this bar any time on my tab," said Gung.

Smoke curled out of his nostrils, which were rimmed with tiny gold rings. The world of Monkey Nose might be in fragments, but the gravity of the music gathered the pieces slowly through the night, bringing an underlying harmony.

A waitress brought Calvino a slip of paper. He opened it and read the scrawl in the dim light.

"Mya's mother sells jewelry in the market. Unsubscribe."

Calvino read the note a couple of times.

"Unsubscribe?" he muttered to himself.

He called the waitress over and asked who'd given her the note.

"Jazz," she said, pointing out the drummer on stage.

Gung had drifted off to another table with his rum and coke. Calvino stood in the doorway and watched the drummer run through one of those two-minute high-speed drum solos where sweat flies off the performer's face and into the crowd. As he finished, the drummer banged his cymbals, making a sound that, though muted, had a head-cracking quality. Calvino and the drummer nodded at each other.

In Calvino's mind there was only one question: unsubscribe from what?

Interviewing people in a bar with a band blaring always turned up a surprise or two—someone with information, biding their time before sending it down the river of tears, believing that it wouldn't make a damn bit of difference. Earlier that night the drummer, who'd sat with a woman straddling him—a woman with silver and gold looped through her ears and around her wrists and ankles, squeezing her breasts against his chest—had brushed off Calvino's questions. But Calvino's timing had been right after all. For a drummer in a band, timing is what it's all about, and apparently for this drummer "fuck everybody" didn't mean "fuck everything."

The drummer tipped his hand as another man who had succumbed to Mya's charm and found that nothing quite like it had happened to him before or since. She'd only been gone a week. Maybe she'd be back and he'd close in for another chance.

The band wanted her back. Gung wanted her back too. She was a big draw. Those left behind were as much in love with the Black Cat as Rob was.

As Calvino paid the bill, Gung came back to the table.

"Monkey Nose plays every Tuesday and Thursday night. Come back. And if you find Mya, ask her about the Big Show, the Lesson and Henry Miller. She's something else, that woman."

He didn't seem that interested in whether Calvino found Rob. Electric bass players weren't that hard to find. But a singer like Mya was. Even though a performer like that always came with baggage, packed with beliefs, emotions and the past, it didn't matter. Everyone at Le Chat Noir wanted La Chatte Noire back on stage.

There was nothing more for Calvino to ask, and he paid his bar bill. Listening to one more Monkey Nose song as he waited for his change, he thought he remembered it from somewhere. The waitress refreshed his memory.

"It's called 'When Can I Kiss You Again?'"

"Romantic," said Calvino, leaving a large tip.

"Not really. It's from Michael Brecker's *Pilgrimage*, the last album he made before he died. He wrote it for his kid, who said those words to him as he was dying of cancer."

41

She disappeared to another table with the tray bearing his tip. You get what you pay for, he thought—isn't that a Calvino's Law? He was no longer sure he remembered the thinking behind that law or whether it much mattered.

Back on the street he waited for a taxi, thinking about inviting Ratana to the bar one night. She rarely got out, and a little live music might be good for her. Then he realized that the last thing he wanted was for someone to fill Ratana's head with riffs about the Lesson in between sets. Or songs that young children inspired in dying fathers. The regulars at Le Chat Noir were the groupies, camp followers, junkies, drunks and men on the make—small-time thugs—that he'd seen around jazz clubs before. They bounced around Bangkok through the night like a bats on sonar, soaring and diving and then sheltering in the last hole in the wall before dawn broke. That was the dark crawl space where the Big Show left them to their own devices.

In the back of the cab Calvino's thoughts drifted to Henry Miller. It'd been a long time since he'd heard that name. The writer was from Brooklyn. He'd written *Tropic of Cancer*, a diary of sexual adventures, as he lived down and out in Paris in the 1930s. Miller's wife had sold her body to support him. Vinny Calvino was also from Brooklyn. He knew of the legend of the writer who had defied morality and the ties of family, marriage and home to break free—to roam the world as a free man. Some men did escape; most didn't. Who were the saddest of them all, Calvino wondered—those without a home, living free under Paris bridges? Or those who stayed behind in their old neighborhoods, trying to imagine what freedom might feel like?

The Dodgers were from Brooklyn, too. They'd all left but hadn't ever found a way to flush the Brooklyn out of their system. It sat in the back of the eyes, the back of the throat, like a tumor waiting to grow, metastasize and spread.

Waiting for the answer to the question, "When can I kiss you again?"

Who could answer such a question? At any turn of the road, Brooklyn could reappear, grab their ass and throw them back where they started, and they'd wake up like the getaway had all been a dream. That's the hold Brooklyn had on people like Henry Miller. Like everyone from Brooklyn, Calvino knew his Henry Miller, the role model who had come to the conclusion that it was better to starve in the company of neighborhood street whores in Paris than to sit around eating bagels in a deli on Decatur Street. Take your life in your hands and run out the nearest exit door—that was the message. Don't look back. Put plenty of distance between yourself and the un-free.

Calvino leaned back, watching Bangkok pass by as the taxi gathered speed—and thinking about Brooklyn. Waste of time, he thought. It was gone. He focused on Rangoon and Alan Osborne's missing son. Maybe the kid was like Henry Miller, and he just wanted to leave his equivalent of Brooklyn and forget that it ever existed. He had the woman of every man's dreams. He could play hero. It made sense. The kid might not want to be found. Why not leave him alone? So he'd lied to his old man about why he wanted the money. Who hadn't done that?

Colonel Pratt would understand his reasoning if he decided to give Rangoon a miss, thought Calvino. But he knew at the same time that Pratt wouldn't buy the premise. Sons and fathers kept in touch. It pained a father to lose a son. There was no greater loss. Well, maybe in Asia they stayed in touch. But in Brooklyn the sooner the son could escape from the old man's shadow, the better. They didn't go missing. They fled for their lives. Explaining that to someone like the Colonel was like talking to a good sleeper about what it's like to have a bad case of insomnia and have your whole life haunted by the futility of sleep.

His cell phone came to life, playing one of Colonel Pratt's saxophone riffs. The music announced the caller.

"I booked us on the afternoon flight tomorrow."

"See you at the airport."

"I'll pick you up. We'll go together."

"So I don't get lost?"

"I know where to find you."

The call ended. Calvino hadn't exactly made up his mind. Unlike Rob Osborne, he could never truly go missing. Not with the Colonel around. No one cares about explanations when they really need you. Good reasons for not going to Rangoon had never been in the cards. Le Chat Noir had given him a reason to believe he could find the two young musicians. They'd got it into their heads that the time was right to escape from the Big Show and at the same time rescue the wood-stealing brother. Rob might be caught up in some political drama that he couldn't get out of. Maybe, like Mya's brother, he was being held against his will. That tiny space of doubt was enough for Calvino as the taxi pulled into the entrance of his condo. Why not help Alan Osborne find his son?

He was on his way to Rangoon in any event.

After all, that's what Calvino did for a living. A Brooklyn boy grown old in Bangkok, living for years off the money people paid him to find someone who had no desire to be found. He had a long career of finding people on the run from the Big Show. Men and women who had no idea how to vanish and leave no trace behind. Unless the disappearing act had been years earlier, he just about always found that they'd left a trail of breadcrumbs. Follow the crumbs and you'd find the bird perched in a tree, thinking he was invisible but standing out like a hooker in a miniskirt skating for the New York Rangers.

But he'd never found a Henry Miller. There was a reason for that; no one but Miller's wife had ever gone looking for him, and she knew exactly where to look. Rangoon wasn't Paris. And this wasn't the 1930s. But he told himself that a Burmese who'd left such a big mark on Le Chat Noir and who channeled Miller was worth the price of a ticket to Rangoon.

He liked the idea that a search for Rob Osborne would lead him to the woman he had watched in a YouTube video on his iPhone. She had the look of a black cat, back arched, eyes intensely focused and nails extended. He paid the taxi fare, got out and walked to the entrance of his building.

Tomorrow afternoon he'd be on a plane. It all boiled down to the simplest of mixed obligations and desires—watch the Colonel's back and somehow, at the same time, look for the Black Cat and Osborne's missing son, who Calvino hoped would be found within walking distance of her litter box.

FIVE

The Traveler's Fish Lunch

RANGOON, HOTEL LOBBY.   Calvino checked his watch. Jack Saxon was running late for their appointment.

Calvino sat on a designer rattan couch with soft white cushions. One cushion closer to the door, Colonel Pratt watched as the doorman scanned the people entering and exiting the lobby. Like airport departure lounges, hotel lobbies are usually filled with bags on carts, porters and security personnel. But no one at an airport gate had ever brought Calvino a tall, smooth green drink with a tiny bamboo umbrella on a tray. He took the glass by the stem and raised it in a toast to the Colonel.

"Welcome to Rangoon," said the young pretty woman from the front desk.

"I thought we already had our welcoming drink," said Pratt.

"I'm not complaining," said Calvino.

"Mr. Jack says he's on his way," she said. "He asked me to bring you a real drink."

Calvino sniffed the drink. Whiskey fired through his nostrils like a slug from a .50 caliber round. Saxon knew his alcohol. He smiled, thinking how Saxon had had the hotel fill the glass half-full of whiskey as a kind of atonement for running late.

Running thirty minutes late, to be precise, for their lunch appointment. He'd sent a text message to Calvino saying that a breaking news story about the British government dropping sanctions had delayed him. Jack Saxon had made a reputation for walking the constantly shifting line of what could be reported in the *Rangoon Times*, one of those frontier English-language dailies that struggled to keep from being shut down.

Saxon had lived and worked in Phnom Penh for half a dozen years. Before that he'd been a reporter in Bangkok, and before that he'd worked as a copy editor in Toronto for an arts and living magazine. An old hand with local knowledge and the kinds of contacts that only journalists and politicians accumulated, to Calvino he was worth his weight in gold. Calvino knew Saxon from his Bangkok days. They'd gone out drinking together and shared a few meals, laughs, stories and women. Two years ago, Calvino had got one of those early-morning distress calls for help. It was from Jack Saxon. His younger brother, Paul, had left Soi Cowboy, got turned around and found himself lost on a dark *soi*. A disoriented *farang* at one in the morning who looks like he doesn't belong or know where he's going is a target.

"Jack has never forgotten what you did for his brother," Calvino said to Pratt.

"He was your friend. I helped him. It wasn't much."

That wasn't strictly true. What Colonel Pratt had done was rescue Paul's ass from a five-year stretch eating red rice and sleeping in shifts along with forty other prisoners in a Thai prison cell. Five years would have been on the light side, but to keep the story simple, five years was the number that Calvino had used on the phone to remind Saxon how helpful the Colonel had been.

Events had happened faster that night than shifts at a Patpong short-time. Paul Saxon had gone through a few beers, left the last bar and walked down a small side street, alone, lost and not used to the heat, when two cops pulled up on a motorcycle. They got off and called Paul over. They searched him. One cop stuck his hand inside Paul's front pocket, staring him in the eye, a little smile crossing his face as he withdrew the clenched hand. As his fist opened, he revealed a couple of pills. He showed the pills to the other cop. He'd been in the wrong place at the wrong time—the definition of a setup. Paul refused to pay the cops twenty thousand baht, about six hundred dollars, to cut him lose. It was Paul's first trip to Bangkok. He was meeting his brother, who was flying in from Rangoon. He didn't understand how to read the situation. Nor had anyone briefed him on the business aspect that came from being ambushed on a dark *soi* with no one around. He called his brother's hotel from the police station. Jack Saxon got Calvino out of bed at three in the morning. At eight o'clock that morning, Colonel Pratt came to the lockup where Paul was being held and talked to a couple of people behind a closed door.

The Colonel paid forty thousand baht out of his own pocket. He said it was from the *farang*. Calvino found out about Colonel Pratt's payment only later, and indirectly. Manee, the Colonel's wife, told Ratana, and later as the conga line reached his office, he found out. By then there wasn't much Calvino could do about getting the forty thousand baht returned. Paul had gone back to the hotel, packed his case and booked a flight to Toronto the same day. Jack Saxon had flown back to Rangoon before Calvino could explain the situation. Calvino gave the money to Pratt in an envelope. Pratt left the envelope on Calvino's desk. For a week the envelope passed back and forth between the two of them, until finally Calvino sent it to Father Andrew in the Klong Toey slums as money to help street kids get out of jail.

Paul had had a short first visit to the Land of Smiles, as the lady in the tourist brochure had characterized it with her "I no bullshit you" smile. Can't imagine why he's never come back, thought Calvino. Two feet of snow in the streets of Toronto would seem like nothing in the life-is-a-bitch department after a few hours in a Bangkok police lockup.

Forty-eight hours after his run-in with the law, with Pratt's help, the brother had boarded a plane to Toronto. All happy tourists in Asia have the same experience; they are invisible in the way that anonymous people are everywhere. The unhappy ones—young men like Paul Saxon, who've found themselves boxed into a corner—those are the ones whose stories crossed Calvino's desk.

"Jack's on the way," said Calvino. "He said to tell the Colonel that he's sorry to keep him waiting."

Two women in the lobby had been distracting Colonel Pratt. As the minutes passed, Saxon's delay had hardly registered as he watched them. He glanced at Calvino and smiled.

"Relax, Vincent. We have all the time we need."

Colonel Pratt had slipped into Thai time, the flow metered by mood rather than established increments. A place where no one counted off the seconds and minutes, and the presence of the two women gesturing and carrying on nearby made for a small, enveloping drama.

Shakespeare quotations ran through Colonel Pratt's head like cherries, apples and oranges on a slot machine.

"'Wine loved I deeply, dice dearly.' *King Lear.*"

It was as if two of King Lear's daughters had inherited their father's rage gene. The two Italian women sat on large rattan chairs with scallop-shell-shaped backs. One appeared to be in her mid-thirties, the other possibility a decade older. Maybe sisters. They wore silk scarves around their necks, necklaces of gold, fine jewelry on their fingers and expensive

Italian shoes. Designer handbags sat atop travel bags with airline handling tickets still attached to the handles. Calvino spotted the word "Roma" on one tag. Already in the lobby when he and Pratt had sat on the couch, they'd been in the middle of a deep, highly emotional conversation with an assistant manager of the hotel, with two guests speaking Italian and gesturing like maestros warming up an orchestra. Just as the two women approached the high-pitched climax of *Cio-Cio San!* from *Madama Butterfly*, the tension in their voices hit the ramp, flying up to the next level of anxiety and hostility.

"We travel more than twenty hours. You say our room is ready. It's not ready. We book a room with a view of the Shwedagon Pagoda. You say you not have. We can't wait. We need to sleep. Now! Do you hear me?"

She looked pale beneath her econ seat hair—matted, and stringy at the split ends.

Everyone in the lobby heard her hysterical outburst—half-wail, half-blowtorch. As she rose to her feet, holding up her hands like a boxer, Calvino tried not to laugh. The assistant manager remained cool, smiling—understandably, as he'd probably been through a lot worse when dealing with the police, military, officials… Anyone powerful enough to kick him in the balls.

They eyed each other, the assistant manager calmly keeping his hands at his sides. His only chance with a woman ablaze on a high-octane slurry of jetlag, frustration, language problems, broken promises and culture shock was to play defense. Would the confrontation turn physical? Or would a miracle suddenly calm her nerves? Calvino saw how close she was to taking a swing. She was so tired it would have been easy for the assistant manager to duck out of the way, but it seemed to Calvino that her awareness of this was making her even more frustrated and angry.

"Think I ought to help?" he asked Colonel Pratt.

"They will find a compromise," the Colonel replied.

Calvino figured Pratt was right. He only had to recall Calvino's Law on gentlemanly intervention in Southeast Asia—never get between people who are spoiling for a fight unless you want your blood on the floor. He watched the women as Colonel Pratt watched the door.

Jack Saxon bounced in with his hand outstretched as he approached Colonel Pratt on the couch.

"Welcome to Rangoon, Colonel Pratt! You got my message?"

"Vincent said you had a slight problem."

"I don't know what causes a newspaper more problems: shootings in the streets or streets filled with people looking to find gold and get rich."

"Jack, you look like you've been sleeping in a pothole," said Calvino.

"Nah, that's no good for my back."

Saxon moved his shoulders forward and then stretched them back, making a bone-cracking sound with his spine. He did a couple of side turns, shifting his body in one direction and then back in the other.

"Excuse me, gentlemen," he said.

Saxon walked past Calvino and the Colonel and stood between the assistant manager and the two Italian women. He kissed the younger of the two on both cheeks and saw the kiss hadn't changed her attitude.

"Bianca, you don't look so happy."

Bianca explained their problem with the room booking. Saxon whispered something in the assistant manager's ear. He turned and left. A moment later, the assistant manager emerged from his office and the women were upgraded to a suite with a view of the Shwedagon.

Saxon's little performance impressed Calvino and the Colonel. In a few moments he'd cut through the runaround and fixed the problem. Saxon then introduced the private

51

eye and the Colonel—as he referred to them—to the women.

"This is Bianca Conti and her friend Anne Russo."

Calvino locked eyes with Bianca just that fraction of a moment to establish a connection.

"*Bella donna*," said Calvino.

She smiled for the first time in the lobby.

"A private eye with a Brooklyn accent, yes?"

Then the women vanished behind a bellhop. Bianca looked back as they turned the corner. She nodded at Calvino.

"Nice demonstration of home turf fixer. Nothing like it when you need a hotel room," said Calvino. "It's the other stuff that gets difficult."

Saxon playfully cuffed Calvino on the shoulder. He'd expected a couple more points from Calvino but settled for the half-star for getting the Italians a room and a full star for the introduction to the good-looking one.

"My brother still tells everyone how the Colonel and you saved him from starring in the Thai version of *Midnight Express*."

"Who's Bianca?" Calvino asked.

"You came to Rangoon to ask about Bianca?" asked Saxon with a crooked smile, shaking his head. "What? You don't get enough action in Bangkok?"

He gave Calvino a playful punch on the shoulder and they embraced for a moment.

"Good to have you in Rangoon. Sorry I was running late." He shook his head and added, "Women, who can understand them?"

Colonel Pratt, standing beside Calvino, chipped in: "Shakespeare once wrote that 'Women speak two languages—one of which is verbal.' Men speak three languages—one of which is silence."

"Shakespeare said men have three languages?" asked Saxon. "Learn something every day."

"Actually, I said that," said the Colonel.

"You might pass that along to your brother, Jack."

Silence was that third language that the spit had to be taught to forget. It didn't take a Shakespearian scholar to tutor a man in detention in the fine art of snitching.

"Paul has never talked about what happened," Saxon said.

Paul had escaped into silence. He'd beat the system. He'd got away, never having been truly tested in a cell where silence no longer a remained virtue. Paul got away without understanding how lucky he was—that most men trapped in the Thai legal system lacked the right connections to get out. Abandoned inside a prison cell, these men waited thinking about their choice of either 'justice' or a deal. The call of freedom drove a man to spit for the deal.

The three men walked from the hotel across the road to a Thai restaurant in a gravel parking lot next to a small lake. The waiter showed them to a big table overlooking the gardens and tropical trees. Colonel Pratt took a menu, put on his reading glasses and looked down the column of photographs next to each item on the menu. He ordered noodles and pork. Calvino pointed at the picture of pad Thai, and Saxon ordered a big plate of boiled shrimp, fish cakes and fried fish cooked in lemongrass, rice and Chinese mushrooms. Saxon had the old journalist's habit of ordering half the menu.

"Hungry?" asked Calvino.

"Starving," said Saxon.

After the waiter took their order, Saxon pulled a notebook from his backpack and thumbed through the pages. He stopped and looked up.

"Jack, next time introduce us by our names. Not 'This is a private eye and that's a colonel,'" said Calvino.

Saxon smiled, raising one eyebrow.

"The first thing you learn in a secretive society is there are no secrets. It's a paradox. The people you don't want to know here will already know who you are. The people who couldn't care less will remember they met a private eye and a colonel in Rangoon. Something exotic to talk about over dinner when they go home."

"They were foreigners. What they say over dinner in Italy doesn't worry me. But there were other people in the hotel lobby," said Calvino, "and that worries me."

Colonel Pratt nodded. "It's a delicate situation," he said.

Saxon pretended to zip shut his mouth and throw away the key.

"Okay, from now on it's Vinny and Pratt. My two buddies from Bangkok."

Calvino suspected it was already too late, but he appreciated Saxon's pledge to rein in his song and dance for future introductions.

"Better," said Calvino.

"Now that that's out of way... the first person Colonel Pratt will meet is Yadanar Khin."

"Who is his father?" asked Colonel Pratt.

Saxon liked that about the Thais. They always knew the right question to ask.

"Yadanar Khin is U Htun's son. U Htun has the rank of general and runs the health ministry. The son sits on a couple of boards of directors. Twenty-seven years old, educated in England, likes imported sports cars and French wine, plays keyboard in a local band, beds beautiful women by the water buffalo wagonload."

"He goes for the low-end market?" asked Calvino.

"Low-end, high-end… An equal opportunity playboy in a buyer's market," said Saxon, smiling.

He flipped through his notebook and ran a finger down the page.

"Tomorrow morning. I'll pick you up at the hotel, Calvino."

"Where are we going?"

"On the trail of the Black Cat and your missing man. The Rangoon Running Club has a weekly run, 10K. I'll introduce you to some people who might have some information. You can run and talk, right?"

Calvino and Colonel Pratt exchanged a look.

"Ten kilometers?" asked Calvino.

"Don't think you can do it?"

"Depends who I'm chasing or who's chasing me."

Saxon smiled. "We can deal with that tomorrow. Swamp Bitch has it all set up."

The Colonel raised an eyebrow.

"It's her running club handle," Saxon explained. "Mine is Pistol Penis. It's a tradition."

A wiry grin crossed Saxon's face.

"Swamp Bitch is a translator. Be nice to her, Vinny. She might be able to find a way for you to attend the trial of Mya Kyaw Thein's brother, Wai Wan."

Saxon registered the slight wince on Calvino's face. He wrote the name down on one of the back pages of his notebook, tore the page out and gave it to Calvino.

Calvino studied the name. He showed it to Colonel Pratt. Under Wai Wan's name Saxon had written, "Yadanar Khin, son of U Htun," an address and a phone number.

"And does Swamp Bitch have another name?" asked Colonel Pratt.

"Ohn Myint."

"You'll get used to the names," said Saxon. "The weird thing about Burmese names is how confusing they are for outsiders. The Burmese don't have family names like in the West. It makes it almost impossible to tell who's related to who. It's like a secret naming society. If you're not a member, you can't follow the membership roster. It confused the hell out of the British when they ran the place. They were always hanging the wrong person. But it's not that difficult to get a feel for. After a few years here, if you pay attention, the names start to sound normal."

"Anything I should know about Yadanar Khin? "

"His mother is Daw Kyaw. If she had a running club name, it would be Fire Dragon Bitch. She is said to have an encyclopedic knowledge of poisons. The rumor is that she used it to clear away her husband's enemies. I let the word drift Yadanar's way that Colonel Pratt is a famous saxophone player and if invited might jam with his band."

The Colonel nodded. "That explains the email I received this morning."

It was the first time Calvino had heard of the email.

"Did he invite you to play with his band?"

"He asked if I'd brought my saxophone. I told him that I had."

Pratt always traveled with his saxophone.

It seemed that even before lunch had arrived, Saxon had squared everything, including getting him a pass to the Black Cat's brother's trial.

"I can't promise a Get out of Jail Free card," said Saxon. "I'm afraid that's a tough one to deliver."

The table fell into silence. Saxon was thinking of his brother in Toronto. Colonel Pratt was wondering whether the invitation to play had really come from Saxon's efforts or another source. Calvino, on the other hand, sat staring at his hands as he thought about running beside Swamp Bitch and tried to guess which part of his body would start screaming first on the 10K run.

A few minutes later Saxon had finished his pile of boiled shrimp and pushed back his plate.

"When I first arrived in Rangoon, an editor at the newspaper gave me a small book of proverbs. He marked one that he said I should pay particular attention to. Calvino, before you go to the courthouse, you might have a look at some old Burmese proverbs. Truth is often found in simple stories."

Reaching into his backpack, he pulled out the book and slid it across the table to Calvino.

"The book has sentimental value. Before you return to Bangkok, I'd like you to return it. I marked the one I like the best. Good luck finding Rob. Find Mya Kyaw Thein, and that'll be where you'll find him."

As Calvino examined the book, Saxon turned to the Colonel.

"Colonel Pratt, I never did get a chance to thank you properly for what you did for my brother. You need anything while you're in Rangoon, let me know."

"Do you know the 50th Street Bar?" asked Colonel Pratt. "I'll be sitting in with Yadanar Khin's band. I hope you'll come along."

A smile started on the right side of Saxon's face and rippled like a racing river until his whole face lit up.

"I play pool at the 50th Street Bar. I've heard Yadanar Khin's band a couple of times. They're not too bad. But Yadanar Khin takes after his dragon lady mother, and that's not a particularly good genetic history to follow."

"What's the name of the band?" asked Calvino.

For some reason the Colonel hadn't asked, or if he knew, he hadn't mentioned it.

"Night Raiders."

Sitting on the balcony of his hotel room, Calvino opened the book Jack Saxon had given him at lunch and took out the bookmark. The secondhand book, old and discolored with a fragile spine, opened to the story that Saxon apparently wanted him to read. Calvino began reading as he eased himself into the chair. The plan had been to meet Pratt in the lobby in half an hour.

It was a Burmese proverb about a weary traveler who stops along the road to eat his lunch. The traveler is a poor man, and his meal is a meager helping of rice and vegetables. Nearby a food vendor is selling fried fish and fish cakes.

Calvino noticed that the food in the proverb was the same that Saxon had ordered.

The stall owner watches the traveler eating as she fries fish over a small grill. The smell of the fish drifts toward the traveler, who squats alone on the side of the road, lost in his own thoughts.

As the traveler finishes his meal and is about to leave, the woman from the food stall looks up from her fish frying and shouts at him, stopping him in his tracks.

"You owe me a silver quarter for the price of one fried fish."

"But madam, I did not eat one of your fried fish."

"You are a cheater," she replies. "A person who takes without paying for what he takes."

"But, madam, I've taken nothing from you. I have not come within five feet of your stall."

"Ha! And you're a liar to boot. I have many witnesses who will testify that they saw you enjoying the smell of my fried fish as you ate your meal. You would not have been able to eat that disgusting mush of rice and vegetables without taking in the sweet aroma of my fish frying. So pay me the silver quarter and don't make any more trouble for yourself."

The confrontation soon draws a crowd. The fish seller plays to the onlookers, who have to agree that indeed the traveler availed himself of the smell of the fish frying. Even the traveler can't deny that he smelled it as he ate. But he insists that he has no duty to pay for that privilege.

The matter is taken to a royal judge, who hears the evidence. The judge deliberates on the matter in a courthouse nestled under the shade of a coconut tree, with chickens pecking for grain along the road nearby. Several minutes pass before he announces his verdict to the parties and the crowd who have accompanied them to the court.

The judge finds that the basic facts aren't in dispute. The traveler's enjoyment of his meal was indeed enhanced by the pleasant smell of the fish frying. He received a benefit. But what is the value of that benefit? The fish seller says the price for a plate of fish is a silver quarter. The judge orders the parties to leave the courthouse and to walk out into the sun. He tells the traveler to hold out a silver quarter in the sunlight so that the fish vendor can grasp its shadow. The judge reasons that if a plate of fish costs one silver quarter, then the exchange value for the smell of the fish must be the shadow of a quarter.

Calvino set the book down and stretched back in his chair. Saxon was sending him a message. First through the food he ordered, then through the story of the peasant who gets into trouble over fried fish he hasn't ordered or eaten. Like open secrets in a secretive society, the message was another paradox.

He looked out at the unbroken forest of trees between his hotel and the Shwedagon Pagoda, the gold-domed top catching the late afternoon sun, casting shadows over the treetops in the distance. Burma was a place of shadows, where hungry men squatted along the road, smelling the fish, while the cooks patiently waited to make their play.

The Black Cat's brother might have been that man on the roadside, caught smelling the cooking fish. His sister was politically active. He figured the Black Cat thought her brother's case had the smell of fish.

She had impressed Gung, the owner of Le Chat Noir, with her views about the Lesson. Maybe she'd been talking about Burmese proverbs, like the one about the poor man and the fish vendor, all along.

SIX

The Rangoon Running Club

A TAXI BEARING Calvino, Colonel Pratt and Jack Saxon pulled to a stop in front of the Traveler's Hotel. They got out and walked toward a couple of dozen people—foreigners and Burmese—dressed in running shorts and shoes, some doing stretching exercises, others clumped in small groups, leaning against SUVs, gossiping and laughing.

Half of the runners looked like old hands in their heavily washed official Rangoon Running Club T-shirts. More than half of them were women. Most of the crowd looked like fit thirties or early forties fighting a rearguard battle against their fifties, clawing back their youth. Saxon didn't exactly fit in. He was older than the others, and he dressed for the occasion with a hill tribe band around his forehead, an earring in his right ear and a silver band around his left wrist, each little pinky nail painted red and big toenails painted green. Some would say he'd gone native. Others thought Saxon was playing out his rebellion against the conformity of a London, Ontario upbringing. Everyone agreed that no one had ever seen hill tribe members who dressed like Jack Saxon. He had his own style, his Pistol Penis identity gear.

Calvino wondered which one was Ohn Myint.

"You never told me how the Colonel and you got Paul out of that mess," Saxon said to Calvino. "He must have some pull inside the department with the big guys. Or the cops are more honest than their reputation."

"Multiple interpretations are what reporters do," said Calvino.

"Funny about that. Paul told me the Colonel paid forty thousand baht, saying it came from me," said Saxon, looking at both Pratt and Calvino.

"Why would Pratt do that?" asked Calvino with his best poker face, covering a losing hand.

Saxon rolled his eyes. "It's a question mark. A puzzle, a mystery."

"One of those unsolved mysteries from the days when most mysteries were never solved," said Colonel Pratt.

"I remember those days," said Saxon. "I miss those days. Anyway, I'd like to pay back the forty thousand."

"Tell your brother not to believe everything he hears," said Colonel Pratt.

Saxon slowly rolled his jaw back and forth, front teeth biting his bottom lip.

"I'd offer the same advice here."

Calvino wore a pair of baggy blue shorts and a T-shirt that said "New York Mets." Saxon led the way through the crowd of runners. A couple of buzz-shaved black youths, no more than twenty years old, were doing warm-up. They were the only ones warming up, and the only ones who looked like they didn't need to. If they'd had "US Embassy Marines" tattooed on those shaved heads, they couldn't have been any easier to spot. The two men shared that combat-trained stare—wary, catlike watchfulness that was really a studied, fully situational evaluation of the opponent's capability—all of it concentrated into a sniper's squinted eye as they surveyed the other runners.

"Those are the winners," said Saxon. "They win today, they're barred from winning for a month. It's hard enough to run 10K with the slight hope you might win, but with these two Americans running, no one else has a chance."

Saxon walked up to one them.

"That's right, isn't it, Randy? You guys never let us win."

"Hey, man, stop bitching. You got it in you. Don't give up on yourself," said the young marine he'd called Randy.

"Yeah, right. This is my friend Vincent. Another Yank. And Pratt, who's Thai."

"Where in the States are you from, man?" the other man asked Calvino, smiling and then sticking out his hand. "Roosevelt's my name."

"Roosevelt, I'm from Brooklyn. Like Henry Miller."

"Henry who?" asked Randy.

"Fool," said Roosevelt, nudging Randy in the ribcage, "the guy who played ball for the Louisville Cardinals. You know, the guy that scored the big overtime touchdown against Florida State in 2002. I was just a kid, but I remember that game."

"Henry Miller… Yeah, the guy who made the big upset. Whatever happened to him?"

"Big upset win and then forgotten. Time does that. Doesn't seem fair," said Calvino. "My friend is a saxophone player."

Pratt smiled and nodded. "I do my best."

The two young men looked Pratt up and down.

"Man, you don't look nothing like a saxophone player," said Randy.

"He plays just like Miles Davis," said Calvino, winking.

"Man, you gotta be joking. Come on, Roosevelt, we ain't finished warming up."

Saxon blocked Roosevelt's path.

"Either of you superstar athletes seen Ohn Myint?"

"Swamp Bitch?" said Roosevelt.

They both smiled at her running club name.

"She's the heart and soul of the club, why we keep on coming back. Ain't that right, Randy?"

"For Swamp Bitch. No one gonna forget her like they forgot Henry Miller," said Randy. "She looks the part."

"Man, she'll take you apart is what you mean," said Roosevelt.

Randy stepped out into the road and pointed fifty meters ahead. A Burmese woman with glasses and flat shoulder-length black hair tied with a blue band into a ponytail, dressed in shorts and white running shoes, stood with her hands on her hips, talking to three men also dressed in running gear. Ohn Myint held court, arms folded, a bottle of water tucked against her chest. Saxon waved at her, and when she didn't respond, he called her name.

"Ohn Myint," he said as they approached, "this is my friend Vincent I told you about."

"What did you tell her?" asked Calvino out of the corner of his mouth.

"Don't worry. Not the truth. I wouldn't want Swamp Pussy to get scared and take off before the race started."

"And this is Vincent's friend, Pratt, a jazz musician from Bangkok."

She offered her hand to Pratt, who shook it.

"I love jazz," she said.

The runners standing in a circle around her turned out to be an oil and gas industry expat, an official from the British embassy and a Burmese businessman whom everyone respected and loved—he'd arranged for the beer truck that would be waiting to sell beer at the end of the 10K run. They looked like men who wore suits and ties all week long but on the weekend changed into schoolboy gym clothes that revealed that they no longer had schoolboy bodies.

One person in the group would take a drink from a plastic bottle of water and hand it to the runner next to him. Hands on hips, squinting at the sun, they shared not just a collective bottle but a shared belief that running once a week would forestall old age. Giving themselves rude schoolboy names, they weren't running to stay fit; they were running against time itself, in a run no one ever won.

Sometimes on a warm, sunny morning like this, a man in such a running group would just keep on running, never looking behind him, and sail toward the horizon, not really knowing why but knowing he wasn't ever going back. Calvino had found one or two missing persons who fit that profile.

He looked at the sky and the bamboo along the road. Birds were singing in the trees, fish swimming in the ponds. The shadow of the thick bamboo sheltered them with a half coin's worth of intoxicatingly fresh air. A couple of the runners stretched their legs. Several young women—schoolteachers, NGOs and an embassy official—wore fresh-pressed shorts and tops and new running shoes. They huddled beside a Land Rover, arms crossed, and talked among themselves.

"Perfect weather," said Saxon.

"I was thinking the same thing," said Calvino.

"You need a name. It's a tradition."

Saxon eyed him for a moment.

"'Kiss My Trash' comes to mind."

Colonel Pratt laughed as Calvino flinched.

"Do I have a choice?"

Saxon shook his head. "'Crack Shot' for your colonel."

"Why does Pratt get a normal-sounding name?"

"You get the running name God intended for you. I am his agent, just passing along your karma. That's why."

With Calvino and Colonel Pratt initiated into the club, Saxon had burnished his reputation as a man who delivered unexpected visitors. Ohn Myint, as the unofficial head of the club, accepted them as an offering to her authority.

Calvino guessed the two went some time back. They had the comfort level, the easy banter and the intimacy even around others that made it likely they got more out of the club than running. Saxon was on the receiving end of Ohn Myint's gossip feed, which monitored who was in and who was out in Burmese society, whose wife had been seen with another general's wife, who had a new deal and where money had gone missing—eddies and flows in the never-ending stream of power.

Saxon, for his part, had a knack for cultivating contacts, and these sources with their inside information were what made him an extraordinary journalist. Together, the two more than doubled the value of their own information. It was a good investment. Sometimes in a hostile environment nothing is more valuable than a solid working connection between a local and foreigner.

Ohn Myint introduced Calvino and Colonel Pratt to the others by their new running club handles. All of them smiled and nodded. If Saxon could vouch for these two outsiders, that was good enough for everybody. Colonel Pratt and Calvino found themselves welcomed into the group.

"Anyone Jack drags in and drops at Swamp Bitch's feet is usually pretty dubious," teased one member of the group. "The last person you brought got lost. We spent hours trying to find him."

"Never did," said another runner.

"They won't get lost," said Saxon.

"Don't worry," said Calvino. "If that happens, we'll buy the beer."

That brought a show of knowing smiles that folded into half sneer. The mood then shifted as Calvino and Pratt were again ignored.

The regulars returned to a conversation they'd been having a few minutes earlier, one of those jags of fear and loathing among expats that are incited by an act of violence against a member in good standing of their community, in this case a Scotsman who was a running club member.

"Derek was attacked *inside* his house," said one of the runners.

All the emphasis was on the word "inside," as if the violence had been worse for him there than it would have been on the street.

"Surprised him, I heard," said another runner.

Ohn Myint had heard from her sources—and the men were all ears—that the assailant had crept up with a ceremonial Japanese sword behind Derek as he sat working at his desk. The sword had been rusted and dull, but sharp enough to inflict five wounds to Derek's head.

"He was *working*," said the runner who had placed a boldfaced emphasis on "inside," pronouncing the word in a shrill, angry tone.

Nothing worse than to be assaulted when working inside, where you also slept, ate, entertained friends, screwed and bathed. The most private of places.

"It could have happened to any of us," said one the men.

He spoke for the group. In their minds it wasn't just Derek who was a victim of violence because it could just as well have been one of them. They couldn't help but think that attack was a message that they could be next.

"A home invasion," said Saxon, as he turned to Calvino, his lower jaw dropped, "with a sword?"

"They catch the guy?" asked Calvino.

"Still investigating," said Saxon.

"After two weeks," said Ohn Myint.

"I saw the photographs after the attack," said Saxon. "He had two puffy black eyes. Blood had filled the white bits. The British embassy has put a lot of pressure on the cops to find the attacker."

"They know who did it," said Calvino.

"The police are investigating," said Saxon, muffling a quiet laugh.

One of the expats moaned that Derek, an experienced oil and gas engineer, had offended a local, causing a loss of face. The attacker was angry, wild-eyed, on drugs.

"You're here to help Derek?" one of the expat runners asked Calvino.

"Don't know him," said Calvino.

"We thought Jack said something about how an investigator was coming along on the run, and he might have an idea of how to get things moving for Derek," said another runner, who periodically raised one knee, grabbed it with both hands, grimaced and then repeated the exercise with the other knee.

"Hey, guys, Vincent's here to see me," said Ohn Myint. "Nothing to do with Derek."

They looked disappointed.

"If you have time, though," one of them said, "you might do what you can for Derek. He's one of us."

Suddenly the runners shot into motion as if someone had fired a starting pistol. They raced to climb inside cars and SUVs that would take them to the starting line. A new white BMW pulled to the side of the road. The window on the driver's side slid down, and an Asian man in a suit and tie waved Colonel Pratt over.

"My contact at the Thai embassy," said Colonel Pratt to Calvino.

"Good, he can take us back to the hotel after the run."

Colonel Pratt pulled Calvino to the side.

"He didn't come to wait. I've got to go."

That was the Thai way. When an official wanted something from you, waiting was impossible. But when you wanted something from an official, the laws of the universe governing time and movement reorganized themselves into a dark force of molasses that no one could influence or fully explain.

"See you later," said Calvino as the Colonel ran across the road and climbed into the BMW.

"Come with me," said Ohn Myint, a.k.a. Swamp Bitch.

She led Calvino over to the British embassy official's SUV, opened the door and pushed Calvino into the back.

"Looks like your friend's gone with number three at the Thai embassy," said the British official.

Burma had only a small network of embassy staff. He used the rearview mirror to catch Calvino's eye. It was a kind of challenge for him to explain why his friend had abandoned the run. An Englishmen would never think of pulling one of their own out before he'd finished the run.

"The embassy is organizing a performance. Pratt plays the saxophone, and he's giving some kind of a concert. They must be going over the program."

The British embassy official smiled in the mirror, one of those English smiles that signals, "You're full of shit, but it's okay because I can find out with a phone call."

"Or he's part of the master plan for a Thai takeover of Rangoon," said Calvino. "It's either the sax or revolution. I sometimes get the two confused."

"A lot of people have that confusion," the embassy official said.

On the long drive from the city to the starting line for the race, the conversation turned back to Derek, the battered engineer. The British embassy official explained his theory about how Derek had caused a Burmese, a fellow runner, to lose face. Derek had been a little drunk and angry, and he launched into a smart-ass riff, ridiculing the man's intelligence, the size of his balls, the legitimacy of his birth and his jungle school education. All of it was good running club banter. But what might play as sport in Scotland or England played on a different frequency in Burma.

The Burmese runner had straggled over the finish line hours after everyone else on the 10K run. A search party had been sent out to find him. They found him drinking tea in a hut with two old men and an old woman with missing teeth and a red betel nut smile. Derek tore into him, calling him an idiot, a jackass and an imbecile. Derek had drunk a lot of beer and the Burmese, head down, just took it all in. Derek's verbal attack and the Burmese man's later physical attack on Derek had left the Rangoon Running club with two black eyes.

"This is the guy Jack introduced to the club?"

Ohn Myint said, "It wasn't Jack's fault."

Calvino thought Saxon would have liked that display of loyalty. He made a mental note—the woman wasn't a bitch. She was straight up, not letting anyone say anything bad about a friend.

On the way to the starting line, they turned down the wrong road, not once, but twice. Twenty kilometers outside Rangoon was a different landscape. They stopped, and the British official asked for directions. The reply was a shrug of the shoulders. In Burmese Ohn Myint asked a young woman in a dress holding a small child on her hip. She translated the instructions into English, and they made a U-turn and headed back in the direction they'd come from. They were the last to arrive at the end of the dirt road. The British embassy official pulled to the side and cut the engine. They got out and walked along the road, which ran between green fields. Toward the horizon was the outline of a village. Other cars had parked, and the runners were on the road, warming up. The men and women who had stood apart before had come together to form a group of nearly thirty runners.

Ohn Myint had been out days before laying the run, marking it with shredded paper and throwing in some false trails to make it interesting.

Jack Saxon had arrived in another car. He waved at Calvino.

"Don't get lost," he said.

"I'll do my best not to embarrass you, Pistol Penis."

Saxon tilted his head.

"Kiss My Trash. Go well. Too bad about Crack Shot."

"Things happen for a reason."

"Yes, they do. I believe that, Vinny."

The countryside stretched out, clean, smooth and green, a place to run off steam, thought Calvino. The thought of running ten kilometers made him sigh. The two US marines pulled up beside him, running in place.

"You can run with us if you want," said Randy.

"We'll see you don't get lost," said Roosevelt.

Calvino smiled. "You go ahead."

Five minutes after the race started, the two of them were tiny dots framed against the sky.

"Big upset, that Henry Miller," he imagined Randy saying to Roosevelt. "Hey, whatever happened to that guy from Brooklyn? I bet he got his ass lost."

Moments after the run started, Calvino had fallen back to the blurry line that divided the slowest of the runners from the fastest of the walkers. Ahead of him he saw Ohn Myint a hundred meters off. Two young female NGOs with pale white skin were ten meters ahead. They looked to be carrying an extra twenty or thirty pounds in bulges around their hips and legs. They performed like the starter car at a Nascar track. Each time he pulled up close, they increased their pace. They might have been overweight, but they could outrun him. His unsuccessful efforts to catch and pass the two women were, he told himself, a greater humiliation than getting lost. He was grateful that the two young marines from the US embassy hadn't been around to witness it.

Five kilometers into the run, Calvino found himself running alone down a narrow dirt road that snaked through a hamlet. The inhabitants were lined in front of their huts, laughing and clapping as he crossed a small bridge. They cheered him as he sweated, face red, legs numb, lifting his arms and flashing the victory sign. He passed a stream running underneath the road that smelled of pig shit. The women wore their best dresses, flowers in their hair, with their children playing in the dirt at their feet. Chickens and pigs caged in pens rested alongside the houses. Older children ran behind him, laughing and cheering, passing him, falling back, passing him again. It made them happy to have a runner they could run circles around.

He had captured an audience simply by running so slowly. The villagers felt he lingered long enough that they almost got to know this white man.

Focus, he told himself. Take it one step at a time. Look happy. Don't think five kilometers left. Just run.

Legs rubbery, Calvino ran, stopped, ran, stopped and then leaned over, hands on his legs, staring at the ground as he struggled to catch his breath.

Sixteenth century, he thought as he looked around him. I've gone back in time.

There was nothing like the countryside outside Rangoon to remind the newcomer that when a country has gone to sleep for fifty years, when it finally awakes, rubbing its eyes, whatever comes down the road—in this case Vincent Calvino—must be a figure from the future. All along the road Calvino stopped to shake hands with the old men, often flashing a gold or silver tooth or reddish lips from betel nut, and the women and children. By the second village, if there had been a by-election, Calvino would have won.

The underdog with grit had universal appeal that extended to the outer reaches of the Burmese countryside.

The main threat was the village dogs that didn't like strangers. Ohn Myint had told the villagers to keep their dogs on chains. Calvino saw them—gnarling dogs collared to trees and posts, showing their teeth as he passed. He couldn't have outrun the most ancient and lamest among them. Their tethers held, but he still shuddered as he ran past the last one that lunged at him.

Shaking all of those hands wasn't enough to wipe away the embarrassment of falling behind a pair of big women. The two marines... Okay, he could live with the fact that a couple of combat-fit twenty-year-olds could leave him in the dust. But it rankled that even the two guava-shaped NGOs had more acceleration, endurance and style than he did. He ran alone. The fat, the old—and, he imagined, cripples too—were all somewhere well ahead of him, crossing the finish line, drinking a cool beer, perhaps wondering if a search party should be organized to find him.

After reaching the seven kilometer mark, Ohn Myint ran back to find Calvino standing in a vast rice field.

"You okay?" she asked. "If you want, I can have a truck come and pick you up."

"No need," said Calvino. "Just stopping to admire the view."

In the distance behind him he saw the walkers—never a good sign if you're a runner. Only it soon became clear that one of them wasn't a member of the club. The man, who approached on a motorcycle, was a military intelligence agent—what the Burmese shortened to "MI." As common as village dogs, only they were never tethered.

"We have a visitor," said Ohn Myint.

The MI agent, in his crisp white shirt and longyi, who'd been sent to spy on the Rangoon Running Club—no doubt investigating Derek's case—rode up the narrow path toward

Calvino and Ohn Myint. Stopping near them, he got off and strolled over.

"Have you been up north?" the MI agent asked.

"North, south, I can't say which direction I've been," said Calvino.

"The northern part of the country."

"You think I should go?"

"What do you think of the situation in the country?"

Calvino smiled. "Friendly villages. One of the village women gave me a peeled orange. And I can't figure that out. Why did she give me an orange?"

The MI agent grinned, his sunglasses covering his eyes.

"Why are you in our country?"

"I'm a tourist. I spend money. I'm hoping to meet a couple of friends. Isn't that a good enough reason? The situation in your country is none of my business. I couldn't care less if you murder each other in your beds."

"Passport," demanded the MI agent.

Calvino nodded. "Runners don't carry passports."

"It's the law. You must have your passport at all times."

"In the shower?"

The MI agent took out his cell phone and talked for a couple of minutes, watching Calvino. When he finished, he lowered his sunglasses. There was a look of absolute hate in his eyes. His boss had told him to let Calvino go. His motorcycle was parked a few feet away in the field where he'd left it. It was orange. All MIs drove orange or gray motorcycles that had the number 4 or 5 on the special license plate.

"Isn't riding a motorcycle on the 10K run against the rules?" he asked Ohn Myint."

"MIs have their own set of rules."

He'd been trailing Calvino through a hamlet and likely had been on his tail from the start of the run.

"He's done nothing wrong," said Ohn Myat.

"What's your name?" he asked Calvino.

"Kiss My Trash. And this my friend Swamp Bitch."

He wrote down the names in his notebook.

"Where are you going?" the MI agent asked her.

"To the beer truck at the finish line."

The MI agent stared at him. "Why are you running?"

"Exercise," said Calvino. "It's good for your health."

The MI agent spit on the ground. Health appeared to be an alien concept to him as he scribbled in his notebook.

"He's an American," said Ohn Myint.

"And who are you?"

"His translator."

"Why do you run?"

The MI agent seemed to be caught in first gear, repeating the same question.

"Good for the heart and lungs," she said in English, and repeated it again in Burmese when it appeared the MI agent hadn't understood.

A small crowd of villagers watched in the distance from the safety of their houses along the narrow, winding road, smiling and whispering to one another.

"How many Americans are running with you?"

Calvino thought of the two ultra-fit marines from the American embassy who had the bodies of whippets and ran like cheetahs.

"A platoon of battle hardened snipers," he said.

It wasn't a word the MI agent understood. Calvino spelled out word "platoon" for him.

"P-l-a-t-o-o-n." He looked at the notebook. "Two O's," he said. "Toon as in cartoon."

The MI agent scribbled "Plato"underneath.

Calvino nodded. "That's it, Plato. The quarterback who played football for Florida State against Henry Miller."

"What is the purpose of running?"

Calvino had already answered the question, and so had Ohn Myint. But the technique was to keep asking the questions until the MI agent received an answer that would fit into his report. That was all that mattered. His job was to produce an answer that he could show his superiors without getting in trouble or being laughed at.

"What do you want to hear?" he asked the MI agent.

"Purpose."

"To lose weight."

The MI agent, slightly overweight, looked at the lines of sweat rolling down Calvino's face.

"But you're not fat."

"My heart is fat."

The MI agent wrote that down.

"I'll talk with you again."

He turned away and walked to his motorcycle.

Ohn Myint nodded. "He'll be back, for sure."

"Jack said you made arrangements for the trial tomorrow."

"It's been arranged," she said.

Hands on her hips, she looked at a runner in the distance ahead.

"And he said you were looking for a missing person, Rob Osborne. Getting the girlfriend's brother out of prison is going to help you find him?"

She asked better questions that the MI agent, thought Calvino.

"Finding Osborne will take time and legwork. I can find him. The problem is convincing him to return to Bangkok."

Ohn Myint sucked her teeth.

"Getting the brother out of prison will persuade Osborne to return?"

"The deal is, I spring the brother, and Mya Kyaw Thein tells Osborne he has to go back and make his peace with his old man."

"Four thousand, five hundred dollars," she said.

"You'll have it tomorrow morning," said Calvino. "Let Mya know what the deal is—Rob goes back to Bangkok to see his father. After he sees him, it's up to Rob whether he wants to stay there or come back."

She surveyed the sky as if looking for an answer.

"I'll let her know."

It was the cost of one man's freedom from prison, the number that would assure that another man, once found, would voluntarily return to Bangkok. Rob Osborne had unsuccessfully tried to borrow the money from his old man. Now the old man would have to pay the amount anyway, with Calvino's fee added as interest.

Some numbers always return, like a swallow to the home roost. But an old saying has it that the presence of one swallow doesn't make for a summer. There was a chance that Rob Osborne wouldn't leave Rangoon without the Black Cat. The price to get her brother out of prison hadn't included her promise to return.

"See you at the finish line," said Ohn Myint.

Calvino watched her pick up speed on the path leading through the field, until her clean smooth stride kicked in. She disappeared around a bend as she entered a road. He sucked in a long breath and put one foot in front of the other, a kind of running that retreating soldiers would have recognized. By now Jack Saxon would be at the finish line drinking his second or third beer. Ohn Myint had taken the baton from Saxon and run with it. The handoff had been made. She would see that the money was delivered.

The way he figured it, Mya Kyaw Thein, or the Black Cat—whatever she wanted to call herself—would find a way to slip into her brother's trial. After all, the Monkey Nose lead singer had left Bangkok to help her brother beat the illegal teak transport rap. It wasn't as if he'd killed someone. Though Alf, the Texan sax player in the Monkey Nose band, had reminded Calvino that stealing a man's horse in Texas was worse than killing a man. What a horse was to a Texan, teak was to the Burmese.

The natural course of events followed a pattern—find the woman, and you'll find her man within fifty meters, lurking in the shadows. Men tend to stay within sniffing distance, Calvino had found, watching and guarding their women. DNA wired them to use their eyes, nose and ears, their senses fine-tuned to the task. When the woman had the agility of a black cat, trapping and caging her wasn't going to end well. The deal Calvino had made with Ohn Myint was his best play. A four thousand and five hundred dollar chip was on the table. Tomorrow the roulette wheel would spin and he'd either win or lose. He was betting that Mya Kyaw Thein's brother would get a tap on the shoulder and then find himself shown to a side door leading to freedom. It's just the way people run after money, he thought. Freedom has a drop-down menu, and price is a central feature.

As he began to run again, he thought how lucky Pratt had been to have an embassy car whisk him away just in time. Had it been luck? Or had Pratt planned it that way? Questions were all he had to sustain him on the last kilometer. The marines would have crossed the finish line long ago. The fat NGOs would be on their second beer, and he'd appear just ahead of the walkers, his head filled with questions and a thirst in his belly.

SEVEN

Calvino's Short Trigger Pull

LATE AFTERNOON, BACK at his hotel, Calvino stood under the shower, trying to wash away the afterburn from the 10K run. Slowly he opened his eyes. Someone was ringing the doorbell for his room. Or was his mind playing tricks? He turned off water. The bell rang again. He hardly felt his legs as he stepped out of the shower and wrapped a towel around his waist to open the door.

Bianca Conti extended her hand. They stared at each other.

"Aren't you going to ask me in?"

Water dripped from his body, pooling on the floor.

"Come in," he said.

She walked into his room, her sleeveless blue dress hugging her waist and hips like a second skin.

"If it isn't a good time, I can come back."

"It's okay."

"Do Americans shower in the afternoon, too?"

"Only after a 10K run."

"You are one of those fitness types?"

He didn't tell her about how Kiss My Trash hadn't exactly won any medals.

Her edge of near-hysterical jetlag madness had passed like storm clouds revealing a bright, promising day. A three-hour power nap had restored her color to a warm honey glow, and her mood had rebooted to a mellow, controlled calmness. She walked straight to the balcony like a catwalk model, slid back the door and walked out. She filled her lungs with air. Slowly she looked back at Calvino, who had begun to pour her a glass of wine.

"Make yourself at home," he said, handing her the wine.

She sipped from the glass.

"The manager told me what happened."

"Did you have to torture him before he talked?"

She leaned with her back against the railing, the sunlit park and lake below behind her right shoulder. Bracelets on both wrists looked to be made of fine silver with precious stones. No wedding ring, but she did wear a gold ring with a large pearl on her right hand. She hooked one calf over the top of the other, relaxed and easy. She tilted her head as she studied him, taking a long look before replying.

"Men always talk when they have a bad conscience."

"That's what a torturer usually says."

"He said this was my room. But your friend Jack Saxon asked him for a favor to give it to you. That is how you got this room."

"The manager blamed Jack?"

"'Blame' is an ugly word."

She held out her glass and he topped it up.

She watched him put the wine bottle back inside, and when Calvino returned, she continued.

"'Wine' is a much better word."

"He must have made a mistake. I know this room was booked for me a few days ago," said Calvino, taking a drink from his own glass of wine.

She extended her glass and touched the rim of his. A nice, clean clink registered, and she smiled.

"Italian?"

"French."

"I mean you. You have an Italian name."

She took another sip and put the glass down.

"My mother was Jewish, my father Italian. I'm a New Yorker."

"I thought you lived in Bangkok, no?"

"When you're born in New York you are a New Yorker for life. That's how it works."

She caught his eye, turning what might have started as a glance into something else. She lowered the glass.

"Back to business. Your friend Jack thought he reserved this room. Or his secretary told him she reserved it. They had you reserved in a room with no view. Jack asked his friend, the manager, to switch our rooms."

"And you've come to take your room."

Bianca giggled like a little girl, something she'd never outgrown.

"It's not necessary. We have another view room. But a Chinese couple will be disappointed. Isn't that how musical chairs works?"

"What are you doing in Rangoon?" asked Calvino.

"Buying emeralds, rubies, opals. I am a jewelry designer. And you?"

He refilled her wine glass.

"A tourist on holiday. All the news of Burma opening up made me curious. I came to have a look around."

"What kind of work do you do, I mean?"

"Private investigations."

"A private eye in a toga? That must be your Italian half."

He grinned, half-embarrassed by his state of undress.

"I wasn't expecting a guest."

"Don't let me stop you from whatever you're doing. I had this desire to stand on the balcony and see..."

She turned away, looking at the view.

"If you missed something by taking the other room."

"I won't turn around if you want to dress."

"I do private investigations," he said as he slipped into his clothes that he'd laid out on the bed.

"Are you on a working holiday?"

He zipped his pants and fastened his belt, leaving his polo shirt out. He sat on the bed and pulled on his socks. After he finished, he watched her long, firm legs, which the sunlight exposed through her thin dress. Why had she come to his room? Was she just passing the time? Why the interrogation about his reasons for being in Rangoon? He buttoned the bottom button of his polo shirt, thinking a woman like this who was in the jewelry business might be someone who could help find the Black Cat's mother, who was in the same business.

"You can turn around," he said.

She waited a few moments before turning away from the view.

"How was does the view compare with your room?"

"I like yours better," she said.

"Do you have plans for the rest of the day," she continued, "work or play?"

"I'm looking for a young musician. His father's worried about him. He's been missing for more than a week, but I think he's somewhere in Rangoon."

"It could take some time to find him," she said.

He shrugged. "It could."

"Meanwhile, if you want to see some sites, I could come along."

The Italian woman who had invited herself to his room was now, after a glass of wine, making a play to become part of his holiday.

"You got off a twelve o'clock flight. You must be jetlagged."

She walked in from the balcony.

"I am meeting my friend for dinner. Join us. Bring along your friend, the Colonel."

She had a good memory for detail. Calvino figured it must be a required skill someone who appraised stones—examining each facet, looking for tiny flaws, remembering the color range.

"The Colonel?"

"The one you were with in the lobby?"

He'd forgotten that Saxon had introduced Calvino by his job description and Pratt by his rank.

"Yeah, the Thai guy. He's playing the saxophone at a club tonight. Join us if you want. Bring your friend…"

"Anne."

"Her name was on the tip of my tongue."

He put on his shoes and combed his hair. He lay down the brush and walked past her onto the balcony.

"It is a great view," he said.

She had slipped out on the balcony and stood close to him.

"What's his name, your Thai friend, the Colonel?"

"Pratt. Everyone likes him, especially women—they seem to love saxophone players. There aren't many Bangkok cops who can play the sax. He's jamming with a local band."

"He's a cop? Is he helping you find the missing musician?"

Calvino shook his head and drank from his wine glass.

"He's doing his own thing."

"Your other friend, Jack, will be there too?"

She cupped her hand over Calvino's hand, resting on the railing. He stared ahead, calculating the situation. He tried to concentrate on the thin traffic on the road in the distance, counting the cars. She stood close, her hip touching his. When he glanced back at her, what caught his attention was a perfectly formed white patch on her skin just below her throat. It was in the shape of a cross. It was the kind of evidence most people overlooked. He wanted to ask her what had happened to the crucifix she'd worn around the throat, about the beach where she'd tanned and whether she'd touched hips lying on the sand next to her last man. But he wasn't sure he wanted to know any of those things. Not yet, anyway. It was better to register the clues and slowly build a profile of this woman who had mysteriously come to his room.

"Jack'll be there, too. Wherever there's a pool table, cold beer and a sports channel, sooner or later you'll run into Jack."

"Jack is a man's man," she said.

Jack Saxon hadn't been in her life more than five minutes, and she already had him figured out.

The sky was washed with streaks of languid orange cloud that brushed the vast tree canopy. Calvino stood next to Bianca on the balcony, looking out at the ancient forest enveloping the heart of Rangoon—a deep green in the fading light. He slipped his arm around Bianca's waist. She leaned in closer, brushing his body with hers. Off to the right was a colonial mansion with a red roof—a portico as erect as a headwaiter at the Savoy—a testament to the past, when British rulers built structures that announced, "We are here," and now added, "Remember that all foreign rulers disappear into the sunset."

"It's all going to change," she said.

"But not tonight," he said.

Rangoon was a vast forest with buildings scattered through it. Calvino tried to imagine a Bangkok-like city sprawling out in place of the trees. The way things worked, he knew she was right. The forest would fall soon enough, and the tall, shiny buildings would take its place.

Not tonight, though. Tonight still belonged to the cartwheeling birds appearing in ones and twos and finally in waves. First the pigeons going to roost, then the swallows, feeding, and finally the bats. They looked out over a city virtually untouched by the world of developers, bankers, lawyers and consultants, with their plans and blueprints for high-rises, shopping malls, condos and supermarkets. Rangoon would soon leave one world and join another.

Bianca slipped her arm around Calvino. They stood holding each other, looking at the sky.

"What happens when the Chinese arrive and want their room with this view?" asked Calvino.

She glanced up at him and shrugged. "They can start a new cultural revolution in the lobby."

He laughed, brushing back her hair with the back of his hand.

"You could give them your room and stay here."

"I don't think Anne wants to share a room with the Chinese."

He'd forgotten about her friend. The phone in the room rang. After three rings, Calvino sat on the edge of the bed and answered it.

"Jack sent me a bottle of Johnnie Walker Black. He included a note: 'I'm working on what I owe you. See you later at 50th Street.' Come up to my room for a drink. I want to hear about the Rangoon Running Club."

Calvino would tell Pratt the truth about the run, and his friend would laugh at the agony of his miserable finish. But that could wait, couldn't it? Calvino wanted to freeze that moment on the balcony, with Rangoon framed against the setting sun as he responded to her touch. He wanted to remember it, file it away like a postcard stored in a box for his old age. But there was no such thing as a working holiday.

"Give me twenty minutes," he said, hanging up the phone.

She reentered the room and headed for the door.

"I should be going."

"Bring Anne along tonight. The 50th Street Bar, about nine o'clock."

"I know the place."

She was out the door before he could ask her about the perfume she was wearing. He'd been around that scent before—fresh lime with a hint of lavender.

After Bianca had gone, Calvino pulled a chair onto the balcony, sat down and placed the bottle of wine on a small table. Stretching forward, he perched his arm on the railing. The hotel was in a part of Rangoon where the elites lived in secluded mansions, hidden in the city forest. Somewhere under the trees, Rob Osborne sat in a room, waiting for a woman to come through the door, thought Calvino. Some were worth waiting for, and every man thought he'd made the right call on the value of his woman. He'd never met Mya Kyaw Thein, the Black Cat, but he had an idea that anyone who'd followed a blogger with a political agenda, a Henry Miller-quoting jazz singer with a brother going to trial in the morning, had to be in love. When that happened, all bets were off. People went missing by the planeload in the name of love.

Romantic madness wasn't Calvino's business. He'd deliver four and half grand to Ohn Myint to spring the brother. That was his business in Rangoon—finding a way to pump money into a system for the result his client wanted.

A day or so should be enough for him to find Rob and watch him get on a plane to Bangkok, he thought. That would be it. Case closed. But something didn't feel right. He couldn't decide why, but he had a nagging feeling that things worked in Rangoon in ways he didn't understand.

Rangoon made a man's mind drift and doubt itself. Was that the reason Rob hadn't contacted his father? Captured by the magic of the place, he'd just forgotten about time,

Bangkok, his father and the Monkey Nose band? Such things happen to people lost in Southeast Asia. People like Rob didn't so much disappear as dissolve into some back alley of a lost place, usually with a woman—strike that; always with a woman—waiting for something or someone: rescue, redemption, drugs, death or enlightenment.

He poured himself another glass of wine. A Bangkok-raised boy like Rob holed up in Rangoon, one of the last places where the sacred dominated the landscape, was running away from home. The light was now fading quickly. It no longer burnt orange under the graying clouds. On the street below cars became visible as their headlights turned on, but there was no real traffic, just one, then two or three cars, then an empty space, and after a moment another car. It was like counting coins in a beggar's bowl.

He'd come to Rangoon because Pratt needed backup. But having arrived, he would do his best to launch a Rob Osborne rescue mission. Calvino remembered what it had been like to strike out in a strange city, to be lost among the losers, dreamers, prostitutes, grifters, godfathers, wanderers and scam artists—the usual crowd who were the first to secure a beachhead in a place with a deep, troubled history and an uncertain future. Places like that never lasted. Sooner or later the modern global generals smelled the money and sent in their officers dressed in suits, who'd been trained to use balance sheets to occupy a territory. That had happened in Bangkok, Saigon and Phnom Penh, and it would eventually happen in Rangoon. There's nothing wrong with the domino theory, Calvino thought; it was tailor-made for capitalism.

If Henry Miller were leaving Brooklyn in our time, Calvino figured, he'd rip up his ticket to Paris and find his way to Rangoon, one of the last romantic oases on earth. On the other hand, the city was already filling up with foreign caravans. Come to think of it, Calvino thought,

Miller would be not only too late, but irrelevant. *Tropic of Cancer*—download it for free from the Internet and then forget where you saved it on your computer. That's how Henry would stop mattering. Saved but unread, except by one exotic Black Cat.

Colonel Pratt asked who was at the door before opening it.

"It's me, Pratt."

Calvino heard the security chain slide and fall. The door opened and Calvino walked in. A bottle of Johnnie Walker Black, two glasses and bucket of ice waited on the table near the balcony. The curtains were drawn. Pratt's carry-on case was open on the bed. Calvino watched Pratt slide the chain back into the slot.

"Still not unpacked?" asked Calvino, staring at the suitcase.

"Got back only ten minutes before I phoned you."

"The Thai embassy is running overtime."

"We drove out to a shooting range. It was my good friend from the embassy who had the idea."

"Did you tell him your running name was Crack Shot?"

The Colonel smiled. "I forgot. He would have liked that."

Pratt hadn't offered the Thai embassy official's name, and Calvino didn't ask. He understood the power and risk of naming people and things.

Calvino sat in a chair, poured whiskey into the two glasses and took a drink from one of them.

"While I was running through rice fields, I was being followed by an MI asshole. As slow as I ran, he didn't even pretend to run. He was riding one of those cheap-ass motorcycles."

"What did he want?"

"He wanted to know why I was running."

"What did you tell him?"

"Doctor's orders. I'm still trying to understand how he found me in the middle of nowhere. I had a tail in the middle of nowhere. I could see him for miles. He made no effort to hide."

Calvino handed Colonel Pratt a glass of whiskey.

"You were running with a group of foreigners. He probably picked you because you were the slowest runner."

"I hadn't thought of that. You're probably right. The lion always takes down the weakest runner in the herd. Darwin said something about that. I think it was Darwin. It might have been Henry Miller."

He drained his glass and poured himself another.

"I have a present for you," said the Colonel.

"I hope it's not jewelry. You know how people talk."

Sitting on the edge of the bed, Pratt pulled a rolled red towel out of the suitcase and unwrapped it, his hand emerging with a handgun.

"Nine millimeter Walther PPQ. German made. Fifteen shot magazine. It has a short trigger pull. Light release. Polymer frame. Good grip and sharp sights set at the factory."

"Are you selling me a gun?"

Pratt removed a second towel, a white one. He opened it and pulled out a second Walther PPQ. He passed the handgun to Calvino.

"This one is for you. I have a couple of shoulder holsters. And let me see..." he said, digging around in the bottom of the case until he found two boxes of ammo. "A box of PMC 115 grain hollow points, and a box of 147 grain gold dots."

Calvino walked over and took one of the handguns.

"Does have a good grip."

He turned the gun over.

"The magazine eject is that slider on the side. Both sides have a slider. Left-handed, right-handed."

Calvino worked the slider with his thumb, and the magazine popped out. It was loaded.

"Didn't you say something about just needing to talk to one or two people and then going back home?"

"I had some information at the shooting range that the people I want to talk to can play rough."

"Imagine that. Multi-million-dollar racket to trans-ship cold pills into Thailand, and to think the people involved might resort to violence if you happen to get in their face. Learn something every day."

Calvino smelled the barrel of the Walther. So far, the early evening had carried the scent of perfume and the smell of cordite from the shooting range. They blended in his nose and his mind like the haze following the sun into the ground. Smells can carry a reassurance, but in this case both smells promised to deliver surprise, pain and regret. While Calvino had been out waving at the local villagers, Colonel Pratt had been testing the sights, grips, range and reliability of the available weapons.

"Better to be prepared."

"Like boy scouts, right? You know what I love most about places like Rangoon?"

The Colonel shook his head as he put on the shoulder holster.

"The Italian women?"

"The Burmese are still in the last century. Except at the airport, do you think you'd find a metal detector anywhere? Even the guards outside the hotel carry AK-47s. Guns are everywhere, and no alarms are going off."

"The Walther's made in Germany. Precision."

"German guns, Italian women… All that's missing is you playing some Joe Henderson on the sax, and we might almost forget why we're in Rangoon."

Calvino turned the gun in his hand. It was an impressive piece of engineering—not unlike the weapons of the people who would be waiting for them outside the hotel, people they didn't know and would never know. If he and Pratt were lucky they'd be done and out of Burma soon. Rob Osborne would go home to his daddy. The cold pill pipeline would be shut down. The Burmese Tropic of Cancer would once again be a tranquil paradise.

If only life worked out that way sometimes, he thought. Even once. That would be enough. In the meantime he was happy to have the Walther PPQ and a box of PMC 115 grain hollow points.

EIGHT

50th Street Bar

CALVINO STOPPED TO massage his calf muscle. It had seized up into a throbbing knot. Seeing his problem, Pratt waited a moment before continuing down the sloped pavement alone, past the uniformed guards with automatic weapons, and stopping at the street.

Calvino consciously tried not to hobble as he stood up and walked to where Pratt waited to hail a cab. A few minutes earlier they had passed three taxis idling in front of the hotel. How Calvino had wanted to climb into one of them. But it wasn't an option. Living with aching calves and legs was the cost of following the standard procedure for choosing a taxi in his line of work. Any taxi parked in front of the hotel might be compromised. Colonel Pratt had learnt long ago that staying alive was tied to avoiding unnecessary risks. Even if it meant a bit of pain had to be endured on the walk to the street, where the drill was to flag down the second taxi that came along.

It wasn't written in any book that it had to be the second car. Sometimes he waited for the third car. Habit and routine were the invisible handmaidens who delivered easy targets to operatives who had the job of tailing them and reporting on their conversations. Calvino's encounter with the low-ranking MI agent had drawn notice that he was at least a subject of interest. People were watching.

On the drive Pratt said little. It was an old habit, riding quietly in a taxi driven by someone who might not necessarily be a taxi driver by profession. Calvino massaged one calf, then the other.

"Still sore?"

Calvino sighed. "A little. I need to go to the gym when I get back."

"You could stop running marathons."

"And give up my place on the Olympic team?"

"That would be a pity," said Colonel Pratt.

The driver glanced at them in the rearview mirror. The taxi drivers in Rangoon, unlike those Bangkok, understood and spoke enough English to follow a conversation, especially one that involved sports.

The two foreigners let their inconsequential conversation drift away into silence during the balance of the twenty-minute journey. By the time they reached the 50th Street Bar, night had set in. The main streets had streetlights, but once the cab entered the side street, the depth of the darkness enveloped it. Outside was a blur of lights from inside houses hidden behind hedges and trees. The bar was buried down a long, empty street, but the driver had no trouble finding it. On the right side bright lights blazed, outlining a modern bar that looked out of place on the street. The bar stood out like a hooker in hot pants and high heels at a church picnic. Parked out front was a long row of luxury sports cars and SUVs, each one in showroom condition and freshly washed, their polished grilles glimmering in the light from the bar. Like an automotive version of a gated community, they faced the street together, leaving no room for intruders.

Pratt climbed out of the taxi and leaned back in for his saxophone case. He'd worn his blue silk shirt and black trousers. He looked more like a businessman than a musician. Calvino slowly emerged from the other side, turned and paid the driver.

"I hope you make the team," said the driver.

"Thanks. They're counting on me," said Calvino.

"You think the driver believed you were Olympic material?" asked Pratt.

"It was low light."

"It was dark."

"Not in front of the bar."

As they passed two of the expensive cars, Calvino stopped. His legs felt better for the stretch. He rocked back and forth on his toes, feeling his calf muscles.

"What do you figure this one cost?"

A silver Lamborghini Murciélago, sandwiched between a new Jaguar and a Maserati, stood out. Pratt walked around the Lamborghini like an earthling inspecting an alien artifact.

"Landed in Bangkok, taxes, shipping, about a million dollars," Colonel Pratt finally said as he walked around to a standstill in front of the car.

"Last time I saw a Maserati in Bangkok," said Calvino, "it didn't look like this. It'd been in an accident. The owner had been racing it on the tollway. Rescue teams arrived with a blowtorch and mechanical jaws. There wasn't much left of the driver."

"I remember that accident. The driver was the son of someone powerful."

"That's called development. Soft loans from Western banks to build expressways so that rich kids can use them as private racetracks when they're bored racing on Sukhumvit Road. And you remember the kid who ran down and killed a good cop, and walked away?"

"'Discomfort guides my tongue and bids me speak of nothing but despair,'" said Pratt quoting Shakespeare.

94

"Shakespeare is what the Burmese have to look forward to?" said Calvino.

"People like the ones who own these cars don't need much help from foreigners, Vincent."

"I never heard you call Shakespeare a foreigner."

"I am not talking about what I think."

It was the Colonel's polite way of saying that foreigners like him usually attributed too much importance to the role of other foreigners in the lives of the rich.

Calvino walked around the Lamborghini, shaking his head.

"Admiring your Italian ancestry, Vincent?"

"Say some guys at Goldman Sachs form a band. They drive out to Brooklyn or Queens for a gig. I could visualize a parking lot outside a bar in one of the boroughs looking something like this. And none of them would be Italian."

The parking lot reeked of cash, privilege and immunity. Cars like these should have a sign installed over the gas tank, thought Colonel Pratt—"fueled by drug money, kickbacks or corruption." Take your pick. Calvino might joke about them, but the people who bought and drove such cars didn't have a sense of humor when it came to the sources of their money. He'd come to Rangoon to deal with the people who drove such cars, and to lower their fuel consumption.

"Looks like you're playing in a band of made men," said Calvino.

The planning had seemed easy in Bangkok. Standing in front of the bar, the full weight of Pratt's mission came home to him—walk into a bar and charm such men into helping him shut down a business that was kicking out vast wealth. He felt stupid.

"The little big leagues are the most lethal," said Colonel Pratt.

"The big minor leagues are even worse."

"Shakespeare once wrote, 'The miserable have no other medicine but only hope.' And robbers of hope are in a league of their own."

Calvino cracked a smile. "Shakespeare comes to Rangoon. Time to check out the players on stage."

They went inside. The door opened into a large room. Pool tables on the left, a large bar in the center, stools on the right, a stage opposite the pool table area and a dozen tables with chairs. The tables had young, well-dressed men and women with perfect makeup and hair—the kind of people who were never seen carrying a paper sack, using a hammer and nail, or unscrewing the back of a motor casing. Most were Westerners, but a few Burmese were mixed in, like a few almonds floating in a bowl of peanuts.

Several white women sat at the bar drinking red wine, talking to the other women, index fingers hovering above smart phones, as bartenders and admirers floated in and out of their field of vision like screen icons.

Calvino spotted Jack Saxon at a corner pool table. Saxon stared down the shank of his pool cue, left eye squinted and breath held, took his shot and dropped the five-ball in the side pocket. As he rose up, his face wore a self-satisfied grin. When he saw Calvino and the Colonel advancing across the floor, his grin morphed into a crooked smile. He pointed his pool cue in their direction, leaned over and took his next shot, a cigarette hanging from the corner of his mouth.

Saxon missed the shot, winced and waved at Calvino. His luck ended, his shoulders slumped forward as if acknowledging defeat.

"Over here!" he shouted, taking the cigarette out of his mouth.

The attractions of the 50th Street Bar were many. It was a place to be seen. Certainly one could drink there while watching the live feed of soccer and cricket matches and

Formula One races—the English taste in sports. You could do some business. You could see who was sleeping with whom this week—one of those old colonial habits that was far more resilient than the empire—or check out who was driving which car. The good life, with an English flavor, had arrived for the children of the few. Saxon led Pratt and Calvino over to the table occupied by the band and made the introductions. Calvino pulled back a chair and sat down, while Pratt leaned his saxophone case against the edge of the stage.

Yadanar Khin stood up and extended his hand to Colonel Pratt. It was soft. He had the hand of a man who'd never known hard physical labor.

"Man, you've got the gift. The Java Jazz Festival album a few years ago blew me away. People probably tell you that all the time. I am honored you're here. When Jack said you were in town and wanted to sit in with us, I thought, that's more than good. That's great."

As he spoke, Yadanar hadn't paid attention to Calvino, who'd been watching him like the chaperon of a teenager with a reputation for getting herself in trouble in the back seats of expensive cars.

Yadanar noticed Calvino's gaze.

"This is my friend Vincent Calvino," said Saxon. "He's in town looking for the son of a friend who's gone missing."

Yadanar gave Calvino the once over, registering his expensive jacket and trousers that helped him blend into the mix of foreigners at the club.

"People get lost in Rangoon. Hope you find the guy. You two know each other?"

He'd turned back to Pratt.

Pratt nodded. "Vincent is one of my biggest fans. Wherever I play, he comes along."

"Like a manager?"

"I screen his groupies," said Calvino.

The Burmese bandleader no longer focused on Calvino. He'd already been assigned to the role of Pratt's flunky. Pratt was the performer, the star, and for the two visitors from Bangkok that was the best result possible.

"We have a lot of musical talent in Rangoon. A couple of months ago, a five-girl band that used to play here got a deal in Los Angeles. We've had talent scouts coming in ever since. Everyone is betting who'll be next to get the big label deal."

Through his family connections in government and business, Yadanar's family owned the day, but that wasn't enough to satisfy him; like the children of oligarchs everywhere his ambition was to possess the night. His tone of voice and gestures toward Pratt were his way of acknowledging that he was in the presence of someone who owned a significant piece of the night. Rangoon was not that different from anywhere else. If you had the power to set business hours your goal was to acquire the rest of the clock. It was old-fashioned greed—predictable, brutal, funny and sad, especially in a world in which most people were lucky if they could rent a moment to call their own at dawn or sunset, feel alive as the world separated day from night, before the Yadanars of the world put their hand out for the rent.

"We're about to start our second set," Yadanar said to Colonel Pratt. "Join us."

The Colonel took out his saxophone and put the strap around his neck. His lips touched the mouthpiece. He worked the buttons. He looked up and smiled. Calvino pursed his lips and glanced at Saxon, who was laughing.

"I left my banjo out in my Lamborghini," said Saxon.

"Go out and get it," said Yadanar.

"Only if Vinny will be my manager."

Calvino grinned.

"Stick to pool, Jack."

Yadanar laughed.

"Hey, Jack, this guy knows a thing or two."

The other members of the band had drifted back to their instruments on stage and waited for Yadanar to take his place at the keyboard.

"Anything special you'd like to play?" Yadanar asked the Colonel, as he rose from the table.

"Pat Metheny's 'Bright Size Life' is as good as any to start."

"You got it," said Yadanar.

They joined the other members of the band on the stage. Calvino sat at the table with Jack Saxon, a few feet away.

The guy is motivated, thought Calvino. He wants to be next to get the ticket to Los Angeles. Being big in the little leagues isn't his dream. Calvino reckoned this might be one of those rare occasions when what a man wants and what he says he wants are the same. He was telling the truth.

Selling cold pills, Yadanar had a lucrative, if shady, business operation that he controlled, and it wasn't enough. He had something in common with the Black Cat, who had her band in Bangkok and her boyfriend—the good life—but that wasn't enough either.

There's never enough for the dreamers, Calvino thought. He had avoided dreams himself, for the same reason he avoided drugs; they jammed the mind with images and thoughts made from the stuff of clouds. He had no reason to connect the two dreamers, except that they were both Burmese and in the music business. Mya Kyaw Thein played in a Bangkok dive for an audience who couldn't spell "Lamborghini." Yadanar hired people to spell it for him, while he waited for a recording agent to turn him into a star.

"Did you ask him about Mya Kyaw Thein, the Black Cat?"

"They run in different circles," Saxon said.

"Circles connect. Sometimes. It was worth a shot. After this set is finished, I'll ask him myself."

Saxon shook his head.

"Be careful, Vinny. This guy has a boldfaced name, and in Rangoon, you need to add italics as well. Don't screw with him."

"All I'm saying is Yadanar keeps score," Calvino replied. "He knows who's working in the music scene. They say the Black Cat has talent. If she's working anywhere in the city, he'd know. If she's in the city and not working, he'd know that too. He can bullshit all he wants. But you know and I know he can call up any woman he likes and invite her over. And what's she's gonna say? No?"

Saxon grinned like he'd just eaten the last piece of pizza lifted from his best friend's plate. But he wasn't looking at Calvino; he was looking at the woman walking into the room behind him.

Turning around, Calvino said, "Looks like I don't have to wait until the set ends."

Shaking his head, Saxon put the beer bottle to his lips and took a long pull.

"When shit like this happens," Saxon said, "I feel sorry for people who don't drink."

Colonel Pratt had his fingers on the saxophone keys ready to play Pat Metheny when there was a change of plans. Mya Kyaw Thein stepped over some wires and picked up the mike, inched across the small stage to Yadanar behind the keyboard and whispered something. He nodded and gestured to Pratt, who leaned over the keyboard to hear the message. Pratt smiled at what he heard. Someone at the bar turned down the volume on the TV. Yadanar introduced Pratt as one of the all-time great sax players in Southeast Asia. His introductory bio left out the part about the saxophone player being a Thai cop. It didn't seem like the kind of detail this particular crowd would want to know.

Most weren't listening to Yadanar anyway and continued talking or running their eyes and fingers over their little screens, looking up only briefly to calculate if they might be missing a chance to see a big league players score.

After the first song, Saxon tapped Calvino on the shoulder.

"You've got a couple of admirers over there."

Calvino turned around and looked at the spiral staircase. Bianca and Anne waved. He waved them over to the table. Each of the women held a glass of wine. A couple of expats hovered near them.

"Bianca and Anne. You helped them out earlier at the hotel," said Calvino.

"I thought they looked familiar."

"I invited them here."

"Looks like they have other ideas."

One of the men behind them refilled their wine glasses.

"Seems those two have no problem making friends."

A waiter brought Calvino a Tiger beer and a glass. Calvino drank from the bottle.

"Pratt should have been a professional musician," said Calvino.

"Cry Me A River" was one of Pratt's favorite standbys. Women in the audience always loved that song, as most women, sooner or later, cried at least a small stream. Yadanar Khin joined in on piano, and the bass player and drummer followed. The Black Cat held the mike close to her mouth and began singing, "You nearly drove me out of my head…"

She'd brought a rich emotionality to the words, making them wet with tears. Every word a woman ever wanted to say to an unworthy man was in that song. All the heartache, tears, regret and sadness poured out of her, filling the bar with a mood thick with pain. She may not have owned the night, but she owned the room. No one spoke; no one played with their cell phones or iPads. Even the pool players leaned on their pool cues, listening. If anyone in the room had ever wanted proof that a woman is capable of crying a river over a man's vanished love, the Black Cat was delivering an explosive and powerful demonstration.

The song ended. There was a long moment of silence. Then the bar broke into thunderous applause. The Black Cat nodded at the crowd. She knew her power. "Thank you. I'll be back," she said, fixing the mike into its stand. Then she walked from the stage to Calvino's table and sat at the chair next to him. Crossing her legs, she jiggled a cigarette from a pack on the table and lit, tilting her head upward and watching the smoke float toward the ceiling.

The whole bar stared at Calvino and the Black Cat as if to say, was this the man who made her cry a river? Was this the man who owned the night?

"I heard you were looking for me," said Mya Kyaw Thein.

"I'm looking for your boyfriend."

"What about Rob?"

"I want to talk to him."

She lit a cigarette and stared at him for a moment.

"I'll ask him."

"That's not the deal," said Calvino.

The Black Cat's nose twitched as she exhaled smoke. She looked slightly irritated but quickly recovered as applause turned into synchronized clapping and shouts for an encore. Yadanar Khin walked down from the stage and offered his outstretched hand.

She looked at him.

"Maybe later," she said to Yadanar. "I've got some business first."

Back on stage, he told the audience, "The Black Cat is taking a short break. She'll be back. What a night! One you are never gonna forget."

This was a woman used to getting her own way.

"Where is Rob?" asked Calvino.

Mya Kyaw Thein looked away like a black cat seeing motion in the shadows.

"Tell his father that Rob doesn't want to see him."

"Rob can tell his father himself. Then it's over. Done."

"Rob said that you used to be a lawyer in New York," she said. "My brother has a lawyer, but he's useless. Ohn Myint must have told you."

"She didn't tell me I'd find you tonight."

"She wouldn't know."

The Black Cat had that right; Ohn Myint wouldn't have fit into the 50th Street Bar crowd. None of these people looked like runners.

"She said you'd help my brother."

Calvino nodded, drank from his whiskey.

"I said that. We also discussed the money. She doesn't want to get involved in that part. I can understand."

"I'll handle the money."

Calvino thought about the way the men around the bar looked at her. She could handle money, men and audiences. It was too easy in a way, and Calvino saw that for men like Mya's brother and Rob, smaller souls, less capable and less sure of themselves, not everything in life had handles. For them it was like catching fish barehanded; most of the time they slipped away.

"I'll bring it tomorrow," Calvino said.

"What about tonight?"

"Tomorrow is better. We meet at the courthouse. Ohn Myint picks me up in the morning. You do whatever you have to do there. Afterwards, whatever happens, you arrange for me to meet Rob."

She snuffed out the cigarette. "You know the amount?"

Calvino nodded. "Four and a half."

She got up from the table, looked back at the audience and flashed a smile—that "you belong to me" smile that entertainers who move audiences to tears turn on whenever they get the feeling that the world is flying away from them. The Black Cat wanted her world. Calvino could imagine her as a political activist. This crowd would have burnt down paradise to please her.

"I'll see you tomorrow," she said.

"And afterwards I'll see Rob. Unless you have some secret reason why that shouldn't happen."

"If you knew anything about Burma, you'd know there are no secrets. Everyone talks to everyone else."

She went back on stage, picked up the mike and sang an Etta Jones classic, "Don't Go to Strangers." She looked at Calvino as she sang, until his glance broke away. He had a sense someone was watching him from the audience.

Bianca stood on the staircase. She flashed him a smile as he turned in his chair. He took a drink from his whiskey glass, got up from the table and walked to the stairs, climbing to the step where Bianca waited.

"You made it," he said.

"You and the singer..."

She broke off in mid-sentence.

"Business."

Bianca led Calvino up the stairs, making a display of taking his hand and lingering a moment so the Black Cat couldn't help but see the man she'd been singing a ballad to was holding hands with another woman. Nothing like the attentions of a sexy woman to bring the other women into play, Calvino thought. Their competitive spirit propelled them forward. It was pure instinct.

"There's someone I want you to meet," she said.

They passed booths and tables filled with customers admiring themselves in mirrors mounted on the brick walls.

Bianca stopped at a booth near the bar end, a secluded alcove where lovers could sit without being disturbed. A well-dressed foreigner in his early fifties, eating a hamburger, sat in the middle of the booth, elbows on the table, chewing and smiling as Bianca appeared. Anne sat next to him, smoking a cigarette, looking bored.

Bianca slid into the booth and introduced him as Arnold or Harold, or it might have been Reynolds. Calvino didn't catch the name. The noise from downstairs made it difficult to hear. But his name didn't matter. Nor did his nationality. He was just another guy who was rich or pretending to be rich, who had charmed Bianca.

"The burgers are great," he said. "You want one?"

Calvino waved off the offer. The man shrugged as if to say Calvino didn't know what he was missing. But Calvino did know what he was missing, and it wasn't a hamburger.

Arnold/Harold/Reynolds told Calvino how he'd worked his ass off to locate a Flying Tiger P-40 because he had a collector in the States willing to pay a million dollars for one. He'd now located one of the airplanes and was looking for a partner to retrieve it. This was a once-in-a-lifetime chance. He confided his insider's information about how the P-40 had been stored in Russia during the war. His previous partner had figured out they could forge the registration plate and pass it off as one of the American Volunteer Group V planes.

During World War II, there had been only a hundred Flying Tiger P-40s in Burma. All but a couple had been accounted for. It was a dangerous business running a scam on people who had spent a lifetime studying the Flying Tigers and knew each and every P-40 as if they were their children. The guy had convinced himself it wasn't a grift. He believed that he'd found the real thing and that it was going to make him rich.

"I specialize in finding missing people," said Calvino. "Unless the guy I'm looking for is harnessed inside the cockpit of a P-40, I'm not interested."

Mr. P-40 fell into an uneasy silence. Grease dripped between his fingers as he finished the hamburger and wiped his hands on paper napkins. Calvino had the impression this setup was Bianca's doing; she must have built him up as the guy to talk to about international business ventures. It could have been a covert sting operation, or she might have been using Calvino to assess the deal. Or they could have been looking for a mark, and Calvino, like a lot of others who turned up in Rangoon, seemed to have money. Whatever the plan had been, Arnold/Harold/Reynolds now looked away, embarrassed. Busted expectation made a man go quiet just as it made a woman turn the emotions into song. At least that's the way it seemed to Calvino as, in the silent interlude, the singer's voice penetrated from downstairs.

The Black Cat—it was difficult to think of her under the name Mya Kyaw Thein—had finished her version of "My Man," and after a couple of beats the audience erupted in wild applause and catcalls.

"That girl can belt it out," said the P-40 con man.

Arnold/Harold/Reynolds was a crook, but even a crook couldn't help but speak the truth about a talented performer. Black Cat made it easy for him and everyone else in the room. She had that rare ability only a few singers had. Something beyond a good voice and good looks. She personalized the lyrics, made the audience feel them, convinced each of them that the Black Cat alone owned the feelings and the words and shared them from her heart.

He's not true. He beats me, too. What can I do? Oh, my man, I love him so. He'll never know. And my life is just despair, but I don't care. When he takes me in his arms the world is bright.

Bianca massaged his leg under the table. The muscles, tender from the run, had knotted.

"Are you all right?" she asked him as he winced.

He put his hand over her hand, stilling it.

"That's better."

Anne and Bianca started a conversation in Italian. Soon both hands were above the table and she carried on the discussion as if she were conducting a band.

Calvino sat back and thought about the performance he'd heard downstairs. Like every person—man and woman—in the room, Calvino wanted to cradle the Black Cat in his arms and whisper, "Baby, you'll be okay."

He thought about going downstairs and telling her that, but he had a gut feeling that, actually, it wasn't going to work out for her. How would it end? The way that kind of thing always ended, in disappointment and frustration. Calvino would go downstairs and she'd be gone. Tomorrow morning, she'd show up at the courthouse and be there waiting for him when he arrived with Ohn Myint, his translator, the marker of trails for the Rangoon Running Club, the fixer who gave the MI agent the language he needed to file his report.

They had business to transact, and that was always a problem. Business poisoned the well where all those feelings waited to be lifted up. He had money to offer—it wasn't even his own; it came from Alan Osborne—and she had a boyfriend she was selling. He thought that a woman could still love a man who was unfaithful and beat her but never a man who had rightly calculated what it would cost for her to betray her man.

Colonel Pratt put his saxophone back in the case and closed it. He was ready to return to the hotel. Calvino flew past him and out the door as the Colonel shook hands with Yadanar Khin and the other members of the band. Mya Kyaw Thein had vanished before the applause ended. No one had followed her out. By the time Calvino had gone downstairs and into the street, she'd gone. No one had seen her get into a taxi or a car or onto a motorbike. Wherever she'd vanished to, she hadn't left a clue—it was the way a black cat disappeared into a dark alley.

Bianca lifted her head slightly from Calvino's chest and looked at her watch in the early morning sunlight reflected from the Shwedagon Pagoda. The curtains were open. The golden temple was a beacon in the distance, and the flame of its color washed over her body. Calvino had kicked off the sheets. Sweat beaded on her breasts and spilled onto his belly as she pulled herself up on one elbow. She tried to make out the expression on his face. His head was turned to the side on the pillow as if waiting for her to say something. Anything.

"Do you ask every woman you sleep with to work for you?"

He cupped his hand around the back of her head and pulled her back onto his chest.

"Only if I think she has..."

"Talent?"

He pushed the hair away from her face.

"Talent for digging behind the lies people tell."

She let out a long sigh and shifted her weight to swing one leg over his. He cried out, reaching down to stop the spasm in his calf from working its way up his leg.

"I forgot. You're a sore runner. Not a sore loser."

She sat up to light a cigarette and walked to stand in front of the window, staring at the dark forest and at the temple, enveloped in a cone of golden light.

"I could help you find this person. If you want me to, that is."

Calvino racked his memory to see if this was the first time, moments after making love to a strange woman, she'd volunteered her services to help him find a missing person. Though it wasn't exactly volunteering. He'd practically asked her to do it. He'd just finished telling her that he planned to follow up a lead on the Black Cat's mother, who had a stall in Scott's Market. He told her he'd learnt from a member of the Black Cat's band in Bangkok that her mother had a shop there and was in Bianca's line of business, jewelry. Scott's Market, or Bogyoke Zay, was a big place with lots of stalls, he'd heard. It could take a couple of days to find the mother, and if he went around asking for her, suspicions might arise and she'd shutter her shop and take a holiday.

He'd also told Bianca that finding the mother was less important now that he'd met the Black Cat. But Bianca had thought he should still talk to the mother.

"If you want to know the daughter, always talk to the mother," she'd said.

She'd sounded very Thai at that moment.

Calvino told himself she was right. It was just that this wasn't something you normally asked of a woman ten minutes after one of those Henry Miller scenes of tearing off clothes, deep-mouth kissing, grabbing and sucking, falling into bed, kicking off shoes and peeling off underwear while choreographing body parts as if the participants were alternating between trampoline jumping and mud-wrestling. The entire performance had taken place within the glow of Burma's most holy and sacred symbol.

"If you want to work for me to find the Black Cat's mother, that can be arranged," he said as she turned around.

She had the confused look of someone who wasn't sure what she'd heard.

"*Work* for you?"

"Were you working for Reynolds... the guy with the P-40?"

"You thought that?"

"He might have assumed that from you bringing me to the table."

"Missing persons, missing planes. I thought he might interest you."

"Wet laundry isn't that interesting," he said.

She had a careless way of being in the world. It troubled him that she failed to understand what is truly worth looking for when it goes missing. Calvino called the confusion the wet laundry fallacy. A person dumped a lump of wet laundry at the door and asked him to believe freshly pressed shirts and pants on hangers had been delivered. He could never trust the judgment of such a person.

"What if I did it as a favor? Like helping out a friend," she said.

Calvino watched her eyes as they stared back at him.

In the mutual mauling, the sex had buried all restraint, shyness, caution and civility. The post-sex intimacy had now flooded over both of them. But the thing about intimacy was that a man's idea of what was in the realm of the possible mostly missed the woman's target by a mile. For instance, about the worst thing Calvino could have said was, "Close the curtains on your way out." Practical though the request would have been, it would have said far too much—that flooding of sunshine on a strange woman's face while his mind tried to remember her more alluring countenance in the boozy darkness of the night before.

For a woman, Calvino thought, what she said and what he said before making love no longer exist after the deed is done. Those words are dead and gone to the past, where they should stay buried. What matter to her are the words that come afterward, the kind of words a woman can set to music and sing. And a job offer to find the mother of a talented and sexy woman who held men in thrall wasn't the kind of overture Bianca was interested in.

"You volunteer to help a lot of people you don't know," he said.

She stared at him, making him feel the sting.

"I only wanted to help Reynolds," she said. "Is that a sin?"

"Where's your cross, by the way? The one you usually wear around your neck."

The deflection caused her to touch her throat. She'd rattled him and he'd bucked back as if he'd taken a hard right hook.

"Are you always on the job?" she asked.

She was right. He was always on the job. Even in bed, the sex had only temporarily substituted itself for the case. He was always working on a case. It was what made him a good PI. It was how he found people who'd gone missing. But it also made him a lousy human being. Most of the time he avoided facing the brutal reality of his nature. Bianca, with the sunburned cross on her throat, had nailed him on the first day they'd gone to bed.

"People have feelings," she said to break the silence.

"It was a crazy idea. I shouldn't have asked you. I forget the Italian word for asshole."

"*Testa di cazzo!*"

"That means dickhead. I remember that from my grandfather."

She laughed.

"He called you that?"

"No. Maybe once or twice. Mostly he used it to describe a neighbor in Florence. Like that guy who was looking for someone to be his partner in the P-40 scam. My grandfather would have called that asshole *testa di cazzo*."

She kissed his chest.

"I'll look for the mother tomorrow," she said. "Now tell me about Thailand. About your life."

"What do you want to know?"

"Do you have a wife?"

111

Calvino grinned, stroked her cheek with the back of his hand. It was such a European question. Not "Are you married?" but "Do you have a wife?"

"That's one missing person I've never been able to find."

"Have you been looking in the wrong places?"

"I live in a wrong place for a wife."

"Bangkok," she whispered, as if that explained everything.

In a way it did.

He liked her. She was quick and bright, and had soft skin, tender lips and flashing dark eyes that locked like a predator watching its prey. He liked the missing cross on the throat of a sinner. They'd made love listening to jazz on her iPad. One of those twenty-four hour all-jazz stations.

"You're thinking about your case again," she said, watching his eyes.

"I'm thinking about what happened in the bar last night. The guys in the band, and how Mya Kyaw Thein appeared out of nowhere and made the whole place stop talking for twenty minutes. About how a few people have vast wealth and can do whatever they want."

He was also thinking about something he didn't want to talk about—had Yadanar Khin, son of a Burmese general and government minister, a keyboard player looking for his shot at the musical big time, told Colonel Pratt that the Black Cat would appear? If Yadanar had been surprised by her sudden appearance on stage, he hadn't looked it. Why was that? After the show, the Colonel had stayed on to talk to Yadanar. Calvino had gone back to the hotel with Bianca and Anne. Anne had gone to her room, and Bianca had gone to his.

She brushed her hand across his face. "You are the quiet one. Missing Bangkok?"

"I always miss Bangkok," he said.

"I'm sorry that I couldn't make you forget for one night."

He reached over for the bottle of wine in an ice bucket, found his glass and filled it.

"Take a drink of this. It's my prescription for forgetting."

She sipped from his glass.

"Take a big drink," he said.

"Are you trying to get me drunk?"

"Wine puts a woman in the mood to tell the truth."

"And for a man?"

"His lies become easier for him to believe."

She drank again. Calvino refilled the glass and put the bottle back in the ice bucket.

"What kind of lies do you tell in Bangkok?"

"Mine are small-change deceptions. It's the ultra-rich who swindle and lie in a class of their own. In Bangkok, when a powerful man builds his big house, he has the builders draw blueprints for secret underground rooms. You see these mansions upcountry or in Bangkok, and you think, these people have some serious money. And that's right, but where is it? Stashed in underground rooms. The generals, the big-shot politicians and the cops use bank accounts only for depositing their salaries. You look at their bankbook and it doesn't look like this is someone hogging a huge piece of the pie. But what you're seeing there is the crumbs. The real wealth is inside Mother Earth. You win wars by tunneling underground. You hide your wealth there. It's the missing piece of the puzzle because everyone is looking above the surface. That's the kind of lie that wine speaks about."

They lay side by side, listening to John Coltrane's *Psalm* album.

"How do you know I'm not after you for your room?"

Calvino finished the glass of wine.

"I hope that's the case."

"What do you mean?"

"As long as I have a room with a view, it means you'll keep coming back."

She kissed him long and hard and wet on the lips.

NINE

When a Facebook Friend Goes Rogue

ACCROSS THE TERRACE a Korean couple stood in the shallow end of the pool on either side of their two-year-old, teaching him how to swim. The kid looked tired, cranky as he kicked his legs. His mother shouted encouragement in Korean, while the father held a hand under his child's belly, guiding him slowly forward. Calvino and Pratt had been sitting on the terrace, at a table littered with papers, for nearly an hour. They knew the family were Korean because, passing their table, the father had held up a piece of paper and said, "The MOU has been approved in Seoul by my boss."

As Calvino watched the businessman in the pool with his wife and kid, he said to Colonel Pratt, "The old hands don't call a memorandum of understanding an MOU anymore."

"What do they call it?" asked the Colonel.

"MOM."

"You want me to ask what that means?"

"Memorandum of *mis*-understanding. The script for the later drama. They call that drama 'MOM.' It's like when you were a kid, and you'd run to your mom and tell her you'd been cheated, and she'd say, 'Didn't I tell to stay out of that neighborhood and not to trust that boy?'"

Hotel guests wandered out from the dining room, balancing large white plates heaped with eggs, beans, bacon and hash browns. Stopping, they scanned the terrace for a place to sit. None of them approached the table where Calvino and Pratt sat. The two men gave off a serious "Don't interrupt" vibe.

At that early hour, only diehard businessmen, soldiers of fortune and fanatics had emerged for breakfast, heads bent over a cell phone or an iPad. They had the same crook of the neck and hunched shoulders as the women at the bar the previous night. No one took much notice of the private investigator and the police colonel from Bangkok. The one notable detail was that neither of them held anything with a screen on it. Two middle-aged men slipping between conversation and silence with no electronic device at hand suggested a social situation that was somehow unsettling.

"You think that kid will ever learn to swim?" asked Calvino.

The Colonel had continued to watch the determined Korean couple.

"Sink or swim. What choice does he have?"

Thai parents would have taken their kid out of the pool after a few splashes and laughs.

"I need to know something, Pratt."

The Colonel set down his coffee cup as the waiter arrived to refill it.

"I didn't know," the Colonel said.

A moment passed.

"How did you know what I was going to ask you?"

"Because it's what I'd have asked you if I were looking for someone and she showed up to sing in a band you were playing with. But I was as surprised as you."

"You think she's involved in the cold pill business?"

Pratt shrugged.

"I don't know. It's possible of course, but unlikely. What does she bring to the party? She's a singer, and a talented one. She's political too. That type is too idealistic for this kind of criminal activity."

The dozen or so tables on the terrace were clustered just far enough apart for private conversation. Around the two visitors from Thailand, middle-aged presidents and vice presidents handed each other their business cards, drank their coffee and checked their email. They Skyped a boss at company headquarters sitting in a time zone where it was night, and somewhere nearby jazz bands played and bartenders poured drinks as couples shifted around the dance floor or slipped away to a hotel room to strip off their clothes. But the company never slept, never had sex, never got tired. It was never satisfied.

"Did you find out anything interesting from Yadanar?" Calvino asked.

"About the girl?"

Calvino's head bobbed like a boxer.

"The girl, your cold pill case..."

"I didn't want to push him. A saxophone player asks one kind of question, and a cop asks another. He's the kind of keyboard player who'd notice the difference."

The world's companies had sent their men to Burma. They sat on the terrace all around Calvino and Pratt, reporting their impressions, loading and dumping data.

"How did you leave it with him?"

"I'm invited back. This time I get my solo."

Company men were awake in the Myanmar Time Zone, and all of them knew their place in the network, linked, talking, filtering information about deals, money and competitors. Businessmen drank their coffee and eyed spreadsheets, financial statements and contracts while fueling up with hotel buffet food. Only the tourists at one table ate the Asian-style breakfast—rice soup with bits of pork and vegetables—slurping it audibly. But they were Chinese and that was to be expected.

"Meaning he doesn't expect the Black Cat to return?"

"You could read it that way. Or he might not know."

Calvino's cell phone rang. He removed it from his jacket pocket and answered the call from a time zone half an hour away. Thailand.

Ratana's voice came through from Bangkok as a uniformed waiter offered more coffee. Colonel Pratt was slicing watermelon with a knife and fork while, out of the corner of his eye, watching some crows near the now-deserted swimming pool. The Korean couple and their kid had gone. That left the birds to hop forward, inching their way to an abandoned table littered with buns from the buffet. Someone had left them in tattered shreds, as if they'd been using them as worry beads.

"You're at the office early," Calvino said. Catching Pratt's eye, he said, "It's Ratana."

"I'm at home. I've been online checking Facebook and Twitter."

Calvino took a bit of cold toast.

"You'd fit right in here," he said.

"Before you say that, you should listen."

"I'm listening."

He chewed on the toast.

"I read a personal message on Facebook from a friend. It was disturbing."

Calvino sighed, took a drink of coffee, noticing that Colonel Pratt was displaying one of his knowing smiles. One of the crows had snatched a piece of bun and flown up to a huge tree ten meters away in the hotel garden.

Calvino had previously told the Colonel how Ratana had discovered Facebook and suddenly found herself with thirteen hundred "friends." They posted pictures of their food, their gardens, beaches they were on, new shoes, children, friends and themselves, and announced where they were at any moment. People like that never went missing. Calvino expected that one of these "friends" had sent her a message about Koh Samui, the vacation paradise in the south, because he'd told her that after he returned from Rangoon he'd take her and John-John, her six-year-old son, there on a long weekend. It was as good a way as any to spend some of the money Alan Osborne was paying him to find his son. He figured she'd asked her Facebook pals for travel advice.

"You found a resort in Samui?"

"I'll read the message. 'Hi, everyone. I'm in Rangoon where I met a stallion of a Bangkok PI. He asked me to help him out on a missing person case. Wow, I get to play a James Bond girl. How cool is that? Working undercover.'"

One of the other crows flew close to the table with the deconstructed buns, eyeing another piece. A waiter shooed it away and cleaned the table.

"Something wrong, Vincent?" the Colonel asked.

The color had drained from Calvino's face.

"I'm glad you told me."

"Be careful, Khun Vinny. The woman's name is Bianca."

"I know," he said.

"She also posted photos with a young Thai guy on the beach. They looked to be more than just friends. He had his arm around her waist."

The edge of disappointment and worry turned her voice into a blade that cut his breakfast appetite.

"Thanks for letting me know."

"Bianca has over three thousand friends on Facebook. And they have friends, who have friends of their own. You'll have to tell Colonel Pratt."

"I get the picture. I've got a problem."

He looked at Pratt as the Colonel lifted his coffee cup toward the waiter.

"So does Colonel Pratt."

He closed his eyes.

"Let's hear it."

"This Bianca also said the Bangkok PI's friend played saxophone at the 50th Street Bar last night. She said he's a Thai cop."

"Keep an eye on your messages, and phone me if she posts anything else."

In the back of his brain the tune of "Big Mistake" was playing to the accompaniment of an alto saxophone. It was a melody that wasn't going anywhere but a blind alley.

"What should I reply to my friend?" she asked.

"Right now, don't reply. Keep quiet."

"That's not how friends treat each other's messages."

"You can make it up to her later. Trust me. Don't say anything. I'll talk to Pratt."

The call ended as Calvino looked across at the Colonel, who couldn't help but read the distress in the American's normally confident face. The crash and burn of self-esteem made someone like Calvino blink.

"You look like you have a problem."

Calvino's face never lied.

"It's possible."

Calvino told the Colonel about Bianca's Facebook posting. The Colonel remembered Bianca from the first day in the lobby where they'd waited for Saxon. She and her friend Anne had a heated argument with the assistant manager. Pratt never forgot a confrontation.

"Bianca went back to your room last night?" asked Colonel Pratt.

"She came in for a drink. How did you know it was a woman problem?"

"Wild guess. And Manee phoned me before we came down. She had just talked to Ratana."

Calvino shook his head.

"You've known all morning and didn't say anything?"

"I was thinking about saying something when Ratana phoned."

"Last night I saw all these women working their iPhones, but did I connect that with me? No. I thought, look at those guys, what suckers. Idiots hanging around women checking them out online. And what do I do? I take one of them to my room. If we'd done it on the pitcher's mound at Yankee Stadium, I'd have had an idea there was an audience watching."

"There is no privacy anymore, Vincent."

Calvino twisted the blade of the butter knife between his thumb and index finger.

"I can't stay here. Not after this."

"I've already looked into changing hotels. But it's not possible," Colonel Pratt said. "There are no vacant rooms."

Every hotel room in the city was booked. Hundreds of business people, government officials and NGOs from around the world had come to the party. Changing hotels meant going to some place outside Rangoon. But the whole point of coming to Burma was to be in the city so they could get their jobs done. Calvino's missing person was in Rangoon. The son of the general who headed the Ministry of Health played in a band in Rangoon. They had no choice but to hold tight, contain the damage.

"I'll ask Jack to find me a room."

"He might have a small guest room you can use. Also, talk to Bianca," said the Colonel. "Let her know her messages are causing you complications."

"She's liable to tell her friends I'm threatening her."

Pratt raised an eyebrow.

"Tell her you found Mya Kyaw Thein's mother, thank her for her offer to help, and tell her you're flying back to Bangkok this evening after your court case."

"In other words, I go missing."

Calvino fell into silence just as Bianca and Anne came out on the terrace and made straight for their table. She was all smiles, makeup on, extra lip gloss, hair on her shoulders, sparkling eyes.

"Hey, join us," said Calvino. "I was just saying goodbye to my friend. I found my missing person. It was a stroke of luck. I'm taking him back to Bangkok on an evening flight. I wish I hadn't found him, in a way. I was looking forward to spending time in Rangoon. But I have another case in Bangkok, and I need to get back there to put out a fire."

Bianca's face clouded. It looked like she was going to cry. Composing herself, she looked at Anne and then Calvino.

"I guess I'm happy it worked out."

"Thanks."

"If you'll excuse me, I need to go to my room and pack."

He left Colonel Pratt with the two women.

"In Bangkok," the Colonel confided, "Vincent's nickname is Heartbreaker. But he probably didn't tell you that. He never does."

"Bastard," she said.

The Colonel had seen that face before. It was the one that had glowed with the white heat of anger in the hotel lobby as the staff kept her cooling her heels while trying to figure out who was going to tell her that her view room was occupied by a private eye named Vincent Calvino.

In the elevator ride up to his floor, Calvino thought about the old days, when a man and a woman simply exchanged first glances, their electrical circuits sparking, picked each other up, made passionate, unrestrained love, fell asleep and then parted to disappear back into their private lives.

His parting with Bianca had been abrupt, like the period suddenly appearing at the end of a sentence that should have kept on going. Bianca had got him thinking about formulating a new Calvino's Law. What he had so far wasn't so much a law as the raw material from which laws are formed: "Before you move on the woman you've locked eyes with, think where that first step might take you. She may not look the type to give you grief, but there isn't a profile you can trust, one that tells you if she'll post your picture and your personal details on her Facebook account. You still want her? Okay, now she closes the Facebook window and opens her Twitter account to spill your details 140 characters at a time. That little step across the room finds a mass audience of strangers. Do you really want the eyes of all those strangers watching your big move?"

Calvino had the answer, but it was too late with Bianca. Some laws can't be applied retroactively. What remained could be scrawled on a restroom wall: "The privacy of the casual affair has been permanently disabled."

He'd been busted. It was something he could live with. But compromising Pratt working in the field was another matter. He used the room phone to call Jack Saxon, who was already at his newspaper office and picked up after the second ring.

"Jack, I need to bunk with you for a couple of nights."

"My place is a dump. I don't have air-con. You'd die of heat prostration."

"I'll buy a fan."

"I have a fan you can use."

Can I leave my suitcase at your office? I don't want to drag it into the courtroom."

"That probably wouldn't be too cool. Leave your bags at the hotel, and I'll pick them up later."

"It's better if I take it to your office."

"Bring them over to my place later, then."

The if-you-must tone of voice gave Calvino pause. How to handle Saxon?

"Jack, it's one case. I travel light."

"Since you're usually on the run, that's smart."

Calvino hung up the phone, took his empty case to the bed and opened it. He crouched down in front of the small safe, feeling the last of the strain in his legs. He worked the combination lock, removed his cash, passport, gun and ammo. After ten minutes had passed he'd closed his case and locked it. He sat on the edge of the bed, looking at the Shwedagon Pagoda, gun in his hand. The gun had a good natural grip. He holstered it and strapped the harness over his back so that the weapon fit snugly under his left armpit.

At the front desk Calvino was greeted by the manager whom Jack Saxon had enlisted to take special care of him and get him a view room.

"I'm checking out. Something's come up in Bangkok, and I need to get back immediately."

"I am sorry to hear that. You've been with us only two nights."

"Great room, too. You might want to put those two Italian women in it."

The manager nodded. "We have three or four bookings a day for that room."

"It's your lucky room," said Calvino.

"I am glad you feel that way. I trust it brought you luck, taking you home early, sir."

Calvino was about to say something more but stopped himself. Leaving a manager with a memorable parting remark was never a good idea in the private investigation business. Slipping quietly away under the cover of a white lie wasn't something a hero did, but heroes didn't snoop around Burma looking for missing persons. Heroes stayed home defending friends, castle and wife, and died by making themselves a memorable target.

Calvino climbed inside the taxi, a wreck of a vehicle with peeling upholstery, broken window handles and a rattling transmission. He gave the driver the address of the *Rangoon Times*. On the drive to Jack Saxon's newspaper, Calvino weighed the odds of Bianca's message causing Colonel Pratt a problem. As far as he was concerned, the Facebook write-up was a major personal embarrassment. Ratana must be disappointed that he'd acted so carelessly. As for the Colonel, the stakes were higher. Burma was a place where MIs watched the movements of foreigners. Bianca hadn't said much about the Colonel. She'd heard him playing the sax. What harm could that information cause? But she'd also said he was a Thai cop, and that wasn't so good.

Colonel Pratt could smooth that over with Yadanar, who would have known that detail anyway. The jazz community knew the Colonel worked for the police. After hearing him play, they forgot he was a cop. But there were other players outside the musical community, and they were the real worry.

He knew that any information about a cop's movements had the potential to cause a problem. The Facebook message linked Colonel Pratt to a certain place with certain people. It allowed anyone with minimal intelligence training to connect the dots. And once enough dots were connected, a picture would emerge of a cop working undercover. Once that happened, the inner network of power players would begin to buzz with paranoia, and sooner or later, they would find a target in their midst and move to zero in and destroy it.

Those players had the resources to stop Colonel Pratt from shutting down the flow of millions of cold pills from Burma to Thailand. Before that could happen, though, someone would need to get lucky. Bianca's Facebook feed had to be accessed by someone inside the network in Burma, a place still mostly closed off from outsiders, where the digital world had only just started to seep in. The risk was small. But even a small increase in risk was not something Calvino could shrug off when it came to his best friend.

His hope was that the intelligence sources of the pill smugglers were as limited as the MI agent who'd cornered him on his run. He tried to imagine that guy reading a feed of millions of Facebook posts and Twitter tweets, and by the time the taxi arrived outside the *Rangoon Times*, Calvino was feeling better. He understood why on the terrace the Colonel had been less upset than he'd expected. Things were getting interesting. Not that that was something either of them really wanted.

There had always been an excess of foreigner-watchers in Burma. But recently the pace of change had not so much quickened as exploded overnight, along with the number of foreigners. Calvino and Colonel Pratt's decision to split up and stay in different places would make the MIs' jobs more difficult. Calvino told himself the damage had been contained. He hadn't come to Rangoon for a holiday. It had been a mistake for the two of them to stay at the same upscale hotel. Besides, the secluded luxury distracted a man from his work.

He breathed more freely as he stood on the curb and watched the taxi pull away.

TEN

Ownerless Dogs Sleeping in The Courtyard

THE *RANGOON TIME* occupied an ugly square box of a building. Its paint peeling and smeared with grime, it faced a church across the road that had the aging, grand style of an old dowager. In contrast, the press, if it ever had a pretty face in Burma, had masked it under a burka of mystery and secrecy for the last half century. Jack Saxon had said the good news about the political changes was that the local press had been upgraded to a hijab.

"One step at a time, and before you know it, we're going to have tabloids with nude women bathing on the Irrawaddy," Saxon had said.

The next thing you know, the press might, like a Saudi woman, demand to drive a car without an escort. As for the church across the street, with its donation boxes, prayers and rosary beads, perhaps it would also wake up, stretch, look around and decide to dust off its teachings. Calvino studied the large bank of stained glass windows facing the road. Messages about an afterlife were old news to him.

The newspaper office was at the end of a wide staircase on the second floor. A slightly overweight Burmese woman, reading a newspaper and picking her teeth like a precinct sergeant, sat behind a large teak reception desk. She saw him come up the stairs carrying a suitcase as if he thought he was arriving at a hotel.

"I'm here to see Jack Saxon," he said.

"Have a seat."

She picked up the phone, keeping an eye on Calvino as she removed the toothpick from her mouth and dialed Saxon's number. Calvino sat in a hard chair, waiting for Saxon to finish doing whatever he was doing before coming out to meet him.

When Saxon finally walked into reception, he looked distracted as he talked into his cell phone. He gestured to Calvino to follow him.

"Anyone ever tell you your receptionist looks like she's straight out of an NYPD borough precinct?"

"Only visiting criminals from New York," said Saxon, without looking back at Calvino.

He closed his cell phone and left it in his right hand as he led the way. They passed a dozen reporters and staff working at desks in a long, narrow room, eyes glued to their computer screens. That guy is posting on Facebook, thought Calvino, as his eyes passed over the screen. He was rolling his bag behind him, and the racket it made had heads popping up.

"Don't mind my American friend. He's mistaken us for the Holiday Inn. It happens all the time."

Calvino smiled and gave one of those borough politician's waves of the hand as if to acknowledge their existence on his way to the big office at the end of room. It was the same wave he'd used so effectively in the villages he'd passed through on the run.

The floors of the newspaper office, an unfinished concrete, could have come from a slaughterhouse. The interior design had the look of a warehouse with long rows of desk banged in. At the end of the room Saxon had a separate cubicle, as befitted a senior editor. On his desk was a red phone. Every call to that number was an emergency from the publisher, a police official, a general or a civil servant. The handset lay on the desk beside the phone. The line was permanently busy.

Saxon laid his cell phone on the desk next to the red phone and sat in his chair.

"You can put your bag here. And you can tell me why you checked out of a hotel that hundreds of foreigners are crying and bribing to get into?"

Calvino rolled his case underneath a long built-in desk trimmed with blue strips to make it look modern. Piles of papers were scattered at both ends. His working space was confined to a small center area.

"The toilet wasn't up to standard," said Calvino.

Saxon's jaw dropped.

"Kiss My Trash—you're kidding! Wait until you see the toilet in my place."

"Can't wait, Jack. And thanks for putting me up."

"You still haven't told me why you checked out."

"It's better Pratt and I stay at separate places."

"You're here two days, and already in trouble?"

"Am I going to complicate your life, is that what you're worried about?"

"You've already complicated it. The question is how much grief can I expect while you're in Rangoon and how much grief you plan to leave behind once you get on the plane. Remember, you go home; I live here."

Calvino nodded. He understood Saxon's position. A man's own troubles in a place like Rangoon or Bangkok were difficult enough, but the shadows left by others putting their noses into the locals' business scaled the risk in ways that were impossible to calculate. How many times had Calvino told someone what Saxon had just said to him? He'd lost track.

"What I have in mind is a guesthouse where I can check in without anyone asking for a lot of personal information, like a passport," said Calvino.

Saxon's face collapsed as he flipped through a notebook, running a finger down the page, turning it before looking up with a big smile.

"There is a place not far from the Savoy Hotel. But you'll hate the toilet."

"I'll use the one at the Savoy."

"I don't think they'd like that."

Ohn Myint's face suddenly appeared inside Saxon's cubicle.

"Ohn, you're exactly on time," said Saxon.

"I've got a taxi waiting downstairs," she said. "We should be on our way."

It was the first time that Calvino had seen her in regular clothes. She wore a freshly pressed longyi and white blouse and had makeup and a light brush of lipstick. Her hair had been combed, parted and tied back in a ponytail. She smelled of perfume and sliced oranges. Her glasses gave her a professional look, like a lawyer or a librarian.

"I phoned her. I hope you don't mind, Vinny. But I've got a ton of work here."

Calvino was on his feet.

"Let's have dinner tonight," Calvino said. "I'm buying."

It was just like Jack Saxon to phone Ohn Myint and reorganize the money pickup. He hadn't mentioned Calvino's name to her directly but said the lawyer going to court was waiting for her in his office. Saxon had assumed the call was being recorded. The link had been made. The MI diehards read the *Rangoon Times* and were aware of the big changes in Burma. They'd been told to expect lawyers, accountants and bankers to arrive by the planeload. But no one in the chain of command had told the MI agents in the field anything about how that would affect their job. They kept doing it as they'd always done. That was the idea, one that would make Calvino a person of interest independent of Colonel Pratt.

Someone would have asked: Who is this foreigner who has wormed his way into a criminal trial of no particular interest? Why is he interested in four ordinary defendants who are on their way to receiving long prison terms?

"I'll look after your suitcase, and I'll see you at the Savoy Hotel at seven."

"You're not coming along?" asked Calvino.

"Two white faces at the court hearing would be a little too memorable."

Calvino picked up his briefcase. Inside he had the cash. The plan was to give the briefcase to the Black Cat at the courthouse. He took a long last look at his suitcase under Saxon's desk.

"I'll handle it," Saxon said. He clenched his jaw and looked at the ceiling. "Remind me to thank my brother Paul for making my life so interesting."

During the taxi ride to the courthouse, Calvino told Ohn Myint the story of what had happened to Jack Saxon's brother Paul in Bangkok.

"I'm old enough to remember a time when a man's character was measured by his willingness to lead a mission to rescue a friend. It was something you did. But that was a long time ago, and not a lot of people think like that any more."

"Does that explain why you came to Rangoon with the Colonel?"

"It explains why you're here in the taxi with me. Jack's your friend."

Calvino looked at the people in the street. He'd been thinking that Saxon had picked good friends, and that that was a good way to judge a person's character.

"People don't have true friends in a lot of places. When friends are considered a kind of subprime emotional mortgage, you're alone. I can't think of a place where I'd want to be that alone."

He waited for her to say something.

"What matters is, you're making this happen," said Calvino. "That's not easy. You feel the rope around your neck."

Ohn Myint had listened carefully but hadn't said much as the taxi entered the northern outskirts of Rangoon. People walked along the dusty road in longyis and sandals before cramped, rundown buildings and one-story shacks baking in the morning sun. The forest had ended as the need for firewood doomed its further expansion.

"Friends help friends," she said, taking the high ground.

"Jack trusts you. That's all I need to know."

She offered a pragmatic, common-sense smile as if to say, "Isn't that obvious? Why otherwise would I be here with you?"

Instead she said, "Vincent, I want to be clear. You deliver the briefcase to Mya Kyaw Thein, and she will deal with it from there. It's been arranged for you to sit in the courtroom. Then we return to your hotel. Tomorrow Mya Kyaw Thein should have her good news."

Her plan suggested that she had no problem drawing a line where one needed to be drawn. Friends didn't push friends over that line. Calvino couldn't blame her. He wasn't entirely certain that if the situation were reversed, he would stick his neck out as far as she was doing. She was right to be careful about accepting new members within a friendship circle. Calvino was just a friend of a friend, though a friend of Jack Saxon's was close enough for her to help. Saxon had told her Calvino was in Rangoon to find a missing son of an old friend and to assist a friend of his who was a Thai police colonel, and she'd decided he was worth helping.

Calvino went quiet as Ohn Myint withdrew into her own world. She had a lot to think about, and he wondered how much Saxon had told her about what had happened with his brother in Bangkok. Calvino stared out the window. People walking along the road or riding cheap Chinese bicycles. Trucks and old buses passed. Lives hammered by sun, dust, poverty and oppression. Blank, empty faces. He thought of Saxon's proverb about the man eating rice and breathing in the smell of fish cooking.

"Mya Kyaw Thein says they grabbed her brother because they didn't like her political views."

"Wai Wan was caught red-handed with a truckload of teak."

"But they catch only a few smugglers. Is teak smuggling suddenly a high priority?"

Ohn Myint sniffed from the dust kicked up by the boys playing soccer.

"If the political situation weren't changing for the better, would she have come back? I don't think so. She'd have been arrested, and they wouldn't have needed to find her riding on a truckload of teak to charge her."

"You don't like her."

Ohn Myint shrugged.

"Like, don't like. I don't know. Some people choose to stay outside a country and throw rocks at the windows. They want people to believe they have all the answers. When the country opens, they want to take all of the credit. It was their rock throwing, they tell us, that did the trick. As for those who stayed behind and quietly worked for change, they don't talk about us. We didn't throw any of their rocks. They come back to tell us that they made all of the sacrifices. But not everyone sees it that way."

"You and the Black Cat should have a talk."

"The whole country is talking. For the first time people aren't scared to say what's on their mind. That is good."

Calvino thought about her answer—noncommittal, impersonal, open and vague. Ohn Myint wasn't afraid to talk to Black Cat or anyone else. Throughout the country others were finding their voice, and no one was stopping them. All those years of the great silence were slowly fading as the volume of voices expanded. The howls from vanguard of globalized riders, the cracked of their whips echoed through the airport halls, the hotel lobbies, bars and restaurants. These foreign voices were everywhere and Rangoon was listening.

The two fell into silence again until Ohn Myint said, "She'll meet us in the courtyard. You can talk to her alone. Ask her yourself."

There was no need to explain why Mya Kyaw Thein would go separately. It was the Burmese way—find your own way to lay down smoke, a small cloud to blur the vision of the MIs. As they rubbed their eyes, a small gap would open and the MIs' targets would dissolve, vanish just as they had appeared, alone, as if carried by a sudden gust of wind.

The taxi driver had no trouble finding the Insein Northern Divisional Courthouse. Like an airport shuttle driver, his internal GPS took him by the best possible route. The location of the criminal court was common knowledge. No one needed a map. It was more than a court; inside this building the regime processed ordinary people into the criminal class and assigned them floor space in the vast prison system.

Many Burmese had relatives, friends or neighbors, sometimes one or two degrees removed, who'd dragged their shackles across the threshold of the court. As the taxi turned into a parking area at the courthouse, a white prison van parked on the side unloaded a batch of prisoners, arms chained, legs manacled, under the watchful eyes of guards.

The prisoners struggled to walk in their chains and their longyis. It required a supreme effort of coordination not to stumble into the prisoner in front or be toppled by the one behind, with everyone falling like bowling pins. Some prisoners had the hang of it more than others.

Ohn Myint paid the driver and they got out in front of the courthouse.

"Where are they taking those prisoners?" asked Calvino.

"They lock them in cages inside. There's a special holding pen on the courthouse grounds," said Ohn Myint.

"Do you see Mya Kyaw Thein's brother?"

She looked at the faces as their taxi pulled away.

"No. I don't see him with that lot. Wai Wan's probably already inside. Vans come in and out all day. If a prisoner has money, they move him from the pen to an office."

Calvino reached for his wallet.

"How much do you need?"

"You can rent the warden's office and he can sit in air conditioning. Fifty dollars. Without the leg irons it's another twenty dollars."

"The à la carte justice system."

He pulled out seventy dollars and pressed the notes into her hand. She shrugged and stared at the money before slipping it in her bag.

"If you have big money, and it's not a political crime, you will get off. Eventually. It takes time in Burma to get charges dropped. Just as it takes time before minds accept change. If you've pissed off someone important, it can get expensive."

Calvino had an idea the Black Cat fell in the category of rock throwers who paid a premium for the windows they broke. As he and Ohn Myint walked up to the courthouse, they watched as the prisoners and their guards disappeared inside. The courthouse was a long, two-story remnant of nineteenth-century colonialism, located off the main road, with railroad tracks running along one side. The British had been masters at building symbols of imperial authority like this one. Now the red-brick vestige of empire served the new oligarchy with the same brutal efficiency as the one it displaced.

The prisoners being delivered to the court were skin and bones. In this building that looked like a ruin, judges tried human skeletons. Calvino and Ohn Myint walked through the archway. Twenty feet ahead, half a dozen numb-looking prisoners were herded down a corridor to disappear around a corner. Ohn Myint hardly noticed them as she led Calvino through a long walkway to a courtyard, following the smell of fried banana, coconut and the hangman's rope.

They arrived at the courtyard to find a hot sun blazing overhead. People took shelter at small wooden tables under large umbrellas. Dogs with festering sores and faces scarred from fighting over scraps sunbathed in the dirt, turning in their sleep like boxers in a coma and ignoring the young boys kicking a soccer ball a few feet away. Near Calvino, a middle-aged lawyer in a white shirt and a black Burmese coat stuffed betel nut between his teeth and gums as he listened to a relative of a defendant moan, weep and collapse into sorrow. Calvino scanned the scene for the Black Cat.

"I'll be back," said Ohn Myint. "Make yourself comfortable. They have tea."

She left to find the warden to arrange for the brother's transfer to more comfortable conditions.

Tea? he thought.

"I'll wait for you here," he said, sitting down at one of the tables.

The Burmese in the courtyard stared at him. No one had seen a white man there for years. They murmured among themselves that Calvino was an omen. Like the villagers

136

on the 10K run, they smiled and nodded, and one of the women got up from her table and brought him a plate of sliced pineapple.

As he sat waiting for Ohn Myint, he ate the pineapple and watched the food vendors, brokers, family members, lawyers, touts and dogs sharing tables around him, under umbrellas, or taking shade under the roof overhanging the corridor. Gradually people stopped staring at him.

The courtyard was part market, part festival—a place of medieval contradictions where harsh justice mixed with food, betel nut and games, fixers and astrologers, amid gossip, secrets, regrets and intrigue. It was also part funeral. A reunion of friends and family and neighbors with a shared bond—one of their own was being thrown into the large meat grinder of the system. At the tables men and women, sad and happy, listless and active, conspiratorial and confessional, drank, whispered and watched for their son, brother, father, uncle or cousin to appear from a holding cell. For people who'd long survived in desperation, anyone like Calvino was a possible source of hope. More plates of fruit were delivered to his table.

Soon he was surrounded with food offerings. Flies buzzed around slices of watermelon, coconut and mango. When Ohn Myint returned, she found Calvino sitting under an umbrella, elbows on the table, his briefcase on his lap, looking over a feast of food at some children kicking a soccer ball in the dirt nearby. She laughed.

"You ordered all of this?"

"I was hungry," he said.

She shooed away the flies with her hand and popped a slice of pineapple in her mouth.

"It's done," she said. "Wai Wan is in the warden's office."

"How's he look?"

"Jack told me you were the sensitive type."

She knew that anyone who, like the Black Cat's brother, had been locked inside the Insein Prison for a couple of months would have joined the brotherhood of the beaten down and haunted, the less than human. That was the whole idea of prison.

"Mya Kyaw Thein should be here any time," she added.

A narrow walkway separated the courtyard from the bank of doors leading to half a dozen courtrooms. When one of the doors opened, the lawyers and relatives of the accused rushed from their tables to crowd in front of the entrance and watch.

Above where Calvino sat, men in uniforms paced across the balcony that wrapped the building's interior, watching the people below. Ever since he'd sat down, they'd seen people giving him offerings as if he were a monk. A white face looked out of place here, where the abundant sunlight belied the darkness of what went on inside the adjacent rooms. Calvino's presence reminded them of the days when it was men who looked like him who'd sat on the bench and judged them. That was another time. In this time and in this place, the power had shifted. The faces on the balcony were those of hard men. The majesty of the courts—judges, lawyers, all the Burmese in uniforms—was built on a bedrock of hard men who carried out their judgments. Men who didn't flinch, who weren't squeamish. The kind of man every regime used to project authority.

Calvino would have stood out as the most likely person to have paid to have Wai Wan transferred to the air-conditioned warden's office. Here was a man who understood how justice worked. There was one good reason not to be poor, one that had nothing to do with buying shiny objects with touch screens; it was about shedding chains for half an hour before facing a judge. Wai Wan could count himself lucky, they must have thought, to have a white man come to the courthouse and pay money for a common prisoner to sit in an important office. Such a man was someone who needed watching.

"When can I see Wai Wan?"

Ohn Myint looked away, thinking for a moment.

"Inside the courtroom."

"How can I do anything for my client if I can't talk to him?"

She shrugged.

"It's the rule. He's not officially your client. It would be good if you didn't refer to him as your client inside the courtroom."

The system seemed to be not that different from a Thai court, Calvino thought. Forget about burden of proof, rules of evidence, questioning the Crown's case, as those approaches were beside the point. Only guilty people were brought to a courtroom. They were there to have their guilt confirmed. Wai Wan waited in the warden's room, having no idea how his fortune had suddenly turned for the better. Soon he'd be delivered to the courtroom and would discover whether his good fortune would continue, bringing him freedom, or his guilt would be rubber-stamped.

"It's better you talk to Wai Wan's lawyer. He can fill you in on the details."

Ohn Myint's job wasn't to defend or explain the system but to translate for Calvino at the hearing. He would say what he wanted to say, and she'd convey the part of it that she thought was appropriate. The prosecutor would say what he would say, and she'd translate that for Calvino in full. And Wai Wan would testify and she'd translate that too. The judge would say little. He would take notes as she translated what Calvino said. The fact that Calvino was to be allowed in the courtroom was already a victory. It was highly unusual and had been difficult to arrange, though she didn't feel it was necessary to explain this background to Calvino.

"This isn't going to work," Calvino said.

"It's up to you. We are here. Arrangements have been made. What is there to lose?"

"I don't think Mya Kyaw Thein's going to show."

"Mr. Calvino, she would do anything for her brother. You shouldn't worry. Let her find you."

"She's pretty good at finding me when she wants," said Calvino.

Relax, he told himself. She'd materialize out of thin air just as she'd done at the 50th Street Bar. Only this appearance would be different. She'd be in the audience this time, for her brother's performance.

He felt a tap on his shoulder, turned around and saw a strange woman looking down at him.

"You don't recognize me? That is the way it should be."

She took his briefcase from the table and walked away. He turned and started to get up. Ohn Myint pulled on his arm, and he sat back down. He watched as she walked several tables away and sat the briefcase down in front of the middle-aged lawyer chewing betel nut.

ELEVEN

The Trial of Pigeons

MYA KYAW THEIN had entered in lockstep with the betel nut vendors who went from table to table—three old ladies under an umbrella. She looked and dressed like she was part of their group. An older woman in the middle of the group carried a large tray of yellow tofu cut into slices. The other two carried plastic stools to set up shop under an old gnarled tree that looked as if it might have been a seedling when the courthouse first opened. The tree and the courtyard had seen generations of defendant witnesses, families and friends of the defendants, touts and brokers, senior lawyers, junior lawyers and Crown prosecutors, all out under the morning sun, sitting around tables waiting for their case to be called.

The Black Cat had slipped into the courtyard dressed like a family member of someone with a court appearance. One of those sad people, dressed in worn clothes and feet caked with dust, who only saw her loved one on court appearance days. She was unrecognizable from the star who had won over the audience at the 50th Street Bar. She had transformed herself into just another faceless peasant. To MI agents milling around the grounds, she would have been invisible.

Wasting no time, she took a stool beside her brother's lawyer, setting Calvino's briefcase down beside his stool.

She found Calvino's eye and gestured for him to join her and the lawyer.

Ohn Myint said, "You're being summoned."

"You're coming too?"

"Yes, I need to talk to the lawyer."

As soon as Calvino sat at the table, Mya Kyaw Thein wasted no time introducing him as her brother's American lawyer. A plump Burmese man with large, round jowls that collapsed like airbags as he leaned over his tea, he listened to Calvino, eyeing him closely. She spoke in English so that Calvino could hear himself described as a New York lawyer who'd flown in to assist in the case. Then she switched into Burmese to talk about the briefcase. Calvino was lost as soon as she spoke in Burmese.

"What's she saying to him?" he asked Ohn Myint.

"She's saying you're from New York."

"She said that in English."

"She's saying how famous you are in New York."

"I'm from Bangkok," he said, "and I'm not famous in New York."

"Too much detail confuses people," she said as Mya Kyaw Thein continued in Burmese to tell the lawyer how Calvino was a celebrity New York lawyer who took only high-profile cases, and that he should understand how lucky he was to have Calvino with him in the courtroom. Once the judge understood that a senior New York lawyer had come to defend a simple Burmese man, he would see that the country really had changed, and the American embassy would send an ambassador from Washington soon afterwards. And there was the matter of cash. It was in the briefcase.

"She's telling him that the American government is watching the outcome of the trial with interest."

"'All that is solid melts into air. All that is holy is profaned,'" said Calvino. "I'd always wondered what inspired someone to write those words."

The lawyer's eyes narrowed as he stared at Calvino. His client had been accused of teak smuggling, and as far as he could see, it was an open and shut case. Why would the Americans bother themselves with the case of a common criminal? He scratched his head and drank his tea, his foot nudging the briefcase.

"It only looks like an ordinary case," the Black Cat said. "The fact that the Americans have sent a top lawyer has to tell you that something important is involved, something not in the file."

Mya Kyaw Thein assured the man that he was still lead counsel and Calvino had come only to offer technical support. He stared at Calvino, wondering how a New Yorker had become an expert in Burmese teak smuggling. The Burmese lawyer, by contrast, looked like he could've been the boy who planted the old tree in the courtyard. After the Black Cat finished her speech, he turned to Calvino.

In English he told Calvino how he'd previously worked as a judge and resigned to take counsel work. He knew a thing or two about how the system worked from the inside. His jowls matched his large, rounded stomach perfectly. He wore a gold stud in the top button of his white shirt.

"I loved Sherlock Holmes and Perry Mason. Do you know their work? Top drawer."

He spoke perfectly acceptable English, stopping to lean over to spit a stream of betel juice into the dirt. Betel juice justice was an old tradition.

Calvino nodded.

"I watched Perry Mason on TV as a kid," said Calvino.

"Everyone in Burma knows Perry Mason," said Ohn Myint.

Perry Mason was something Calvino's parents and grandparents had discussed over the kitchen table in Brooklyn. The ancient courthouse and now Perry Mason confirmed that he'd passed through an airlock to another time and place, where Raymond Burr defended criminals in black and white on small screens.

The old ex-judge tugged at his gold-framed glasses as he reached for a pen sticking out of the pocket of his black coat. Calvino watched as he unscrewed the cap. He imagined him sitting on the bench performing the same ritual. The lawyer wrote slowly on a notepad, using a deliberate, discursive lettering that had otherwise left long ago with the British. At the end of the note, he wrote a number. He screwed the cap back onto the pen as he reviewed his note. With a satisfied nod, he returned his pen to his coat pocket and handed the paper to Calvino, who read what the ex-judge had written:

"Your Honor, your dismissal of charges against Wai Wan will show the American government your fairness and courage and demonstrate for the world to see that Myanmar's courts can be trusted to deliver justice."

Calvino reread the note.

"That's it?"

But somewhere between the lines was a number with a dollar sign in front of it: $4500. Not a particularly round number, one might say, but that would be to miss the point. The digits added up to nine, and the Burmese were fond of the number nine because it represented good fortune. Ne Win, the old dictator, had once issued a decree requiring that all Burmese currency be reissued in denominations divisible by nine. Ne Win was the same strongman who had once sat atop a white stallion that was loaded onto a military aircraft so that horse and rider could circle Rangoon nine times. A fortune teller had told Ne Win that in a dream he had seen a powerful general riding a white horse in the sky over the city, and that that man could never be defeated.

Calvino passed the note to Mya Kyaw Thein. She displayed no emotion as she read it. The money was already at the lawyer's feet, and Calvino had his script. Ohn Myint had kept her distance, drinking tea and watching the boys running after the soccer ball. To be that young and innocent, to lose oneself in a game seemed magical to her, like running. Her thoughts drifted to the weekend and the new 10K route she would mark. Maybe Saxon would come along and help this time.

The lawyer slid a piece of betel nut inside his mouth, smiling with red teeth as Calvino finally nodded. The Burmese lawyer had been a judge for thirty years before retiring to private practice. In his view the case had been resolved, and that's what judges and lawyers did—resolve cases.

"Yes, that's it," said the lawyer. "Keep the note. If you have any questions, please ask me."

The ex-judge smiled like a fat-bellied cat that had scored a sparrow. He liked an audience, especially one with an attentive foreigner. With the business out of the way, he began to recount his memories from his days on the bench. With sad eyes, his jowls shaking as he moved his head from side to side, he confided how hard it had been to sentence men to death.

"Sending a criminal to the gallows is a terrible responsibility."

He chewed his betel, lost in thought while retaining his executioner's confidence. He sat erect like a judge on the bench, a professional, a man at peace with working inside the criminal justice system.

"What is the exact charge against Wai Wan?" asked Calvino.

He had no illusions that the executioners in this part of the world worried themselves about technicalities. But he knew that when the executioner's men were asked, they could play the law game as well as the best of them.

Calvino made his next move: "What elements does the Crown have to prove to convict him? What evidence do they have to connect him to the crime, is what I am saying."

That wasn't what they heard him saying. What they heard was someone from New York asking irrelevant questions. None of that mattered. Would someone tell this American lawyer this wasn't New York, and proving or disapproving hadn't mattered once the young man had been caught up in the machinery? The gears of the system had meshed, tearing and ripping, running automatically, and it was difficult to remove a man stuck inside.

Calvino wanted to ask more questions of the hanging judge, but before he had a chance, the lawyer raised his hand.

"As lawyers we know you have a right to know. So I will tell you what the Crown has proved so far. It's all about a permit. If you have one, okay. And if you don't?"

He flashed his hanging judge half-smile.

The lawyer bent to the side and spit a glob of red juice in the dirt. He wiped his mouth with a folded and pressed white handkerchief that he produced from his black coat and then told Wai Wan's story. Wai Wan and three other men had been charged with the illegal transportation of teak. On the outskirts of Rangoon, a cop on a motorcycle had pulled over their truck, examined the cargo and found teak doors and window frames. The cop asked to see the teak transportation permit. Wai Wan shrugged. He didn't have one. The cargo owner hadn't gone to the Forestry Department and applied for the permit. Neither had Wai Wan. He admitted that. But he was only a driver, hired labor. He wasn't in the teak business; he was in the trucking business. Applying for permits wasn't something a driver did. This was something the teak dealer arranged.

However, the owner wasn't on trial. She had paid a large bribe and walked away free and clear. The driver, the spare driver and two passengers, who didn't know the truck carried teak, had been charged and faced ten years in prison. They had no money to buy their way out.

After the lawyer finished, Mya Kyaw Thein stared at Calvino.

"You see? Do you understand?"

Calvino nodded that he got the message and, smiling, signaled that he had his to deliver.

"He's got a permit problem, and he's also got a sister who wrote anti-government blogs, and that may have had something to do with the charges."

"That's speculation, Mr. Calvino."

"Does it matter now? Aren't we done here?" asked the Black Cat.

Both men looked at her, and Ohn Myint turned away from the soccer game to look at the Black Cat too. She was right about that, thought Calvino. There wasn't anything else to say. The deal was done; the game's outcome was set.

Mya Kyaw Thein's brother had been set up while the teak owner had walked. What was happening to Wai Wan peeled away layers of injustice. But the ex-judge was likely right, Calvino realized—to point at corruption was just speculation. Wai Wan was doomed the moment the teak truck without a permit was stopped and he and others were left holding the bag. It had never been political. That had all been inside the Black Cat's mind.

Wai Wan's case was a petty-ante nothing of a case. What he'd done and what would happen to him didn't matter. His misery was no more than a paper cut in a wall of raw meat ten miles high and five miles wide. Yeah, it was unfair that the rich owner walked, but no one cared about such a tiny injury. In the scheme of things, Wai Wan's life and freedom didn't have much value. Calvino had started to understand what the ex-judge had been trying to tell him all along—the brother's case could be fixed for a small sum of money because he was a nobody facing an ordinary criminal charge. If his case had truly been political or the authorities were gunning for the Black Cat, they wouldn't have settled for a lousy four and half grand.

Ohn Myint spotted Wai Wan among a group of prisoners on the walkway.

"We need to go to the courtroom," she said.

Wai Wan and three other manacled men were led into the courtroom by two police officers in gray uniforms as a vendor lowered her tray of sliced watermelon toward a granny in the crowd with watery eyes and missing teeth. Behind the prisoners the guards took their place just inside the door. Ohn Myint walked alongside Calvino, the Burmese lawyer and his junior, a young Burmese woman who'd said nothing at the table. When Calvino looked back, the Black Cat had vanished. The ex-judge led the way to the defense counsel's table. He and his junior sat at the counsel table, and Calvino and Ohn Myint sat on chairs behind them.

The accused shuffled across the untiled floor to a low wooden bench placed against the wall facing the high bench—it looked like a close cousin to the reception desk at the *Rangoon Times*. The chained men moved in single file and sat down in unison on the bench. A few months in prison had taught them the value of coordination.

The opposing counsels' wood tables faced one another. The middle-aged lead Crown prosecutor had just entered. His assistant seemed to be freshly graduated from law school and wore two bangles on her left wrist, one blue and the other orange, as well as a gold ring on her middle finger and gold earrings. The two prosecutors leaned together and whispered as they glanced in Calvino's direction. His presence puzzled them.

In between the tables, a court reporter sat dwarfed behind a large black typewriter that would have been old in Orwell's day. It had a long carriage to allow the user to find the key for each letter in the Burmese alphabet. Facing the prisoners and with his back to the high bench, which blocked any avenue of escape, he was like a bombardier, totally alone and exposed.

The courtroom had no seats for family, friends, the press or the curious retirees who in Western countries found courtrooms a form of entertainment. Calvino saw Mya Kyaw Thein moving in and out of the doorway along with a host of other relatives and friends of the men inside. They took turns, rotating after a couple of minutes, letting another set of eyes watch. She caught her brother's eyes, and he smiled.

Behind the large teak bench was an empty high-backed chair made of leather. Everyone had taken their assigned places except the judge, and the room of people waited in silence, shuffling papers. The open windows behind the defense table allowed traffic sounds to filter in from the road behind the row of palm trees. Wai Wan's lawyer pulled on his black gown. Outside the courtroom, a rooster crowed as if signaling a false dawn, when in fact the crowing coincided with the arrival of the judge.

The judge walked through a doorway framed with faded yellow curtains that were tied back. He appeared in black robes and wearing a *gaung baung* with green trimming. Everyone stood.

He entered in a dignified fashion, sitting on his throne-like chair behind the towering teak bench. On the wall in a gold frame hung the country's coat of arms—roaring lions, red on white. The judge looked like the awe-inspiring Wizard of Oz staring down at the Scarecrow, the Tin Man and the Cowardly Lion in handcuffs on the wooden bench below. A murmur arose outside the courtroom as word spread that the proceedings were about to start. People from the courtyard crowded into the doorway. The soccer game stopped.

A calendar was nailed above the half-partition that separated the courtroom from the one next door. There was no clock. One of the guards found a key on a thick ring of keys and unlocked Wai Wan's handcuffs. He was the first to testify. He walked to a platform and stepped up, facing the judge, but still much lower than where the judge sat. He swore an oath to tell the truth. He swore by placing his hand on a lacquered palm leaf with Buddhist scriptures written in Sanskrit and wrapped in a red cloth. He swore to the Buddha to tell the truth. During the swearing the feathery beating sound of bird wings nearly drowned out Wai Wan's voice. No one paid any attention to the far wall, where at the top a row of windows with torn wire mesh had become a nesting place for birds. As Wai Wan swore his oath, pigeons fluttered and cooed, flying in and out from the courtyard side.

The ex-hanging judge slipped on his official white hat, a *gaung baung*, casting him in the role of the good guy in the drama. The junior lawyers and the Crown counsel wore pink versions. The hats were frayed and yellowed around the rim, as if they'd been handed down for generations without ever being laundered.

Wai Wan gave his name, his father's name and his mother's name. The three other defendants leaned forward on the wooden railing in front of their bench, listening to Wai Wan testify to events he'd spoken about many times. His voice droned on as if he were reading from a script. He explained how his truck had been stopped forty miles outside Rangoon. A policeman on a motorcycle had pulled him over. It was night. They had almost reached their destination when the police officer had asked for their papers.

Wai Wan had been behind the wheel of the truck carrying the teak cargo. He had stopped at eight checkpoints and been waved through. There hadn't been a problem. After the ninth toll-gate, though, he saw in his rearview mirror that the truck was being tailed by a sole motorcycle cop. Something had gone wrong. He'd done nothing and had nothing to hide. He was a truck driver. He hauled cargo. Owners phoned him and gave him work. He assumed the paperwork had been done. That was the owner's job. They did the paperwork, he drove. Officers manning eight toll-gates had sent him on his way to Rangoon. Not one had asked to see a permit. Besides, he was a little fish. Trading teak was a big-fish business. The biggest teak traders were sending truckloads across the border to China. It was an open secret.

As Wai Wan testified and the birds glided in and out of the holes in the broken wire mesh—sparrows and pigeons— the sound of the clattering old typewriter and the echo of the same machine from the courtroom next door created a dull ache of sound as if the suffering of the defendant's voice had inhabited it.

From the doorway Calvino saw Mya Kyaw Thein's face among the crowd. She blended into the background. Calvino saw her and wondered how much the thoughts of Henry Miller mattered to her at that moment. The author who had roughed it in Paris had never been in a Rangoon courtroom. That was an order of magnitude beyond what Miller could have imagined. The criminal proceedings involving her brother had delivered a nugget of meaning; she'd learned the ultimate definition of being down and out. She struggled with what she saw and fought with all of her will not to make a scene. She told herself that she must be patient, that everything would work out. Wai Wan would be set free. What she saw before her was a brother she hardly recognized. He was like a living dead man, pushed down so far that it might already be too late to get him back to the surface. Her eyes showed an emotion Calvino hadn't seen when she was performing on stage the previous night. In the door of the courtroom the Black Cat wore a look of perfect hopelessness, a look that spoke of pure, distilled despair.

Two men, one old and one in a gray and pink shirt, pushed their way into the doorway, taking Mya Kyaw Thein's place. The old man, who wore a peaked, billed cap, stared at one of the prisoners who sat against the far wall on the low bench. One of the young men stared back. They looked like father and son.

The senior defense counsel asked Wai Wan questions. The defendant appeared frightened, angry, frustrated and humbled. He stared straight ahead, giving his answers in short bursts, as if each word was the result of painful labor. His short hair made him look severe. His yellow thick-cloth shirt and green longyi hung on his slender body as on a scarecrow. He noticed that his sister was no longer watching from the doorway, and what little morale her presence had given him vanished. He was alone in a room with officials and guards, the hard core, whose reserve of sympathy had been exhausted long ago.

The prison guards, in their gray shirts, blue trousers and sandals without socks, looked bored in the back of the room. One of the guards had his shirt unbuttoned and wore a thick gold chain with an amulet attached. He mocked Wai Wan, rolling his eyes. The patch on his uniform had a large white star on a field of red, blue and yellow. Two stripes, blue, ran underneath the star.

Wai Wan had changed his story from the one he'd given at an earlier hearing. In his previous testimony, he'd left the owner out of the story. It was his way to protect her, and in return she'd promised to stand by him and the others, paying what was necessary to get them released.

She had lied about her side of the bargain. She'd never intended to help him or the others. When he'd found out that he'd been set up as the fall guy, his world had collapsed. He'd wanted nothing more than to get his revenge against the teak wood owner who had double-crossed him. Now he was discovering that not only had he been used, but it was too late to switch stories. The shock was that the court wasn't interested in the truth but only the discrepancy between his two versions of the story.

The clerk at the typewriter typed as fast as a World War I machine gun, every word like a bullet mowing down an advancing infantryman. Wai Wan got emotional, saying he'd gone through a number of toll-gates without a problem. It was after the ninth toll-gate that the police motorcycle had followed the truck and pulled him over. No one cared that the officials at the other toll-gates must have been paid off. That made the guards in the back finger their amulets and snicker. The case wasn't about the officials who'd taken a backhand payment; the case was about Wai Wan driving a truck filled with teak wood without a transportation permit. Other people might have been dirty, but that had no bearing on the case.

He told the judge that the owner had promised to get him released if he didn't mention her name. This was why, for this hearing, he had decided to have his own lawyer rather than the one hired by the teak owner.

"I was hired to drive a job. I didn't do anything wrong. I drove a truck. That isn't a crime, is it?"

He'd worked for the same lady before. She would call him from time to time with a job. There had never been a problem. He drove the truck. She paid him for his services. What was in the truck wasn't his business.

Then it was the Crown counsel's turn to cross-examine Wai Wan.

"How long have you been a driver?"

"Eight years."

"What kind of license do you have? Does it permit you to drive a heavy vehicle?"

"Yes, I have a license to drive a heavy truck."

The clerk called time out, pulled out the pages separated with a sheet of carbon paper, peeled them apart, took out the carbon paper and slipped it between two fresh sheets of paper and back into the carriage. The maneuver was done in one sweeping motion. He adjusted the paper and nodded that he was ready, and the cross-examination resumed.

"Your truck was filled with teak."

"The owner told me she'd done the paperwork. I believed her."

"Do you have any proof of what she said?"

"Proof?"

"Evidence?"

A soft hiss of a no issued from his pressed lips.

"When you were arrested, did you communicate with the owner?"

He nodded. "Yes, over the phone."

"What did she say?"

"That she would come and get me released."

"And did she come?"

"No. The forestry official held me in a cell. He interrogated me, and I told them what the owner told me to say."

"Do you have any evidence of what the owner told you to say?"

Wai Wan slowly bowed his head, defeated, boiling with anger, trying not to catch the eye of his sister in the doorway. He wouldn't want her to see him in utter submission, helpless as a whipped slave.

One of the cops leaned forward on a wooden railing. One hand rested on his chin, and with the other hand he worked a key to the handcuffs to pick at the edge of the Crown counsel's table, slowly peeling it back as if he were unwrapping a gift.

"Before, you told the court you said that you acted alone. Now you say someone instructed you by phone what to say to the forestry officials. How can the court believe this testimony?"

When a man has been betrayed, his face shows a peculiar pain of shock, disbelief and hatred. Wai Wan had been sucker-punched. The Crown counsel continued to punch, but there was never any contest, as in a prize fight when the fight has gone out of the opponent and it's only a matter of time before he collapses.

The trial was going in the wrong direction. Calvino had had enough. He stood up and nodded at Ohn Myint.

"I want you to translate what I am going to say."

"I would like to request that your honor subpoena the owner of the teak and the owner of the truck, if it is a different person."

He stopped and let Ohn Myint translate.

The judge looked over his glasses at Calvino as if the British invaders had returned on the wings of the courtroom sparrows.

"Request denied."

Calvino locked eyes with the judge and broke out into a smile.

"Second motion. That I be allowed to approach the bench for a conference."

The Burmese lawyers exchanged glances. No one had ever requested a private conference with a sitting judge. What could the foreigner's intent be? The judge sat through what seemed a long period of silence. Finally he waved Calvino to step forward.

"In New York we keep it simple. I was going to ask you to dismiss the case against this man on the grounds of lack of intent."

Calvino pulled out the note the ex-judge had written and read it word for word:

"'Your Honor, your dismissal of charges against Wai Wan will show the American government your fairness and courage and demonstrate for the world to see that Myanmar's courts can be trusted to deliver justice.'"

After he finished reading the note, Calvino handed it to the judge, returned to his chair and sat down.

All eyes turned to the judge. He seemed to recognize the handwriting. On the note, and on the entire wall.

TWELVE

View from the Balcony

JACK SAXON HAD booked Calvino a room at the guesthouse under the name Richard Smith. The room, cramped, hot and dark, smelled like a livestock holding pen and was only slight smaller. Calvino stood in the doorway surveying the bed, the chair, the closet and the bathroom door, painted pink. He walked over to the window and pulled back the curtains. The view was of a brick wall two meters away. Closing them again, Calvino walked to the front of the bed, leaned over and tried the mattress. Soft as overcooked pork bellies. He sat down on the edge. As soon as Rob Osborne was on a plane to Bangkok, he'd find another place. For now it would do.

It was time to go to work. He studied the room from every angle—entry, exit, electrical, lights, water, floors and closet. It was the kind of hotel room where the police found a body stuffed in a bag, hands cut off, with a shaved, bearded head stuffed in a separate burlap bag. And they'd joke about the pink bathroom door.

And they would know they'd never catch the mad butcher who had carved up the body. Because tracking a murderer who'd left his victim in a place like this was a waste of time. The victim would have likely used a phony name like Richard Smith. No one could ID him. John Doe murder files everywhere were stuffed in the back of a file cabinet in the drawer marked "Nobodies Killing Nobodies When They Were Drunk and in Arm's Reach of a Knife." A bit long for a file name, but once they'd found a body in a room like this, the cops only had to go through the motions of opening a file, one that would gather dust.

Saxon had left Calvino a note on the chair. Calvino picked it up and read it.

"Welcome to the real Burma. See you later. Your case is in the closet."

Like the note Calvino had handed to the judge, Saxon's note didn't open with a name or end with one. Anonymous notes were short on such details. Who else but Saxon would have rented him a hellhole and then put his case in the closet so other guests wouldn't steal it and sell his clothes to buy booze or drugs?

Calvino went to the closet and pulled his suitcase off the top shelf. The closet had that old man's stale smell of cat piss and day-old dried sweat. He put his case on the chair and sat on the bed, opened it and took out his clothes and his handgun. Strapping on the holster, he checked the chamber of the Walther and slipped it into place. He went to the closet, took out his jacket, put it on, checked himself in the mirror and locked the door behind him.

Back on the street, Calvino checked out the narrow driveway leading to the guesthouse, turned left at the street and began walking to the Savoy Hotel. Across the road he saw a cloud of swallows swarming out of the Shwedagon, visible at the horizon. The birds blackened the sky. He stopped to watch, shading his eyes with his hand. The thick soup of birds darted, flitted and danced across the sky as a single interconnected, flexible unit. The setting sun cast shadows, but where the swallows flew, the sky remained a bright aqua. As he watched, he thought about his hotel room with the balcony overlooking the pagoda—the one he'd checked into as Vincent Calvino—and the distance he'd flown solo from the pagoda to a backwater nest registered under the name Richard Smith.

A couple of minutes later, Calvino walked into the Savoy Hotel driveway, pushed through the entrance door and entered the bar. He looked around but didn't see Colonel Pratt. Instead he saw what wasn't in the bar. There was no table with beaten-up alcoholics, their livers screaming like a retired traffic cop with nightmares of escorting kids caught in heavy traffic. There were no characters who'd fallen under the wheels of life. Everyone looked as if they'd checked in under their real name and had real lives that didn't require carrying a handgun.

The tables were occupied with respectable types: expat diplomats, businessmen, NGOs, translators and teachers. A few more people sat at the bar engaging in polite conversation. These were the kind of drinkers who got all of their vaccine boosters every year, exercised, avoided meat and cigarettes, paid their taxes and read to their kids at bedtime. Saigon, Bangkok and Phnom Penh all had similar bars for the same crowd of swallows. It was a place for drinkers to step out of the harsh reality of the culture and language and pretend among themselves that they were together in their own country, a city they liked, where they were safe and everyone was pretty much like them.

Calvino figured the bar catered to customers who came early and left late, long enough to drink and sober up again before stepping into the Rangoon night.

He passed a wall of brass fittings that suggested an old English country pub. Behind the bar hung photographs of fishing boats. The bronze bell above the bar had an open invitation to ring it and buy a round for customers. Only true drunks rang the bell, and by the look of it, the bell hadn't been rung in some time.

One drink reorder later, Colonel Pratt walked in dressed like a businessman in a suit and tie. He was heeled, too. He went straight to the bar and sat on the stool beside Calvino. He didn't look like a saxophonist. And he didn't look like a cop. Colonel Pratt had transformed himself into the role he saw scripted for him by circumstances. It wasn't just the clothes; it was the style, the attitude and the way he walked that created the illusion.

"Sorry, I'm late. Jack phoned me," he said, ordering a beer. "I went around to have a talk with him."

"Jack's been a busy boy. He got me a room."

"How is it?"

"It's a different view from the balcony," said Calvino.

"Everything go okay today? At Jack's office and at the trial?"

Calvino nodded, lit a cigarette and ordered a third round, telling himself that he had to slow down. He snuffed out the cigarette. It promised to be a long night, and he'd be going to neighborhoods he didn't know, surrounded by people he didn't want to know.

"What'd Jack want?" asked Calvino.

"He had some advice."

"He's a journalist, not a doctor or a lawyer."

Colonel Pratt raised his glass of Tiger beer, and Calvino touched the rim of his whiskey glass.

"He said it would be a good idea if I hired a local to do surveillance work."

"Good idea. Put a tail on Yadanar."

"Only there's a little problem," said Colonel Pratt.

Calvino didn't say anything. What was there to say? Being alive and on assignment in Rangoon was a guarantee of problems, and like the swallows from the Shwedagon they came in swarms. The Colonel saw Calvino wasn't going to ask him what he meant.

"You want to know the problem?"

"I'm waiting to hear."

"Rangoon doesn't have private investigators."

It was like going into McDonald's and being told they didn't sell French fries.

"And you thought I might be able to find one for you?"

Colonel Pratt drank from his glass.

"You are good at finding missing persons. There has to be one private eye in Rangoon. Think of him as missing. Find him. It's a simple surveillance job. I need a local who knows the city. You don't. I don't. And there isn't anyone else."

He was right; they needed local resources. It was the difference between success and failure.

"I'll find someone."

Just as Calvino was on the cusp of solving one missing person case, the Colonel handed him another one. The hard-to-find were popping up like mushrooms at dawn hiding in a fine mist.

"You're still busy with the Osborne case."

Calvino smiled. "Looks like I'm finished with it tonight. I've booked his flight to Bangkok. I have the ticket. What I don't have is him."

"Is that a detail or a problem?"

"I'll let you know. It looks straightforward. But the kid has been hiding out in Rangoon for a reason. Why would he do that? Because he's worried that I'm looking for him? I don't think so."

"It's not over," said Colonel Pratt.

"Not until he's on the plane to Bangkok."

"Any plans to meet him?"

"Tonight in Chinatown. That's the plan."

"Why don't I come along?" said Colonel Pratt.

Calvino toasted his friend.

"Tomorrow I'll have a look around for a local investigator."

Saxon had given the Colonel some good advice. A local private eye in a foreign jurisdiction was a guy who made his living because he had access to inside information about important people. If it had been easy to find a private investigator, Saxon would have had his number or known someone who did. The fact that he hadn't passed a number along to the Colonel gave Calvino a doomed feeling. The starting Yankees pitcher walks three consecutive runners, and the coach pulls him, gives the nod to the pitcher's brother, who walks out to the mound on crutches. That's how Calvino thought of himself, a guy put in the game because there was no one else to pitch.

"Improvise," said Colonel Pratt.

"That works with jazz. I'll see what I can turn up."

Calvino began to explain how the judge had dismissed the criminal charges against Wai Wan. He'd used the old Asian standby—throw the case out for lack of evidence. The police officer on the motorcycle who'd arrested Wai Wan, or someone who professed to be that officer, said he couldn't be sure Wai Wan was the driver of the truck. The cop also testified he was absolutely certain about the identity of the remaining three prisoners. They had sat quietly against the wall—a relief driver and two passengers. The owner was out of the case. The driver had got a pass out of jail. That left three poster boys sitting on the low bench, backs to the wall, reminders so no one forgot that, at the end of the day, someone is always needed to hold the bag.

Calvino paused, held up his glass and tried, and failed, to catch the bartender's eye, even though he was standing close enough for Calvino to smell the garlic on his breath. The man stood behind the bar staring into the distance like he'd been hit by an alien ray gun in an old science fiction movie. Calvino turned to see what had captured the man's attention and saw that the bartender wasn't the only one who'd stopped breathing and talking.

A knock-down beautiful Thai woman had entered the room. Standing near the door, she looked around as if looking for someone. A sea of hopeful faces with sloppy choose-me smiles stared back. She'd stopped every conversation in the bar.

Calvino's jaw dropped as he saw her cross the room to stand just behind Pratt. This woman had a knee-liquefying beauty that made a man's legs turn to rubber stumps as his jaw involuntarily opened like that of a moron who'd stumbled onto a porn site for the first time. There was a small class of women who made knees quiver, but only once or twice in a decade did the cartilage in a man's knees appear to uncoil, boil and dissolve.

"Is something wrong, Vincent?"

Calvino signaled with his eyes that Pratt should turn around and take a look at the woman hovering a couple of inches away from his left shoulder. He'd been thinking about Calvino's courtroom experience. When he turned on the stool, he saw what had caused the room to go silent.

The woman was young. Pratt guessed she stood at about 165 centimeters, and with heels, over 170. Her thick black hair extended to her waist, which was as narrow as that of a political prisoner attached to a feeding tube. She had intense and expressive large brown eyes, full, glossy red lips and the kind of long, shapely legs that come from hours of daily exercise. Calvino guessed she was in her mid-twenties. She wore no wedding ring. She tapped Pratt on the shoulder with one of her fingernails, a long, slender stiletto tap that a man paid attention to. She had the Northern Thai white skin, the kind that Thai men slit throats for, and a smile that caused other men to stare with utter amazement and envy that the woman had chosen Colonel Pratt. What did that man at the bar have that they didn't?

As soon as it was clear she was with someone, the conversations resumed.

"Hello," said Pratt in English.

"Do you mind if I sit down?"

Pratt looked at her, smiled.

"Have a seat." He turned away, talking to Calvino. "The brother walked out of the courthouse a free man?" asked Pratt.

He'd put her on ice. It was an old habit. Like a good cop, he had learnt long ago to control distractions, making it clear he'd decide the timing.

"There was some paperwork, but that didn't take long. They're flexible about that. Pratt, there's someone who wants to say something."

Calvino glanced over Pratt's shoulder. He was talking but no longer concentrating on anything other than the woman hovering near Pratt, waiting for him to give her a moment. Finally, she spoke to him in Thai.

"I wonder if I could have your autograph?"

If one question could give a man face, this question gave Pratt the equivalent of a Jupiter-sized one.

"You must be mistaken," he said.

She tilted her head to the side, brushing stray hair from her face.

"I heard you playing last night at the 50th Street Bar. I went back to my hotel and searched your name on Google. What a surprise! You are a famous jazz saxophone player from my country. You make me very proud to be a Thai. I saw you at the bar. I hope that you don't mind."

"Are you joking?" said Calvino. "Of course he doesn't mind. What do you want to drink?"

There was no trouble getting the bartender's attention.

"This is my friend Vincent Calvino."

She stretched her hand out to Calvino.

"Pleased to meet you. How lucky you are to have such a talented friend."

"He reminds me every few hours," said Calvino. "Just in case I forget."

"I don't think you've told me your name," said Colonel Pratt.

With a woman who looked like this one, a name seemed unnecessary.

"My friends call me Kati."

"What's your Thai name?" asked Calvino. It bothered him when a Thai woman called herself Kati or Joy or June.

Leaning forward, she whispered, "Titiporn."

If there was ever a reason for a Thai woman to use a *farang* name, she had it nailed. Calvino roughly estimated her breasts to fall in the region of 38C, raising a man's temperature to about the same figure in Celsius. With a name like Kati she was sure to have stories of intensive questioning by immigration officers at international airports. But that would have paled against the attention her real name would have attracted in an upscale expat bar in Rangoon.

"That's a beautiful name," said Pratt.

"Memorable," said Calvino.

"What would you like to drink?" asked the Colonel.

Kati, who preferred that name to Titiporn, sat at the bar next to Pratt.

"I hope I'm not interrupting anything," she said.

"Vincent was telling me about visiting the historical sights in Rangoon."

"The Shwedagon is so beautiful," she said. "But I prefer Wat Po in Bangkok."

"I agree," said Colonel Pratt.

"Are you playing at 50th Street again tonight?" Kati asked. "If so, I'll go to hear you again. You play like a dream from heaven."

A mouthful of whiskey shot out of Calvino's nose.

"Did I say something funny?" she asked uncertainly.

Calvino grabbed a bar napkin and wiped his nose.

"You wouldn't happen to be on Facebook?" asked Calvino, raising an eyebrow.

He glanced from her over to Pratt, whose nose was next to Kati's hair. She flashed a smile as she shook her head.

"I don't really like social media. Do you?"

"It has its moments," said Calvino.

"I know someone who could make a fan page for you," she said, looking up at the Colonel.

"I'd click 'Like,'" said Calvino.

Kati reached into her Gucci bag and took out a pen and a notebook.

"If you could give me your autograph, I'd treasure that. If you have a photo of yourself playing the sax, that would be something I'd keep forever."

"Heaven" and "forever," thought Calvino. Kati had a long-term vision of things connected with Colonel Pratt.

"*Gin kow ru yung?*" asked the Colonel.

"Have you eaten yet?" as Calvino knew well, is one of the most caring and friendly questions any Thai can ask another, framing a genuine concern.

She flashed a smile and touched his arm. "*Yang kha. Hiew.*" she said. "Not yet. I'm hungry."

This from a woman who, like the man in the proverb Saxon had shared with Calvino, probably lived off the smell of food. Kati looked like someone with the money to buy a boatload of fish.

"And you?"

"Vincent and I are going out for dinner. Join us if you like," said Pratt.

"That's so kind. But I would be interfering with your business."

"It's okay. Isn't it, Vincent?"

"Not a problem. We're going to Chinatown."

Her face brightened. "I love Chinese food."

"To an Indian restaurant," said Calvino, watching her smile dim.

In all the many years Calvino had known Colonel Pratt, this was the first time he'd ever witnessed him inviting a total stranger to join them for dinner. If there was going to be a first time, Kati was a good choice. Pratt already had that faraway look of an expat who'd taken an airport taxi to Soi Cowboy and bar-fined the first dancer who'd sat on his lap and provoked thoughts of marriage and children before the ink on his visa stamp had dried. Pratt had that struck-by-lightning look. Calvino saw the signs. When a woman like Kati walked into a man's life, he discovered he'd been living no more than a zipper's length away from the kingdom of mind-controlled morons ruled by women with improbable names. It was hard to watch Pratt dropping IQ points faster than a plane with stalled engines losing altitude.

"Pratt, there's something here that doesn't seem right," Calvino, leaning in, said softly to Colonel Pratt, who suddenly no longer understood English.

"Right, wrong. We are talking dinner in Chinatown. Give Rob his plane ticket, and we go to 50th Street afterwards."

"Okay," Calvino said to both of them, "why not make a night of it?"

"Thank you. I'm so excited," she said, giggling as she touched Colonel Pratt's shoulder.

Kati looked like a woman who could keep a high level of excitement rolling right through the night, thought Calvino.

He watched as Kati's hand lingered a moment too long on the Colonel. Pratt accepted the gesture like a celebrity accustomed to hands reaching out and pressing to confirm the idol was flesh and blood. Musicians on the road have a basic code of conduct: bring the sexy members of the audience to an emotional frenzy and then, after the show, reap the rewards by playing the game of not letting them go and pushing them away at the same time. Pratt had never fallen into that way of life. He was too much of a cop and a family man. At least that's what Calvino had believed all of these years. The saxophone allowed him to vent, to release and let go. It had never been about the women. But men changed, lives changed, and women like Kati didn't fly out of a famous temple at dusk every night of the week. She was a bird in the hand.

Calvino asked the bartender for the bill. He paid for the drinks, thinking of a laundry list of issues he had intended to discuss with Pratt about the Chinatown meeting. Sometimes it was better not to plan and to just let things work out on the fly. She'd also be at the 50th Street Bar later. That didn't leave much opportunity for talking about the local private investigator. The chances were that everything would fall into place. Besides, Kati was a goddess, and all other business suddenly seemed much less pressing.

Cold pill smuggling and missing people had filtered out of Colonel Pratt's consciousness as he sat at the Savoy Hotel bar beside the attentive Kati, her legs crossed on the stool, talking in Thai about jazz. Kati had mastered that fine art of watching a man with doe-like eyes, hanging on his every word as if everything he said was a riff on the secrets of the universe. She sighed like a schoolgirl when he signed his name in her notebook. Colonel Pratt had stumbled across a Thai name in her notebook that had disturbed him, but there was nothing like a beautiful woman to make a man to file away his suspicions for another day.

"We can go, Pratt," said Calvino, standing up.

"I did mention it was Indian food, didn't I? Do you like Indian food?" Colonel Pratt asked Kati.

"I love it."

She lied with a grace that impressed even Calvino. He was pretty sure that Pratt could have said, "We're going to eat fried rats and house lizards," and she would have loved that too.

"Right," said Calvino, "and we'll be meeting another friend."

Rob Osborne was hardly a friend. But this remark sounded better than, "We'll be meeting a missing person whose father fronted $4,500 to spring his son's girlfriend's brother from prison."

In the private investigations business there was always a chance that a meeting over a missing person could go pear-shaped. But he had no reason to expect it in this case. The Black Cat, in his mind, had been using Rob all along to get her brother out of prison. Mission accomplished, why wouldn't she deliver him? It had been Colonel Pratt's idea to go along as backup. They both carried concealed weapons. The Colonel had been shot a while back, and whenever that old scar started to itch, he said it was a warning. Meeting Rob Osborne in Chinatown had him scratching that old wound. Turning a missing-person meeting into a social occasion didn't seem like the right way to scratch it. But sometimes one itch replaces another, and Kati had a barroom of men itching.

Mya Kyaw Thein had said Rob Osborne would meet him in Chinatown. She'd given Calvino the name of the Indian restaurant and told him which table to sit at. She kept her promises, she'd told him. Getting Rob to meet Calvino, she assured him, was nearly as difficult as springing her brother from Insein Prison. She refused to say how long the meeting would last or if Rob would return to Bangkok. He could deal with that. However the meeting ended, Calvino could report to his father that he'd met with Rob, and he was no longer being held against his will or in any serious trouble.

The Black Cat hadn't committed to showing up with Rob. That was something she hadn't worked out with him. But it didn't matter, thought Calvino. It might be better if she didn't turn up. His old man wanted Rob. The woman, in Alan Osborne's world, was a distraction, a person of no interest outside the fact that she'd lured his son into hiding. Mya Kyaw Thein had been bitter about Alan Osborne's ill treatment of his son and her. She hadn't mentioned that her boyfriend had punched his father in the face. Besides, it had worked out well for her in the end. Without Rob running away to Rangoon, the old man would have never paid the money for her brother's release.

Calvino walked behind Colonel Pratt, who had Kati in tow. He felt like the manager of a rock star. The Colonel had won a prize at the Java Jazz Festival a few years back, which had led to more engagements and prizes in Macau, Singapore and Hong Kong.

Colonel Pratt was a cop who played the saxophone as a hobby to release pressure from the job. Things and people change. The Colonel had started to think of himself more as a saxophone player whose hobby was policing. Calvino had witnessed the shift over the last year. After Pratt had been shot, he had thought about things in a different way. He'd never seemed happier. There was no boss in jazz. He turned a blind eye to the politics inside his department, where corruption money kicked upstairs, letting connected people walk free. He told himself that people inside the jazz culture were made of better stuff. His music made other people happy. He could riff and improvise and no one lost face, no one got hurt. When was the last time he'd done that as a cop? Pratt had asked Calvino that question not more than six months ago.

"Midlife crisis, Pratt," he'd said. "You'll out grow it."

"Music is the best life. I have no desire to outgrow it."

Kati—the Thai woman also known as Titiporn—was

another good reason for Colonel Pratt to think of himself as a musician. No cop with his head screwed on right would have invited a strange woman to a meeting in Chinatown while packing a weapon because a scar itched. Women like Kati made a man forget about planning, forget about concentrating on who was on the scene, who was waiting in the shadows, and what firing position to assume in case of an ambush. Kati made him like a bomb unit commander who felt safe with a phony detector because he had faith things would all work out somehow. A beautiful woman could make even a cautious man like the Colonel feel safe when he should have been on high alert for danger.

Kati had threaded her hand through Pratt's arm as they walked away from the Savoy Hotel to flag a taxi on the street. Calvino made a point of staying a couple of steps behind them. The sky was pitch dark. Heavy traffic passed as they looked for a cab. The Shwedagon Pagoda swallows had flown elsewhere, looking for food while avoiding predators, or folding their wings in a flutter of sex.

As they got into a taxi, Calvino sat up front with the driver. A small, dark man with glasses and a silver front tooth, he reminded Calvino of the judge who had presided over the trial earlier that morning. In physical features, they were largely indistinguishable. That was a dangerous way of thinking. Calvino thought about the line written by Orwell: "You turn a Gatling gun on a mob of unarmed 'natives,' and then you establish 'the Law.'" Whether Burma was opening up or not, the local history had shown that the natives were perfectly capable of turning the Gatling gun on their own.

THIRTEEN

Chinatown and Dragon Dancing

EITHER A MAN finds a way to own the street where he lives or it will end up owning him. Wai Wan's trial proved that the wisdom applied in Burma. It was his absence of Rangoon street smarts that made Calvino uneasy. Colonel Pratt had the same instinct about their own presence in Rangoon—we don't know these streets, and we're in over our heads, so hire a local.

Kati and the Colonel spoke in soft tones, having switched to Thai in the back of the taxi. Calvino sat in the front with the driver, who looked straight ahead at the road. One street after another, and none of them had any recognizable feature. He had no idea whether the taxi was headed to Chinatown. He sat back and thought about Rob Osborne and how things had gone his way so far.

New York taught its children a couple of early lessons. One of them was never allow yourself to become complacent. The other was stay clear of strange neighborhoods unless you've got a rabbi on board to vouch for you. Calvino had never forgotten these lessons, but his gut told him he was about to violate both.

"You all right up there, Vincent?" Colonel Pratt asked from the back. "You're being very quiet."

"I have no idea where we are," said Calvino.

"We're on Lanmadaw Street, and he'll turn right onto Maha Bandoola Road. When we reach Latha Street, that's Cherry Mann," said Kati in English.

For someone who didn't like Indian food, she had a GPS fix on the location of the Cherry Mann restaurant.

"How did you know that?" asked Colonel Pratt.

"I go shopping in Chinatown," she said.

"We won't get lost, Vincent," said the Colonel.

They settled back into their Thai conversation in the back.

Getting lost wasn't what worried Calvino. He still hadn't got over the way the Black Cat had manipulated the location. Letting her choose the meeting place gave Rob a tactical advantage. She'd insisted. Her choice of place—though she'd said it was Rob's decision, not hers—or forget about a meeting. A small voice in the back of his head repeated another wisdom: Never let a woman choose where to meet a lover who has gone missing.

When the taxi turned right at Maha Bandoola Road, they found that a power shortage had left the street in darkness. It was like driving through a tunnel. The dim light from the cab's interior gave the driver a ghoulish look. Calvino tried staring out the window, but he was looking into a black void. Out there in the darkness were the men who "owned" the street. Calvino knew that who owned the streets and the neighborhood wasn't something that could be figured out by reading the title deeds. That kind of ownership required force and brutality, and there was a chain of owners, one stacked upon the other, the boss above more powerful than the one below. To get those relationships straight required insider knowledge of the flow and movement of people, who was on the take, who was muscle and how the money circulated. Stuff that happened in corners and alleyways served a purpose. But an outsider had no access to the chain of command.

The streetlights came on, and a group of Chinese New Year dragon dancers appeared in the headlights. The taxi slowed down. Dancers passed on both sides of the car. There'd been no sign welcoming them to Chinatown, but they were there. The sidewalks were crowded with restaurant tables of celebrating Chinese. Candles and gas lanterns flickered, throwing star-rays of light on glasses and bottles of whiskey.

The taxi pulled to the curb as Maha Bandoola Road intersected with Latha Street. The three of them got out of the taxi and walked in the street. Calvino strode next to Colonel Pratt and Kati was on the Colonel's other side, holding his arm. They navigated around cars double-parked in front of restaurants. Calvino looked for a sign or a building number. The lighting was strictly Third World; the streetlight had a faint amber glow, but its illumination never managed to touch the ground. They stepped from pools of dim light into large shadows that swallowed up the buildings.

"Cherry Mann. Mann, like man and woman. The number is 88," said Calvino.

"That's a lucky number," said Kati.

"Can you read the number on the building?" asked Calvino.

Colonel Pratt squinted at a building.

"We're gaining on 88."

They walked through a large sinkhole of darkness and found a series of restaurants on the pavement, no-nonsense outdoor eateries with dozens of tables. The smell of whiskey and beer mingling with duck and steamed rice filled the air—but not for long, as they passed a rancid open sewer smell that made the bile back up in Calvino's throat. He looked at the surroundings. A series of dark alleys ran off both sides of the main street. Further down the road, the traffic jammed bumper to bumper behind a small convoy of rickshaws. It was the kind of spot where anyone could watch people coming and going without being seen. The kind of place the Black Cat had chosen told Calvino that somewhere among the Chinese signs, businesses and shophouses, Rob Osborne watched and waited. He'd be spitting distance away.

Calvino stopped a rickshaw driver and asked which restaurant was Cherry Mann. The rickshaw driver shook his head. He pointed in the opposite direction. They had walked the wrong way from the Latha Street intersection.

"Are you meeting someone?" asked Kati.

"Vincent's friend," said Colonel Pratt.

The last thing Calvino took the Black Cat for was his friend.

"We've gone the wrong way," said Calvino, gesturing impatiently with his hands to the sky.

Neither Kati nor the Colonel seemed to mind. With a beautiful woman on his arm, a man is never lost. They stood in the road deciding what to do next.

"It's this way," said Calvino, leading the way down the road.

At night the area had the closed-down, shuttered look of a place under siege. People were holed up inside their rooms, hunkered down as if in bunkers, knowing in their gut that night was the most dangerous time for people squeezed into a ghetto. After dark, over the sound of the TV, that aching voice gnawed at them, wondering just when trouble was going to explode. Roundups start at night. Expulsions and beatings love the cover of darkness too. Living in a ghetto like this, people could hear the tick-tock of someone else's clock beating in their heads.

They found it a few minutes later. The Cherry Mann restaurant extended over the pavement with rows of tables, all packed with locals, drinking and eating. Waiters ran back and forth with orders, wiped down tables to seat the next customers and disappeared into the kitchen facing the street. The clientele relaxed, smoked, joked and talked in that liquor-loosened way—loud, boozy, with a machine-gun kind of laughter rattling across the tables. Calvino walked ahead of Colonel Pratt and Titiporn—he liked to use her Thai name. It rolled off the tongue. He figured the Chinese at the tables would like it too.

He pushed through a knot of Chinese who had taken their party to the next step. They spilled into the street, joining others on foot, in cars and on motorbikes, and drinking whiskey in sidewalk restaurants celebrating the New Year. The smell of firecrackers and money drifted above this group of slavering drunks who laughed and spit chicken bones beside their tables, where rats timed their bone runs with precision. Colonel Pratt and Kati fell back, cut off by the crowd. Calvino ploughed ahead with shoulders and elbows.

Finally Calvino saw her. Mya Kyaw Thein, the Black Cat, sat alone at a small table, like the last man in an overrun platoon waiting for reinforcements to arrive. She'd worn vastly different outfits at the bar and the courthouse, so Calvino wasn't surprised to find her dressed in Chinese polished red silk with a fire-breathing green dragon stitched over her heart. She was the kind of woman who had a costume for every stage. Seeing Calvino, she stood up and waved.

"I thought you'd never come," she said.

"We got lost," he said.

"A private investigator who tracks down missing people getting lost in Chinatown? That's almost too funny," she said.

She smiled as if genuinely amused.

"Being lost and going missing are two different problems," Calvino said.

"Unless you're like Rob and you are both," she said.

Mya Kyaw Thein spotted Colonel Pratt and Kati as they emerged from inside the restaurant. They had gone inside Cherry Mann for an inspection. Kati said she never ate at a restaurant without first checking out the state of the kitchen. Kati in her high heels and short skirt had Chinese heads snapping hard enough to sever them at the spine. A waiter tripped and spilled a mutton curry down the back of an old man, who yelped as if someone had shot him.

"Who is that with Pratt?"

"Kati. She's a big fan of his."

"Are you crazy? What is she doing here? I told you to come alone."

"I told you that Pratt was coming."

Colonel Pratt made a point of hanging back. They stayed near the entrance of the restaurant, talking and gesturing at the glazed ducks in the window. The Colonel watched the area around the Black Cat's table, waiting for a signal from Calvino.

"How many more people did you bring?"

Her good-natured humor about his getting lost had vanished. She became a different person. Tugging at her Chinese collar, she became all business, her nerves on edge.

"What kind of trouble's Rob in? You just said he was lost and missing. What's that supposed to mean?"

He'd asked this question before and never got a straight answer from her, no matter what costume she'd been wearing. Maybe there wasn't one. Or maybe there was, but she thought—out of loyalty, perhaps?—that it was better to let Rob do the explaining.

"She has everyone on the street staring," she complained. "A couple of the old men look like they've stopped breathing."

Red-eyed drunks drooled in their soup as she passed, clinking glasses or bottles, belching and swearing to each other that Kati was an omen for an auspicious New Year.

"She's here. Deal with it," said Calvino.

He glanced at Colonel Pratt and nodded.

The Black Cat's eyes danced around the tables of Chinese men who followed Kati with their greedy eyes.

"This isn't gonna work. No way Rob is going to risk coming with an audience watching our table."

"Cool down. Have some food. Let it play out. So tell me, how's your brother doing now he's out of prison?"

Wai Wan minus his leg irons was resting at home. But she'd got his point; they'd made a bargain, and he'd come to collect what was owed and due. She sat back in her chair quietly, arms folded, the wheels turning inside her head.

She was about to say something, one of those things people regret saying, when she sucked in her breath and said instead, "Could you ask your friend to not sit at the table?"

"It's too late for that," said Calvino. "He's with me. Dealing with trouble is something Pratt does well. And you said Rob had trouble. Pratt's my backup. As a singer, you should appreciate the need for a good backup. Or else you die."

She bit the corner of her lip.

"Okay, I'll deal with it."

It was too late for her to say anything else. Colonel Pratt and Kati had arrived and hovered beside the table as a waiter looked for two stools. The Black Cat welcomed them by taking a sip of water. Her eyes had already followed her thoughts beyond the crowd and into the street. She looked up at Kati, who smiled as she sat on one of the stools.

"I recognize you. You're the singer from 50th Street last night. I'm so honored to meet you," said Kati. "The audience at the club loved you. I loved you. I'm so glad to tell you in person how great you are. I feel that I know you. It sounds stupid, but it's true."

Perched on the plastic stool with her short skirt hiked to her upper thigh, she squeezed in close to the Black Cat.

"Kati hasn't eaten dinner," said Colonel Pratt.

"I'm not really that hungry," said Kati.

At a table in the next row, a Chinese businessman sent a waiter their way with a bottle of whiskey. He put it in front of Kati. The waiter pointed at the patron with a gold tooth sticking out of a smile that threatened to rip the man's face in two.

The Black Cat opened her handbag, removed her cell phone, turned around on her stool and faced the road as she dialed. There was a long pause before she turned to face Calvino. Then she slowly shook her head.

"He says he won't come unless it's just you. He's scared."

"Why is he scared?" asked Calvino.

"He has issues."

"Why? His old man?"

"It's beyond that."

That ended any hope of the night ending in a straightforward way. Calvino's hunch that Rob wasn't a missing person but a man in hiding had been confirmed.

"Beyond what?" he asked.

"He has a problem?" said Colonel Pratt.

The upper end of things signified by that simple word encompassed the full range of hurt and grief.

"Big time," she said, locking eyes with Calvino.

Calvino saw the same intense emotion he'd witnessed in the courtyard earlier that day and on stage the previous night.

"Why don't you tell us why Rob's afraid?" asked Calvino.

"It would be better if he told you."

"Ask him to join us. Tell him we're here to help him. He'll be okay."

The Black Cat clutched her cell phone like it was a small bird fallen from a nest. Gently, lovingly, she gestured with it, as if the piece of shiny black plastic had a long story to tell, if only you could dial the bureau of truth. But that line was always busy.

She spoke in a whispered voice over the phone.

"He wants to meet only you," she finally said to Calvino.

She locked eyes with Colonel Pratt.

"Nothing personal, Pratt. I liked how you played last night. The thing is, none of this has anything to do with you. My boyfriend knows you're a cop. He says he can't handle talking to a cop. Not now anyway."

The small talk had ended. Colonel Pratt understood that there was a problem and he wasn't part of the solution. There were far too many eyeballs feasting on Kati and watching their table. The men ate rice and mutton with their hands, sticky, wet fingers jabbing at the air.

"We'll be on our way," said the Colonel. "I hope you come back to the bar tonight to sing. I'd like to hear you again."

"That'd be great," she said with audible relief.

Calvino smiled. Colonel Pratt had handled the moment with perfect pitch.

"My name is Kati. I love your voice," said his companion, bridging her hands together to form an elegant *wai*.

"Glad we met, and maybe I'll see you later," said the Black Cat as she auto-dialed Rob's cell phone number.

"See you later," said Calvino.

Colonel Pratt smiled as he rose from the table.

"Happy New Year!"

"Year of the dragon," said Calvino. "Isn't that a lucky year?"

"They're all lucky if you get through them," said Colonel Pratt.

Kati pulled at her skirt as she rose from the stool, and it seemed for an instant that half of Chinatown failed to exhale. She put her arm through Colonel Pratt's, and they walked away. The Colonel had accumulated a big enough face from the sea of Chinese diners that his head could have been a float in Macy's Thanksgiving Day Parade. He led Kati through the narrow gap between the tables, and soon they disappeared into the crowd.

There goes my backup, thought Calvino. He'd ordered the mutton and some vegetable dishes. The bowls on the other tables showed grease floating like oil slicks over the food.

Lowering her cell phone, the Black Cat said, "Rob's on his way."

That last call to Rob confirmed what Calvino suspected— that he was nearby, watching. What demon had lodged in Rob's mind? Calvino casually thought that, whatever it was, he wasn't in the business of taming demons. Wai Wan had passed freely through eight toll-gates, but it was at the ninth one where the motorcycle cop had followed him and changed his life. Whether a man had ever really cleared the ninth toll-gate was never an easy question.

The dragon dancers came out of the darkness. First came the sound of their drums, accompanied by cymbals and gongs. Calvino had a closer look at the Black Cat's costume; it was the same design as those of the dancers. She'd dressed so she could melt into the dragon dance.

A couple of dozen dragon dancers wound through the street on the right. They came down Maha Bandoola Road, making the rounds from shop to shop, banging drums and gongs until the owner made a donation. Someone tossed firecrackers behind the dancers. Calvino saw the flash from a hundred tiny explosions in the road. The diners at the tables laughed, showing their teeth. The Chinese savored the sound of exploding firecrackers and the smell of gunpowder. The banging of gongs and drums grew louder as the young men and women covered in dragon costumes moved in closer, darting in and out of the road. The large red dragon mask with huge eyes and gaping mouth reared up and down near Calvino's table. One of the men in sneakers and white shirt shoved a donation box in front of him. As Calvino dropped in a five-dollar bill, he saw a foreigner move behind the dancers, stop for a moment and then walk over and sit at the table.

As the dragon dancers continued down the street, Rob watched, biting his lower lip. He'd dressed in white silk like the other dancers. His head was covered with a smaller version of a dragonhead mask. Slowly he peeled off the mask to reveal a *luk-kreung*—or half-breed, as his father called him—looking as if he'd seen a ghost. In the dim light, Rob easily passed as a Chinese dragon dancer. Only he was taller and had broader shoulders than most of the Burmese or Chinese.

Rob drew in a long breath as sweat streaked his face and dripped down his neck, glistening hot even in the dim light. His hair, long and braided in strips, hung around his head like a curtain on a Somali warlord, and he had a full black beard. He had the kind of presence that indicated an ongoing relationship with trouble. Calvino had thought that trouble's name was Mya. But a man could never be certain whether trouble had an extended family. There was an echo of his father's face, mainly in the eyes and the way his mouth clenched like an angry fist looking for a soft gut to land in.

"I can't stay long."

"You want something to eat?"

Rob waved off the offer. He sat down at the table. The Black Cat reached out and brushed his face with the back of her hand. She'd been eating mutton curry and rice with her forefinger and thumb, the traditional Burmese style. He grabbed her hand and licked her fingers. She looked suddenly sad and distant. It was the same look Calvino had seen when the Black Cat had stood in the courtroom doorway watching her brother testify.

"You want something to drink? A beer? Whiskey?"

"I told you, man. I can't stay here."

"Your dad's worried about you."

"I'm overwhelmed by his paternal instinct."

"He'd like you to go back to Bangkok."

"He can go fuck himself."

"Your father's not well."

"He's dying. Don't you think I know that? So fucking what? Everyone dies. He's taking his sweet time at it. You can tell him that."

An old Thai expression came into Calvino's mind as he studied the contempt on Rob's young face—*thom namlai rot fah*, "spit at the sky"—a hard-hitting phrase that described a certain way of showing disapproval. It fit Rob, as it fit a slave sending a message to his master. The man under the thumb of another spit in the sky because in his universe that was where the master lived.

"Why so bitter? Did he beat you as a kid?"

"I wish he'd given me that much attention. Why did he send you?"

"Maybe he wants to say sorry for that. Fathers can't help making mistakes that mess up their son's lives. Why should you be any different?"

"It's too late." He squeezed his girlfriend's hand. "You can tell him that."

"What kind of trouble are you in?"

Calvino hadn't wanted to ask the question because once he had information about a man's demons, his approach to the ninth toll-gate, that information pulled him inside the circle where the demons lived and did their business. And no one who'd taken a moment to think about it voluntarily entered another's ring of fire unless he was a friend.

"The kind that never lets go."

A black Lexus had double-parked next to a Range Rover and a Toyota SUV, and two men in street clothes got out and walked between the cars, straight to the table. One grabbed Rob by the back of his shirt and pulled him up from the stool. His partner held a handgun. In the dim light Calvino saw the gun come out in a flash.

"You make a big problem," said the Burmese in English. "Now you come with us."

The Black Cat turned into Mya Kyaw Thein and spoke to the men in Burmese. It sounded like a plea, the tone of a beggar requesting mercy. But the submissive tone of voice never works with gunmen, Calvino thought, whether they're in Rangoon, Bangkok, Phnom Penh or Saigon. Calvino didn't know any place in the region where such a pitiful tone would deliver any response other than a leering smile. She'd have had a better chance if Mya Kyaw Thein had switched back to the Black Cat and belted out "Cry Me a River."

"It's okay, Mya. Don't get involved." Rob looked at Calvino. "Tell my father you saw me."

More firecrackers exploded a couple of feet away as the two men frog-marched Rob, shoving him through a gap in the tables. An elbow brushed a glass and it dropped on the pavement, shattering into pieces. The kidnappers kept their man moving. One of the Burmese thugs, dressed in a black T-shirt and cargo pants, held a handgun waist-high, out of sight. Calvino saw the barrel of a black 9mm touch the small of Rob's back. His companion had an arm around Rob's arm, pulling him along. A knocked-over dish hit the pavement. Like the glass, the broken plate drew no notice amid the blaring music, blurry voices with smudges of laughter and a background of traffic noise, gongs, drums and firecrackers. The two gunmen walked unhurriedly—the hallmark of professionals—glancing back now and then, and except for the tables they'd bumped into, no one noticed what was going on.

"Rob…" Mya said and then broke off her thought, switching into Burmese to shout at the two men who'd moved away from the table.

Neither of the men replied. Calvino grabbed her wrist as she got up.

"Wait here," he said. "Let me handle it."

Calvino waited until the two men and Rob had disappeared behind the Range Rover. The rear of the Range Rover obscured their line of sight back to the table. Calvino waited until they couldn't see him before rolling off the stool and dropping to the pavement. He crawled forward three feet through the cigarette butts, chicken bones and spilled curry before rising to his feet and, hunched over, running to take cover in the front of the Range Rover.

Rob stood in front of the Lexus, where he switched into fight mode. He took a swing at one of the men and tried to make a break into the road. The two muscled goons, who had relaxed half a notch, thinking they had him under control, were caught off guard. They caught up with him a few meters away and wrestled him to the ground, punching him in the kidneys with a couple of well-positioned body jabs that would sap the fight out of any man.

With the Lexus engine running, lights switched off, the driver sat alone behind the steering wheel, watching the struggle. Calvino pulled his Walther out of the holster and slipped in alongside the Lexus. He tapped on the window. The window slowly lowered. Reaching in to grab the driver, Calvino hit him hard on the head with the butt of the Walther and then opened the door from the inside. The driver tumbled out onto the street with a thump. Calvino dragged him free of the door and climbed in front.

Now the two goons had dragged Rob back to the Lexus, and he was making it hard work to shove him in the back seat. They'd had enough. Both men turned on Rob with their fists, beating the shit out of him. One of the blows hit Rob hard in that sweet spot on the bridge of the nose. He doubled over as a mess of blood and snot fell into his hands along with a muffled scream. Working Rob over served its purpose; his disorientation made it easy to bundle him into the back of the car.

Inside the Lexus Rob kicked at them with his legs, but his power was spent, and his will drained. One of the men held him in a hammerlock as his buddy worked his fists on Rob's midsection. By the time they'd finished with Rob, he slumped forward. The men taunted him in Thai.

One of them tapped Calvino on the shoulder and said in Thai, *"Pai rew-rew"*—Go fast. Clearly the goons weren't Burmese. Like a twitch on a poker player's face, a man's "tell" always gave him away if others at the table could read it.

"Pai nai?" asked Calvino in his most guttural Issan accent.

The two men froze, exchanging puzzled looks, as if the other one might have a clue what was happening in the front seat. A new player sat at the wheel, and he spoke Thai with a *farang* accent. In the heartbeat of a rabbit chased by a fox, Rob and Calvino made a play. The only one they had.

Rob butted the gun hand of the man seated next to him. A shot from the 9mm shattered the windshield to the right of Calvino's head. The other goon jammed his elbow into Rob's side. He screamed in pain. The gunman held the 9mm with both hands, looking for movement in the front seat. Calvino stayed absolutely still. Just as he squeezed the trigger, Rob kneed the shooter's gun hand. The 9mm kicked, blew a hole through the front seat. The sound of firecrackers outside masked the shots. Calvino had dropped to the floor.

In the dark, Calvino found what he was looking for. He used the space between the driver's seat and the seats in the back to make his move. Violence happens in seconds that seem to take an eternity to pass. Calvino squeezed off two rounds, hitting the shooter in the chest. He slumped against Rob, who used him as a shield against the surviving thug, who'd pulled out his own gun and was now looking to shoot Rob. The second thug then emptied two shots into the front seat, inches above Calvino. His gun jammed, and Calvino sat up, leaned through space between the seats and shot the gunman twice in the head.

A moment passed.

"You okay, Rob?"

Nothing came from the back seat but a long empty silence punctured by gongs and cymbals and drums from the street outside. The scent of fresh blood rose from the bodies and filled the Lexus with the gut-retching smell as it combined with the gore and gunpowder. Rob had blood smeared on his beard, face, neck, shirt and pants. He looked like a slaughterhouse worker who'd just ended a double shift.

"Christ, you killed them!" he said, sitting between two dead men. Blood seeped into the dead men's clothing from their wounds.

"I asked if you're okay."

Rob nodded, the color drained from his face. Shaking, he pushed the body from his lap, leaning it against the side window.

"You hear them speaking Thai?" Calvino asked.

The kid had gone into shock. His ears still hadn't cleared from the guns going off in the confined space. His mouth opened, but this time nothing came out. He had that glazed-eye look of someone in shock.

"You'll have to tell me what that was about when I can hear again," said Calvino.

Inside his head a thousand drum band played the close-range 9mm bogey.

"Let's get out of here," said Calvino.

Calvino shoved the door open on the driver's side. Next, he popped the glove compartment, grabbed the papers inside and stuffed them in his pocket, and climbed out. He walked around the front of the Lexus, memorized the license plate number and circled the vehicle to check the perimeter before opening the back door. He waited until another group of dragon dancers had passed, their sound still muffled in his head. His ears felt like they were stuffed with sticky rice and cotton. He didn't hear the 250cc motorcycle that pulled to within a foot of the door. He had his Walther in his hand and was about to raise it when the motorcycle rider removed her helmet. The Black Cat saw the gun.

"It's me," she said.

He could see that and holstered the handgun.

"Can you take two on the back of that thing?"

She had left the table right after Calvino and gone to her Honda, parked twenty meters away.

"Is Rob okay?" she asked.

"Ask him yourself," he said, pulling Rob out of the back seat.

He was a mess—bloody and muttering, shaking his head like a crazy man. He swallowed like a man trying to clear his ears on a long-haul flight. But the main outcome was Rob Osborne had survived. He was no longer missing.

"Rob, get on," she said.

Calvino helped him as he struggled to lift one leg over the motorcycle. Rob wrapped his arms around her waist and leaned his head on her back.

"You want to take him to your place?" asked Calvino.

She shook her head. "That won't work. Get on, we'll take him to your place."

There was no time for argument. Calvino got on and gave directions to the guesthouse around the corner from the Savoy Hotel.

The Black Cat in her red silk Chinese costume steered her Honda Dream through another group of dragon dancers. To Calvino the sound of their drums and gongs seemed to be a long way off, but the drummers were only a few feet away. They left the Lexus behind in the shadows and finally in the dark as the motorcycle gathered speed. The night air felt cool on their faces. The sounds of the traffic seemed indistinct against the ringing echo of gunfire that bounced off deep edges inside Calvino's brain.

Something had gone sideways faster than the fingers of a *katoey* pickpocket on a crowded, dark street. But the kid was alive. He was alive. And the sweet scent of the night filled Calvino's lungs with the freshness and renewal of a man who was glad to have survived himself. His ears started to clear. He had the giddy feeling of having walked out of a firefight alive. Nothing was ever sweeter than the moment of feeling the pulse of life when, by the law of averages, it should have stopped.

Rob had gone missing for a reason. That didn't matter now. He had him on the bike.

In missing person cases, he knew, there is always a reason—money, mental illness, anger or hurt. Or someone has got into something way over his head and people with guns have called his hand. But there was plenty of time later for reasons, he decided, as the heady experience of sheer life amazed and conquered all else.

FOURTEEN

Dreaming of Electric Eels Hatched from Mooncakes

CALVINO HAD GONE up to his room first to pull a shirt from his suitcase. Returning downstairs, he used the shirt to cover up Rob, who leaned against the motorcycle in the driveway. Showing up covered in blood would have invited a police report.

Inside the lobby the old woman at the reception desk watched them come through the door.

"Motorcycle accident," said Calvino.

The receptionist noticed the ghost-like whiteness of Rob's face.

"Does he need a doctor?"

"He's fine," said Calvino.

Mya Kyaw Thein said something in Burmese about how someone had cut in front of the motorcycle, but his condition wasn't serious. He'd only been shaken up. That seemed to satisfy the receptionist, who studied Rob over her glasses. She returned to reading a book, the Georgette Heyer novel *Death in the Stocks*.

"My secretary thought Andrew Vereker deserved to die," said Calvino.

The old woman glanced up from the book.

"Lots of people deserve to die, but the ones who deserve it are rarely the victims," she said, displaying a command of English found in Bangkok five star hotels.

Once they entered his room, Calvino switched on the light and pointed to the bathroom door, telling Mya Kyaw Thein to take him inside and clean him up. She started to say something but stopped herself. Taking orders from anyone wasn't something she was used to. Whatever the emotions brewing inside, she let the moment pass and led Rob into the bathroom and washed his face, pushing his head down to the sink. She wiped his neck with a towel as they emerged. Most of the blood had been cleaned away. But his clothes still smelled of fresh blood and gunpowder. The bruises on one cheek and the busted nose looked bad. Rob sat on the room's one chair.

"Cool," he said as he looked around him, blinking, fidgeting with his hands and groaning from the kidney punches. "I'm basically okay."

The room had twin beds with threadbare sheets and pillows, flattened and yellow, and old headboards that looked like teak. The room was a dump, but it pleased Rob, who'd been sleeping rough in the basement of an abandoned house—Rob's last address in Rangoon. He'd been on the run, and it had been a good place to hide out.

"You sure you don't want to take him home with you?"

Mya Kyaw Thein glanced at Rob and back at Calvino.

"I can't. My mother and my brother and sister don't know I have a boyfriend."

"Probably not a good idea, then," said Calvino.

Rob had taken off Calvino's shirt and dropped it on the floor. His own, blood-splattered shirt certainly wouldn't have given the right impression to the Black Cat's family.

Calvino flicked a switch, setting the blades of the overhead fan to rotate slowly.

"Make yourself at home."

"I haven't slept in a real bed for a week," Rob said. "Ask Mya."

He was one of those men with the habit of referring to his girlfriend or wife for confirmation, as if a simple fact could never otherwise be accepted as true.

"A week is a long time to be hiding out in a city you don't know," said Calvino.

"I managed. Thanks to Mya. Isn't that right, Mya?"

The Black Cat squeezed his shoulders.

"You're safe now. That's what matters."

"Am I?" he asked, looking up at her.

She nodded, brushing the back of her hand against his cheek as he purred like a cat.

With a sigh, Calvino recalled the luxury hotel he'd left. It was as if he'd taken an elevator down to the basement while Rob had gone from the basement to the penthouse. Only the two destinations were the same place. Everything depends on where a man's elevator has brought him from, Calvino thought ruefully.

"You saved my life," Rob said.

"That's right. I did," said Calvino, unscrewing the cap of a bottle of Johnnie Walker Black Label.

Pouring himself two fingers, he raised the glass toward the two of them.

"Here's to being alive."

He threw the full storm into the back of his throat and swallowed.

"My father drinks whiskey like that. Neat, in one go."

Calvino eyed him as he refilled his glass.

"No-stopping-to-breathe drinking," said Calvino.

"I never heard binge drinking called that before."

"Now you have."

Rob's nerves showed in his hands. Calvino watched him play with a lighter, the cigarette in his mouth bouncing up and down with his hand, doing a tango. The Black Cat helped him light the cigarette.

"You've got a real hang-up about your old man," said Calvino.

Rob took a long drag on the cigarette, sucking in a lung of smoke before handing it to Mya Kyaw Thein, who helped herself before passing it back.

"If I'm going to stay in this room with you," said Rob, "I want one thing understood. I don't want to talk about my father. Are you okay with that?"

"Is that so?"

Calvino looked at his glass, then back at the kid.

"Why don't you tell me about the men who jumped you tonight? What are you mixed up with that makes a couple of Thais want to kill you in Rangoon?"

Rob shrugged, his head lolled against Mya Kyaw Thein. Two cats rubbing against each other set off the purring sound that came from Rob's throat.

Then Calvino could see that Rob's adrenaline had kicked in again. His mind had flashed back to the Lexus, to getting beat up and watching two men get shot.

"Hands still shaking?" he asked.

It wasn't really much of a question. Hands answered for themselves.

"How about we call your old man? You tell him you've decided to stay in Rangoon to finish up some business. When that's done, you'll phone him again."

The bass guitar player for Monkey Nose had a fresh streak of blood leaking out of his nose. He looked like a suicide bomber who, after setting off the bomb, had through a miracle walked out of the rubble.

"Do it, Rob. Go back to Bangkok. Get Alan off your back. Sooner or later, it's the only way, baby."

Rob watched as Calvino phoned his old man.

"Alan, I got someone who wants to talk to you."

Calvino held out the phone. Rob licked his lips, his hands trembling. He stared at the cell phone the same way he'd stared at the gun earlier that evening. It was hard to tell what part of him hadn't been traumatized. He glanced over at Mya Kyaw Thein, who gestured at the phone and then back at Calvino. He could hear his old man's voice coming out of the speaker.

"I don't have all fucking day. Are you there?"

The kid sighed long and hard, took another puff of the cigarette and glanced at the door as if he was going to bolt. Calvino stepped in front of the door—though, really, what were the chances of the kid running out the door and disappearing in the street? About the same as Cherry Mann getting a Michelin star, a blind, barefoot Chinese lawyer appointed to the United States Supreme Court or Calvino winning a 10K race against two US embassy marines. Rob was bluffing. He stalled for time, praying his old man would hang up, staring at the phone as Alan's voice spewed out a steady stream of threats and insults, tiny and distant as if from an echo chamber. Trapped. First into going to a meeting at Cherry Mann, then muscled inside a Lexus by thugs and now stranded in a run-down guesthouse with Calvino and the Black Cat waiting for him to take the phone. Rob saw with clarity that he had no place to run.

He took the phone from Calvino and raised it to his ear.

"Yeah, I'm okay. Just hanging out. Mya and me have some business to finish. When that's done, I'll give you a ring."

Calvino finally broke into a smile, raised his glass.

"What's the doctor say?" Rob continued. "They said you had a year over a year ago. Like you always said, what do those quacks know? Right. I gotta go."

He handed the phone back to Calvino.

"He's no longer missing, Alan. What I mean is my job's done. If he goes to Bangkok, that's up to him. You'll have to work that out with Rob."

He didn't wait for Alan to react. He terminated the call and slipped the cell phone into his jacket pocket.

Calvino reached for the Johnnie Walker bottle as he perched on the edge of one of the twin beds. He listened to the tap leaking in the bathroom. The rhythm of the drops filled the void. They'd shifted down from an accelerated pounding of the heart to second gear, finding a speed slow enough to turn the corner and ponder what to do next, where to go and how to play out what had taken place.

"What happens when the police find those two men?" asked Rob.

"Will they come looking for you?" asked Calvino. "Not likely. Still if I were you, I'd think Bangkok might be a better place to be."

"I didn't kill them."

"They planned to kill you."

Rob pushed his tongue against the inside of his cheek— one side, then the other—as he thought about what had happened in the Lexus.

Men like the two Calvino had killed always had stories— contradictory, sad, dangerous, punctured with the usual laughter and joy. The police would examine the bodies and write an ending for their stories, but in Calvino's experience police write-ups usually left out the most important things about the dead person. Police reports everywhere, he thought, are pretty much variations of the same story: victim drove up the wrong side of the hill at night and slammed into a semitrailer with its lights off. Two gunshot deaths in Chinatown on New Year's would offer the cops a laundry list of convenient theories to choose from: gambling debt, drugs, gangland dispute or robbery. In Thailand, the police always seemed to advance two theories in such deaths: personal conflict or business conflict.

The Black Cat rocked Rob's head back and forth as she sat on the edge of one of the beds. She looked like a dragon dancer nurse's aide.

"You sure you don't want a drink?" asked Calvino, holding up the bottle.

She shook her head.

"I saw how you looked at Pratt's groupie," she said.

"And how did I look?"

"Interested. Jealous."

"Kati is too high-maintenance."

"Every man at the restaurant wanted her. You're saying you didn't?"

"As a woman, you'll understand the difference between being wanted and being maintained."

As he said it, he couldn't stop himself from glancing over at Rob, who clung to her.

Calvino let it ride because it didn't matter what she thought. He raised his glass to drink and then snapped his fingers until he had Rob's full attention. He was done playing along with them and their little act of mutual comfort, fear and sorrow.

"Tonight isn't really about Kati or Pratt or me. It's about two dead thugs who got themselves killed on their way to kill you. Why don't we stop singing the daddy-hates-me blues and talk about what the two of you are doing to piss off important people? I don't think it's your song selection. Tell me, what is it? Which one of you wants to start with something called the truth? Reach down. It's inside you, though you haven't taken it out in some time. Start tonight. Start now."

Like most stories involving a Lexus, two thugs and guns, the story came down to money and power. As in every part of

Asia, the money god exacted a price for salvation, which was what true believers call payday. The idea of unsubscribing from the ruling system, going down and out with Henry Miller, had been a noble, romantic notion sixty years ago. Since then, nobility and romance had lost their virginity and become streetwalkers.

The Black Cat opened up first, and as she talked, Calvino thought he understood how a few artists had an ability to go deep down into where their demons hatched plans and pull them up to the surface, wailing and shrieking. She was taking him to that place.

"My grandfather, who owned a bookstore in Rangoon, was a good friend of Yadanar Khin's grandfather. Yadanar Khin's grandfather was a military man. He rose through the ranks to become a general. My grandfather had a different karma. He was arrested and thrown in jail, where he died. Yadanar Khin's father, like his father before him, became a soldier. He was promoted to be a general and now is a minister in the government. His family is rich. Mine is poor. We needed money for my brother. Rob tried to help. His father refused, even though Alan Osborne's father had known my grandfather and had been a regular at his bookstore."

She gestured toward the Johnnie Walker bottle, and Calvino poured her a glass. The Black Cat sipped from the glass and put it to Rob's lips. He took a swig.

"I'd heard that Yadanar Khin had good connections. His family made money from all kinds of deals. When he found out I was a singer, he said he'd see what he could do. A Burmese band had just signed with an American label. He wanted that for himself. He thought I was his ticket. I said his family owed my family. He said, 'Bullshit. What's that got to do with me?' I told him I had a boyfriend and was already in a band in Bangkok. He said there might be another way to do business, seeing that I lived in Bangkok and had a relationship."

"Is this why Rob had two Thais trying to kill him?" asked Calvino.

Rob lifted his head from her lap.

"She told me not to get involved."

Calvino watched him sit on the bed next to her.

"But you insisted," Calvino said.

"It wasn't a big thing. I was supposed to pick up a suitcase and deliver it in Bangkok."

"What was inside?"

"Cold pills. Over-the-counter medicine for hay fever or a cold."

"Pills that drug dealers buy to make *yaba* out of," said Calvino, referring the crazy-making local variety of methamphetamine. "You know that, don't you?"

It wasn't that he wanted to know whether Rob had bought into Yadanar's story that he was taking cold pills into Bangkok for people with a runny nose and fever. He wanted to know whether he would lie about it.

"I guess so," he said. "But that's got nothing to do with me. The stuff I brought in was for a clinic in Korat. I wasn't giving anything to a drug dealer. I delivered to a doctor. Jesus, what's wrong with that?"

"You didn't think, why does a doctor in a clinic need me to bring a suitcase of cold pills when he can order them in Thailand?"

"It's a quota or something. I don't know. All I know is what was written on the packets. 'Cold pills.' Nothing dangerous."

"After what happened tonight, do you still believe that?"

Rob exhaled a long breath.

"I know, man. I know."

"Those two guys weren't sent around to pop you over a suitcase of cold pills. There's got to be something else you need to tell me."

Mya squeezed Rob's hand. He raised his head from her shoulder and took another drink of the whiskey.

"Yeah, there was a small thing that happened the last time I picked up a case of pills."

"The last time? Meaning you made a number of trips for Yadanar Khin and his boys?"

"Only three. Not so many. I told them after number three that was my last time taking the shit into Bangkok. I made that clear. Ask Mya. Three times was our deal. After that, they were supposed to pay the money for Wai Wan to get out of Insein."

As with most stories, this one had holes and parts that didn't fit in, like clouds and tree branches that had been crammed into a jigsaw puzzle to complete a skyline that now looked upside down.

"You were running pills before your old man turned you down for the loan?"

"One run before. Two runs after. Yadanar Khin's old man had the power to lift the phone and get Wai Wan out with one call."

The beef with his old man hadn't been the only reason Rob had run away from Bangkok. The old man had no idea. The young man that his father thought of as a street entertainer had been walking the shadow line, looking for the fast, easy money.

Rob had hit the usual dead end. He wanted out in a line of work where "no way out" was the rule.

"But a problem came up when they wanted you to make one more run."

"It was more than that. I saw someone I shouldn't have seen."

"Who was that?"

Rob took another drink and stretched his arms, folding one around the Black Cat's shoulder.

"Yeah, I ran into a guy named Narit, who used to hang out at the Black Cat Bar in Bangkok. I met him there once. His old man had an import/export company in Bangkok. Something to do with electronics for car transmissions assembled at some industrial estate on the Eastern Seaboard, in Chonburi Province. He also had an uncle who was on the board of a hospital and just bought an S-Class Benz. The night I met him, his uncle had let him borrow the car and we walked out front, where he'd parked it, and he took me for a ride on Sukhumvit Road. After that, Narit had a few drinks and bragged about the important people he was connected to, and told me that if I ever had a problem, I should let him know.

"On my last run, it'd been arranged for me to pick up the suitcase at the usual place here in Rangoon. I go there and I run into Narit. He's not happy to see me. In fact, he's pissed off, asking what the hell am I doing there? Was I following him? Looking to make trouble?

"And I said, 'Man, I'm just picking up a case and taking it to Bangkok. What are you doing here?'

"And Narit says, 'I think someone told you I'd be here, and you're playing me for a fool. You think I'm stupid?'

"It got heavy. Narit pushed me hard, almost knocked me down. I recovered and pushed him back. He bounced off a shelf of pills, knocking off a dozen boxes. It made him lose face.

"He pulled out a knife, and I said, 'Hey, man, what are you going to do with that?' And he said, 'Tell me why you're setting me up.' And I said, 'You're *prasat daek*. Shit crazy. I had no idea you'd be in Rangoon. How would I know that, man?'

"And he said, 'Exactly how did you know that?'

"Finally I turned and walked away. He said, 'Hey, I thought you came for something?'

"And I said, 'I changed my mind. I got the wrong address. See you around.'"

"What was the address?"

"I heard you on the phone tell my father that my case was closed. So why do you want to know about this, man?"

Calvino looked hard into his eyes.

"I'm square with your father. But you're not square with me. Last time I remember, you were in the back of a Lexus with a couple of heavies who looked like they had some serious plans to cause you a universe of pain before they finished you off. And it ain't over. Unless you want to spend the rest of your life in this room eating what someone slides under the door, you need to keep me on your side.

"You want to go back. But right now you can't. Narit's told you that if he finds you back in Thailand you're a dead man. If I'm wrong about that, you don't have to give me the address."

"The covered market at 27th Street. Stall number A782. That makes us square," said Rob.

Calvino leaned forward from the edge of the twin bed, his face a foot away from Rob's, and said as his cell phone rang, "I'll get back to you on that."

It was Jack Saxon on the line, though he didn't give his name.

"Richard Smith, you should come over and let me buy you a drink. Sulking alone in your room is no way to spend time in Rangoon."

Saxon had started the conversion without any introduction, jumping in midstream and expecting Calvino to follow.

"I'm a little busy, Jack."

"Did you make it to Cherry Mann?"

"Yeah, Pratt and I found it."

"You sat down at a table with that sexy little singer you've been dreaming about, at twenty-one hundred hours?"

"About then."

"Not long afterwards two Thais were shot dead. Funny coincidence."

Calvino paused, waited. Saxon had gone quiet.

"What do the police say?" Calvino said, breaking the silence. "Could have been a botched robbery. New Year's, a lot of gold and money changing hands."

"That's what the police told my man. I'm curious to know if you heard the shots."

"With firecrackers going off and drums and gongs, I couldn't hear anything but people hacking and spitting chicken bones."

"You've been around. You know the difference between the sound of a gunshot and a firecracker."

"Jack, there was a lot going on."

"Did you find the missing kid?"

"I found him."

Calvino shot Rob a look. But it was Mya who found Calvino eyes. He locked eyes with her for a moment too long before breaking off.

"So you had a happy ending."

That was an old-hand expression for finishing with a bargirl.

"'Happy' isn't the word I'd use."

"That's disappointing. I'm at the bar in the Savoy. Come over and let me buy you a drink, and you can tell me why you think those two dead Thais were involved in a Chinatown heist."

"I was only guessing the motive," said Calvino.

"Just like the police. But my man said it looked like a professional hit. Both were shot at close range. One in the head, the other in the chest. The driver knocked out beside the car."

"You're writing a story, right? Add this to it. You open up the country, and the next thing you know, the bad blood pours in and someone gets killed in the line of duty."

"What duty would that be?"

"The faithful working to keep the margins of profit moving up. Before the thaw men like this could kill each other, and no one on the outside knew. Now the whole world is looking down the streets, asking questions. Be careful, Jack. No place opens that fast."

"You sound like someone from the government."

"As I said, I'm busy. We can talk tomorrow."

"One more thing, Vinny. I found a private detective. He just opened shop. If you want details, I'll be at the bar."

Saxon ended the call smiling, helping himself to a bowl of potato chips on the bar.

Calvino rose up from the bed, slipped on his jacket and took a step over to Rob to check his nose and face.

"You'll be okay. Listen, I've got to go out for an hour. I'll be back. If there were a mini-bar, I'd say help yourself. But there ain't one. Help yourself to the whiskey. I'll bring back some food. By the time I return, I'll have figured out what to do next."

Ten minutes later Calvino slid onto the stool beside Jack Saxon at the bar. Saxon turned and looked over his glasses at Calvino the way a teacher looks at a student who has tried to sneak into class twenty minutes late.

"Whiskey," said Calvino. "A double Black Label."

"What happened to your suit?"

Saxon reached over to run his finger over Calvino's right sleeve and then put it in his mouth.

"Mutton curry. You must have been eating with your fingers. You got enough on you. It looks like the cook exploded an old bull ram at your table. But I digress. You left your room to keep me company or at least long enough to ask me for the details on the Burmese gumshoe."

"No one has called a private investigator a gumshoe for fifty years or more."

"We were behind the times in my part of Ontario."

"And now that you mention it, what's the name of this gumshoe, and where can I find the little hole-in-the-wall office, his fedora sweat-stained, hanging on an umbrella rack?"

"His name is Naing Aung. You'll find him in a walkup on 27th Street. His shop is the fourth door on the left, as you walk in from the Scott's Market end. If you pass a Hindu temple on your right, turn around and go back. You've walked too far."

A smirk streaked Saxon's face, and he shook his head.

"He's new to the business. But I think he'll be okay. I verified him myself, Vinny."

"What do you mean, verified?"

"I asked him to follow you. He tracked you and Pratt and some beautiful Thai woman to Cherry Mann. I had to know if he was any good and what kind of moves Pratt and you might throw at him. I told him that guys like you and the Colonel never go anywhere in a straight line just in case you're tailed. But you didn't lose Naing Aung. I thought that was a good recommendation."

"What else was in his report?" asked Calvino, sipping his whiskey.

"He said you got lost."

"I was avoiding a tail."

Saxon pursed his lips, frowned, before breaking into a big smile.

"Naing Aung didn't see it that way. But it doesn't matter. You've got your private eye. I'd say we're square."

Saxon raised his glass and waited for Calvino to raise his.

"Square and an IOU if you need something in Bangkok."

"If I ever have someone who goes missing there, I'll give you a bell."

FIFTEEN

The Chinese New Year Tail Job

CALVINO CARRIED TWO plastic shopping bags out of the Savoy Hotel bar. One bag was heavy; inside were two one-liter plastic bottles of Coke. In the second bag were twin orders of pasta with pesto and two orders of rocket salad with sliced tomatoes. The smell of pasta filled the air, and for a moment he was back in Little Italy on the outskirts of New York's Chinatown, near where downtown bankers and lawyers sat in their Manhattan offices figuring out how to invest in Burma.

He walked back to the guesthouse carrying the bags. The old woman behind the reception desk glanced at him as he turned to walk up the steps. She lowered her glasses.

"Mr. Smith buys his dinner at the Savoy Hotel," she said.

It was unusual behavior for one of her guests, for whom the pleasures of the Savoy were normally far out of reach. She gripped another Georgette Heyer novel. He caught the title—*The Toll-Gate*.

"How's the book?"

"Stolen gold, highwaymen, mysterious strangers," she said.

"Makes you feel right at home," he said.

"Mysterious strangers and a missing toll-gate keeper," she said.

"I'm familiar with the plot," said Calvino.

"I thought you might be," she said. "Even though you don't look like a reader."

"I've been reading Orwell."

"That man had no romance in his books."

Calvino thought about it; she was right. Orwell was a lot of things, but a writer of romance novels wasn't one of them.

"But he had a lot to say about the toll-gate keepers."

Her tired, old eyes wrinkled as she smiled.

"Rangoon is packed with crooks," she said. "What you have in those bags smells good."

Calvino wasn't certain what she was hinting at—a free meal or hot money, or if she was just bored, having read the newspaper three times, and was hungry for conversation.

"Anyone come around asking for me?"

"Are you expecting more guests in your room? We have a house rule about guests bringing in other guests. I'll have to charge you."

"If anyone comes around asking for me, tell 'em I checked out. "

He winked at her.

"Like the missing toll-gate keeper," she said. "What would you like me to tell these Bow Street Runners who are after you?"

"Tell them I was headed to the airport."

"Are you?"

"I'm going upstairs to eat."

"And then you're going to check out?"

Calvino set the bags down and took out his wallet.

"Let me start over."

"No need. I understand," she said, as Calvino slipped her a twenty-dollar note.

The receptionist had a sly moxie that complemented her silver hair and satin-slippered shuffle. She sat behind her desk clutching the novel with gnarled hands that were speckled with liver spots the size of dimes and nickels. She put *The Toll-Gate* down, slipped her reading glasses back on, and examined the twenty. She turned it over, put it to her nose and smelled it. The old lady could have passed as one of the blue-haired ladies who played the slots at Atlantic City and who constantly craned their necks, keeping a cocked eye on those around her. Who was winning, who was losing was all the information she was interested in. She hadn't quite made her mind up about Calvino.

Calvino switched on the light as he entered the room and closed the door. Rob was stretched out on one of the twin beds with one arm folded behind his head, smoking a joint, wearing a set of earphones, his head moving to the beat of the music. He wore an old, thin bath towel. Bloodied jeans and shirts were heaped in a pile beside the bed. Women's underpants and a bra lay in the mix of clothes. And the second bath towel was draped over a chair. Either Rob was a secret cross-dresser, or he'd recovered enough strength to ride the Black Cat. Rob looked up from the bed as Calvino set the plastic bags on a table. The bathroom door was closed. Light seeped from under the door.

"Is Mya in the bathroom?"

With the earphones on, Rob heard only music. Calvino opened the bathroom door, had a look around and switched off the light. Empty. He closed the door. It was easier than removing the earphones and repeating the question.

He opened the plastic bag and took out the packaged pasta and salad. The smell from the hot pasta drifted and caught Rob's attention. He removed his earphones, swung his legs over the side of the bed and padded across to the table to look at the food.

"Hungry?"

"Starving."

"When's the last time you ate?"

The kid unwrapped the plastic knife and fork from the package.

"Couple of days ago."

"Where's Mya?"

He shrugged, shoveling the pasta into his mouth and drinking from the large plastic bottle of Coke.

"She went out."

"That's obvious. Where'd she go?"

"I can't remember. Her mother's house, or maybe to 50th Street."

"Is she coming back?"

"I dunno. She was pretty upset about what happened tonight."

Rob eyed the second container of pasta.

"You gonna eat that?"

Calvino shook his head. "It's yours."

"Thanks," said Rob, popping the lid on the Styrofoam container. He took another large swig from the Coke bottle, belched and spooned in a large mouthful of pasta. He watched as Calvino crossed the small room to the closet, where he pulled out a clean shirt and trousers before disappearing into the bathroom. After a shower, Calvino came out dripping wet, trying to decide which of the two used bathroom towels to use to dry off. He chose Mya's towel from the chair, tossing it back over the chair when he'd finished. It still had her smell. Rob had finished the second pasta and crawled back onto the bed.

"When's the last time you slept?" Calvino asked.

The kid was already half-asleep. Bathed, fed and tucked in, he clung to the soft bed like a drowning man who'd been pulled into a lifeboat. He hadn't even had time to put the earphones back on.

It was past midnight as Calvino climbed out of the taxi at the 50th Street Bar. Even from the street he could recognize one of Colonel Pratt's sax riffs. The piano and guitars played in the background, giving the Colonel space to do his thing. The same flashy cars were parked in the same places. It was like returning to a high-end showroom.

Colonel Pratt had finished his solo as Calvino entered the bar and was taking a bow in front of a table where Kati stood and applauded. She might have been the Colonel's biggest fan, but he also had the rest of the house shouting for an encore. He spotted Calvino as the American crossed the floor toward the stage.

Calvino leaned down to Kati to say, "Have you seen Mya?"

Kati shot him a look that he read as an unmistakable "No, I haven't seen the bitch." The question was asking one cat to account for another prowling the same neighborhood. Maybe she did go to her mother's house, Calvino thought.

Colonel Pratt came up for air after another two-minute solo to the sound of more applause. He lowered his saxophone and smiled at the crowd. No cop had ever heard that amount of applause in a lifetime of work.

Yadanar Khin looked up from the piano keyboard and announced a twenty-minute break. Unstrapping his saxophone, Colonel Pratt stepped down from the stage and walked over to the table where Kati sat, beaming like a lighthouse. Calvino joined them, sitting across from the Colonel. Yadanar Khin was on his way to join them as well when a customer pulled his elbow and sat him down at another table. Two other band members followed the piano player. That left Calvino with Colonel Pratt and Kati and three empty chairs.

"Did the kid show up?" asked the Colonel.

"He's no longer missing."

The Colonel broken into a smile as Kati put a hand over his in one of those preemptive "he's mine" gestures.

"Good," said the Colonel.

Kati sat like the holographic angel on a Christmas tree—beautiful, glowing, impressive and totally still. Not a word came out of her mouth.

"I phoned his father in Bangkok, and they talked."

"That must have been a touching moment."

"The kid refuses to go back to Bangkok."

"He's going through some difficult identity changes."

Calvino thought that those words described Colonel Pratt more than the kid.

"He's staying with me at the guesthouse until I can figure out what do to with him," said Calvino.

He wasn't comfortable with Kati listening in on their private conversation, but Colonel Pratt hadn't given him much choice. Not at Cherry Mann, not at the 50th Street Bar. The way she was shadowing the Colonel made Calvino wonder if he should leave the two of them alone. He saw no point in going into details with a stranger at the table.

Calvino figured Colonel Pratt must have sensed he was only sharing a minimum of information. Why would an experienced cop like the Colonel sit back while Kati moved in so close? A broad like her throwing herself at a middle-aged cop who played the saxophone might happen in the movies, but what had happened in Chinatown had been real. The point was, his friend hadn't been there to back him up, and Calvino felt the sting of disappointment. The Colonel had never let him down before.

"How'd he end up in your room?"

"Let's say, we bonded like blood brothers."

"He could use an older brother. Someone to give him advice."

"We could all use some advice."

It was an opening to talk about Kati, but it wasn't the place or time. She was hanging on to him like a vine twisted around a bamboo.

"I've got a lead on a couple of things…"

Calvino stopped himself, rose from the table and motioned for Colonel Pratt to follow him outside.

They stood in front of the luxury cars. The valets recognized them, turned away and went on with their business. Neither Calvino nor the Colonel fell into the category of luxury car types; they'd arrived in beat-up old taxis. Parking valets, Calvino thought, always get instant updates on the pecking order.

"Pratt, I want to help you," he said. "I don't know who this Kati is. What she is to you, or you to her. Whoever she is, I'm not comfortable talking about business around her."

The Colonel walked down the street to where the light faded to darkness. Calvino followed.

"You think that I'm stupid?"

"I never said that."

"But you thought it."

"Every man around is tripping over his dick to get next to her," Calvino said. "I'm not saying I don't understand the attraction. I do. But you can't work a case with a woman who draws more attention than a suicide bomber in a swimsuit and an explosive vest."

"It's a honey trap, Vincent. I saw it coming. I have to play it the way I see it. I need to know who's running her and what they're after. If I throw her out, they'll do something else. It's better to keep your enemies close so you can watch what they're doing."

Calvino stepped forward and hugged him.

"Great. Honey. They set the trap, but you saw it coming. For a while… You know, for a minute or so, I thought…"

"Forget it. What have you got?"

"A couple of Thais in a Lexus grabbed the kid. I shot them. They gave me no choice. They drew down on me. As I said at the table, the kid's at my room. Also, I talked with Jack, and he's found a local private investigator who can do the work you've got in mind."

"How does Jack know what I have in mind?"

"He doesn't. It's a figure of speech. He knows you need someone for surveillance. I thought I'd go and check him out."

Colonel Pratt turned, looked at his watch and glanced at the entrance to the bar.

"I've got to get back. Let's meet the private investigator tomorrow morning."

"Not a good idea, Pratt. A *farang* and a Thai show up asking him if he's up to running a surveillance detail on some important people. Rangoon's a small, tight place. People talk."

"Okay, set it up, and I'll take it from there."

The small changes had been adding up in Colonel Pratt's life, only Calvino hadn't wanted to see them. Working in a corruption-ridden department had never been much fun for an honest cop like the Colonel. The saxophone had been a hobby for years. Sometimes a hobby takes on a life of its own and becomes, not a pastime or a temporary escape, but a new path. After he'd won an award at the Java Jazz Festival, some doors had opened for Pratt. He'd been invited to play in Singapore, Hong Kong and Brunei. His assignment to the job in Rangoon had also resulted from his music career. To those around him, he seemed too good on the saxophone for it to be a cover. After one set, members of the bands he sat in with forgot he was a cop. That was the idea.

"The kid gave me some information about some cold pill smuggling operation he got involved in. That's why he nearly got himself killed earlier tonight."

That caught the Colonel's attention, and he stopped.

"Did he give you any names?"

"A guy named Narit that he'd met before in Bangkok. He ran into him here by accident during a pickup of pills he was taking to Thailand. It happened in a covered market."

"He gave you the location of the market?"

"Twenty-Seventh Street, the same street as Jack's private investigator."

A taxi pulled up. Four young foreigners got out and walked toward them. One of the men stopped in front of Calvino.

"Are you working the door?"

Calvino smiled. "Ten dollars each."

The foreigner reached for his wallet.

"Put away your money. Go on in. Enjoy yourself."

The party of four walked into the bar.

"That wasn't necessary," said Colonel Pratt.

"I wanted him to remember me. In case I need him later inside."

"Back to Rob Osborne and the cold pills."

"I like the idea of the private investigator being on the same street as the market where Rob went for his drug pickups. That should make his commute for the surveillance a stroll in the park," said Calvino as another taxi passed on the street, only to be swallowed up in the darkness a moment later.

"I might not need him. I can go to the market myself."

"DIY surveillance work in a foreign land is an old blues song about a man who comes to a tragic end. I'm surprised you don't know it."

"After what happened to you in Chinatown, it's a good idea if you don't show your face where these people do their business."

Calvino had knocked out the driver before he'd had a good look at his face.

"The ones who could ID me are dead. There's no risk."

They could hear that band had started up inside the bar. Colonel Pratt looked at Calvino for a long moment.

"Thanks, Vincent. I'd better get back inside."

"One more thing, Pratt. You left the restaurant when we were in Chinatown. It's been eating me."

"You didn't know?" asked the Colonel.

"Know what?"

"We had a tail."

Calvino looked at his hands, then at the ground.

"I didn't pick him up."

"I thought you knew. That you made up the story about getting lost for Kati's benefit."

Calvino shook his head.

"No, I was lost, Pratt. I didn't pick up the tail."

"He was a little Burmese guy with a strange haircut. Thirty, thirty-five years old, wearing a cheap polo shirt with an alligator logo and a checkered green and yellow longyi. From the way he moved, he either wanted us to know we were being followed or he was stupid."

"Or he was new to the business. Shit, how I did I manage not to spot him?"

The jazz piano drifted into the night. The band had started the set without their saxophone player. It didn't worry the Colonel. He kept cool as he glanced at the door.

"Kati's difficult to ignore. The guy tailing us spent a lot of time looking her up and down. I figured if we left you, he'd follow me. And he did. Or I should say he followed Kati. Don't forget that Mya was clear that her boyfriend wouldn't show up if we stayed."

"You did the right thing, Pratt. I handled it."

"I'm sure you did," he said.

"The Walther did the job."

"If you don't mind, I won't pass along your thanks to my friend at the embassy."

Calvino put an arm around Colonel Pratt's shoulder.

"You really had me thinking…"

"You thought I was head over heels for Kati."

"Kati. I hate that nickname. Ninety percent of the time, with a woman named Kati, what you see isn't what you get. You never see it coming. And, yeah, I did think that. But I also missed the tail in Chinatown. You ought to think of telling me to go back to Bangkok."

Pratt hugged him.

"Stick around. Things are starting to get interesting."

For the first time since Kati showed up out of the blue, Calvino was confident that the Colonel was firmly anchored in reality. Some people had underestimated the Colonel in the past, and Calvino now had to admit he'd been one of them.

"See you around," Calvino said.

Calvino watched the Colonel walk back into the bar. He hailed a taxi headed his way. It stopped, and Mya opened the back door and got out.

"How about I buy you a drink, and you tell me how you got Rob into the cold pill business?"

"Some other time," she said.

They stood in the street staring at each other.

"You've had a long day. Your brother in leg irons. Your boyfriend nearly killed by thugs. As a friend of mine said, things are starting to get interesting. So what's next, Mya? Back in Bangkok at Le Chat Noir, your boss told me you'd adopted Henry Miller as your patron saint. He said Miller's philosophy of fuck everything appealed to you. As a freethinker, a political activist and a blogger. But it turns out you're going for the brass ring. Not fuck the system, but how do I get inside it? And who do I take with me, and who do I leave behind?"

"I'll make it right for Rob," she said. "I owe him that much."

"You owe him, you owe me, and your brother owes you. It must get confusing. You ever sit down and write down all the debts and credits?"

"I can finish up on my own," she said in what sounded like a sincere voice. "What you did tonight isn't something I'll forget."

He thought about it. How everyone had this sudden need to be square. Jack Saxon wanted to know if he was square for his brother's rescue. Rob wanted to square with him after what happened in the Lexus. Even Pratt talked about squaring things. The problem was Rangoon. It was a place where the toll-gates had just opened, the gatekeepers were missing or on the take, and everyone who passed through found themselves inside a world where the squares, circles and straight lines operated according to different principles of social and political geometry. No one was square, but everyone was trying to square the circle and thinking they'd succeed.

Looking at the Black Cat's face, backlit from the bar, it was hard to read her emotions. Her tone hinted that she measured things, men, performers and opportunities with the same ruler she'd been trying to break and throw away. But she'd run into a hard lesson of adult life: some rulers were harder to break than others—and the money ruler was the last one anyone broke. They kept that one safe. It was instinct, automatic behavior, hardwired from birth. And that was the ruler that made most men easy marks, and most women slaves. She'd wanted to walk away from it as Henry Miller had done. Times had changed. Even Henry Miller had a price, and in Rangoon, whatever that price was, someone would have found it.

As they stood talking, Calvino had a vision of the old woman behind the reception desk at the guesthouse, who apparently had made some wrong plays along the way. In the street was a young woman who had reached a toll-gate, and if she looked behind, she would find that she had someone tailing her.

When that happened, which way was she going to turn? And who was she going to turn to?

"See you," she said, and walked into the bar.

Believing in the power of the wrong kind of man was a fast start down the road that led to an unmarked dead end. No amount of backing up would allow such a woman to return to the main road.

"Good luck, Mya!" he called after her.

She stopped, turned around.

"Don't get too close to these people. You have no idea what they can do."

SIXTEEN

The Urgent Astrologer and Private Investigator

A MIDDLE-AGED MONK, his polished globe of a head reflecting the sun, sat on a wooden stool and watched a street tailor at work behind a sewing machine, repairing the monk's bag. The bag had a Buddha image stitched on the front. A young boy and his father also looked on as the tailor operated the machine's pedals, the blue veins of his gnarled bare feet pumping up and down as if he were on a treadmill. Sewing and making merit for the next life looked a lot like running in place. The boy, nine or ten years old and dressed in bright green trousers, ran over to buy a sweet from a Muslim vendor and then returned to his father's side.

Calvino had walked the length of 27th Street, checking out access points and getting a sense of the character of the neighborhood and the kind of people who worked and lived there. He'd already passed Naing Aung's office, next to the Urgent Photo Studio, and continued walking until he'd reached the main road. He'd arrived there in time to watch a mass of people shove and push to get off a bus as others sought to squeeze through the same entrance to get inside.

The tailor was finishing his work on the monk's bag as Calvino retraced his footsteps along the crowded street to the Scott's Market end of 27th Street. Most of Naing Aung's neighbors ran luggage, bag and lottery shops with small offices wedged in between on the ground floor. He passed a couple of the grizzled owners, chewing betel nut and spitting as they shuffled in front of their shops in sandals and longyis, looking up and down the street for a customer.

A vendor selling roller luggage and shoulder bags in large stacks gestured to Calvino in vain to enter his shop. Calvino walked past a carpet shop plunked in the middle of the bag stores that displayed red and blue rugs hung from the ceiling like prototypes of Third World flags. He stopped to look at welcome mats draped over a table at the front. A young woman yawned as she passed the shop, asking him for money; she carried a bundled-up infant. Calvino gave her a couple of hundred-kyat notes. Next door to the carpet shop was a small office, where several young women huddled over a hand calculator and worked on open ledger books laid out on an old wooden desk. One of the men used a screwdriver as three or four office girls watched him repair an old rotary phone.

Down the road was a Hindu temple that Jack Saxon had mentioned as a landmark not to pass, or Calvino would have gone too far. A simpleton lounged in the doorway staring at the sky. He begged for small change before an Indian chased him away.

Calvino wasn't lost. He cased Naing Aung's neighborhood on the old theory that birds of a feather nest closely together.

Having gained a sense of the area around Naing Aung's office and the covered market, he found himself in front of the old wooden staircase leading from the street to the third floor office. A painted sign in italics read:

The Urgent Astrologer and Private Eye Office of Naing Aung.

The "Private Eye" part had been added to the existing sign recently. Bits of corrugated metal with the name of his fortune-telling business had fresh red paint that made the letters jump out like the cover of Mao's little handbook. Calvino looked down to the foot of the staircase, where half-dead fish listlessly swam in a pot of water. The building was in a row of houses and shops. Next door, an old woman worked the foot pedals of an old sewing machine. The sewing machine and its operator both looked as if they were from another time. He wondered if she and the barefoot tailor at the opposite end of the street had long ago made a deal to divide up the neighborhood and keep out any competition.

"Naing Aung, is he a good man?" he asked the old woman.

She looked up from her sewing machine, where she'd been working on a handbag for a young girl in a school uniform. She lifted her eyes upward in the direction of the stairs.

"Fourth floor. You come for lottery number?"

"I heard he has all the lucky numbers," said Calvino.

"Never give me one," she said, turning back to her sewing.

When Calvino reached the fourth floor, he came to a door with the same words as the sign on the front of the building. This time they'd been printed in boldface and all-capital letters. Calvino opened the door with the opaque glass window and walked inside, expecting to find a reception area. Instead he walked straight into Naing Aung's office. He was perched behind his desk, leaning forward on his elbows, his fingers touching in a bridge below his chin. Calvino knew it was the private investigator from Pratt's description of the man who'd followed them to Cherry Mann. He wore the same polo shirt. When he stood up to shake hands, Calvino saw that he was wearing a green and yellow longyi. Also in the room was a matronly woman, powdered and perfumed, dressed in an orange sarong crisscrossed with silver. Gold and silver bangles clinked like wind chimes as she turned around on her chair.

"*Mingalabar*, Mr. Calvino. Please take a seat," he said.

The Burmese greeting meant, "It is auspicious to meet you."

"Daw Aye Htay is my client. She is sharing her dreams from last night."

"*Mingalabar*," said Calvino, though he doubted the auspiciousness of meeting Naing Aung, the astrologer turned private eye.

Calvino had forgotten his dreams from the previous night. In fact, he never remembered dreams. What he remembered were living nightmares, such as the image of two men in the back seat of a Lexus trying to kill him.

"I can come back," said Calvino.

"No, no, please sit down. We are almost finished, aren't we, Daw Aye Htay?" the Burmese PI asked the large Indian woman. She made a noncommittal grunt.

Naing Aung read it as a yes and added, gesturing toward the door, "Please, take that chair."

Calvino sat back in a wooden chair, arms folded, waiting for Naing Aung and his client to finish the consultation or her dream analysis or whatever business they had been conducting before he walked in. They both stared at him, not in a curious or suspicious way, but more with the stalled look of two people trying to reestablish a psychic space that had evaporated. Naing Aung closed his eyes and held his arms out like a shaman performing a religious rite, one designed to open the woman's dream like an oyster and look for the pearl inside.

Calvino had always wondered what went on inside an astrologer's office, and now he had a ringside seat to find out. So this was the man who'd followed them to Chinatown, the person Jack said was the only private eye in Rangoon. As unlikely a candidate as Naing Aung seemed, Pratt needed local knowledge and talent, and all roads led to this office.

The Indian client twisted ample hips and stomach around to better study Calvino. Middle-aged, her large, round face was set off with a pair of armor-piercing brown eyes with heavy eye shadow that gave her a raccoon-like appearance. On the desk, sticks of incense had burnt halfway down inside small bronze bowls festooned with fresh flowers. A plate of cut banana and coconut sat nearby. Behind Naing Aung, a foot-high porcelain statue of Buddha in one corner and a statue of the Hindu goddess Indira in the other flanked his desk like guardian angels.

Daw Aye Htay said nothing as she worked prayer beads between her fingers, the low sound of a chant coming from deep inside her throat. Odd, thought Calvino. The two spoke Burmese in muffled tones, but from the sound of it their conversation was a negotiation having to do with the stranger seated on the chair behind them. Naing Aung had birth charts, diagrams and books opened on his desk. He said something in Burmese, and Daw Aye Htay extended her hand. Drawing his forefinger over lines in her palm, he smacked his lips and nodded and then shook his head. Letting go of her hand, he consulted one of the charts.

Colonel Pratt had said Naing Aung had strange hair. What the Colonel had omitted was that the private investigator's haircut looked like the flight deck of a damaged aircraft carrier. Calvino had been in other PIs' places of business. None had prepared him for Naing Aung's "Urgent Astrologer and Private Eye Office." He tried to imagine how the Colonel would have taken it all in—the investigator chanting over incense sticks, hunched over his charts, incense smoke drifting across the desk, as the woman with the worry beads, mouth firm, waited for the chants to deliver a message from another world.

She had a long wait.

Naing Aung finally looked up, switching to English as he spoke. He explained to Calvino that they'd been discussing events in her life and the meaning of her dreams. She'd already spoken to her children, her sister and a monk about her dreams the previous night. Naing Aung, apparently, was the last person on her dream list. But as Calvino would soon find out, sharing dreams is an utterly natural part of a Burmese day.

"Tell Mr. Calvino your dream," Naing Aung said. "He's a private eye from Bangkok. If you agree, Mr. Calvino."

Calvino didn't see much of an option. He could walk out of the office and report to the Colonel that Jack Saxon had recommended someone who was in the snake-charming business, or he could play along and learn if Naing Aung had any actual investigative skills. Having already climbed the stairs to the fourth floor, Calvino flipped a coin in his mind.

"Let's hear the dream."

"What day of the week were you born on?" asked Daw Aye Htay.

"Tuesday," said Calvino.

"The same day as me," Daw Aye Htay said, showing some expensive gold and silver fillings as she smiled. "Tuesday is good."

She pulled her chair around so that she could see both Calvino and Naing Aung by shifting her head. Then, showing a measure of pride as she looked at Calvino, she began her story.

Daw Aye Htay had bought a goat from the slaughter-house. It had been a rescue mission. She'd planned to take it to a temple and free it in the temple grounds. Her family accompanied her on the day the goat was to be released. At the temple they watched a family of monkeys scramble around the grounds begging for food. People gave them guavas, bananas and candy. Mother monkeys clutched their young to their breast with one hand while reaching out with the other for a sweet.

There was a reason behind the temple visit. The family driver had taken the Toyota Camry out and been in an accident, hitting a pedestrian on the road. The police had arrested the driver and hauled him off to jail. The accident had happened in front of a hotel on the way back from picking up the family's son from school. The news filtered in from an MI who lived in her neighbor's house. She told her brother to go and wait at the ICU. At the time she was more worried about her son.

The pedestrian injured in the accident turned out to be a mentally ill monk. The family driver, an ethnic Indian, sat in jail waiting for help from his boss. The Burmese in prison hated the Indians. Sectarian grudges and suspicions ran deep in Burma. Ethnic cleansing flared up with disturbing regularity. Daw Aye Htay's face turned fearful as she whispered to Calvino that her name was surely on some extermination list, and come the awful day the Burmese rose up and slit the Indians' throats, she would fare no better than a Rohingya trying to escape slaughter in some muddy village deep in the heart of the Arakan region.

Her fear of ethnic persecution extended to her driver, who, she was convinced, would die a terrible death inside a Burmese prison. He would be killed by knife-wielding Burmese convicts, the murder covered up as some natural cause such as a heart attack. Daw Aye Htay was sure this would be her driver's fate—unless, of course, he had money and connections and paid the medical bill and gave compensation. Then jail might be avoided. But the driver was a poor man who depended on his income to feed his family. If he went to jail, his family would have nothing. They'd be in the street, going around hungry like wandering ghosts. The mentally ill monk's family had started a crusade to squeeze money from them because they were poor and saw a chance to get rich.

She had bought the goat because the driver had been born on a Tuesday, and the goat was also Tuesday-born. Naing Aung had confirmed this was the right animal for the dates concerned. If it had been a Thursday, like Naing Aung's birthday, then it would have to have been a monkey. On the other hand, the crazy monk was a monkey-born person. That was a consideration, too.

Daw Aye Htay also had a monk advising her. He had actually phoned her four days before the accident happened to recommend she free the goat. Naing Aung had thought that three goats would be better than one. She'd had conflicting advice. The injured man's family was now trying to blackmail her, to extort a large cash settlement. Daw Aye Htay's family all thought that such a demand amounted to theft. But they also agreed that a debt was owed to the monk. And even though the man was crazy, evil and cunning and came from a bad family, he was still a monk. As for why this accident had come about, everyone told her the same thing—she owed the injured monk because in a previous life she had committed some misdeed. In this life, it was her karma to pay off that debt. She had already paid the monk's family three thousand dollars. The family wanted more, seeing the accident as a cosmic lottery win. There was no limit to their greed.

Day and night, hospital nurses and staff waited hand and foot on the monk. They came to his bed and *waied* him. His family had already started a lawsuit. They even tried to drag him out of the hospital in the hope that he might die and they'd get more money. The doctors, worried about tarnishing their own karma, refused to sign the papers to let him be discharged.

It was her son's dream that had convinced Daw Aye Htay not to pay any more money or release any more goats in atonement. From the time her son was an infant, she'd known he was special. She'd had a vision then of a small boy wearing white clothes who came from a green bamboo forest holding a gong, which he struck with a small golden mallet. Her son had said in his childlike voice, "All people beware that I'm coming." Behind him a monk followed.

Even when he'd been a three-month-old baby and she was breastfeeding him, her son had come into her dreams. Every time the mother ate something that wasn't good— raw fish in particular—he gave her a dream not to eat raw fish. The son found his way into the visions of friends, who phoned her to ask whether she'd eaten raw fish. "How did you know?" she asked. "Your son came in my dream and told me."

After she had finished her tale, Naing Aung sat back in his chair.

"Daw Aye Htay wants me to investigate the wife and brother-in-law of the monk," explained Naing Aung. "They are up to monkey business. If I can find evidence of dirty books in their house, then the family will go away. Otherwise, it will drag on, and that is bad karma."

An astrology and private investigation mind-meld, thought Calvino.

"How do you know he has dirty books?"

"I felt a vibration," said Naing Aung.

"Pornography and sex toys?" asked Calvino.

An astrologer turned private eye who could go to the lengths of planting pornography, as it seemed Naing Aung was prepared to do, suggested he was thorough in his planning.

Naing Aung was no longer listening to Calvino. He clutched hands with Daw Aye Htay, her eyes closed, and they murmured a Pali chant. When they finished, Daw Aye Htay stood up from her chair, rotating the worry beads between her thick fingers as she swept out of the office.

He heard her heavy descent on the creaky staircase and the rattling of her bangles.

"Do most of your clients come to you to talk about their dreams?"

"Yes. That's my business. My first question for you is, what is your dream?"

"To find a local private investigator who can handle a surveillance job."

"I am your man," said Naing Aung.

Calvino saw a number of problems with no solutions. Someone who read dreams and competed with monks over the number of goats to set free was bound to have unusual ideas about how to gather evidence or run a stakeout. He couldn't decide who was the crazy one—Daw Aye Htay, Naing Aung or himself for not calling off the interview and following the Indian woman down the stairs.

Calvino hadn't introduced himself.

"You probably wonder how I knew that your name is Vincent Calvino."

"It came to you in a dream?" said Calvino.

Calvino thought Naing Aung raised an eyebrow, but he wasn't certain. The astrologer's eyebrows had been shaved off and painted in heavy black eyeliner in a high black arch, and when he raised one or both of them, the movement registered only in a tiny upward tic that could easily be missed.

"It came from Jack Saxon."

"Other than Jack and the woman with her driver in jail, how many private investigation clients have you had?"

"My client list is expanding daily. I can show you my appointment book and you can see for yourself."

He dug through the pile of papers on his desk. Producing a black-covered book, he opened it.

"Business is booming," he said with a sigh. "So many foreigners are coming to my country and wanting investigators. There are none. I am the first one. The tide has turned, the good days are coming…"

He paused, grinning with the threat of continuing his string of clichés.

"Jack, for instance. He gave you a case."

Calvino wanted to test him.

The astrologer's right hand touched his artful eyebrow, like someone who couldn't resist touching fresh paint.

"Jack assigned me the task of following Mr. Vincent Calvino and his friend Pratt to Cherry Mann restaurant and reporting back with my findings."

"But you screwed that up."

Both eyebrows raised in unison.

"I did not."

It was clear why he'd touched his eyebrow. It seemed that when he lied or evaded a question, he had a slight nervous tic that even a painted eyebrow couldn't fully disguise.

"You lost me at Cherry Mann."

Naing Aung lowered his head, eyebrow ticking as he stared at the incense burning in the bronze urn.

"Mr. Saxon gave me thirty dollars to follow you to Cherry Mann, plus taxi fare. I saw that you got lost. I told Jack you couldn't find the restaurant. I put that in the report. He gave me a ten-dollar bonus for that information. Jack said nothing about what to do if one of you left Cherry Mann. Mr. Pratt did leave. I followed him and the woman he escorted. That cost Mr. Saxon another fifteen dollars, plus expenses."

"Other than following me and planting some pornography in a monk's sister's house, have you had any other experience in surveillance work?"

"*Perry Mason*. I've seen every one, and read all of Sherlock Holmes. Mr. Mason and Mr. Holmes are the best teachers in the world. My astrology experience has also prepared me to become an investigator."

"I'm not hiring you to follow the stars," said Calvino.

"But, Mr. Calvino, the stars follow you."

"I need a surveillance detail on a stall in the covered market across the street. You report who's buying pills and who's delivering pills."

He passed a slip of paper with the stall address on it over one of the astrological charts on the desk. Naing Aung looked at the address, tapped a long little fingernail against the side of one of the bronze bowls where the final embers of some incense sticks smoldered, and nodded.

"That would be the stall of Mr. Thiri Pyan Chi. He's a very important man."

"You know him?"

"I know everyone who lives and works on 27th Street."

"Your dreams must get kinda crowded."

"Sometimes there's a traffic jam," said Naing Aung. "How many days do you want me to watch him?"

"Three days. And I want you to report on everyone who comes and goes, and their activity. Got that?"

"All day?" He rubbed his chin, squinting at his diary, flipping the pages and clicking his tongue. "I have so many appointments."

"What time does the market open?"

"Early morning."

"When does it close?"

"Five in the afternoon."

"After hours, does anyone go in or out?"

"It's locked up." He tapped the diary. "Tomorrow, for example, I have an appointment with a client at 11:00 a.m."

"Change it."

The astrologer used his long pinky finger to lift a fallen ash from the bronze urn and dropped it in the wastebasket.

"But it's an auspicious time. That can't be changed."

"Can you get someone to work with you?" asked Calvino.

Naing Aung thought that was a strange question. An astrologer was plugged into the cosmos through his superior psychic powers. Such powers were never shared with another astrologer. That was bad luck and bad business. By extension and logic, a private investigator should handle the details of his clients personally.

"I prefer to work alone."

"But you have appointments. And you can't be in two places at the same time. I've walked around the market. There's an entrance from 27th Street and another entrance in the back where the trucks, cars and motorcycles park."

"Or I could retain my appointments and sit right here," Naing Aung said, gesturing at his window, which looked down at the street, "and watch the market."

He was quite proud of himself for coming up with a clever solution.

"That's what Sherlock Holmes would do. He'd stay close to the scene and observe from a distance so as not to expose himself."

"He had Watson."

"I have you."

"There are a couple of reasons why that won't work."

The Burmese PI found himself glancing out his window as he calmed his eyebrow tick. The covered market was visible below. It would be difficult to get much in the way of travel expenses on this job, and he was thinking how best to increase his rate as compensation.

Calvino waited for a reply, thinking Naing Aung was running manpower estimates through his head.

"I have a friend who can watch the back," Naing Aung finally said.

"I want to meet him."

Calvino wondered if Naing Aung had picked up from Perry Mason or Sherlock Holmes the idea that watching the back of a market was not nearly as important as having someone watching your back.

As he looked out the window, Naing Aung found a solution to his problem sitting at a roadside table drinking tea.

"I will introduce you to my colleague."

Calvino smiled. "Now we're getting somewhere."

Naing Aung, a head shorter than Calvino, walked beside his new client, greeting shopkeepers and vendors as they edged their way down 27th Street. Skynet TV dishes angled out from third and fourth-floor balconies. A Muslim with a white skullcap and white cotton shirt and trousers, his beard flecked with gray, shook Naing Aung's hand as they passed.

"My colleague is from America," he said. "Mr. Calvino.

"Will the American buy my sweets? It is my dream."

The Muslim made a sweeping gesture with his hand at a large glass case filled with candies. His gold-framed glasses rested heavily on his nose. Calvino thought the vendor was going to start talking about his dreams too when a taxi honked, edging forward slowly to clear a path among schoolchildren walking two and three abreast toward the main road.

Moving on, the two men passed several lottery vendors. "Moe Yan Lottery Enterprises" was painted on a sign hanging in front of one of the shops, the white frame chipped along the edges. The pitch was the same as at every shop: "Make yourself a billionaire." Not a dollar billionaire, but a kyat billionaire, and that was a wholly different scale of wealth. Every other shop was a lottery shop. The signs promised a way out of poverty.

"My clients ask for lucky lottery numbers. They dream of a number and phone me to ask if it is lucky."

"Do they ever win?"

"You don't need to win to believe. All believers are winners. This is the wisdom of our fathers."

Naing Aung had managed to sum up the whole machinery of astrology and religion without the hint of an eyebrow tic. To give him credit, thought Calvino, he did seem to believe that what he said was true.

Opposite the Hindu temple on 27th Street, four lottery shops competed for customers. In the lottery trade, a shop positioned opposite a temple presented the faithful with a gateway to test their good fortune. Naing Aung is right, Calvino thought. Belief in luck is powerful—and good business.

The Burmese PI walked slowly as he explained about Khin Myat, the man Calvino had seen him staring at through the window. Eight years of working as a freelance journalist in New York, taking translating jobs here and there, had given Khin Myat time to witness how the truly rich in America lived—though it was mainly from TV that he knew them. He'd taken an American wife, who worked as a refugee counselor for an NGO—that's how they'd met— and they had settled in Queens. Her much larger income had supported him after they married.

Sarah—that was his wife's name—had ended up dumping him for a union official she'd met at an Occupy Wall Street protest. Sarah had told Khin Myat that she was washing her hands of refugees—too much baggage. Khin Myat had found a job at Walmart spying on shoplifters and worked double shifts, building up lots of overtime.

Poor Khin Myat hadn't seen it coming, that this wife would leave him. Sooner or later she'd get bored with her union official—Naing Aung had consoled his friend with this thought many times. Wives changed… governments,

233

too. Khin Myat read about the political changes in Burma and went to a travel agent and charged a one-way ticket to Rangoon to his wife's Visa card. He'd confided in Naing Aung—or so the latter told Calvino—that he'd rather slam against a brick wall as his own master than scan security-camera feeds in Walmart for the rest of his life.

Naing Aung guided Calvino past several storefronts. Squeezed between the lottery shops was a roadside café with wooden tables, red plastic chairs and locals drinking tea and eating sweets and fruit. Naing Aung greeted another young Burmese man dressed in blue jeans and a New York Mets T-shirt. He turned to introduce Calvino, but before he could open his mouth, Khin Myat turned to Calvino with a handful of lottery tickets.

"How many do you want?"

Shock crossed Naing Aung's face like someone watching a car about to smash into a crazy monk on a pedestrian crossing. He gestured with both hands, waving them at Khin Myat.

"What?" asked Khin Myat, trying to read his friend's lips. "No lottery ticket? Okay."

Khin Myat shook his head as he laid the tickets on a table. He registered his defeat by drinking from his teacup. Naing Aung glanced sheepishly at Calvino to resume his introduction.

"Mr. Calvino, meet my good friend and colleague Khin Myat. He lived in New York. He was born on a Monday."

"I was born in New York on a Tuesday," said Calvino, smiling as he extended his hand.

Burmese names, Calvino understood, are chosen according to the day of the week a person is born on.

"New York was confusing. The names never corresponded with anything important like the day of the week," said Khin Myat. "But after a few years I said, hey, why should a name go with the day of the week? It got me questioning myself."

"About the meaning of dreams?" said Calvino.

"Man, how did you know that?"

"So now you sell lottery tickets," said Calvino.

It was the kind of disparaging remark that Khin Myat remembered Sarah, his wife, saying.

"I'm helping out my uncle."

He gestured to a lottery ticket shop across the street.

"You know the street?" Calvino asked.

"Better than you know New York."

"I haven't lived in New York for a long time. I couldn't say I know it. You've been away a long time. Things change. People come and go."

"Not in Burma. Nothing changes that fast. Same people, same faces, mostly the same family businesses."

Calvino thought he had a point. Rangoon had an air not so much of timelessness as of an old streetcar crawling slowly up a hill, one that you could get off for a while and catch up with a bit later, without missing a beat.

"I need a second pair of eyes for a few days."

"Doing what?"

"Watching the covered market."

"I can't do it myself," said Naing Aung.

Khin Myat fingered his book of lottery tickets, sucking his teeth.

"Are you some kind of cop?"

"I'm a private investigator," said Calvino. "I find missing persons."

"Like on TV."

"Nothing as romantic as TV. Watching is boring, and people lose interest."

"I could watch security tapes for hours and never take a break."

"I mentioned to Mr. Calvino that you are observant," said Naing Aung. "Sherlock had Watson—a point made by Mr. Calvino. I can't deny that Watson was essential to his success."

Khin Myat had two natural, non-twitching eyebrows, and that was a good start, thought Calvino.

"Man, Sherlock Holmes lived a hundred years ago. If you watched *CSI, The Wire, The Sopranos*, you'd know no one solves cases like that anymore. You need technology to rock 'n' roll. Isn't that right, Mr. Calvino?"

Khin Myat swirled the dregs of his tea in the small cup, tipped the cup over on the table and fingered the leaves.

"You can read tea leaves, or you look at the evidence of who put the poison in the cup. It's not the same thing."

Calvino wanted to give him a bear hug.

"Can you two work together?" Calvino asked.

They exchanged a knowing smile. One man sold lottery tickets on the street, and the other sold winning numbers, stitched together by the invisible thread of greed and opportunity.

"Good, then we can all work together."

"I work well with Americans," said Khin Myat.

Naing Aung's eyebrow did its familiar tell, suggesting he wasn't happy with the way his friend was positioning himself as the superior investigator.

"If you'd worked that well with them, you'd still be at Walmart."

The moment of tension between them passed as a young woman turned up at the table, chose one of Khin Myat's lottery tickets and paid him the money. She had the confidence of a regular customer.

Upon his return to Burma, Khin Myat had found that his time in America both helped and hurt him. As a young Burmese, he fell into the class of what the locals called returnees, the men and women who had filtered back to

Burma after the first hint the place was opening up. Ohn Myint was another example. Her nickname, Swamp Bitch, Jack Saxon had said, voiced an attitude the other Burmese mainly kept to themselves about the returnees. Their time spent abroad made for feelings of jealousy and envy, combined with a lot of misinformation about the "good life" elsewhere.

"Khin Myat left America very rich," said Naing Aung.

"I wish it were true. Unfortunately it's bullshit. You ever hear of anyone reviewing security tapes in a Walmart office getting rich?" asked Khin Myat. "Since I came back a couple of months ago, I've been selling lottery tickets for my uncle. If I were rich, why would I bother?"

Naing Aung held out a cup and poured himself tea.

"Because even the rich need to feel productive. They need to do something for their family."

Khin Myat stabbed a finger into the tea leaves on the table and held up his finger for Calvino and Naing Aung to see the leaves stuck to it.

"The rich don't have to raise a finger, and if they do, it's to order a servant to run to the table to clean it."

He popped his finger in his mouth.

"I clean my own hands."

"When I was transferred to the security department," he said. "I made minimum wage. You know what living on minimum wage in America means? Food stamps. You live in a small room in a bad neighborhood. So I came home, thinking it had to be better."

He'd followed up leads in Rangoon but they'd led nowhere. He'd then drifted back to 27th Street, where his uncle had an office and a lottery ticket business. Khin Myat found himself ahead of his time. He had no idea when the rising tide in Burma would lift small boats like his.

Meanwhile, Khin Myat was not a rich man. It also turned out that he and Naing Aung had a family history from 27th

Street. Naing Aung had wanted him to invest in his new private investigation business, only Khin Myat had said he had no money. The astrologer had taken that statement as a negotiating posture. He'd assumed Khin Myat wanted to drive down the price. Calvino had given them their first chance to actually work together.

"Tell Naing Aung that not everyone in New York is rich. He won't believe me."

"New York has poor people," said Calvino.

Naing Aung wrinkled his nose. It was a conspiracy.

"Maybe that's true. But any Burmese who lived eight years in America is rich."

"That's wrong on so many levels, I don't know where to begin. Just because I lived in the States doesn't mean that I've got money. I had to pay taxes, insurance, social security, a mortgage and gasoline. By the end of the month, I hadn't saved anything, and even worse, I had credit card debts piling up."

Khin Myat turned to Naing Aung. They'd had this conversation before and likely right in front of the same Hindu temple.

"Naing Aung, do you pay taxes in Rangoon? Do you know anyone who pays taxes? Who do you know who pays for insurance or social security? You don't. No one you know does. You are the one who should be rich. In the US you make all that money, but you blow it on shit no one thinks about here. Man, being rich isn't something they know anything about."

"You want the job?" asked Calvino. "Fifty bucks a day."

"Plus expenses," said Naing Aung.

"I'm in. Just tell me what I've got to do, Sherlock," he said, looking at his friend, who had used his long pinky fingernail to peel the skin from an orange and now popped a slice into his mouth.

"Your fee can be a down payment on your junior position in my private investigation business," said Naing Aung.

He'd already done the calculations.

Khin Myat scratched a two-day stubble on his cheek as his eyes narrowed. He watched Naing Aung lick the juice from his finger after devouring another slice of orange. Naing Aung ignored the disdain in that look as he wiped his hand on his trouser leg. Calvino wondered if Khin Myat had shot such a glance at his Walmart supervisor the day he told him that he was quitting and returning to Burma, and the supervisor had replied, "You'll be sorry."

"Just tell me what you want me to do," he said to Calvino.

"It's a stakeout."

Khin Myat laughed.

"I was born to watch."

SEVENTEEN

The Cold Pill Stakeout

AT ABOUT 10:00 A.M. business at the 27th Street covered market picked up. Customers wandered in from the street, and the big customers parked their pickups and vans in the back and used the rear entrance. Khin Myat ran a thumb through the thick wad of lottery tickets he'd taken along on the job. He remembered from TV that people watching other people needed a cover so they wouldn't be noticed. Khin Myat didn't need to invent a cover. People on the street knew that he sold lottery tickets on the street for his uncle.

He wandered through the parking lot in the back, showing the lottery tickets as he walked. He watched as medical supplies were unloaded, stacked on carts and then pulled into the market, the wheels clanging as they bumped over the uneven concrete floor. Nothing looked out of the ordinary. He followed one of the carts inside. It was just another business day, with local customers and merchants exchanging cash for merchandise. It reminded him of watching endless hours of security tapes when nothing happened except someone pulled a box of corn flakes off a shelf and put it in their basket.

Sometimes a tourist might walk down one of the dark corridors and take a couple of photographs before turning around and walking back to the street. Local housewives wandered inside to shop for bargains at the stalls selling women's and children's clothes. Calvino had been smart to hire him and send him inside, Khin Myat thought. He moved down the corridor and no one paid any notice. Seeing he had lottery tickets, most turned their backs as a sign they weren't interested.

The real business took place in the rows of stalls with medical supplies and drugs stacked in shelves. Clerks squatted on stools in front of their shelves and waited on customers who pointed at boxes.

Khin Myat milled among the shoppers in the market that first morning, looking for the stall whose number Calvino had given him. Hands hanging at either side of his longyi, he occasionally raised a fistful of tickets toward someone at a stall, and they would gesture for him to keep on moving. Calvino hadn't used the term "surveillance detail." He'd kept it simple, saying he needed both an inside and an outside pair of eyes. Calvino had picked Khin Myat as the inside man, and Naing Aung was to work out of his office as he listened to the dreams of his clients.

Khin Myat had been one of the first people to enter the market when it opened. He continued wandering past the stalls, skirting the phantom shapes of old Chinese bicycles leaning against a wooden platform. The concrete floor was cluttered and dirty. Shoes and sandals were shoved under stools in front of the stalls. Workers helped themselves to water from large plastic jugs as he passed.

The interior of the covered market was medieval. Nothing like it existed in places like New York. Birds nested in the ceiling, and cats stalked the dark lanes between the stalls. He wished he had a pair of night vision goggles as he finished one lane and turned to enter another one.

If Rangoon had a heart—though no one doubted that it had a head—the covered market was likely it. It was a land of spirits, superstitions, family and neighbors sharing their dreams with each other and with astrologers, monks and gurus, all looking for a winning lottery ticket number and all within the shadow of a sacred Hindu temple. You could also buy any modern drug you wanted there.

The vendors at the quieter stalls slumped over their newspapers, eating curry and rice as they waited for customers to shuffle up and point to a box of drugs or a modern medical device. Khin Myat continued, largely ignored as he wound his way along the market stalls. All around him was merchandise intended for those whose health had failed—the injured or maimed, the frail or disabled. He passed through a fleet of wheelchairs ready to roll through a world of demons, portable toilets for pit stops in the unrelenting search for ghosts, crutches to keep up with a fast-talking fortune teller, blood glucose monitoring systems as a hedge in the world of faith healing, scales for weighing medicine when brewing up herbal recipes and slimming belts to strap on before entering a ritual of black magic.

Every disease, condition, genetic malfunction or accidental injury had an infinite choice of remedies. Wholesalers, retailers, doctors, healers, nurses and hospital workers all shopped at the market; so did junkies, quacks and hypochondriacs. It should have been a fertile ground for lottery ticket sales.

"Things are upside down everywhere," Khin Myat muttered to himself, holding up his sheaf of lottery tickets. "But in Burma they're so confused that no one can tell the arms from the legs."

He stopped beside a row of products near the stall Calvino had told him to target. He picked up a green box labeled "essence of chili," looked it over, put it back, picked up a bottle of cod liver oil and finally one with garlic oil. Sitting at the stall, a small man removed his glasses, put his newspaper aside and arranged his longyi like a barnyard bat looking to drop from the ceiling and sonar out for a snack.

"This might be your lucky day," Khin Myat said. "Buy a lottery ticket and become rich."

"Are you looking for something or just wasting my time?"

Khin Myat returned to examining the labels on boxes. After a moment the man asked him again what he was looking for.

"Medicine for my mother. She has a bad cold," he said.

"A good son would take her to the doctor and not hang around a market trying to sell lottery tickets," he was told.

He'd received similar messages from a couple of other vendors. He should visit a proper pharmacy and not a wholesale market. What kind of a man was he? He must be one of those returnees who'd returned to make money and leave their mothers to die alone at home.

Several times Khin Myat caught himself just as he was about to defend his dignity and mother by telling the merchant that he was on an important assignment. Instead he wandered off, cursing under his breath. This part of a stakeout he'd never seen on American TV—the dead time, the sheer boredom of it, standing around and trying not to be noticed. The sick mother story had backfired. He trimmed his story to the bare minimum and concentrated on selling lottery tickets to a bunch of hardcore merchants who watched him with steely eyes as he circulated past their shops.

Calvino had told him to observe the activity, not just at the target stall, but around it. Khin Myat began to take notes of what he found displayed on tall, rickety wooden shelves in the nearby stalls. He noted the names on the boxes of drugs: Moxiget, Oncet, Loram, Diabenol and Solvin. He walked on past stalls specializing in medical instruments: chrome hammers for testing reflexes, long tapered scissors with gold handles, a large corkscrew device that looked like an instrument of torture, wraps for shoulders and knees, scales for weighing medicine, thermometers, bandages and canes. Wooden shutters for locking everything up at night were pulled back, and their padlocks hung from thick rings. The security system to protect the inventory was basic. He turned the page in his notebook and kept on writing.

Khin Myat closed his notebook, stuck it in his back pocket and rocked back on his heels as he looked around. The most striking feature of the interior area around the medical equipment and medicine stalls was the silence. It was the kind of stillness normally induced by anesthesia in an operating room. Words were exchanged in the hush of a hypnotist. There was none of the loud crying out or jostling that happened around the stalls that sold clothes, bagels, lottery tickets, flowers, peanuts and other food. He'd never been on a stakeout before and wondered if his experience was normal. Calvino had said, "Keep your eyes peeled and ears open." He'd been more specific than that, adding, "Watch everybody who stops at the target stall, photograph them with your cell phone, and if anyone walks away with a large quantity of drugs, follow him and see where he goes."

The second time he walked down the lane with the target stall in the middle, Khin Myat slowed down and picked up a box of Actifed. The clerk, a middle-aged woman, sat on a beach chair, half secluded behind the large counter. She nursed a baby.

"Khin Myat?" she asked with a kernel of doubt in her voice.

Hearing her call his name, he jumped as if he'd been tasered. He knew that voice from the past. He stepped closer and stared at the woman's face. She saw his puzzled expression.

"It's me. Su Su."

And so it was. Su Su had been in his class twenty years

before. She continued to nurse her baby, waving to Khin Myat.

"Khin Myat. Everyone in the market is talking about you."

He frowned.

"What are they saying?"

"They want to know why your uncle's business is so bad that he sent you to walk up and down the market all morning and selling only two tickets."

"I sold three."

"Three months ago, Khin Myat, I had a dream that you had come back from America."

"I'm back."

"With your wife?"

"That's finished."

"Sorry," she said, shifting the weight of her baby, moving her from one nipple to the other. "At first, I couldn't believe my eyes. I saw you wandering around the market like you were lost. And I said that's Khin Myat selling lottery tickets."

He clenched his jaw. It was very difficult to bear this humiliation. He swallowed hard.

"Things are not always what they appear to be."

She shook her head.

"You were always a mysterious boy," she said. "And if they survive, boys like that grow into mysterious men. That's what my father always said. Come and sit with me and I'll tell you what I dreamt last night. It may have meaning. Perhaps I should buy a lottery ticket."

He decided to accept her invitation for two reasons. First, she was someone from his old school, and he hadn't seen her in twenty years. And second, her stall was directly across from the one that Calvino was seeking information about. He climbed over the counter and sat on a stool beside her.

She explained that she had named her daughter after an angel, the same name as a dove—*mair jopew*, a female dove. As she rocked her baby, she told Khin Myat of her dream.

"Two nights ago a *mair jopew* had flown down from heaven, and not just any heaven, but the highest of all the heavens. The dove took me and my baby on its back and flew to the north, toward a temple in the remote mountains. I wasn't afraid even as I looked down at a huge forest around the temple. On the ground I found myself surrounded by many kinds of animals: peacocks, monkeys, snakes, hippos, goats, deer and many kinds of nesting birds, all mingled. I saw a python over thirty feet long, a snake that could talk to other animals. The python rose up as I came near, but when it saw that I held my baby, it said that I could pass. Dogs ran up and greeted my daughter with a low-pitched cry of joy, but I saw they paid no attention to the other children who came behind us. A monk came down the path toward us, and when he reached me, said I'd been expected. He said that the temple I was about to enter was more than two thousand years old. Centuries before, the pagoda had been abandoned, but a *waysar*, a monk possessing supernatural powers—mind reading, flying, dream channeling—had cleaned it up, repaired it, and brought it back from the dead."

She adjusted the position of her baby, wiped its mouth with a cloth and sipped tea, pouring a cup for Khin Myat.

"That's it?" he asked.

She had more and had waited for him to show interest in hearing the rest.

"The *waysar* had enlisted local villagers to help him rebuild the high wall surrounding the grounds and paint it red, and the stones were placed one by one by hand and painted as he had said to do. Soon another monk joined us and gave me coconut juice. The two monks led us inside a sala where the *waysar* waited in front of an enormous Buddha. This monk, who knelt on the floor, stood up and faced me. I looked at his face. It was you, Khin Myat, and you said that you had come from America, that your journey had led you to meet me at the temple, and that we would meet again. Do you have a ticket ending in 945?"

Many people wanted that number. He checked the lottery tickets.

"I have one with 379."

"Not so lucky," she said. "But for old times' sake, I will buy it."

Khin Myat thought his first private investigation job was going quite well. Though the people working in the market might not be fully understood by someone like Vincent Calvino, Khin Myat could see right through them. He was one of them. Su Su had been a classmate. Not only had she bought a lottery ticket, but she was giving him a platform from which to do his surveillance. He decided to press his luck with Su Su.

"That stall over there," he said, nodding in the direction of the target stall, "it doesn't do much business. They must be unlucky."

Su Su changed the baby's diaper before laying her down on a small cot.

"Don't say that, Khin Myat. Thiri Pyan Chi is the owner, and he's very lucky. He took over from his father, who died three years ago. He has very good customers in Korea, Singapore and Thailand. People say he's rich. He drives a Lexus. His son drives a Camry, and his wife is friendly with the wives of important people. Looking at his stall, you can't see the money. But it flies like a bird into his pockets."

"He does business with the Thais?"

"I know a worker whose name I won't mention, but he brags that their best customer is a Thai."

"Wheelchairs and canes?"

She laughed. "Medicine for some of the big hospitals. He has a large supply contract. It's a secret. My friend told me that the boss told him not to discuss the business with anyone. But I told him that I wasn't just anyone. I was Su Su."

"Medicine for polio, high blood pressure and the flu?" said Khin Myat.

"Mostly cold medicine. It's from a company called Coldco. Thiri Pyan Chi imports it from China."

"The Chinese medicine arrives every day?"

He acted confused.

Touching his shoulder, she said, "No, silly. On Wednesday afternoons a shipment arrives. Khin Myat, why all of these questions? Don't you have to sell the rest of those tickets or your uncle will take a cane to you?"

"I am no longer a boy, Su Su. My uncle would never dream of caning me. Not today or any day. I felt a cold coming on and thought it might be good to have some cold pills. Besides, I thought selling a few tickets in the market would be a good business plan."

"You don't need to buy cold pills from Thiri Pyan Chi. I will give you Actifed. How many do you want?"

"One package is enough."

She stretched behind her to pull down a box, reached inside and, pulling out a packet, gave it to him.

"You said Wednesday afternoons. Is that late afternoon?"

"Around closing time. Just after the train comes. "

"Are these big shipments of pills or just a few boxes?"

She shrugged, checking on her baby in a cot.

"Do you think I have time to count Thiri Pyan Chi's inventory? I don't work for him."

"At school, you noticed everything. I guess you changed."

Across her face came the look of someone searching for a way out of a dead end she'd found herself in.

"A couple hundred thousand pills."

"Every week?"

"Yes."

"By train every week? On Wednesday?"

"You know the train station behind the market? The shipments come through the station. It's only three hundred meters away."

He was forever being given these familiar details as if he were an outsider. Returnees were thought to have forgotten their knowledge of the country, and Khin Myat struggled not to lose his temper. He swallowed hard.

"Isn't that a lot of cold pills?"

"Not if you have a bulk sale customer. Most of us sell bulk. It's how we make our living. The aunties and schoolgirls who come through would hardly support our families."

In her dream, when Khin Myat had appeared as a specially gifted monk, he had asked many questions. It seemed perfectly normal to Su Su that, having appeared in the flesh, he would ask many more. She couldn't wait until closing to tell her husband, brother, mother and neighbor how Khin Myat had appeared at her stall and tested her with questions that only she could answer.

"You didn't see the shipping label on the boxes going to Thailand, did you, by any chance?"

"Khin Myat, you've not been fooling me. You are digging for information for someone. I could see that from the way you were prowling around the market. What is it exactly you want?"

He leaned over and touched the baby's forehead with his pinky finger, leaving a tiny tealeaf stain.

"That's a blessing for your daughter. My dream last night said I must do this blessing today."

He thought Su Su might swoon. She clasped her hands around his.

"Thank you, Khin Myat. I always said you were a good boy. I knew you would come back. I can see from your face that there is something troubling you. You can tell me. We are friends."

"I'd really like to know the name of the person in Thailand that Thiri Pyan Chi ships those cold pills to."

She flashed a smile and nodded.

"They aren't shipped to a person. He ships them to a company—G.A.J. Electronics Ltd., at Warehouse 189A, Bonded Industrial Estate, Chonburi Province, Thailand. I see it on the packing labels every Wednesday. Regular as clockwork."

"You haven't changed, Su Su."

Her large eyes wide open, she smiled at him.

"I am glad you're back, Khin Myat. But my dream told me to expect you. And here you are at my stall blessing my baby. I want to buy two more lottery tickets. You choose the numbers for me."

Calvino grunted as he listened to Khin Myat's oral report. He trained his binoculars on the entrance to the Pha Yar Lan train station. They stood on the second floor balcony of Scott's Market next to the retaining wall overlooking the street below. At the entrance was a black hole in the ancient stone wall separating the market from train station.

"You appeared in this woman's dream?" asked Calvino.

Khin Myat nodded, observing how Calvino studied his face to see how much of this dream business Khin Myat believed in.

"We were at school together," he said, to change the subject. "I hadn't seen her in years. Hadn't thought about her. There she was in the stall opposite the one you sent me to watch."

"That was good luck," admitted Calvino. "Had she changed much?"

Calvino answered his own question: "People rarely change. You ever notice that?"

Khin Myat watched as Calvino slowly moved the binoculars along the lane leading from the main street to the passenger entrance from the market into the train station. He paused, lowering the binoculars to examine the SUVs, cars, pickups and vans parked along the lane. He looked for a familiar face.

"Su Su was always different from the other children. But most of my friends are different from me now," Khin Myat said.

"There's your clue. It's not that they're different. You're the one who's changed. That rare thing called change is what New York is known to do to a man," said Calvino, lowering the binoculars and turning to look at Khin Myat.

"I saw my wife with the union official at Occupy Wall Street one Saturday afternoon. They were holding hands. They looked happy. I went back to looking at security tapes that night but couldn't get that image out of my head. So you're right. New York does change a man."

It was closing time at the main market, and vendors were packing boxes and crates into their vehicles. Not all that much had changed from 1926, when the British had built the market complex. Before Orwell had arrived in Burma, the resident administrator named the market after a colonial official who had introduced the Burmese to football. The father of Burmese football received the red card after independence, and the market was officially renamed Bogyoke after General Aung San, the short-lived father of the country and also the father of "The Lady," Aung San Suu Kyi.

Aung San had died young and heroically, leaving a romantic legacy. Calvino told himself he'd left it too long to die young. The young were men like Khin Myat and

251

Naing Aung—full of life and wanting to live forever. They believed in luck and dreams. He envied them.

"Have you checked in with Naing Aung?" asked Calvino.

"I thought I should call you first."

"You did the right thing. Your information stays between the two of us. Understood?"

"You don't trust Naing Aung," said Khin Myat.

"I trust you."

Khin Myat shuffled his feet and looked down, half-guilty.

"I need to tell you something," he said.

Calvino leaned against the wall.

"What do you have to tell me?"

"I give lottery numbers to Naing Aung in the morning before he sees his first client. Then, when he has a consultation, he has a vision and tells them a number, one that I've given him. Afterwards, they come to my table, see the number and buy the ticket. I give him a percentage of the sales."

"I'm glad you told me," said Calvino. "I pretty much had Naing Aung's number from the first time I saw him. Let's keep our information about the stall between the two of us."

"Understood."

Calvino raised the binoculars and scanned the lane. He caught sight of Colonel Pratt walking on the pavement. He saw the Colonel raise his cell phone to his face. Calvino answered the call.

"Turn to two o'clock," said Calvino. "First staircase on your right."

Ending the call, he put a hand on Khin Myat's shoulder.

"You did the right thing telling me, coming clean. Not that I don't trust Naing Aung, but I don't want his assignment to start appearing in his dream analysis. That could cause a problem."

"Investigators are paid to avoid problems."

Calvino liked the innocent charm of Khin Myat.

"If that shipment of cold pills arrives, I'll see that you get a bonus."

"I'll split it with Naing Aung."

"That's up to you. But I ain't saying anything to him."

Colonel Pratt appeared at the top of the stairs. His first words were addressed to Khin Myat.

"Are you sure about the address on the box?"

Calvino had gone over the name and address in Thailand several times with Khin Myat, but the Colonel wanted to hear it straight from the source.

"That's what she said. I didn't personally see it. Like I told Mr. Calvino, the woman who did see it, my old school friend ever since she was a child, has a good eye for detail. If she says she saw something, I believe it." He smiled. "But it doesn't matter whether I believe it. It's whether you do."

The Colonel had already had someone pull records of corporate directors and shareholders from the Ministry of Commerce. G.A.J. Electronics Ltd. listed two shareholders connected to well-known names in business and political circles. The proxies never fooled anyone who knew who the proxy stood for. But to be wrong in an accusation of this kind was career suicide. To be right, unfortunately, was even worse.

Colonel Pratt looked at his watch.

"What time does that train arrive?"

"In thirty minutes," said Khin Myat. "Unless it's late. Then maybe one, two hours."

It was the kind of open-ended answer that, like a dream, had many interpretations, and a Thai fully understood that each one was as probable as the next.

EIGHTEEN

Pha Yar Lan Train Station at Scott's Market

FROM THE NARROW lane leading to the train station entrance, Calvino turned and shielded his eyes as he stared up at the second floor balcony that ran along the side of the colonial-style market building. Khin Myat leaned over the balcony railing, with his own binoculars, watching Calvino standing to the right of a column. Calvino swept the balcony, freezing on Khin Myat, catching a glint of sunrays from the glasses.

Calvino continued his sweep of the area. From where Khin Myat was positioned on the balcony, he had an unobstructed view of the train station entrance, a narrow gate carved into the high stone wall. If Khin Myat saw something that looked out of the ordinary, a face that looked out of place or anything his guts told him something wasn't right, Calvino had told him to call him and report.

"What exactly do you mean by 'out of the ordinary'?" Khin Myat now asked, speaking into the phone while looking at Calvino below.

Good question, Calvino thought. In Burma he had no benchmark to judge what was extraordinary.

"There's no rule. You'll know it when you see it."

He ended the call, and glancing up, saw Khin Myat waving. As a rule members of a surveillance team didn't wave at each other. But only so many contingencies could be planned for, and the street inevitably delivered surprises that hadn't been expected.

When in doubt, Calvino fell back on Justice Potter Stewart's definition of pornography—"I know it when I see it"—because sometimes only ad hoc rules deliver the right outcome.

Colonel Pratt stood beside a small clothing shop, looking at the merchandise displayed in the window. Calvino walked up and stopped beside him.

"Thinking of buying Kati a dress?"

"It's not her style," said Colonel Pratt.

They stared at a traditional dress with gold sequins, worn by a dummy with a cheap black wig that had slipped to one side, covering one eye.

"Time to meet a train," Calvino said.

Calvino glanced at his watch. They had plenty of time to kill, so why wasn't he feeling more relaxed? It had to do with the setup. Relying on lottery ticket vendors and astrologers like Khin Myat and Naing Aung for information was loaded with enough downside to make a descent from Everest look like a walk through Kansas in comparison. He and Colonel Pratt were strangers to their newfound Burmese colleagues. Men like Thiri Pyan Chi were neighbors to these men, members of the same 27th Street tribe of merchants and vendors. Double-crossing a tribe member, even when he's a criminal, might come with some heavy costs.

"I keep asking myself if the astrologer would tip off Thiri Pyan Chi," said Calvino.

Pratt nodded and turned away from the window display, saying, "We'll find out soon enough."

Pratt and Calvino walked side by side down the lane, which was narrowed by rows of cars parked on both sides. They came to the entrance, which could have passed as a gateway into a medieval dungeon, with its heavy iron gate hanging on thick hinges in the stone wall. The sound of trains arriving drifted from the other side.

Wai Wan's trial had taught Calvino a lesson about the perils of toll-gates when moving cargo along Burmese highways. Contraband shipments ran a gauntlet of officials, and that was expensive and dangerous. But one lone cop was all it took to scuttle a shipment. A jealous competitor, a business rival or an old enemy seeking revenge only had to find that one cop and slip him some money, and a semitrailer-sized hole appeared overnight in the balance sheet. Then it was stop and seize, cat and mouse, payoffs and jerkoffs, as grudges and double-crosses piled high like old inventory no one could put a value on anymore.

The Burmese system had been built on violence. It proved the old adage that it was far cheaper to pay one man to blow up a bridge than three hundred men to build one. Violence and the threat of violence, knitted into the distribution system, made for an elite clan of rich psychopaths. It was also why Burma had few modern bridges.

Thiri Pyan Chi had found an alternative highway for smuggling his cold pill shipments into Rangoon right under the noses of the authorities: the train. Pha Yar Lan train station was his lucky ninth tollgate.

"We don't engage them," said Colonel Pratt, "or interfere."

"Not much point," said Calvino.

"No point at all."

"I'll play like a tourist taking some photos on the platform."

Pratt thought Calvino didn't look like a tourist.

"Tourists don't take photographs of boxes being unloaded from a train."

"I'll be discreet," said Calvino, smiling.

"Some foreigners never pass as tourists."

"You're saying I stand out?"

"If you take pictures, you'll be noticed."

"It wouldn't be healthy to be noticed by Udom Thongsirilert," said Calvino.

Colonel Pratt nodded. Udom Thongsirilert, an influential Thai from Buriram, ran a number of legit Thai companies—specializing in transport, event planning, luxury imported cars and electronics—along with a couple of illegit ones. The legit companies provided a way to launder his large profits from the smuggling of cold pills. One of his legit companies sold the cold pills to clinics and hospitals. The pills went in one door and out another to Udom's transport company, which hauled them back over the border to Burma to the string of *yaba* factories. The route was intentionally serpentine as with most clandestine businesses, a direct line of supply led to a prison cell. More circuits also meant more profit for the transport company.. Colonel Pratt had been sent to Burma to gather intelligence to close down Udom Thongsirilert's Burmese smuggling operation.

"I'd like a look at the shipping manifest," said Calvino.

"I'd like to look inside the boxes, but that's unlikely to happen. We'll watch them, follow them out and find out how they ship them into Thailand."

"Did I mention that the Burmese guy who sells the cold pills out of the market happens to drive a Lexus that matches the one in Chinatown?" asked Calvino.

Colonel Pratt stopped to look around at the cars and pickups before his eyes rested on the wall they were about to disappear behind. He turned to Calvino.

"I'm sorry about what happened at Cherry Mann."

"You pulled the tail off. You made the right decision. You didn't know it was Naing Aung, an astrologer. We could have had one of Udom's people following us."

"I thought there was something strange about that guy."

"The eyebrows," said Calvino.

"What about them?"

"He shaved them off and painted them on again with black eyeliner."

Colonel Pratt smiled and entered first through the station gate topped with iron spikes. He followed close to a couple of Burmese to avoid drawing attention. Calvino waited to the count of ten and walked through. As he emerged on the other side, the Colonel stood on the concrete platform holding a Burmese newspaper about twenty meters away. He blended in like a local commuter. Calvino turned and walked ten meters in the opposite direction. A crowd of about a hundred people was stretched out along the platform.

The Pha Yar Lan train station was usually invisible to outsiders. In Rangoon only locals took trains. One day that would all change, but that day was still long off. Calvino examined the faces among the crowd. Not a single foreigner on the platform. He felt a gear grinding in his gut—the place where porn and fear both registered a vote. Once they'd entered the station, Khin Myat lost the ability to watch their back. While on the train station platform, they were on their own. Colonel Pratt pretended to read the newspaper with his back to the platform wall. His eyes moved across the platform, the dual tracks and the surrounding wall to the terrain on the opposite side of the tracks, where a line of trees ran down a steep embankment. Calvino hovered near a column as a dog came up and sniffed his leg. Even the dogs smelled the scent of a foreigner, he thought.

Colonel Pratt mentally flipped through his checklist of contingencies. For one thing, the people bringing in the shipment might slip out without using the main gate. But spotting these alternative exits was even more important because he and Calvino might have to use one fast if things turned ugly. The first priority of going into a dangerous unknown place, he knew well, was planning an avenue of escape. Once they were on the run, it would be too late.

Calvino waited until the dog moved away before walking to the end of platform. His white face stuck out among the Burmese sitting, standing, squatting or milling around. Like a tourist from Iowa on New York's E train, even under a low-hanging hoodie it required only a glance to peg someone who was from out of town. He tried to act relaxed, stretching his arms, glancing at his watch, pacing as if waiting for the train. Not belonging to the commuter set on the platform wasn't something he could disguise. After a few minutes, though, people stopped staring. They adjusted to the presence of a foreigner pacing to the edge of the platform and looking down the tracks, playing the role of an impatient visitor waiting for a train.

The pedestrian bridge across the tracks looked like an empty painting against the sky. No one used it. Climbing up a long flight of stairs only to climb down another one made no sense when you could just step down from the platform and walk across. A couple of schoolgirls loitered on the tracks between the platform and the embankment on the opposite side, leaning in close to whisper with each other and giggling as they stole looks at Calvino. Other commuters, apparently worn down from a long day's work, loitered in the no man's land between the train tracks. On the far side several young girls squatted on the tracks with their tiffin boxes at their sides, reflecting the sunrays.

Calvino could see Colonel Pratt holding his cell phone between his ear and shoulder, head buried in the newspaper. He didn't look in Calvino's direction as he spoke. Calvino wondered who he was talking to—his wife, Manee, or Kati, the super-fan who'd been super-glued to him before like a bandage on a hairy leg. Neither man acknowledged the other. Khin Myat had warned Calvino and the Colonel, in his way, that the train wouldn't be on time. None of the trio had had to state another possible setback: that the shipment wouldn't be on it when it did arrive.

The worst part of the wait was killing time and trying not to be noticed as the minutes were murdered one by one.

A steady stream of tired vendors and shoppers filtered through the entrance from the market, lugging bags and boxes. Like the courthouse, Pha Yar Lan station hadn't changed from Orwell's time. Colonial architecture and infrastructure handcuffed the struggling nation to a dead empire. The Burmese wandered like survivors of some terrible conflict among the buildings built by their former masters. The concrete and brick walls of the train station's interior, decaying, unpainted, covered with moss and gnarled vines, had witnessed more than one crime in their time. The cold pill smugglers joined a long column of criminals who understood that the Burmese railways had been built by the British to carry booty and contraband. Why wouldn't Yadanar, Udom and Thiri use the same railway tracks to carry on the tradition?

Calvino struggled to think of a distinction between the colonial masters and the businessmen who'd followed them. He looked across the embankment to the opposite side, where among the trees and weeds a man relieved himself, his back turned to the platform.

A couple of brown dogs, led by the one that had sniffed his pant leg before, sauntered along the platform, tails wagging, snouts down, sniffing for scraps. Train platforms, like airport departure lounges, Calvino thought, are life suspension spaces, places where people wait for transportation to arrive so their life can start up again. The difference between powerful and rich and powerless and poor showed on the faces around him. Those who wait for public transportation have a sad, weary resignation; those whose transportation waits for them belong to a different species.

Life comes equipped with two standard options, thought Calvino, as he looked down the track at Colonel Pratt and saw that he was no longer on the phone. A man is born to wait for the train, or he finds a way to make the train wait for him. Calvino knew where he belonged in the scheme of things. His life was not that different from those of the people waiting beside him. Most people accept that in the grand scheme of things they were born to wait. But sometimes when the young catch a glimpse of the long wait ahead of them, they find that hitching a ride on *yaba* makes waiting disappear. That's the attraction in it, he thought, the escape hatch from the boredom of the long wait.

Crows circled in the cloudless sky overhead, cawing as they roosted in the treetops above the embankment. The crowd stirred as an ancient locomotive slowly came into view. The train stopped on the opposite side of the platform. The conductor's left hand eased the brake lever. The wheels screeched, metal against metal, as the train finally stopped. People with bundles and bags climbed on, stepping up gracefully in their longyis as they moved over the tracks and up the stairs to the carriages.

A few minutes later a second train—Number DD 933—pulling six orange and brown striped carriages, stopped at the station. Passengers leaned their heads out the windows, smiling and waving to people in the crowd. A couple of schoolgirls in uniform ran to climb into a carriage, giggling and shoving. They had no need to rush. The conductor sat in the front cabin lost in thought as he smoked a cigarette. His blue-uniformed assistant squatted in front of the engine, whipping out a lighter and leaning the cigarette pressed between his lips into the flame.

At the far end of the platform three men approached the end car with a trolley. With the help of a man inside, they formed a line, passing boxes from one to another and finally to a man who stacked them on the trolley. Colonel Pratt walked down the platform past the men.

The boxes had printed labels with Thiri Pyan Chi's name and market stall address. The Chinese brand name and logo for Coldco was stenciled on the side of each box. The Colonel counted forty boxes stacked in rows on the trolley. He'd researched the packaging and number of pills inside a standard shipment box. One thousand cold pills were inside each of them. Forty boxes translated into forty thousand pills. A degree in chemistry wasn't necessary to calculate that the amount of pseudoephedrine inside the shipment would make a batch of *yaba* to supply a small stadium of teenagers. Still, the shipment was only a bucket in the sea of cold pills flowing through Thailand.

Colonel Pratt had confided to Calvino a couple of facts about Udom's operation that he'd learnt at his intel briefing, including how his department had traced orders for ten billion cold pills from one of Udom's electronic companies directly to the Chinese manufacturer. The Colonel's boss wanted the answers to two questions: who had helped Udom arrange the supply route from China into Rangoon, and who were his Burmese friends who were working out the shipments from Rangoon to Thailand? The Colonel had initially thought that finding out about the train shipment would allow him to crack the case, but even if the train were a hundred carriages long and they were all filled with cold pills, it still couldn't be what they were using. Pratt ran the figures through his head. Using trains shipping one trolley's worth a day, it would take seven hundred years to complete that order.

When he saw the trolley with the forty boxes, he was disappointed. The shipment was more likely than not a local resupply to Thiri Pyan Chi's market stall. He also sold cold pills in quantity to hospitals and clinics in Rangoon and possibly some upcountry as well. Colonel Pratt felt frustrated as the trolley rolled past. It had been a huge waste of time.

As Colonel Pratt turned and walked back to Calvino, one of the workmen, carrying the last box from the train carriage, stopped in his tracks. He dropped the box and started shouting in Burmese. It wasn't like there were any other Westerners he might have confused Calvino with. He was the only one on the platform, and the man had got a clear look at him. Calvino had walked close enough to also recognize the man behind the wheel of the Lexus with two soon-to-be-dead Thais in the back.

A Chinatown reunion with the Lexus driver wasn't what Calvino had expected. He'd clipped the driver on the head and dragged him out and dropped him in the road. But something in the back of Calvino's mind had told him the driver must have seen him approaching in the rearview mirror. Getting hammered on the head with the Walther hadn't blurred his memory, apparently. Three of the men started after Calvino, who had already pushed through the passengers and headed for the entrance.

The men left the cold pill boxes behind along with some paperwork. Colonel Pratt backtracked and grabbed the papers. A young man with his arm around the waist of his girlfriend stared at him, shaking his head. An awkward moment passed as the two men locked eyes. The young man broke the solemn spell with a wide smile and wink. His girlfriend nudged him and nodded. One of the workers turned just before the entrance, looked back at the train and huddled for a split second with another worker. Someone must have remembered there was no one to prevent people from stealing the whole lot. One worker ran toward the trolley, shouting at people to back away or there would be trouble. Colonel Pratt noticed a detail in the warning. The man wasn't threatening to call the police. No need for that. Everyone knew that "trouble" was a word expandable to cover most kinds of suffering. They backed away.

Colonel Pratt joined several people who passed through the entrance and back into the street alongside the market. When he looked up at the balcony, the Colonel didn't see Khin Myat, who was supposed to be keeping a lookout. He scanned the street and a laneway that disappeared inside the central market but saw no sign of Calvino.

It hadn't been an ordinary delivery. The men and the shipment had nothing to do with Udom, Pratt realized. The driver of the Lexus worked for Thiri Pyan Chi. Colonel Pratt had assumed Thiri Pyan Chi was Udom's man, an assumption that Udom likely shared. While there was a connection between the covered market stall owner and the two Thai men Calvino had killed in Chinatown, it wasn't clear how Udom's smuggling business fit in.

Calvino made his getaway from the train station as the driver and two of the other men gave chase. They ran straight into a couple of foreign businessmen, who walked in front of them, absorbed in conversation. They looked the foreigners over before pushing them out of the way. Calvino had a head start.

Colonel Pratt emerged as the men ran after Calvino. He followed them, thinking one of them might be in a position to "spit" some answers. Or were they just hired hands, knowing nothing?

As the men pursued Calvino into the market, the Colonel entered a tea shop and took a seat near a window overlooking the street. Eventually, after the thugs had failed to catch Calvino, they returned to pushing the trolley down the road. Two of the men, sweating from the sprint after Calvino, walked alongside the trolley, steadying the boxes. The trolley needed three men to navigate the uneven brick road. They pulled it to the back of a Lexus, and the men loaded the boxes of cold pills inside. After one of them closed the back hatch, two of the men climbed inside, and the man who had spotted Calvino got into the driver's seat and pulled the Lexus into the road. They left a fourth man behind with the trolley to return it to the covered market. They worked like a team who had the drill down. Hard-handed men working with armed-unit efficiency. Not one slacker. Men like that never came cheap.

Five minutes later Colonel Pratt looked outside the tea shop and saw the back door of a parked Toyota open and Calvino roll out, squatting down low and holding his cell phone. Slowly turning around, he smiled at Pratt.

"Nothing better than a little rest in the back seat of Toyota Camry."

"Your 10K run whipped you into shape," said Colonel Pratt as Calvino took the seat next to him.

"That guy was behind the wheel of the Lexus in Chinatown. I clipped him pretty good."

"Not something a man forgets."

"Apparently not," said Calvino.

Colonel Pratt pulled out the invoice he'd nicked from the cold pill shipment and smoothed it out on the table. He put on his reading glasses, read, turned it over and read some more before looking up at Calvino.

"This confirms a theory I've had about Yadanar. He's Udom's middleman, and he uses Thiri Pyan Chi for the heavy lifting. It turns out that Thiri Pyan Chi has another partner, whom I suspect Yadanar doesn't know about."

When ROI—return on investment—motivates violent men to do business together, Calvino thought, it's only a matter of time before the battlefield is marked, the landmines are set out and the ambush zones are patrolled.

"You know this secret partner?" said Calvino.

"I had a call from Bangkok."

"While we were on the platform," said Calvino.

Colonel Pratt had run a background check with the department on the two dead Thais in Chinatown, expecting to turn up a link to Udom or one of his companies. They'd drawn a blank. There was no connection. But the investigator in the department had found out something interesting.

"The two men in the Lexus were on the payroll of Somchai Rungsukal."

"Who's he?"

"An upcountry man of influence," said Colonel Pratt.

"What were Somchai's men doing in the back of the Thiri Pyan Chi's Lexus, working over Rob Osborne?" asked Calvino.

"You might want to ask Rob that question."

"This sounds like a heart is about to be broken," said Calvino, reaching over and pouring tea into a cup. "God, I got thirsty in the back of that car. I'm still sweating."

Sweat dripped off the end of his nose and onto the table.

"Kati wants to join you on the 10K run on Sunday," said Pratt.

"*Join* me?"

"She brags to her friends that she has a date with Kiss My Trash."

Colonel Pratt possessed an irritating memory for names and faces.

"What made you suddenly think of her?"

"You mentioned broken hearts and it made me think of her."

"Did she say why she wanted to run the 10K with me?"

Colonel Pratt poured tea in his cup and studied Calvino for a moment. He took a sip and put the cup down.

"I asked her to follow you and see if you dropped any packages."

"She bought that story?"

Colonel Pratt nodded as he looked at the bottom of his teacup, reading the leaves. Calvino had a flashback to Khin Myat sitting in front of the Hindu temple, sticking his finger in the wet tea leaves and studying the pattern.

"Kati has formed the bad habit of buying any story, if the price is right."

"What you're saying is that you've found her price," said Calvino.

"She works for Udom. He sent her to Rangoon, Vincent. He suspected Yadanar had opened another channel into Thailand and was double-crossing him. Kati's job was to get close to Yadanar and the people around him."

"Instead, she decided to go for the saxophone player."

"Udom has people in my department. He found out I'd been sent to Rangoon to deal with Yadanar. That caught Udom's attention. My boss in the department wanted to close down Udom's business. Udom couldn't decide who was a bigger problem—Yadanar or a Thai police colonel on assignment in Rangoon to upset his business. Someone was messing with his cold pill monopoly. If Yadanar was cheating him, he'd handle that in the standard way. Udom had his own way of finding out if someone was shipping cold pills to other sources in Thailand. Yadanar was the man. It couldn't happen without him knowing about it. Udom is a true believer in the double-cross, having been something of an expert in the fine art himself. Kati's main job was to compromise me so I'd be sidelined, my boss would take the heat, the investigation would be taken over by Udom's allies and everyone comes out happy. Except I'm left holding my saxophone and not much else."

"I thought she was a honey trap. And I also thought you'd reverted to an eighth-grade hormonal rush."

"Udom wanted video, photographs of the two of us naked. Not for blackmail but to take me out of his hair with the department. That first night I saw the setup. I let her believe she had me trapped. I saw an amateur take her own hook and line and run into the deep water. I wanted to see how far out she'd swim out before I reeled her back."

"Shit, Pratt. You really knew?"

Calvino remembered the Colonel's performance of the star musician enveloping his latest hot fan.

"You're not bullshitting me because you think I'll tell Ratana, are you? Did you sleep with her?" asked Calvino.

Colonel Pratt sat behind his tea, looking at Calvino, who wiped the sweat from his neck with a paper napkin.

"I told her I loved my wife. I let her know that I had only one chamber in my heart. That is a message no Thai woman can resist because they never hear a man tell them that. It converts the seducer into the seduced. I showed her photos of Manee, the two of us together. I showed her photos of our kids. I scrolled through a hundred photos on my cell phone, looking at Manee the way a teenager looks at a girlfriend. Kati turned away from the display screen and said that she had something important to tell me.

"But first I had to promise not to hate her. I told her that I could never hate her. She said that she couldn't go through with something sinful with a man like me. The karma would be too awful. I asked what kind of sin? She cried. After she wiped away the tears, she said she'd been the star 'pretty' at Udom's events company, the highest paid pretty on the payroll. No man had ever resisted her.

"Udom had put her on a couple of assignments. She always succeeded in compromising the man. She'd thought until the end that I'd weakened, and she'd earn a large bonus. All that was missing was an X-rated video of the two of us. She cried again, this time for herself. She said that she was sorry. She didn't know what she'd tell Udom. And would I please help her. That's when I had the idea for her to go on the run."

"You asked her to follow me on the 10K?"

Colonel Pratt nodded, swirling the last dregs of tea in the bottom of the cup.

Looking up at Calvino, he said, "I told her you could help her."

Calvino glanced at the window. A couple passed by, sharing ice cream.

"Help her with what?"

"Help her find out who in Burma is helping Somchai Rungsukal run cold pills into Udom's turf. Udom would be happy to act on that information."

"And Kati believes I know the inside man?"

"Maybe not the inside man, but the inside woman who knows the story."

Colonel Pratt saw no need to be more specific.

"Okay, so I get her an appointment with the Black Cat. Does that mean Kati cancels the run on Sunday? Because that would be fine with me, if you know what I mean. I'm still recovering from the last 10K. I got a cold sweat with those guys at the train station. My legs are still sore from the last run. They should've caught me. I don't know how I got away."

"It's hard to know. What I do know is, a woman like her runs on hope. That's longer than a 10K. She's on Udom's personal treadmill, and that means her marathon never ends. No matter how fast she runs, she never gets square with him. Hope is all she has left to hold on to."

"That's all any of us has."

Hope, Calvino thought, has an on-and-off relationship with the word "square." No matter where a man looks, geometry between people runs in odd angles, almost no perpendicular lines, with the result that "hope" can sound like no more than the name of an old ghost town or an actor who died a long time ago.

"You'll set it up?" asked the Colonel. "And you might ask Rob Osborne if Somchai Rungsukal is a name that rings a bell. Someone in Thailand had a reason to have him killed. Ask him if it was Somchai. Then ask the Black Cat. One of them will be lying."

Calvino thought about the Black Cat stalking a mouse, backing it into a corner, playing with it, until playtime was over and dinnertime had begun. Catching her in the small hollow of that in-between time was the challenge.

"I'll see what I can do," said Calvino.

NINETEEN

George Orwell's Favorite Bookshop

GEORGETTE HEYER'S *The Toll-Gate* lay open on the reception desk as Calvino walked into the guesthouse. She had to be a Georgette Heyer fan like Ratana, thought Calvino. A lit cigarette burned in a glass ashtray. Down the short corridor he saw a light under the washroom door. He leaned over and took his key off the hook. The sound of a toilet flushing followed him up the first steps on the three-flight walk to his room.

He used the key to open the door and quietly shut the door behind him as he entered the dark room. In the shadows Rob rocked back and forth, his arms folded over his chest as if to comfort himself. He'd pushed the chair in front of the window, his eyes fixed on the windowless brick wall of the building next door. Calvino placed a hand on his shoulder.

"Are you all right?"

He felt Rob's shrug in the darkness.

"Weird shit. You see it, right?"

Eyes glazed, wide open, seeing stuff on the wall that came from his mind and thinking it real, he looked up at Calvino, but in the darkness it was hard to make out the expression on his face. Calvino walked over and sat on the edge of the bed, taking off his jacket. He smoothed it and carefully laid it beside him. He took the cap off a bottle of whiskey and poured himself a drink.

"You want something to drink?"

Rob was non-responsive, eyes paranoid.

"You don't look so good."

"I'm not giving you any, so don't ask," said Rob.

"I'm not asking, but what aren't you giving?"

Rob's altered mind had been enhanced, and it wasn't from whiskey. Whatever he'd taken, it didn't seem to be agreeing with him. Paranoia and drugs go together like rum and coke, Calvino thought. The classic sign of someone high is their illusion that someone is going to take away their drugs. Calvino sipped his whiskey.

"I'm not going to take your stuff, Rob."

"How can I trust you? You killed those two men."

"Somchai Rungsukal sent them because you double-crossed him. That's how I see it. What do you see on the wall outside?"

Fear showed everywhere on Rob. In his eyes, in the twitch of his mouth. His mind was tricking him, telling him the things he saw were slowly cutting through the window pane, would enter the room and surround him, and he couldn't move. Rob was both a man terrified of leaving a shabby room and a man terrified to stay in the room. Fear pinned him to the chair.

"You know Somchai."

Calvino looked for a reaction.

Rob stopped rocking and extended his hand.

"Give me a drink."

Calvino poured whiskey in a glass, got up from the bed and put the glass into both of Rob's hands. He drank like a thirsty child.

"You were running pills for Somchai."

"Half of the men in Thailand are called Somchai. I know half a dozen Somchais, so what?"

"We can narrow it down to one man, the one you've done mule work for out of Rangoon."

Rob searched for Calvino's eyes.

"He sent those men to kill me?"

"You know the answer, Rob."

"It's not over, is it?"

A new tidal wave of fear washed over his face. This time it wasn't paranoia but a genuine understanding of his situation.

"What kind of shit did you take?"

"Acid."

"How did you get acid?" asked Calvino.

It might have been from the old lady at reception, dealing on the side, but much likelier it was from Mya. Calvino figured the old lady who lived in the world of regency romances would have thought of acid as something thrown to disfigure a face.

"I borrowed two tabs from a sea lion in the smuggling game."

"Does the sea lion have a name? Play a musical instrument? Speak Thai? Give me a hint, Rob. I like games as well as the next guy, but I don't have a lot of time to play right now."

Calvino waited for a response that made more sense. He wasn't certain if Rob had the capacity to respond. He drank his whiskey, thinking he might be in for a long night.

"Mya's dumping me."

"She told you that?"

Rob slowly turned away from the window.

"She got the family bookstore back, the one on 42nd Street."

"Yeah?"

She couldn't scrape up the money to spring her brother from prison, but she'd found the resources to acquire a building in the heart of Rangoon? Calvino knelt down beside Rob and touched the rim of Rob's glass to his own.

"Here's to books and black cats."

"It happened a few days ago. I found out today."

He paused, lost in his thoughts.

"Her mother and brother have moved in upstairs."

"How she'd manage that?"

Rob's mouth felt dry. He licked his lips, swallowed hard.

"Yadanar fixed it."

"What makes you think she's going to break up with you?"

"She said she bought the bookstore for us. She said it was a new start. It was like a new life for the two of us in Rangoon. But I don't believe her. Mya did it for Mya."

His mouth trembled as he stared at the wall across the way.

"When I look at the wall outside, I see stuff falling apart. I see people drifting away from each other. They can't stop it from happening."

"But you haven't split up."

"Not yet," said Rob, shaking his head. "I'm watching the wall, and you know what I see? I see Splitsville station one more stop down the track."

His lips trembled. They were dry. He licked them, swallowing a mouth of Johnnie Walker.

Rob made the sound of an old steam locomotive train whistle.

"Train pulling into the station."

"Stop feeling sorry for yourself," Calvino said. "You've got a life back in Bangkok. I can get you on a flight tomorrow. What do you say? Fresh start."

Calvino refilled the empty glass as Rob stared at the brick wall out the window. Dark shadows sprawled in a tangle of blurred webs. A sudden agitation propelled Rob to lurch forward and gesture with his fist.

"Somchai, I'm not afraid of you!" Rob shouted, the veins in neck thick and bluish under his pale skin.

His eyes moved in a hellish frenzy, the torment of the vision burrowing deep into his psyche.

"There's no one there."

"You're not looking. There! Do you see him?"

He twisted his hand into the shape of a gun and pretended to fire it at the phantoms dancing on the wall opposite the window.

"Out of ammo," said Calvino.

Rob lowered his arm and stared at his hand as if it were a smoking gun.

"Still loaded."

Rob smiled and dropped his arm by his side.

"Mya promised to clear me with Somchai. But she doesn't know the Thais. You can't fix things with Somchai."

"Maybe she'll come back later and surprise you," said Calvino.

"She sleeps above the bookstore. It's her dream. I'm not in it."

"People change."

Rob glared at Calvino.

"You sound like my father."

"There's something you're holding back, Rob. What'd she say before she left?"

"She said it was okay for me to go back to Bangkok. That I'd be okay. How can it be okay if she stays here? Do you get that? I don't," he said, slurring as his voice slowed. "Somchai said he'd kill me. How can she fix my problem? Can you tell me that?"

He sighed, staring out the window.

"Why don't I talk to Mya?"

He turned in his chair.

"That'd be good. Talk to Mya."

He ducked down and then dropped to the floor, his hands over his head as if under attack. Calvino lifted him back into the chair. Rob flinched as he glanced at the wall again, recoiling as if he struck by a round. He clenched his teeth, raising his fist toward the wall.

"Fuck you! I'm not afraid."

"I don't see anyone," said Calvino.

"But he'll be back."

The dogs of fear pulled on the muscles of Rob's face like a dogsled, twisting it.

"You still have your gun?" Rob asked.

Calvino nodded.

"Do you still have yours?"

Rob held up his hand in the shape of a gun, slowly raising it until his forefinger pointed at his temple. He dropped his thumb like the gun's hammer.

"Bang!" said Rob.

"Reload and keep cool. I'll be back."

"That's what everyone always says."

Calvino opened the door.

"I'm going to Mya's bookstore. Want anything to read?"

"A book about dreams. The one Mya said she was going to write."

The Irrawaddy Bookstore had been doing business on 42nd Street between Maha Bandoola Road and Merchant, around the corner from the Strand Hotel, for as long as anyone could remember. It was an institution. And like all institutions it had a history of grand heights and abysmal lows.

Calvino found the shop nestled like a chipped antique cup in the palm of a withered hand. The old colonial-style building, with shops on the ground floor and living quarters above, had decayed into squalor. The neighborhood survived on life support, living off memories of a glorious past. Looking at the street, Calvino could foresee that foreigner developers would soon stand on the pavement, figuring a way to buy up the buildings for renovation and resale, or better yet, to tear them down and put up chrome and glass high-rises with names like Imperial Suites and Empire Tower.

In one corner of the bookshop's front window, a small hand-printed sign was taped to the glass with the message "Irrawaddy Bookstore. Est. 1934." He looked up at the balcony and pulled on a thin rope that hung down to the top of the door. Improvised doorbells with pulley ropes hung from the balconies of most buildings in the neighborhood.

"We're closed," a voice shouted down a moment later.

Calvino backed away from the building and looked up in the dark. A light came on in an upper window. It was followed by a second light. He saw people sitting on their balconies in the next building. In fact, most of the balconies had people sitting on chairs, talking and watching the street. The hot evening had driven them outside.

Calvino cupped his hands and shouted, "Mya, it's Vincent. Can we talk for a few minutes?"

The Black Cat leaned over the railing, making out Calvino's form among the shadows.

"How did you find me?" She laughed at her own question. "But that's what you do. Find people who are missing. I'll come down."

A couple of minutes later the Black Cat stood framed in the door, braless in a white spaghetti-strap top over tight jeans, faded at the knees, and knee-length black leather boots. Her hair was pulled back into a ponytail. She looked younger without the makeup and eye shadow.

"I guess you want to come inside," she said.

"I won't take much of your time."

She gestured for him to enter the ground floor, where the bookstore operated. She walked to the wall and flipped on the lights, which flickered before settling into a dim yellow glow that showered the bookcases along the walls. The curtains in the front window had been left pulled back. Outside, Calvino saw an old woman looking at books displayed in the window. She smiled and nodded at him and walked on. Others came and stared. None of them smiled or stopped for long to look at the books. They were more interested that the bookstore had lights on at this time of night.

The Black Cat's boots clopped on the wooden floor-boards. She disappeared behind the impressive teak counter. An old cash register sat on top, its vintage keys ringed with faded gold. She sat on a stool. He imagined her grandfather had sat on the same stool in his day.

"You've talked to Rob," she said, thumbing a cigarette out of a pack.

"You shouldn't have given him the acid."

Sitting motionlessly, she lit the cigarette. She studied him while exhaling smoke from her nostrils.

"Why would you think I'd do that? Because I'm in the entertainment business?"

"Because he asked you to," he said. "And you thought it might do him good. A trip is a cheap ticket away from reality."

"So they say."

"When I left him, he still hadn't escaped."

"Rob gets depressed a lot."

Calvino let it go and made a point of looking at the books displayed on a table below the window. There was a strange collection of titles—*Legal Ethics*, *Elder Law 3rd Ed.*, *Immigration Law 4th Ed.*, *Regulated Industries 4th Ed.* Several biographies. And a series called "For Everyone" with volumes on Einstein, Chekhov and Tagore.

"No Henry Miller? No George Orwell?"

"They're on order," she said.

"Something's bothering me," he said. "Your brother was in prison. You couldn't get together four grand plus to spring him, but you bought your grandfather's old bookstore. I must be missing something. Bar girls pull this stunt in Bangkok. 'Brother in trouble. Give me money.' But she's got a house, a condo and a Honda Accord she's not telling you about."

"No money changed hands for the building," said Mya.

"Someone gave you this building?"

"Someone gave it back."

She saw him pull a doubtful face.

"It's like this. After 1988 my family backed the wrong side. The wrong side is always the one that loses. Our side lost. So my mother put the title of the building in my aunt's name."

"Your aunt backed the winning side," said Calvino.

The Black Cat nodded.

"It's taken a while for your aunt to give it back," said Calvino.

"One condition was for my brother to get out of prison. My aunt said that would be a sign, meaning the time would be right to return our property. My mother agreed that, without the auspicious sign, transferring back the deed could spell disaster. Winners never want to be losers. They don't want to deal with losers. Or think about them. She waited until we could show we were also winners. We all waited. My brother is out of prison and my aunt returned the deed."

"You're not going back to Bangkok," said Calvino. "You've told Rob."

She nodded. "I told him."

"No more Monkey Nose? No more 50th Street Bar? You plan to pull on your boots, sit on your grandfather's stool and sell books?"

"I told Rob he can go back to Bangkok. No one is going to hurt him."

"Has Somchai Rungsukal put that in writing?"

"Rob told you about Somchai? Why am I not surprised?"

She removed the braid holding her ponytail in place, letting hair fall down over her shoulders.

"It was Somchai's men who jumped Rob in Chinatown. Did you set him up?"

She butted out her cigarette, shaking her head.

"No, I had no idea that was going to happen."

"What did you think was going to happen?"

"It was a mistake."

"It didn't play out the way you'd planned? Maybe Somchai told you that he only wanted to smooth things over. No hard feelings. But you had some doubts, and that's why you asked me to come around to meet Rob. For protection. Backup in case, as you say, you made a mistake."

She brushed her hair back from her face, never taking her eyes off Calvino, who'd picked up the Chekhov bio. He leafed through a few pages before putting it down, waiting for her to say something. Now that he'd laid his cards on the table, she saw a winning hand. She held a busted flush.

"I have a feeling you're making the same mistake again," said Calvino. "You've worked out a deal. How does that work, when Somchai wants him dead?"

"It works because Somchai's a businessman. Rob dead will cause him a lot of trouble he doesn't want. He's got that message. Letting him live makes him a lot of money. And he's got that message, too. Men like him choose money over trouble."

Calvino thought about what she'd said. It had the ring of truth. Guys like Somchai had much the same wiring. He lived like Udom inside a world where violence and the threat of it served a business purpose. Businesses need stability in the illicit world as well as the licit one. Men in that world stayed alive by paying attention and respect to someone bigger than them, more violent, more ruthless and connected. That was the best path, the one less likely to lead to a sheer drop from a cliff.

"What is Somchai afraid of?" asked Calvino. "That Udom's going to visit him in his dreams?"

"In a way, yes. Dreams explain choices."

"Henry Miller walked into your dreams and said, 'Hey baby, put on your dancing shoes.' You're getting back your bookstore, and Rob Osborne walks away a free and clear man," said Calvino.

Years ago, every upcountry girl who worked a bar dreamt of owning a mini-mart. The saddest part of poor people's dreams was how modest, how threadbare, they were. Dreams woven into a garment that easily fell apart.

"You're making fun of this. You shouldn't."

To the Burmese dreams weren't a laughing matter. She was right; he wasn't taking it seriously. Dreams as a social currency. It wasn't something he'd encountered before— searching for reality inside magical and imaginary worlds, dense and filled with possibility. When he talked with the Burmese in the real world, they dragged their dream scripts with them, using them to direct their actions. He hadn't decided yet how to deal with Burmese dream sharers and dream merchants. The Burmese, once they started in on their dreams, gave off the "uncanny valley" vibration—that disturbing feeling that someone or something stumbled upon in the real world isn't quite fully human or slightly more human than it should be.

Calvino looked at Mya, smoking, dreamy-eyed, watching him as he stood across from her. She saw that he hadn't quite reached the point of deciding what to do next. Most foreigners who entered into the modulated reality of Burmese dreams found it repulsive and ran for the exit.

"Tell me about your dream," said Calvino.

If stepping into that imaginary world was what was needed to learn Rob's future, he was willing to pay the small price.

"What you need to know is the dream of my aunt, my mother's elder sister."

"And afterwards, you'll tell me yours."

She shook her head, leaning forward, one elbow against the cash register.

"Not my dream. My mother's dream comes next. The one she had on the same night as my aunt," said Mya. "They came together in each other's dreams."

When a woman says her mother and her aunt literally shared a dream, there was only one response: "How did that happen, exactly?"

He thought about Rob dropping acid to reach his own dream state, where visions of the impossible flickered like puppet shadows on a brick wall, firing up all of his senses and remaking the world.

"It started with a barking dog," the Black Cat said with a Cheshire Cat grin.

A golden retriever howled in the middle of the night. It wasn't the normal sound of a dog playing or greeting its master. The dog stood guard at the gate. Not long after, a neighbor's small terrier joined in with a tenor howl. Soon the whole neighborhood of dogs bayed in a chorus as if the ghosts of All Souls' Day had misread the calendar.

The incident with the barking, yapping and howling dogs occurred at two in the morning on the third day after the cremation ceremony of Mya's grandfather. On that day five monks arrived at the house, walking in single file. They stood at the front gate at five in the morning, waiting for an invitation to enter the compound. On the fourth day, Mya's mother forgot to provide a meal for the dead. It had been so hectic, with the monks and all, and she'd been tired, exhausted by grief. Up to that day her five-year-old daughter, Mya, had also left food before a photograph of her grandfather, but that day she hadn't.

Three monks came to Mya's mother in a dream and told her she'd forgotten to leave a food offering. No one had looked after her father's spirit, and he came into her dream to say that he was hungry. She saw her father in a vision, inside the crawl space between dreaming and consciousness. He was sitting with her mother in the bookstore, behind the cash register, smoking a cigar. He had a book open on the counter. He read and smoked just as she remembered him doing, when she was a young girl and she and her sister let their father read to them each afternoon after school.

The bookshop exploded in a blaze of colored feathers. A goddess riding on the back of a peacock settled down next to her father. When the goddess opened her bag, she extracted two fish, a goldfish and a catfish, a female and male.

The goldfish talked to her from inside the well. The catfish had died. Holding the dead fish in a pot and raising it to a monk in the sky, she looked to the sea. There she saw crocodiles and dragons, and another monk who'd been alive from the time of Buddha. He held a fan and stood watching the horizon. A group of yogis walked down the road to the temple. She dreamt of a dragon goddess in lace, her hands in a wai, and on her head was an entangled mass of green snails.

She shared her dream with her daughter and sister over morning tea. She decided to save money to contribute toward paint for the new stupa. And she fasted and prayed, working the prayer beads as she chanted. She donated money for the prayers so that merit would be sent to her father. She lighted candles in front of his photograph. Three days a week she ate no meat.

The next night, she dreamt of a *nat* who'd been in the room beside the garage, next to the window in the back. The *nat* wore lots of jewelry. The spirit was a man around forty years old, but she couldn't see his face in the shadows. People from the spiritual world waited for her. She gave merit for them, waiting for them to come. For three days she didn't tell anyone. She was too scared. For three nights she was too afraid to get up at night. On the third day she told her sister. Now they were both frightened. The dragon goddess was her guardian angel, and whenever she was insecure or had a problem, she called her name and asked for help.

She didn't know the way of replying to someone inside this invisible world. Suffering and in great sorrow, she wandered in a world without form, looking for her father for another three days and not finding him.

She wanted to cleanse her body of meat. She sought purity.

She had a string with 108 beads. No, it was actually 111 beads. Each one as black as pure evil, but when she rotated the beads quickly, she found they turned white like an elephant's tusks, pure as ivory. She showed the beads to her sister, even though she knew she must be humble and unassuming. It looks like your father's work, a monk said. The sister's son, Yadanar Khin, smoked a cigarette at the piano. She heard the music rise but she couldn't smell the smoke. The sister's husband in his general's uniform stood with the remote pointed at the TV, watching a pirated tape of a reality show.

The sister watched as her father stared at her husband in front of the TV. Her marriage to a soldier had been a huge disappointment. He had left the bookstore to Mya's mother. A statement affixed to the will had said, "Your husband will find you many buildings. The bookstore and house are to belong to your sister." But when the troubles came in 1988, the deed was signed over. It had been a victory for her. The father had come to tell her the trouble was long past. She must return the property.

Mya's mother had also seen their father in her dream. He'd told her that the blood of the Buddha family will come together, not in this life, but in the bloodline carried by the *nats*. People will gather around and form a community. They would never go to hell. They would be spared the fate of mortals eaten by worms. Instead they'd live in nirvana.

The sister collected eight leaves from the grounds of the Shwedagon Pagoda. They were best collected on a Saturday. As her father instructed in the dream, she then put them under the mattress and slept over them every night. One day she called Mya's mother for the first time in many years. It was at six o'clock, to say she must see her immediately. On the way to her house, her driver, an Indian, hit a crazy monk who wandered into the road. She left the car and phoned her son Yadanar, who came in a sports car and took her to see Mya's mother. They discussed the meaning of the dream. They phoned a monk and asked for advice. That night the sister placed fresh leaves under the mattress. The next morning she found two dead cockroaches there.

The house was broom clean, spotless. There was no way the insects could have crawled into the bedroom from the garden. They must have hidden in the leaves placed under the mattress. On a Thursday a monk came to her house and asked her, "Are you okay?" He knew that she wasn't. That was why he had come.

She told him about the dream, her sister's dream and the accident. The monk said that he had stopped them from being hurt in the accident. He'd had a vision as it happened and intervened. And he told her that we must all die; even the Buddha had to die. Before we die, though, we must be useful to people who are lost. He also said that the father had sent a message about unfinished business with a sister and that the elder sister would know what was intended by that message. Mya's mother had kept faith all of these years that her elder sister would tell her when she received the sign.

The morning her sister arrived with Yadanar, Mya's mother knew that her sister would bring the title deed. Yadanar waited until the two sisters were deep into discussions about the dreams, and then he gestured for Mya to meet him in the garden. It was in the garden that Yadanar said he had a plan to tour with his band and wanted her to join as a singer. He pressed her, saying the house deed could easily be reclaimed. His father had the power to do anything. She should know that. She asked if he could fix a problem her boyfriend was having. Naturally, Yadanar asked what kind of problem, and she told him about how Somchai had come around to the club in Bangkok. He always came with three or four friends, and they had got to know each other. It turned out he was doing business in Rangoon and wanted to let Rob in on a good opportunity to make money.

"I was having problems raising money for my brother," Mya explained to Calvino. "Rob went to his father. The bastard wouldn't help even though he was filthy rich. Rob said he'd help out Somchai. Only it turned out, Somchai didn't want Rob for bringing back a few pills. He wanted him making a couple of regular runs each month. Rob thought about it and told Somchai he wasn't interested. Next thing, someone tried to kidnap Rob. I think Somchai wants to kill him."

"What kind of business was Somchai running?"

"Cold pills. He said there was no problem. "

"No problem? Then why the need to smuggle them into Thailand?"

"It's complicated."

"You're saying Yadanar found a way out of the mess for Rob?"

She got up from the stool and walked around the counter, stopping in front of Calvino.

"You don't want to get too far into this. It's done."

"What's done?"

"Yadanar said, 'If I fix this, you'll sign an exclusive with me.' He owns me for a year. Rob kicks free of his problem."

"Rob isn't taking it well," said Calvino. "He asked me to pick up a book about dreams. The one you said you were writing."

"I'm still working on it," she said. "Every night there's more material."

In Mya's dream she saw Rob looking out a window at a blank wall and seeing himself with Monkey Nose playing back at the club. No singer, just three guys trying to get through a set with the audience talking and forgetting they were playing.

Calvino left five dollars for the biography on Chekhov and slipped the book in his jacket. It would give Rob something to read and think about until Calvino could get him back to Bangkok.

"Does Rob know that you and Yadanar are cousins?"

"At first he was relieved," she said. "But it didn't last."

Another man might be competition for the affections of a woman, but a man who was part of the family and who wanted much more could never be defeated. Calvino started to understand why Rob had dropped the acid and saw fantastic visions. Psychologically, he'd always been better suited to live in the demimonde of Henry Miller's world—his father's world—only to discover he'd been isolated, left struggling inside a Dorian Gray underworld, chased by murderers.

TWENTY

A Windowless Room on 42nd Street

IT WAS AFTER 2:00 in the morning when Calvino quietly unlocked the door to his room at the guesthouse and slipped inside. Before he found the light switch on the wall, an old, foul smell mugged him in the dark. He kicked the door closed behind him and moved to the side. Like most flophouses at night, the room floated in near darkness, black enough for any occupant to qualify as legally blind. He reached inside his jacket, pulled out the Walther and crouched low, listening and waiting for his eyes adjust. Nothing moved. He heard pipes rumbling in the ceiling. He inched forward, staying low, until he reached the chair in front of the window.

Slowly he rose to his feet, leaned forward and pushed back the curtains. Light from the outside filtered through, revealing Rob's body, slumped to one side in the chair. Defying gravity, caught in one of those stop-action controlled falls, he looked pinned in place like a collector's butterfly. Calvino felt for a pulse on his neck. The skin felt clammy. Pulling his hand away, he holstered the Walther.

Calvino made his way back to the door and switched on the light. The first thing he saw was how blood had pooled on the floor around the legs of the chair. A pillow with a black burn mark partially covered a gun. Crawling around in the dark, Calvino had managed to track through blood, staining his pant knees and cuffs. Bits of stuffing from the pillow hung from the entry wound in the side of Rob's head, making it look a little like a burrow hole used as a bird's nest. The pillow would have muffled the sound of the shot.

Calvino went into the bathroom, took off his trousers and washed the blood and brains from them. He put them back on and walked back into the bedroom.

Suicide? When the world lost its power to enchant, and imaginary and real enemies merged on a dark brick wall, killing oneself floated to the top of the option list. But just because suicide was an option didn't mean someone like Rob would have acted on it. Calvino searched the room again. The kid had been depressed and talked about Mya dumping him. Young men have killed themselves over rejected love from the beginning of time. Rob was a perfect candidate for a suicide verdict. Only it didn't wash with Calvino. He asked himself, when did anyone ever put a pillow against his own head before blowing out his brains? And who ever tossed his own room before killing himself? The sheets had been stripped from the twin beds and thrown on the floor. The mattresses were pulled off the beds and cut open, the springs and stuffing spilling out like the guts of an animal hit by a speeding truck. Someone had been looking for something.

Calvino walked to the chair and had a closer look at the body. Rob's right hand hung lifeless above the gun. The hand of the deceased and the weapon used to inflict death matched in the perfect suicide arc; it looked like the gun had dropped on the floor after the shot had been fired. The last image he had of Rob was of him miming suicide by gun.

"What's happened here, Rob?" Calvino muttered, sitting on the edge of the bed with no mattress. He ran a hand through his hair. A man's fist doesn't turn into a gun.

Dreams are dreams, play is play, and dead is dead. Calvino pulled out his cell phone. Colonel Pratt came on the line. There was a lot of background noise.

"I'm looking at a body with a bullet wound in the head," said Calvino. "It's the kid."

"Hold on," said Colonel Pratt.

The Colonel walked outside the bar and kept on walking until the noise streaming from the club was swallowed up by the night.

"Are you okay?"

First, control the situation by establishing the caller is safe. Even with Calvino, the police training automatically took over.

"I was out when it happened."

"It must be connected with what happened in Chinatown," said Pratt.

"Whoever it was knew what they were doing. They made it look like suicide. Anyone profiling Rob would buy the suicide theory."

Calvino sounded frustrated, angry and desperate.

"That's what thugs like that do, Vincent. I'm sorry about the kid. He got involved with people he should have avoided. And once he took that step, he was a dead man walking. Rob knew the score. Be honest with yourself. You saw this coming."

Colonel Pratt had put the words as clearly as a man could, words that described Rob's world and his short-lived place in it. Hard words, and only a few of them had been needed because the truth boiled free of the frills.

"I shouldn't have gone out."

"Sooner or later it would have happened. Head toward my hotel. Phone me when you're about to arrive. I'll go outside and meet you. That way it will look like we've come in together. Half an hour."

As Calvino started to put the cell phone into his jacket pocket, his hand found the book inside. Pulling out the Chekhov biography, he recalled the playwright's famous gun rule—show a loaded gun on the stage, and there's no choice but to use it later in the play. Did the rule apply to a gun made from a fist? As in Chekhov's time, the rich didn't need to search their dreams for hints on how to steal and exploit. They did it with eyes wide open.

He slipped the book back into his pocket and quickly packed his clothes in his suitcase. He removed the visible evidence that he'd ever been in the room. No one would be dusting for fingerprints. No Burmese CSI investigators would be arriving to search with a fine-tooth comb for hair, skin or saliva. The death scene would get the usual procedure—the what-you-see-is-what-you-get system of investigation—and what the police would see would depend on who paid them to see or not to see. Someone would dream the death, and the dream would be the report that had the weight to close the case.

Calvino took a final look at the body. How would he explain what happened to Alan Osborne? He thought that was likely the one person who would comprehend the situation—understand the ties between players in the visible world and criminal gangs. Those worlds were so tight that a razor blade couldn't be slipped between them.

It was late, and he passed no one on the stairs as he descended to the lobby. Whoever had shot the bullet into Rob's brain had known what they were doing. In the bookstore he'd heard about Yadanar's pledge to protect Rob. Nothing was going to happen to him. Promise. She might have told him where Rob was staying, thinking he would send someone to watch over him. But Calvino had no evidence she'd said anything, or if she had, that Yadanar had a reason to have Rob killed. Other than Mya, the only other people who knew Rob's location were Colonel Pratt and Jack Saxon. Neither the Colonel nor Saxon would have told anyone. Calvino felt an aching feeling that he'd overlooked something; he suffered from the worst of all anxieties—the possibility of another that he had overlooked. The prospect haunted him as he walked towards the guesthouse.

Arriving at the lobby, Calvino walked to the reception desk. The old lady refused to look up from her novel. He cleared his throat. She ignored him. Her steadfast refusal to give him even a sideways glance surprised him. They had spoken more than once. It was small talk, granted, but they'd made enough of a connection for her behavior now to seem odd. Calvino was pretty sure that out of the corner of her eye she had seen him as he approached. Her faced was twisted in frightened mask, capturing the expression of someone who desperately wanted to crawl out of her skin, but there was no other skin to crawl into. She was attempting to pretend that Calvino had never arrived at the guesthouse.

"Still reading *The Toll-Gate*?" he said. "I thought you'd have finished it by now."

Slowly she raised her eyes from the book and looked at him over the top of her reading glasses. There were bruises on the right side of her face. Georgette Heyer's novels hadn't prepared her for life in the twenty-first century.

He stood waiting for her to collect her thoughts.

Finally, she blinked away tears and whispered, "Go."

No bill, no request for money. No nothing except that one small word that spoke a library of twisted suffering.

"They threatened you. Beat you up," said Calvino. "I can help."

"Like you helped the boy in your room?"

It was true that what had happened to Rob wasn't exactly a recommendation of Calvino's ability to protect anyone. There was nothing he could do or say to change things now. Whoever had killed Rob had covered the bases. That's the way they wanted things to play out, he thought. They had closed the business with Rob. Finished, over and done with. Calvino was nothing to them. If he were smart, he'd walk away—and they expected he'd have no other choice, and that would be the end of it. They would have told the old woman at reception to play along, and the moment she'd put up the slightest resistance or asked the wrong kind of question, they'd taught her the lesson of simple obedience.

It didn't take a genius to figure out their script. The Richard Smith whose phony name was on the registry was a young *luk krueng*, a half-breed, with braided hair and a beard. He had the look and the lifestyle of a terrorist. She'd found him dead inside the room. She would say he had appeared depressed. How was she to know he'd used a phony name? He'd looked like a drug addict and kept to himself. She had no idea why he would have killed himself. No, she hadn't heard any shot. And no, she hadn't seen anyone go into or out of his room.

Walking out of the lobby, it hit Calvino. Whatever deal had been done was in place. All he had to do was walk out the door and not look back. Not ask questions, get on a plane to Bangkok, return to his life and dream of new cases. His options were limited. He wasn't Richard Smith, and he had a dead man in his room. If it wasn't suicide, they'd be happy to let him take the fall, and for a moment he saw himself back at the courthouse. Only this time, he wouldn't be a privileged guest but another shackled prisoner in the dock. No one would be in the room seeing that he walked out a free man.

The killers were covered, unless Calvino was stupid enough to think the ball was still in play when the game was already over. They figured him for a survivor, a private investigator who found missing people and so understood the nature of violence. Stick with the suicide theory and it would be a smooth, easy resolution. It wasn't all that hard to make a murder look like a suicide, especially if the dead man was no more than a kid, someone who tested positive for drugs and had a history of running in circles where people die young. The police report would have enough evidence to support suicide. Unless Calvino wanted to make trouble, hang around and contradict the cops. Then they'd find his gun. Find out his real name. Maybe link him to the two men killed in Chinatown. No one wanted Rob to be a murder victim. That would look bad for the country's opening party. Calvino felt he'd been lowered into a tight-fitting box, and the lid had been screwed shut.

It was 4:00 a.m. when Calvino pushed his suitcase into the back of a taxi, climbed in and asked the driver to drop him at the Shwedagon.

"I want to feed the monks," he said.

It was too early in the morning for the driver to offer him a free ride to shop for discounted jewelry. As Calvino sat in the back of the car, he thought about Mya and Yadanar. Whether they had already been told what had happened to Rob.

After the taxi stopped beside the pagoda, he pulled out his case, waited a couple of minutes and then hailed another taxi. He leaned into the window and asked the second taxi driver how much to drive to Kandawgyi Road and drop him off at the entrance of Bogyoke Aung San Park. The driver sucked his teeth, looking Calvino up and down and noting his suitcase, and quoted three dollars. Taking a foreigner from Shwedagon to Kandawgyi Lake—one of the features of Bogyoke Aung San Park—made him scratch his head.

"I had a dream about making merit if I fed the ducks at dawn," Calvino said.

The foreigner made sense.

"Get in. Two dollars, okay?" the driver said.

Colonel Pratt had walked out of the hotel, crossed the street and was waiting when Calvino's taxi stopped at the entrance to the park. He waited until Calvino had paid the taxi and it had driven away before approaching him. Seeing the Colonel, Calvino shifted the suitcase to his left hand and extended his right hand to his friend.

"Sorry to pull you out of bed," he said.

They walked along the pavement leading inside the vast garden. They had the park to themselves. Walking over to a bench, they sat down and Calvino looked at the lake in the darkness. A few lamps at the far end illuminated the water. It was a dead-quiet time in Rangoon, an hour of the morning without people or car sounds, just birds roosting in the treetops and the sweet scent of flowers on the cool breeze.

"I told Mya after you called me. We were about to do a final set," said Colonel Pratt.

"How did she react?"

"She sang that song of hers. There wasn't much of an audience left by then. The bar wanted to close down. Yadanar wouldn't let them. He wanted to play all night. Cocaine makes four in the morning feel like noon. She got on the stage and sang 'My Man.' There weren't more than five people in audience, but she had them on their knees. She put down the microphone, walked off the stage and out the door."

Calvino's cell phone vibrated inside his jacket and he fished it out. Mya's voice came through from the other end.

"You heard," he said.

He looked at Colonel Pratt as they sat on the park bench.

"Okay, we're at Bogyoke Park, sitting on a bench overlooking the lake. You'll find us."

Half an hour later she walked up behind them silently, circled around the bench and stood looking at the lake, hands in her jean pockets. She'd been crying and didn't want them to see.

"Tell me what happened."

She turned and walked over to Calvino and sat beside him.

He told her how he'd found the body after he'd left her bookshop. Whoever had killed Rob had made it appear as if the gunshot had been self-inflicted. They'd terrorized the old woman at reception into a story that Rob had checked into the room under a phony name, dropped acid, put the gun to his head and pulled the trigger.

Colonel Pratt asked, "Would Rob have killed himself?"

She leaned forward, looking at the lake and the first crack of light on the horizon.

"No way. He wouldn't have had the courage."

"Didn't your cousin Yadanar promise nothing would happen to him?" asked Calvino.

She glanced at him, her eyes red as if on fire.

"I don't think..."

"Think what? That he knew this would happen and let it?" asked Calvino. "This isn't a dream, Mya. Rob's brains were splattered against the wall of the room."

"Easy, Vincent," said Colonel Pratt. "Rob was a Thai. I'd like to talk with Yadanar, not as a saxophone player but—"

"As a cop," she said, finishing his sentence.

"As a human being," he said. "But not at the bar. It's not the place."

"Tonight Yadanar has a birthday party at his house."

"He mentioned it," said the Colonel.

"You don't need an invitation. You can just show up."

"He should be relaxed in his own house," said Calvino. "We should go. I have the perfect gift for the birthday boy."

He removed the Chekhov biography from his jacket pocket.

"It's a real paper-and-ink book. You don't see many of them anymore."

She recognized the book that Calvino had bought earlier that night from her bookshop. The Black Cat rose from the bench.

"I've got to go," she said, fishing a key out of her jeans. "You'll need a place to stay. Here's the key to the bookshop. There's a cot in the back. My grandfather used to sleep in the shop."

Calvino extended his hand and she dropped the key into his palm. She must have told Rob that he couldn't stay there, Calvino thought. The Black Cat must have read his mind.

"Rob wanted to sleep upstairs in my room. I'm sorry I told him that was impossible. He might still be alive if I'd let him."

"Or you might both be dead," said Colonel Pratt.

A wave of grief swept across her face, and her shoulders slumped.

"I've got to go."

Colonel Pratt looked at the Chekhov biography and the bookshop key sitting on top.

"Something's not right, Vincent," said Colonel Pratt, watching the Black Cat disappear toward Natmauk Road. "She's just found out about Rob, and now she's given you a key to where she lives and invited us to a birthday party."

"She feels guilty," said Calvino.

"She didn't ask what will happen to Rob's body. Some women can fake grief. It's not that hard."

"You think she was faking it?"

The Colonel shrugged.

"I kept looking for some evidence of shock or remorse or sadness, and what I got was social arrangements."

"They said Henry Miller wasn't sentimental either. But here's the key," said Calvino, holding it up. "Maybe it's her way of showing that she wants to help. To make up for not taking Rob in."

"There's something wrong."

Colonel Pratt had something else to say but stopped himself.

"Don't go if you think it's a setup."

"You'd go on your own?" asked the Colonel.

"Yeah, I would. And I'll stay at her place. I need to explain to Rob's father that she offered something important. She asked a foreigner to stay in her shop. That's a big deal. She was one of the last people to see Rob."

A rim of orange light broke beyond the lake and the trees. Colonel Pratt muffled a yawn.

"Maybe she's playing it straight."

"Let's give her the benefit of the doubt," said Calvino.

"You should go back to Bangkok. There's a morning flight. I've done about all I can here. I don't see that it's any different for you."

"I'm starting to see the potential in Rangoon. I need a couple of more days. I could head back now. I could. But the kid was killed in my room," said Calvino. "When that happens to a man, he has to try to find some reason for it. I need to know, Pratt."

Calvino shrugged as Colonel Pratt got up from the bench.

"I thought you'd say something like that," said the Colonel.

"That doesn't mean you shouldn't head back. You have reports to file, people to see. And you have a room with a view. You should catch the sunrise."

"What if she set up Rob, and now she's setting you up?"

"She'd have to dream it first," said Calvino.

"It's a risk," said Colonel Pratt. "You can joke about it. But that's not wise."

"You've been hanging out with Yadanar. Have you closed your deal with him?"

"It's in the works."

The yellow dome of the Shwedagon lay outside the Colonel's hotel window, waiting for him to sit on the balcony and enjoy. But he was in no mood for sunrises or temples as he trundled back to the hotel. Calvino watched him follow the same path out of the park that the Black Cat had taken. He sat alone in front of the lake, remembering the brick wall on the other side of the guesthouse window, with Rob's hallucinations scribbled on it like psychotic graffiti.

Calvino had never slept inside a bookshop before. This shop came frontloaded with a full buckshot of history and ghosts. There was a small bedroom the size of a large closet in the back. The cot was pushed against the wall. His rooms were shrinking in size and view. This one had no window. It was a cell with a cot, a sink and a hot plate. When he slipped in after dawn, he lay back on the cot, watching a small lizard staring down at him from the ceiling, and the next thing he knew, he was in dreamland, walking among peacocks, lions and chattering monkeys.

He stumbled into a thicket, tearing his trousers, but battled through, coming out into an open field. He had no idea what the place was called, nor could he recognize any of the faces, bright with laughter and singing. It was a birthday party, and women were dancing and clapping their hands. He was the only foreigner present. Mya was dressed in black leather, cat whiskers painted on her cheeks, her eyelashes thick and black. She stalked and circled and pounced on the piano player.

Yadanar picked her up and swung her around as if she were a small child. They both laughed, and everyone applauded and started singing "Happy Birthday." Rob appeared with a birthday cake with more than thirty candles burning bright. Calvino ran toward him, calling his name. The faster he ran, the farther away Rob was, until all Calvino saw was his arm stretched out and his fist shaped like a gun. A large crowd followed Rob. He fired a shot out of his finger as if it were the barrel of a powerful gun. The echo of the shot shattered the silence. The crowd had surrounded an old male elephant stuck in a muddy field. The old bull bellowed and trumpeted and stomped its enormous feet. Calvino watched the bullet spinning in midair, suspended, and Mya jumped up and tried to pluck it from the sky, but she failed. Instead the bullet disappeared into the skull of the elephant. The animal made one last trumpeting sound and fell over dead.

The crowd applauded. Yadanar launched into "Cry Me a River" on the piano, and Mya began singing into the mike.

When he woke up, the Black Cat stood at the end of the cot, holding a cup of coffee.

"You were calling my name," she said.

"I had a dream. You were singing. An elephant was shot dead."

A smile crossed her face.

"Tell me. Tell me everything."

TWENTY-ONE

The House Filled with a Thousand Paintings of Dreams

COLONEL PRATT SHARED a taxi. The Colonel picked Calvino up a block away from the bookshop on 42nd Street. The driver, a Rangoon native, looked at the address for Yadanar's house and said he knew it. Mya had written the address down in Burmese, having left for the party earlier. She hadn't wanted to arrive with them.

Yadanar's house was in an area most people knew about but had never seen with their own eyes. The dreams people had inside those mansions were filled with monkey kings, peacocks, crocodiles, gold lions and pigs and dogs squealing through halls of power, pagodas, cemeteries, battlefields and bedrooms. The very rich and powerful dreamt their dreams inside these vast old houses left behind by the British and inside modern futuristic domes inspired by visions of the colonial rulers' grandchildren. Yadanar's mansion was traditional, a relic of colonization, built on the edge of a densely forested area and situated halfway up a hill that overlooked the Shwedagon Pagoda. His father had acquired it ten years earlier. Yadanar's family lived in another mansion nearby.

As the taxi turned up the hill, the night closed in. There were few streetlights to break the uniformity of the dark tunnel of trees. The road seemed to close in on Calvino like a nightmare. The houses were hidden behind high stone walls. The interior roads had few signs posted, perhaps to deter the intrusion of strangers. The driver, though, turned from one small lane to the next without difficulty. He knew where he was going.

"Some neighborhood," said Calvino.

The Colonel sat quietly in the back.

"Pratt, you're too quiet. You're thinking about going home tomorrow?"

"The birthday party might not be a good idea."

Calvino had heard the same reservation early that morning beside Kandawgyi Lake. The time lapse hadn't changed Pratt's opinion.

"You've bonded with Yadanar, right? You're going to see that he breaks into the jazz scene. You're' going to help him realize his dream. Tonight he'll announce in front of all his friends that he's going on the road to be a superstar. You'll tell him his name will be on the lips of people in Hollywood and New York. Give him a big face. Then we can go home. When Yadanar owes you, he pulls the plug on cold pill smuggling into Thailand. He wins, you win. Case over."

"And if it doesn't work out that way?"

"We can worry about that bridge when we come to it."

"When I came here, no one had any idea how involved he was, or about his connection with Udom. It would be foolish to think that Yadanar will easily let all of that money go somewhere else."

"You don't trust him?"

"Would you?"

Two security guards posted at the front gate sat on plastic stools, smoking cigarettes. Each was heavily armed. The distinctive shapes of two AK-47s revealed themselves in the light pooling from the pillar-top lamps on either side of the gate. Both guards snapped to attention as Colonel Pratt and Calvino approached. The guards used a walkie-talkie to confirm that Colonel Pratt and Calvino were on the guest list. One of them opened the gate, and Calvino and the Colonel walked down a long dark driveway. The interior of the compound was as densely forested as the neighborhood outside. The property felt lonely and isolated as they passed through it together.

"When I lived in Queens, we were always careful about walking into someone else's neighborhood."

"Most places, it's the same," said Colonel Pratt. "You go into another man's territory without his permission, and next thing there's a battle."

"Luckily, we're invited guests."

Colonel Pratt hardly listened as he scanned the wall for exit points.

"Not all invitations are to be trusted, Vincent."

They walked along a private drive that rose over a small incline and curved slightly to the right. Then for the first time they saw the mansion, which showed lights behind the curtained ground-floor and second-floor windows. The sounds of piano, drums and guitar grew louder. Pratt stopped to consider the lay of the land. It was an enormous mansion, with two stories, verandahs, large arched windows and a driveway filled with the same cars that had been parked in front of the 50th Street Bar.

The front door of the mansion could have passed for the gate separating Pha Yar Lan train station from Scott's Market. The door stood open to the night. Calvino pushed it open wider and walked in first. Clusters of young people stood in corners, sat on sofas, walked between rooms or stood with drinks and food that were delivered on trays by three or four circulating servants. They didn't recognize anyone among the faces until Jack Saxon's head popped out of a doorway.

"Vincent, did you have any trouble finding the house?"

"As easy as finding Insein Prison," he said.

Ohn Myint poked her head out beside Saxon.

"Swamp Bitch!" said Calvino.

Colonel Pratt did a double take.

"Remember? It's her running club handle," said Saxon, seeing the Colonel's embarrassed look. "I'm called Pistol Penis."

"And Vincent, remind me of your handle, again," the Colonel said.

"Kiss my Trash," said Ohn Myint. "Though Jack said he wanted Alien Warrior instead. It was already taken by one of the US marines."

"How could I forget?" asked the Colonel, smiling as he started to relax. It was good to see Jack Saxon among the faces, and the translator who had managed to get Calvino into the courtroom.

"Yadanar's busy at the moment," said Saxon. "Let me take you on a little tour of the house."

Saxon ushered them into a large sitting room, where a saxophonist was playing some Dexter Gordon variations to piano accompaniment. Couples sat on the floor, chairs and sofas, lost in the music or talking and drinking. A large joint passed from hand to hand as clouds of smoke gathered above the partiers' heads. The walls were covered with paintings. More paintings were stacked in the corners or leaned against furniture and walls.

"Family dreams," said Saxon, as he saw Calvino studying one of the artworks.

"There was a painter in my family," said Calvino. "My grandfather was from Florence."

"As far as I know, Yadanar hasn't ever been out of Burma, and he's certainly not related to any of the painters whose work you'll find in this house. Some of them are quite famous. His maternal grandfather was a famous bookseller in Rangoon. He had a shop on 42nd Street, not far from the Strand Hotel. Orwell used to go there to buy books. There's a rumor he wrote one or more short stories in the room in the back."

"Didn't Orwell write about an elephant?" asked Calvino.

Saxon smiled. "You Americans really should read more. Did Orwell write about elephants? Does the American president have a helicopter?"

The landscapes in the paintings were jammed with images of temples, wandering monks, flying bearded beings—half-human, half-horse or lion—white elephants, unicorns, flying fish, lush gardens, children playing games, old people, dead people, warriors in ancient uniforms, stupas and market stalls heaped with precious jewels. Most of the paintings were dreamy, surreal visions—the stuff that Rob had described as he stared out the window. The painters had borrowed from Salvador Dalí, lifting his melting-clock faces, seconds dripping onto the backs of exotic animals. Abstract figures, some with horns or wings or tails, floated among the clouds and stupas.

"Wild, crazy shit, eh?" Saxon asked.

"And yet there's a sameness to them," said Colonel Pratt.

"Like temple artwork," said Calvino.

"I'm no art expert. Yadanar says every painting in this mansion came from somebody's dream."

Saxon peeled off to whisper something to Ohn Myint.

Returning a couple of minutes later, he said, "Follow me. There's more. A lot more to see."

Saxon led them past a series of rooms, unused bedrooms warehousing hundreds of paintings. Flipping on the light, Saxon stepped into one of the rooms. No one was inside. There was a bed with paintings stacked on it. Empty closets had been used to store more paintings, leaning them one against the other like folders in a filing cabinet.

"Every room is like this. Filled with paintings. Or musical instruments or books. Sometimes all three are mixed together. Yadanar's grandfather was a bookstore owner."

"You already told us that, Jack," said Calvino.

"I repeat myself when I'm stoned. What I was trying to say is the grandfather wanted all of his children to love the arts with a passion."

"Looks like he got his wish," said Colonel Pratt.

"The grandfather should have been careful what he wished for," said Saxon, "because getting your wish granted can be a curse."

"The same with dreams," said Calvino.

"Same, same," said Saxon. "You haven't heard the story?"

Calvino shook his head.

"Ohn Myint, tell them the story about the paintings. The one you told me."

There was nothing shy about Ohn Myint. She was direct and looked them straight in the eye, the way she'd looked in the eye of the MI agent on the 10K run.

She explained how Yadanar's mother, father, aunts, uncles and cousins exchanged dreams, the images jumping along the family tree like wood lice. The dreams were written down in a book kept at the 42nd Street bookshop for years. Dreams were written out and given to painters, some of the most celebrated of Burmese artists, who took very little in exchange for their work for Yadanar's family. Yadanar's mansion housed paintings that went back more than sixty years. The grandfather was obsessed with finding a family member to become the curator of the paintings. He wanted to skip a generation, and that meant Mya or Yadanar's generation, his grandchildren.

Looking around the mansion, it was clear that the family tradition of curating dream art had passed to Yadanar when he was a small boy. Dates of the passage of the art to his side of the family had some curious features. In 1988 the grandfather had died, and the bookshop deed had been passed by Mya's mother to Mya's aunt—Yadanar's mother. Also in 1988 Yadanar's father's advancement up the ranks in the military stalled. He felt that the grandfather's bookshop had been a curse on his career. He wanted it shut down. He also wanted the paintings. Once he had succeeded in acquiring all of the paintings from his wife's family, his career took off in the army, and he became a high-ranking official in the military government. The rumor was this good fortune had come about after he had gained possession of all of the paintings.

The grandfather had expressed to his wife that Mya, his granddaughter, should inherit the paintings. She could sing like an angel. She loved books and hanging out in the bookshop. But his dream hadn't come to pass. Why had Yadanar's family gone to the trouble of taking the bookshop and the artwork, and preventing Mya's return from Thailand?

Marrying a soldier had disappointed the grandfather, who had banished Yadanar's mother from the family. If only he'd lived long enough to see that his grandson would be artistic, a lover of art and music.

The paintings had long enjoyed a legendary reputation for foretelling. The owner of them had a portal into the future. According to Mya's aunt, her husband, the general, used the paintings to make his plans. He gave information as favors to his superiors. They won lotteries, promotions, beautiful women and business deals. He never publicly admitted to what others would call black magic, but he never denied the use of the paintings for fortune-telling, either.

When Ohn Myint had finished her story, Saxon said, "The Burmese are big on dreams. Carl Jung was Burmese in a prior life."

Ohn Myint drifted off for a drink. The three men stood around looking at the paintings. Neither Colonel Pratt nor Calvino could see how the future unfolded in the images.

"Let's go meet the curator," said Saxon.

On the way upstairs they passed Khin Myat. Calvino stopped on the stairs at eye level with him.

"Didn't expect to see you here," Calvino said. "You remember Colonel Pratt."

The last time they'd seen Khin Myat, he'd been on the balcony watching them go through the gate of Pha Yar Lan train station.

"I didn't expect to be here. Yadanar's birthday party is also his going-away party. He invited old school friends, people he'd lost touch with."

Su Su, the woman from the covered market, came down the stairs and stood behind Khin Myat.

"There you are," she said.

"Catch you later," Khin Myat said in perfect idiomatic American English.

Saxon raised an eyebrow. "I'm impressed."

"How so?" asked Calvino, assuming he was referring to Khin Myat's linguistic skill.

That wasn't the case. Saxon was accustomed to hearing returnees speak in perfect English.

"Vinny, you know more people here than I do. And I live in Rangoon."

"You need to get out of the office more often, Jack," said Calvino.

Before Saxon replied, the Colonel, who'd been watching the faces come and go, gestured to Saxon, who leaned in closer.

"Have you seen Yadanar?" he asked.

Saxon held up a finger, signaling to wait one minute. He disappeared up the staircase, and when he came back he had Yadanar at his side.

"Pratt," said Yadanar, "I hope you had a drink and some food. A little later, I thought we might play a set. If you have time."

"I didn't bring my saxophone."

"I have one you can use."

Yadanar grabbed the arm of a passerby, saying, "Take my friend to find a saxophone."

"And I'll catch up with you in a couple of minutes," Yadanar said to the Colonel.

Calvino and Colonel Pratt exchanged a look of two men trying to read the mind of the other.

"I'll wait for you here," said Calvino.

The Colonel broke into a smile. He was amused by the thought that Yadanar might have as many musical instruments scattered through his house as he had paintings. Calvino saw the smile and thought that Colonel Pratt was handling the party better than expected. His cop's haircut and conservative shirt and trousers, along with being more than a generation older than most of the people in the house, made him stand out like a father at a high school prom. He'd done his best to blend into the crowd. He'd warned Calvino that a cop wandering through rooms of guests smoking dope and doing drugs had the potential of going pear-shaped. In Burma that was the one shape of fruit that was best avoided. But he'd relented. After all, Saxon owed him for helping spring his brother. That was the only piece of evidence the Colonel clutched to himself against the possibility that he was walking into a setup.

Colonel Pratt worked his way through the groups of smart young people at Yadanar's birthday party, and the escort assigned by Yadanar led him into a room with three saxophones on a table. The Colonel picked up one of the instruments and played a couple of runs. He continued with the other two saxophones, taking his time to choose among them.

As Colonel Pratt was picking a saxophone, Calvino followed Yadanar down the upstairs corridor, passing several closed doors.

"Where's Mya?" Calvino asked.

"She's here. Waiting for you."

"Jack says this is your going-away party. Mya says it's your birthday party."

Yadanar approached a door at the end of the corridor and stopped in front of it.

"They're both right," he said.

A Burmese man stumbled out of the room, wiping sweat from his face. The blood had drained from it. He looked ghost white.

"This is Thiri Pyan Chi," Yadanar said.

But Thiri Pyan Chi didn't stick around to exchange business cards. He rushed past them and down the corridor and disappeared down the stairs.

"He's in a hurry," said Calvino.

"Like everyone in Rangoon. And that is a problem. I'm afraid your friend Rob got mixed up with a Thai named Somchai. He's been in town to see Thiri Pyan Chi. I asked Thiri Pyan Chi to invite Somchai and his two bodyguards over to his house for a business discussion. I sent over a few men to bring the four of them to my party."

"Thiri Pyan Chi was running a business with Somchai behind your back," said Calvino.

"That's just one of his big mistakes," said Yadanar. "I told Thiri Pyan Chi how disappointed I was to find out about his side deal with Somchai. You know what he said?"

"He was going to tell you when the time was right."

Yadanar's face lit up.

"I like you, Vincent. You understand how Burmese people think. Mya told me that about you. She was right to invite you tonight."

Calvino caught a glimpse of Thiri Pyan Chi wandering around downstairs, ready to vomit. He looked like he was going from one wall of dreams to another, looking at angels, demons, fairies, gods, warriors and peacocks.

Calvino and Yadanar still stood in the corridor outside the door Thiri Pyan Chi had emerged from.

"He doesn't look so good," Calvino said.

"People who fuck up never do."

Calvino thought about Thiri Pyan Chi downstairs, eating snacks, drinking his way to some courage and trying to engage in conversation among the guests whose faces looked ten, twenty years younger than his own. No doubt he felt like a senior citizen.

It was nearly midnight.

"Time for the party to start," Yadanar said.

Yadanar opened the door and nodded as Mya rose from a sofa and walked toward Calvino. She wore blue jeans with tears in the knees and a fresh black T-shirt that had Burmese script on it, and underneath—"STOP Killing Press." Red was used for the word "STOP" and white for "Killing Press." Her political activist self had surfaced and found its way to Yadanar's party.

Calvino understood why Yadanar had sent Colonel Pratt off to find a saxophone. He hadn't wanted a Thai police colonel inside this room. Two men, apparently Yananar's good friends, stood aside to reveal they weren't alone. Seated on the floor, tied up with black duct tape, were three men, their heads covered with white cloth bags. Above them was a large mural that covered most of the wall.

"You like the painting?" asked Yadanar.

The artist must have devoted weeks with his paints laid out on a table in the room, painting *nats*—the whole pantheon of Burmese spirits—as they hovered over the floating lotus on a languid, crystal-clear lake, diving and flying through an enveloping, brilliant blue sky. Canary-eyed dragons flew above an open sea. House lizards as large as dragons crawled over a table with books, incense sticks and candles. Bats, owls and eagles darted in and out of bonfires. Rows of monks disappeared along the shore into an infinity of mirrors. Dismembered bodies littered the sandy beaches with large tree roots extending into the earth. Elephants on stilts walked over a wooden bridge that led to an ancient temple.

"My mother had this dream many years ago."

The hooded men whined like beaten dogs, their muffled voices sealed by duct tape.

"Is this the Burmese way of dealing with party crashers?" asked Calvino, watching as Yadanar moved closer to the prisoners on the floor.

Yadanar glanced back.

"I like that. Yeah, that describes them exactly. Party crashers. They weren't invited and decided to sneak in and help themselves. Isn't that right, asshole?" he said, kicking one of the men in the ribs.

The kicked man let out a loud, throaty groan of pain. Calvino had begun to wonder if the men, the setup and Mya in the T-shirt were all part of the artwork. The look he'd seen on Thiri Pyan Chi's face, the fear in the eyes, his shaking hands, hadn't been those of an actor performing a role. He'd been terrified.

Sitting apart from the three men on the floor, an Asian woman was also tied up with a pillowcase over her head, her skirt hiked up to her thighs. Yadanar lifted his shoe and jabbed the shoulder of one of the bound men on the floor.

"This one is named Somchai. He's a Thai who came to visit my country. He read somewhere that Myanmar was open for business, and everyone was invited to come and

312

look around. We are the new land of opportunity. But Somchai made a big mistake. He didn't do his homework. He thought, I don't know any of those people in Rangoon, and you know what? If I don't know them, then they probably don't know each other. Would he think that in Thailand? I don't think so. Somchai lacked a basic understanding of the situation. He had no idea—nor did he care to find out—who holds the real power, the man you must see before you make your deal. Just to be on the safe side that you're not stepping on toes. You want to know how stupid Somchai is? He recruits a man whose girlfriend is connected through her family to the top. But he doesn't have a clue.

"People in her extended family control the export side of the retail pharmaceutical business. Why wouldn't he think, Myanmar, another country, yes, so shouldn't I find out who are the people in my country, Thailand, doing business with that family in Myanmar? Could someone important like Khun Udom already have the business covered? If he didn't know Khun Udom was in the business, then he had no brains and should have stayed home. No, he left home and came here to export cold pills. What does he do with the pills? He puts them in circulation in Bangkok, and Udom phones me and asks me why I'm setting up a second channel into Thailand. Why am I sneaking around his back, cheating him? And I tell Udom that is news to me. I am a person of honor. My family are people of honor. We keep our word. Before you came into the room, I asked Somchai if he ever bothered to read the newspapers in Thailand. The Thai government apparently doesn't like the amount of cold pills entering the country. Udom was asked to lay off the business. He did. But pills still showed up. He took the heat. And then he blamed me for causing him a problem. But it wasn't Udom. It wasn't me. It was this little shit named Somchai."

Yadanar slapped one of the hooded men in the head. Calvino assumed that one was Somchai. The blow knocked the man to his side.

"Thiri Pyan Chi has told me everything about you, Somchai. You didn't figure that one either. What a dickhead. Always ask around about the guy you are thinking of going into business with, and ask yourself who is he, and why doesn't he have a business going with someone bigger than you? You don't marry someone on your first date. Your timing is terrible. You could never play the piano with such poor timing. I asked you before, 'Don't you read the papers?' The Thai government is investigating the import cold pills business. They are digging for information. They are looking for someone to hang the blame on. And then you arrive at the party.

"A good businessman knows not only when to enter a market but when to leave it. Udom is a very good businessman. He's been our partner in China. He loves us. We told him not to worry. We'd shut off the cold pills going into Thailand. And we'd put him in some new projects. Seaside resort developments are a good investment. You build places for the rich to lie on the beach and relax. Instead, what does Somchai do? He kills Rob Osborne. Because he thought he was a threat. Rob a threat? Somchai's lack of judgment knows no end. He got it in his head Rob would talk about his business to other people. Rob made him nervous. Maybe Rob would tell his girlfriend he'd threatened him. But did Somchai care? He didn't. Until someone told him that Mya and I are family. But then it was too late. He'd already killed him. Or maybe he knew and just didn't really care that I'd be very unhappy. I'd promised Mya that her boyfriend would be safe. But Somchai made me a liar. We keep our family promises.

"Now I have Udom screaming at me. I have my cousin saying I'm a lying shit. And all of this comes around my birthday. I thought to myself, what would make me happy on my birthday? And I said to myself, 'Let's have a conversation with Somchai and his Thai colleagues. Sort this out. Start the new birth year on happier ground.'"

Talking to a room where three men and a woman sat gagged and bound, Yadanar had created a perfectly attentive audience. No matter how long Yadanar paused, no one cut into the silence with a question or comment. One of Yadanar's friends handed him a flute of ice-cold champagne, and he took a sip. He pointed the glass at the woman on the floor.

"She pulled the trigger. Blew out Khun Rob's brains, didn't you?"

Mya stepped forward and pulled the pillowcase off the woman's head. A gag, stained with blood, muted her shouts.

"Kati?" said Mya.

She looked at Yadanar.

"She killed Rob?"

"I'm afraid she did," said Yadanar.

Kati's face was bruised, swollen. A large red welt had risen on one cheek. Her eyes were puffy and black. Her front teeth, visible above the gag, were jagged stumps. They'd done a thorough job of beating her. The beauty had been erased from her face, leaving a mask of horror.

"She decided to help Somchai out by pulling the trigger. None of the men in this room said she was lying, that one of them pulled the trigger. She shot him because that's what Somchai asked her to do."

Yadanar walked to a cupboard, unlocked a drawer and removed a nickel-plated handgun, a Colt .22 with a long silencer fitted to the barrel, and showed it to Calvino.

"She killed the man you were looking for," said Yadanar. "Do you want to do the honors on behalf of his father?"

"I don't shoot women who are tied and beaten up," said Calvino.

"Right," Yadanar said.

Turning to Mya, he flipped the gun around. Grabbing Mya's right hand, he slapped the gun into her palm. Her fingers wrapped around the grip. She pointed the long-barreled Colt .22 at the floor.

"It's my birthday," said Yadanar. "Calvino doesn't have the stomach for it. Will you avenge Rob's death? You should be the one. You know why? She told us she found out Rob was hiding in your room from you. She heard you talking to the Colonel at the 50th Street Bar. You looked surprised. Shocked. That's what happens when you treated a strange woman like she's wallpaper. Foreigners regularly do that with Thai girls, am I right? Think about it. Is this your karma? The moment must be in one of our family dreams. One recorded in some painting stacked in some room of this house."

Calvino looked away. Staring at Kati, broken and terrified, full of pain and suffering, only made him feel sorry for her, and he didn't want to feel any pity for a murderer. He understood now that Yadanar had an even better reason to separate Colonel Pratt from him. No one wanted a police colonel to witness what would be done to a woman who had gambled her life and lost with her bet on a stupid man. Bad things turned up in the real world and landed at the door of a woman who'd never given a thought to the real odds of things going completely wrong. It wasn't something she'd remotely thought could happen. Luck had always been with her.

"Don't, Mya."

Mya avoided looking at Calvino. Instead she stared at Kati, crying and begging, in between her wails and sobs.

"A beautiful woman like Kati always gets what she wants from men, and when she wants it," said Yadanar. "Somchai was young, handsome as a leading man, and he dressed with an elegant hi-so club style. He talked her into shooting the guy. Just do it. Boom. You got close to him because you're a woman, a pretty woman, and maybe he thought you were a part of his dream, a hallucination. And you blew out his brains, making it look like suicide. Isn't that what you told us earlier?" Yadanar sighed. "Not that she wanted to tell the story. But she finally got around to telling us everything."

Mya walked over to the corner where Kati sat. She saw Kati's eyes balloon in size as she aimed the Colt .22 and pulled the trigger. The silencer masked the shot. The bullet entered Kati's skull above her right eye and rattled around and around inside her skull, scrambling her brain tissue into a soft yogurt. She fell back against the wall with the mural, splattering blood on angels and fairies hovering on a grassy knoll. Mya lowered the Colt .22 and crossed the room while everyone watched. Stopping at the cupboard, she dropped the gun in the drawer.

She turned to Calvino.

"Back in Bangkok, you tell Rob's father that no one got away with killing Rob. His killer was taken care of. You tell him that Mya made certain herself."

The three men on the floor squirmed, blubbering, crying and pleading.

"We'll take care of them later," said Yadanar.

He opened the door for Mya, who strolled out in her activist T-shirt. Calvino caught up with her and grabbed her arm, spinning her around.

"That was your 'fuck everyone' statement?" he asked.

"I can't think of a better one, can you?"

She broke free and rushed down the stairs.

Yadanar stepped to Calvino's side, holding a glass of his birthday champagne.

"My cousin was headstrong even as a kid," said Yadanar. "I liked her T-shirt this evening. STOP Killing Press. How appropriate for a revenge killing."

"I didn't think she'd pull the trigger," said Calvino.

"To be frank, neither did I. She exceeded my expectations."

Yadanar had seen her impact at the 50th Street Bar on the first night she'd walked on stage and left the audience screaming for more. She was an entertainer, a performer, who was only alive when she stood before an audience. Calvino started down the stairs, squeezing between couples. He looked for Colonel Pratt in one room, then another, until he heard the sound of a saxophone, drums and a violin coming from down the hall. The Colonel was inside, playing the borrowed instrument. After the music finished, the Colonel walked over to Calvino, smiling. Playing the saxophone had him in the groove, the zone, the eye of the storm—a place that had many names, and a place where a man could exit and no one could touch him. Calvino gestured for his friend to step outside. Colonel Pratt removed the strap of the saxophone, swung it over his head and walked out of the room. The other players looked after him, shrugged and kept playing.

They walked down the corner and into the kitchen, past the fridge and into a pantry. Calvino shut the door.

"You were right about the birthday party having risks," said Calvino.

"You were right about the girl," said Pratt.

"Which one?"

Colonel Pratt looked surprised.

"Which one? Is there more than one?"

Calvino recovered himself.

"Not really. There's the Black Cat, of course. Who did you think I meant?"

"I thought Kati would be here tonight," said Colonel Pratt.

"You thought that she worked for Yadanar," said Calvino.

"A reasonable assumption," Colonel Pratt said. "Unless you've got some information you want to tell me."

"Only she didn't work for Yadanar. She worked for Somchai."

"Worked? She quit?"

"She's out of the picture."

Calvino picked up a thick loaf of bread. Without thinking, he took a knife and hacked off a hunk. Then another piece, until the entire loaf was in pieces.

"You never know where a woman like that will land."

"She didn't say goodbye."

"She might have. But you just didn't hear it."

"Why'd you cut the bread?"

"I must have seen it in a dream."

"Maybe we should get out of here."

"I'll go back to the bookstore for my things."

"But Mya promised to sing tonight. I promised her I'd stay for that," said the Colonel.

Calvino wanted to tell the Colonel what the Black Cat had done to Kati. But he left him with the impression that Kati had checked out of the party early. He just told the Colonel that he'd overheard her admit she'd been Somchai's squeeze.

"Are you sure?"

Calvino nodded. "Afraid so."

The Colonel hadn't known. And he didn't want to know. It was enough for the Colonel to file her away as the kind of woman who was the small change that moved from one high roller's pocket to the next. She'd been like most of the pretties who worked the auto shows. Her life's ambition had been to find a man who'd buy her all the stuff of her dreams. Somchai had been tied up on the floor a few feet away, and the only dreams left were those in the large mural above their heads. Some dreams weren't for sale.

The house was filled with the new generation. The sons and daughters of politicians, businessmen, godfathers and generals, people who had gone to school together and were now linked by power, marriage and wealth. Yadanar's little speech inside the room had been an indictment of Somchai's ignorance, and the consequence of ignorance when doing business in Myanmar was a death sentence. Figuring out where one belongs is always the first order of business. The room was filled with people who were one, large extended family. What family didn't have morons, renegades, traitors or cheaters? There was always a struggle under the surface, until someone felt lucky and tried to ambush the pack from behind.

Colonel Pratt returned to the music room to play for the guests. People laughed and hugged and danced. When the song ended, Calvino moved through the crowd to stand next to the Colonel as Yadanar stood on a stool, his hands raised, asking for everyone's attention.

"I have a birthday announcement. Good news," he said. "Where's Mya?"

She was found in the back of the room on a sofa.

"Come up here with me."

He waited until Mya was next to him.

"We have been invited to perform in Bangkok. Pratt, Mya and the rest of our band are going there."

"Did you know about this?" Calvino asked the Colonel.

Pratt slowly turned his attention from Yadanar.

"I'm afraid I did."

The room of people applauded.

"Our country is opening. We will take the message of a new beginning for the Burmese people to the larger world. We are changing. We are part of the new Myanmar."

There was more applause. One of the band members handed Mya a mike, and soon her voice echoed through the room, out the hall and throughout the house as she sang "Every Step of the Way." Yadanar accompanied her on the piano. It was just the two of them playing in the music room, before an admiring crowd of people invited to a birthday party. A going-away party.

On the way out of the grounds, before they had reached the gate and the security guards with the AK-47s, Colonel Pratt told Calvino that he had found Yadanar's price, the amount that would guarantee no more smuggling of cold pills into Thailand. The promise of a chance at the musical big time had been it. No guarantees, but a chance. Then the matter would be in the laps of the gods. The deal was good enough for Colonel Pratt to return to Bangkok and let his boss know the cold pill smuggling operation had been closed down. The "closed" sign was hanging in the window. The owner had turned his back on pills to earn an audience with his piano and his cousin's voice. Udom no longer had his Burmese source. It was as if the electrical generating plant had been shut down. Blackout.

TWENTY-TWO

Bangkok: The Living Room

IT WAS CLOSING night at the upscale nightclub, located in a five-star Sukhumvit Road hotel. Yadanar wore a newly tailored tan suit, a purple silk shirt and alligator shoes with shiny soles. He sat behind a grand piano, smiling at the audience, hands dancing across the keyboard as Colonel Pratt finished John Coltrane's "My Favorite Things"—which he dedicated to Manee, his wife, who was sitting at a front row table. Two members of the 50th Street band, one on drums and the other on guitar, accompanied the Colonel. Mya perched on a stool to one side, holding a mike and tapping her booted foot to the beat.

As the Colonel finished, Calvino, Ratana and Manee all rose in unison, clapping. The rest of the audience followed. Alan Osborne, wearing sunglasses, sat in his chair, gimlet-eyed. He reached over and pulled Calvino's sleeve.

"Sit down, Calvino. Being an unpaid shill is terribly demeaning. At least peasant farmers demand to be paid before they applaud some third-rate politician."

Calvino couldn't make up his mind whether Obsorne's nasty, bitter streak, his lashing out, was connected to the grief from losing his son, or if it had always been there, part of his natural instinct, the way he lived in the world.

"He deserves it," said Calvino, leaning down.

Osborne wrinkled his nose and waved Calvino away.

"Says the slave to the master."

At the next table, Udom sat in the company of a politician, a general and an official from the health ministry. Udom rose and walked to the stage. He presented Pratt with a large bouquet of orchids. They exchanged *wais*. Two of the Chinese businessmen at Udom's table stood and applauded as Udom took the mike from Mya.

"Khun Yadanar is like my son. His father, like my brother. We love and understand each other."

He hugged Yadanar and then walked back to his table.

Calvino had watched over the past couple of weeks after returning to Bangkok as old alliances had fallen apart and new ones had emerged. Information drifted in from Jack Saxon, and the Colonel had his own pipeline—one that was made of glass, so he could see the faces as they passed through.

The Thai and Burmese cartel bosses had rushed to plan resorts in the newly developing country, and casino gambling interests had acquired a rim of land that swung along the Burmese coastline, a pristine jewel of a beach. Chinese money circled Udom and Yadanar's families. Competitors tested weak points in their relationship and their networks. The new group had formed as the old business was abandoned. After all, it was only business. Nothing in business—not the concessions, the personalities or the families—was forever. There was no forever equation in illicit business any more than in the so-called licit ones. A man made as much profit as possible and moved on as political pressure to share the spoils became irresistible. Friends who helped the venture, the ones in power, always asked for larger and larger slices of the business.

Businessmen helping politicians was the right order of things. Udom and his partners easily made the transition from cold pills to saunas and slot machines. They knew that money, like a raging river, found its own pathways and was unstoppable, cutting through anything in its path.

The audience chanted for an encore. Mya came back on stage and sang, "When You're by My Side," with Yadanar accompanying her on the piano. She sang the words with soft, intense feeling that lit up the audience, leaving the women in tears and even the men with moist eyes. It was the rendition that would turn up for a lifetime within their dreams.

Since he'd returned, Calvino had had a recurring dream. He was next to Colonel Pratt when they were caught in a crossfire, ambushed by a group concealed in the vendor stalls of the covered market in Rangoon. They should have been dead. In the weird reality of the dream, a shootout had erupted. Pratt had taken cover behind a wheelchair, and Calvino had crawled behind a desk stacked with boxes of cold pills. All hell had broken loose as two of the gunman ran down a corridor firing. More had joined in the running gun battle, shooting anything that moved. Colonel Pratt and Calvino killed three, possibly four heavily armed men. They'd stumbled into the group, who'd arrived pushing trolley carts down one corridor. The carts were stacked high with boxes of Chinese cold pills. The gunmen wore strange rubber masks with large holes cut out for the nose and eyes. The rubbery faces were recognizable—famous gangsters like Al Capone, Marlon Brando as the Godfather, death masks of ancient kings, generals and warlords.

After the shooting ended, Calvino stripped the masks off each body as Pratt looked on. Underneath were more rubber masks—of Somchai, Rob and the men he'd shot in the Lexus. Then he saw another body. Kati's limp, long fingers pressed into a *wai*, her bikini top pulled down exposing one breast, her unblinking eyes open, staring at a box of cold pills. The damp, sickly smell of decomposition filled the space.

When he'd woken up, he'd opened the blinds and stared out at Bangkok at dawn. He wouldn't want a painting of that dream, he thought. When he thought of the hundreds of paintings in every room of Yadanar's house, he doubted the wisdom of preserving such dreams. Forgetting dreams is what keeps us anchored to reality, keeps us human, he thought, watching the sunrise over Sukhumvit Road.

When he'd told Pratt about the dream, the Colonel had said that the point of the artwork in the mansion was the opposite of Calvino's view. If the stories unfolding in dreams were inescapable in the waking world, the best defense was to surround yourself with a full index and plan for what fate had in store.

"Forgetting your dreams can't change the fact that they were real in your mind or the future possibility that they will be real again," said the Colonel.

"Not so," Calvino had said. "Dreams are the brain's one-stop Laundromat. They wash the dirt and grime out so our brains are clear and fresh the next day."

"I don't think so, Vincent," Pratt had said.

They'd left it at the impasse, as Calvino saw no point in arguing the point. He was more interested in the deal Pratt had brokered with Yadanar Khin. The Colonel had straight-out told Yadanar that he couldn't make anyone famous. No one had that power. No one but Lady Luck could touch someone with her magic wand. Over time the local papers had run fewer stories about the cold pill scandal until not even a slight vapor trail had been left. That jet airliner had long passed overhead and disappeared out of sight and out of mind. People had moved on to the latest object flying overhead, threatening to turn their lives upside down, and never stopped to look back and ask, "Whatever happened to those cold pill smugglers?" That question wasn't asked.

Someone could have asked Yadanar, behind a piano, about the cold pills. No one did. No one would. He'd been on that plane. But no one can see who is inside a plane leaving the vapor trail overhead. As Mya finished, another round of applause followed. Yadanar rose from the piano and took a bow. Mya went to his side, and they took a bow together.

"With all this bowing," said Alan Osborne, "You'd think they were bloody Japanese."

Calvino had seen Osborne wiping away a tear. The old man, filled with bluff and bile, tried to hide a simple act that made him human because he never identified with the essence of humanity. It was found inside its tears.

"They're on their way to Jakarta and then New York," said Calvino.

"Hellholes, both places," said Osborne.

On stage Yadanar looked the part of a professional entertainer. The Black Cat, with her killing smile and angelic voice, created an audience of captives who would have done anything she asked. His good looks and hers helped seal the deal. Pratt arranged for them to receive an invitation to the Java Jazz Festival. Calvino had a relative named Nero who had real estate on the Lower East Side of New York. Nero was connected. He was able to arrange a night at the Blue Note. Negotiations had been completed for a TEDx performance in Singapore. A week after leaving Myanmar, Yadanar had put a couple of light years' distance between himself and the cold pill smuggling operation. The Americans had given him and Mya a visa. Everyone wanted to do business and play friendly.

The bodies of Somchai and his crew had been dumped into a deep channel of the Irrawaddy River. Kati's body had been stuffed in a barrel, filled with cement and shoved over the side of a boat in the same spot. Nobody inside Myanmar had looked very hard for them. They were foreigners who had come and gone. No one in the country cared what might have happened to them. The Thais remained silent.

Not a bubble rose to the surface to burst with Somchai or Kati's name. It seemed that everyone who remained alive was happy. But it is always a mistake to find happiness in silence. There are always unhappy people waiting in the margins.

Thiri Pyan Chi had got himself ordained as a monk, a tried and true way to escape the law enforcement system that involved voluntary impoverishment, celibacy and chanting morning and night. As he sat under a blue umbrella with a blonde and a tall tropical drink, his bald head glistened in the sunlight. The statues at the pagoda gave him a case of "uncanny valley" revulsion. They seemed like dolls whose too lifelike human appearance caused him to vomit his ham sandwich into the dirt.

After the applause died, Yadanar joined Udom's table and Mya pulled back a chair and sat beside Alan Osborne.

"You sing beautifully," Osborne said.

Mya had no idea that this was from a bitter old man who never gave a compliment.

"Rob wanted to come home," she said. "He just didn't know how."

"My father was born in Burma. In a way it was home for him. I think of Rob as having gone home. But thank you," he said.

Those were two of the most difficult words for someone who identified with the official class and looked with disdain on "Kipling's natives." He looked at her a long time, reached forward, pulled her head to his lips and kissed her forehead. Calvino had told him that she'd settled things in Rangoon. But he'd left out exactly how. It was best that way. Alan was as careless as he was bitter, and a bitter, careless man never keeps secrets, at least not for long.

Colonel Pratt put his arm around Calvino's shoulder. It wasn't a Thai thing to embrace a friend. Thailand wasn't Spain or Argentina.

"When you see too much, it takes time for the image to pass away. But it will pass. You have to believe that when the train enters a tunnel, it will come out the other end."

"You sounded great tonight," said Calvino.

The Colonel removed his arm.

"If my playing were that great, you'd have come out of the tunnel. The words are nice, but they don't ring true."

"None of what happened there rings true, Pratt. Mirrors clouded with smoke and dreams."

"That is a good description of Myanmar."

Calvino suppressed a yawn behind his fist.

"It's past my bedtime."

"Before you go, see that it's right between Rob's father and Mya. You'll sleep better after that."

Calvino liked his friend's loyalty. The Colonel had emerged from the tunnel and only wanted the same for him. Each night Calvino struggled to stay awake until utter fatigue wore him down and dragged him under the radar of what he could control. As he drifted, the surface was no longer solid. Rangoon carried him back through the land of dreams and deposited him at the foot of its dreamers.

Calvino eased into a chair beside Mya, nodding hello to Alan Osborne.

"Stay away from Calvino. He'll only get you in trouble," said Osborne.

It was his English way of showing affection.

Her lips slowly stretched into a smile as if he somehow amused her, or she'd been amused by her own image of him bearing no relationship to the actual man.

"Mr. Osborne, thank you for coming tonight. I know you're not well."

Calvino watched as a tear slipped down Alan Osborne's cheek. He made no attempt to wipe this one away.

"You can sing. I can grant you that."

There wasn't any response that would take away the old man's guilt. Mya leaned forward and hugged him.

"Rob loved you," she whispered.

"That's a lie. A noble one, but that doesn't make it any less false. He tried to love me and found what most people have found, nothing to love."

"He never gave up trying, and to me, that's the meaning of love," she said.

Alan Osborne's face collapsed, and he wept. The conversation around the table stopped. Calvino helped Osborne from the table. He walked him out to his silver Benz, watched him unlock the door. Osborne opened it, leaned inside and pulled out a box.

"Go ahead, open it."

Calvino lifted the lid and removed a book.

"It was Rob's. I think he'd like to know that you have it."

It was a first edition of Orwell's *Homage to Catalonia*, signed to Lionel Osborne.

"Orwell gave that to Rob's grandfather."

The conversation at the table was in full swing when Calvino returned and sat at the table.

Colonel Pratt turned to him and said, "Vincent introduced me to an astrologer in Rangoon. He was a meditation expert. And his knowledge on *nats*, what the Burmese call spirits, was solid. He'd made a study of organic foods and diets. And he promised that if I followed his advice, I would immediately improve my saxophone playing."

Naing Aung was an expert at many things, thought Calvino.

"Naing Aung used his multiple talents to open a private investigation business."

"Does that mean you might start astrology as a sideline?" asked Ratana. "I'm joking. A foreigner can't get a work permit to become an astrologer. I remember checking that point for one of our clients some years ago.

"Vincent as an astrologer would be an exciting idea," said Manee.

Drinking from his whiskey glass, Calvino glanced at the Orwell novel, which he'd laid on the table. When he looked up, he was surprised to find all eyes around the table staring at him, waiting for a reaction. He was from New York and by default was expected to finish Ratana's setup. Over the years she'd fed him the lines, and he'd never missed an opportunity to unearth the deeper joke inside. But the transmission lines had been knocked down in his dreams, and in the uneasy twilight awareness of the moment, he told them what he hadn't told Colonel Pratt.

"Naing Aung's crystal ball had some help. He had a friend who staked out a table in front of a Hindu temple. The friend sold lottery tickets. The friend would whisper the numbers of several tickets, and then Naing Aung would give those numbers to his clients asking for magical lottery numbers. They would leave Naing Aung's office and then 'find' the numbers on the table across the street in front of the Hindu temple. A good racket. They could have been Wall Street bankers.

"An investigator deals with sleaze. It's unavoidable. But a sleazy investigator sells out his clients. So I'll be sticking to the investigations. I'll leave reading the future to others."

No one laughed. No one got the joke because the illusion had been broken.

The Colonel acted quickly to change the mood of the table by telling Ratana and Manee about Naing Aung's version of his destiny to become Rangoon's first private eye. From the Colonel's tone of voice, it was clear this story was being told to cleanse the air—the dead, stale air that Alan Osborne had left behind, the same air that Calvino had breathed into the story of Naing Aung's fraud.

Calvino listened as Colonel Pratt told the story he'd heard Naing Aung tell in Rangoon. It was a story of a monk who had sent a message to all of his disciples that he'd left the temple with his entourage. Everyone who did meditation received his message through his special powers to communicate thoughts. Meditation started on a Monday and lasted nine, eighteen, forty-five or eighty-one days. Every day they lit candles in front of an alter that held a Buddha image and the monk's photograph. Meditations were transmitted messages to the *nats*, who acted as guardian angels. For six months they read the twenty-four verses of the Buddha teachings, nine times a day, each reading requiring ten minutes. Some people used only one one-hour reading per day. The main point was the repetition. After nine days what the vision owner desired was realized. Naing Aung had performed the rituals to ensure that his private eye business would be a success. At the end of the ninth day, Vincent Calvino had showed up at his office with his first real case. Naing Aung believed that his guru had the special capacity to read each person's destiny. He also believed that people's destinies were intertwined.

Naing Aung's dietary advice to the Colonel had been straightforward—rice curry, vegetables, no meat, no cakes or cheese. Small snacks all add up. Before a performance, he shouldn't eat anything that needed to be chewed. He should mix the food and eat it as a slurry. A monk who had mastered his body ate only five spoonfuls of the slurry. Of course, that was an extreme meditation practice, which only the brave could hope to continue for more than a couple of days. To stay on the right diet and meditate was the way to send merit to the whole world.

Once again the laughter returned to the table. It caught Udom's attention. He rose from his VIP table and walked over to where Colonel Pratt, Calvino and the others sat at the second VIP table. The room of people watched the

VIPs huddling together. They watched them during the performance, too, taking their cues from their "betters." They applauded when the VIPs applauded, laughed when they laughed, ordered wine as they ordered.

Udom sized up Calvino, taking measure of the *farang* seated before him at the table. The shape of the head, the lips, eyes, height of the forehead, his watch and clothes. Patterns emerged that meant a man could be trusted. Calvino also sought to read the mind working inside Udom's skull. The *jao pah* smiled, thinking the *farang* saw only what the Thais chose to let them see. They never worried about a man like Udom, who looked like a happy businessman. There was nothing of the gangster about him.

Yadanar didn't like being left stranded with Udom's flunkies, so he walked over to join the conversation at Colonel Pratt's table.

"Mya is my cousin," he said to Ratana. "Her mother and my mother are sisters. She is like my sister."

Udom heard the remark and turned to Yadanar.

"And Khun Yadanar, you are like my son, your father, like my brother. We love and understand each other."

He'd had a lot to drink and his words slurred a little.

"My home is also your home," said Yadanar.

"And my home is your home," said Udom.

House exchange, thought Calvino. He smiled, watching them express the depth of their relationship. They lived in houses built with underground bunkers stacked with cash, the walls covered with art, yet in a sense they were one large house. Yadanar's mansion was buried deep in forested enclaves, surrounded by high walls and men with automatic weapons watching the gate. The men who ran the world lived in such houses. When Somchai had gone up against them, he'd hit the full force of power and influence, the weight of money that condemned him to the bottom of the Irrawaddy River, where he and Kati and his *luk nong* slept—

though still appearing in the dreams of the rich, who paid artists to paint their afterlives in murals and on canvases.

Calvino picked up the Orwell book and left the table. Half an hour later, back at his condo, he sat with a drink and read about Orwell in the Spanish Civil War until he fell asleep in his chair. After the Bangkok night had long disappeared and the sun had cleared Queen Sirikit Centre, he woke up. He had several missed calls on his cell phone. Ratana, Pratt, McPhail had all phoned. The phone had been in silent mode. He opened his iPad and checked his email. A dozen messages, but the one that caught his eye was from Jack Saxon.

He read Saxon's message. Then he opened the *Bangkok Post* website and read the breaking news story on the scroll. Yadanar and Mya, the Black Cat, were dead. It had happened while he'd been asleep, dreaming. He reread the story.

New York–Bound Burmese Entertainers Killed
Dateline: Bangkok

Two Burmese nationals named Mya Kyaw Thein, aged 26 years old, and Yadanar Khin, aged 32 years old and the son of General Tayza, Minister of Public Welfare, were killed in an apparent car bomb attack. They were traveling to a club on Ratchadapisek Road when the explosive device was set off by remote control. The police suspect a cell phone was used. The explosion was reported at 2:30 a.m. Wreckage was scattered over a hundred meter radius. Police believed as much as 50 kilos of explosives had been used. The military said they had intelligence that similar explosive devices were used in recent violence in the three most southern provinces.

Asked whether the bombing was connected to the insurgency in the South, the police spokesman said they suspected a personal or business conflict lay behind the killings. They were investigating both possibilities. But they weren't discounting an escalation of Muslim terrorists to strike targets in Bangkok.

There was a photograph of half a dozen police smiling as they stood around the crater left by the bomb. One of them was holding a GT200—a device used by those with more faith than sense to detect bombs. Calvino examined the photo. Nothing about the car appeared car-like. It was hard to know what kind of car it had been. If the bomb had done that to steel, clearly nothing of Yadanar or Mya's remains matched a human being. Atomized—machine and bodies.

Rescue teams had arrived in their pickup trucks and vans. The fire brigade had turned hoses on the smoking ruins in the street. Charred bodies were cradled in the mesh of metal and glass and upholstery.

Expectations of Burma's new opening were running too far ahead, as if the flowers had bloomed before the seeds had been planted. The old garden still held the ground, gnarled with old growth, weeds and thorns, and untamed lanes. And the way through the forest was through dreams tethered to a chain of other dreams.

Revenge floated above that old garden like a mist.

Calvino opened two more emails from Jack Saxon. The last of them was a forward Saxon had sent, originally sent by "Anonymous." Someone had gone to the trouble of reworking lines from a famous W.H. Auden poem and posting them on the activist website where the Black Cat had uploaded her political tracts. The revised poem read:

In the nightmare of the dark,
All the dogs of Burma bark,
And the big families wait,
Each sequestered in its hate;
Intellectual disgrace
Stares from every human face,
And the seas of pity lie
Locked and frozen in each eye.

ACKNOWLEDGMENTS

My friend Geoffrey Goddard showed me sides of Rangoon that I would never have found on my own. Geoffrey introduced me to many people, including Khaing Tun—Khine—who answered many of my questions about current political and social developments and gave me a deeper understanding of the changing expectations of the Burmese people as their country opens.

A number of people read earlier drafts of *Missing in Rangoon* and offered comments, suggestions and advice, and the book is stronger because of their efforts. I'd like to acknowledge with gratitude the efforts of (in alphabetical order) Denny Baun, Kevin Cummings, Peter Friedrich, Michaela Striewski and Frank Vatai. They undertook their task with genuine dedication to helping me realize the potential of the book. The defects and flaws that remain are mine alone. As hard as I strive for perfection, I inevitably fall short. I accept that fate as it reminds me that I am chained to the frailty of the human condition like everyone else.

With special thanks to Martin Townsend, copy editor extraordinaire, and Busakorn Suriyasarn, proofreader and editor, for her advice and cultural expertise.

The book draws upon real events at a time of change inside Burma, but the characters and story are fiction. A novelist makes things up, and sometimes the result is more real than real life. If I've come close to convincing you the story is real, then I've accomplished what I set out to do.

PRAISE FOR THE VINCENT CALVINO P.I. SERIES

One of "100 Eyes of Mystery Scene Era" in the 100th issue of *Mystery Scene Magazine*

"Moore's Vincent Calvino novels ... are crisp, atmospheric entertainments set in a noirish Bangkok."—*The Guardian*

"Vincent Calvino is one of the most notable detectives of modern crime literature."
—Harmut Wilmes, *Kölnische Rundschau*

"A vivid sense of place ... the city of Bangkok, with its chaos and mystery, is almost another character. Recommened."
—*Library Journal*

"If there's a new book by Christopher G. Moore, the Bangkok-based Canadian author, I'll read that, particularly if it's a Calvino private eye one. His novels, set among louche expatriates in a semi-criminal nocturnal demi-monde, managed to put Bangkok into a context for me when I was spending time in S.E. Asia. He leads you into hidden establishments and constructs, some palatial, some mean hovels in hidden side-streets, to which only a cat could find its way and that by accident."
—Peter Stark, *Quarterly Review*

"Vincent Calvino is a terrific character who could only have been drafted into action by a terrific writer."
—T. Jefferson Parker, author of *L.A. Outlaws*.

"Underneath Bangkok society is a deeply encrusted demiworld of hope, despair, corruption and courage that Moore ... paints with maestrolike Dickensian strokes."
—Thomas Plate, *The Seattle Times*

"Think Dashiell Hammett in Bangkok."
—*San Francisco Chronicle*

"A worthy example of a serial character, Vincent Calvino is human and convincing."—*Thriller Magazine* (Italy)

"Vincent Calvino [is] the Thailand-based reincarnation of private eye Sam Spade."—*Cliffhangers*

"Moore is a stylist much like the writers of the early to mid-20th century who kick-started the P.I. genre in America. He writes with the angry and sad voice of Ross Macdonald and the flow of and beauty of Raymond Chandler. Penning his books in the third-person, he uses allegory and symbolism to great effect. The Calvino series is distinctive and wonderful, not to be missed, and I'm pleased to see that it is finally becoming better known in the States."
—Cameron Hughes, *The Rap Sheet*

"I have come late to Christopher Moore's PI novels featuring Vincent Calvino. And that's been my loss ... Calvino is the hard-boiled successor of Philip Marlowe, a damaged, beaten-down but never beaten protagonist who doesn't know when to quit. The Bangkok he inhabits is full of life, corruption and broken dreams. Moore drags you in to experience all of it ... His writing recalls the gritty noir of Chandler and the intrigue of Le Carré with a dry humour thrown in."—Chris Bilkey, *Crime Buzz*

"Calvino is a wonderful private detective figure! Consistent action, masterful language ... and Anglo-Saxon humor at its best."—*Deutschland Radio*

"Every big city has its fictional detective; and Bangkok's is Vincent Calvino."—*Bangkok 101*

"The hard bitten detective is real, and grittily impressive ... Unlike many other fictional detectives, he doesn't play in the manicured imagination of an armchair novelist. He's real."—Tarun Cherian, *Deccan Herald* (India)

"It's easy to see why Moore's books are popular: While seasoned with a spicy mixture of humor and realism, they stand out as model studies in East-West encounters, as satisfying for their cultural insights as they are for their hardboiled action."—Mark Schreiber, *The Japan Times*

"Although they are fiction, the Vincent Calvino novels record the main events that have rocked the history of Thailand's capital. Moore's insights into the Thai society, economy and politics make the Calvino series a valuable radiography of what Bangkok looks like through the detached eyes of an expat living in Thailand."
—Voicu Mihnea Simandan

"Moore's work recalls the international 'entertainments' of Graham Greene or John le Carré, but the hard-bitten worldview and the cynical, bruised idealism of his battered hero is right out of Chandler. Intelligent and articulate, Moore offers a rich, passionate and original take on the private eye game, fans of the genre should definitely investigate, and fans of foreign intrigue will definitely appreciate."
—Kevin Burton Smith, *January Magazine*

"Moore's flashy style successfully captures the dizzying contradictions in [Bangkok's] vertiginous landscape."
—Marilyn Stasio, *The New York Times Book Review*

SPIRIT HOUSE
First in the series
Heaven Lake Press (2004) ISBN 974-92389-3-1

The Bangkok police already have a confession by a nineteen-year-old drug addict who has admitted to the murder of a British computer wizard, Ben Hoadly. From the bruises on his face shown at the press conference, it is clear that the young suspect had some help from the police in the making of his confession. The case is wrapped up. Only there are some loose ends that the police and just about everyone else are happy to overlook.

The search for the killer of Ben Hoadley plunges Calvino into the dark side of Bangkok, where professional hit men have orders to stop him. From the world of thinner addicts, dope dealers, fortunetellers, and high-class call girls, Calvino peels away the mystery surrounding the death of the English ex-public schoolboy who had a lot of dubious friends.

"Well-written, tough and bloody."
—Bernard Knight, *Tangled Web* (UK)

"A thinking man's Philip Marlowe, Calvino is a cynic on the surface but a romantic at heart. Calvino ... found himself in Bangkok—the end of the world—for a whole host of bizarre foreigners unwilling, unable, or uninterested in going home."—*The Daily Yomiuri*

"Good, that there are still real crime writers. Christopher G. Moore's [*Spirit House*] is colorful and crafty."
—*Hessischer Rundfunk* (Germany)

ASIA HAND
Second in the series
Heaven Lake Press (2000) ISBN 974-87171-2-7
Winner of 2011 Shamus Award
for Best Original Paperback

Bangkok—the Year of the Monkey. Calvino's Chinese New Year celebration is interrupted by a call to Lumpini Park Lake, where Thai cops have just fished the body of a *farang* cameraman. CNN is running dramatic footage of several Burmese soldiers on the Thai border executing students.

Calvino follows the trail of the dead man to a feature film crew where he hits the wall of silence. On the other side of that wall, Calvino and Colonel Pratt discover and elite film unit of old Asia Hands with connections to influential people in Southeast Asia. They find themselves matched against a set of *farangs* conditioned for urban survival and willing to go for a knock-out punch.

"Highly recommended to readers of hard-boiled detective fiction"—*Booklist*

"Asia Hand is the kind of novel that grabs you and never lets go."—*The Times of India*

"Moore's stylish second Bangkok thriller … explores the dark side of both Bangkok and the human heart. Felicitous prose speeds the action along."—*Publishers Weekly*

"Fast moving and hypnotic, this was a great read."
—*Crime Spree Magazine*

ZERO HOUR IN PHNOM PENH
Third in the series
Heaven Lake Press (2005) ISBN 974-93035-9-8
**Winner of 2004 German Critics Award for
Crime Fiction (Deutscher Krimi Preis) for best
international crime fiction and 2007 Premier Special
Director's Award Semana Negra (Spain)**

In the early 1990s, at the end of the devastating civil war
UN peacekeeping forces try to keep the lid on the violence.
Gunfire can still be heard nightly in Phnom Penh, where
Vietnamese prostitutes try to hook UN peacekeepers from
the balcony of the Lido Bar.

Calvino traces leads on a missing *farang* from Bangkok to
war-torn Cambodia, through the Russian market, hospitals,
nightclubs, news briefings, and UNTAC headquarters.
Calvino's buddy, Colonel Pratt, knows something that
Calvino does not: the missing man is connected with the
jewels stolen from the Saudi royal family. Calvino quickly
finds out that he is not the only one looking for the missing
farang.

"Political, courageous and perhaps Moore's most important
work."—*CrimiCouch.de*

"An excellent whodunnit hardboiled, a black novel with a
solitary, disillusioned but tempting detective, an interesting
historical and social context (Kampuchea of after Pol Pot),
and a very thorough psychology of the characters."
—*La culture se partage*

"A bursting, high adventure ... Extremely gripping ... A
morality portrait with no illusion."
—Ulrich Noller, *Westdeutscher Rundfunk*

COMFORT ZONE
Fourth in the series
Heaven Lake Press (2001) ISBN 974-87754-9-6

Twenty years after the end of the Vietnam War, Vietnam is opening to the outside world. There is a smell of fast money in the air and poverty in the streets. Business is booming and in austere Ho Chi Minh City a new generation of foreigners have arrived to make money and not war. Against the backdrop of Vietnam's economic miracle, *Comfort Zone* reveals a taut, compelling story of a divided people still not reconciled with their past and unsure of their future.

Calvino is hired by an ex-special forces veteran, whose younger brother uncovers corruption and fraud in the emerging business world in which his clients are dealing. But before Calvino even leaves Bangkok, there have already been two murders, one in Saigon and one in Bangkok.

"Calvino digs, discovering layers of intrigue. He's stalked by hired killers and falls in love with a Hanoi girl. Can he trust her? The reader is hooked."
—*NTUC Lifestyle* (Singapore)

"Moore hits home with more of everything in *Comfort Zone*. There is a balanced mix of story-line, narrative, wisdom, knowledge as well as love, sex, and murder."
—*Thailand Times*

"Like a Japanese gardener who captures the land and the sky and recreates it in the backyard, Moore's genius is in portraying the Southeast Asian heartscape behind the tourist industry hotel gloss."—*The Daily Yomiuri*

THE BIG WEIRD
Fifth in the series
Heaven Lake Press (2008) ISBN 978-974-8418-42-1

A beautiful American blond is found dead with a large bullet hole in her head in the house of her ex-boyfriend. A famous Hollywood screenwriter hires Calvino to investigate her death. Everyone except Calvino's client believes Samantha McNeal has committed suicide.

In the early days of the Internet, Sam ran with a young and wild expat crowd in Bangkok: a Net-savvy pornographer, a Thai hooker plotting to hit it big in cyberspace, an angry feminist with an agenda, a starving writer-cum-scam artist, a Hollywoord legend with a severe case of The Sickness. As Calvino slides into a world where people are dead serious about sex, money and fame, he unearths a hedonistic community where the ritual of death is the ultimate high.

"An excellent read, charming, amusing, insightful, complex, localized yet startlingly universal in its themes."
—*Guide of Bangkok*

"Highly entertaining."—*Bangkok Post*

"A good read, fast-paced and laced with so many of the locales so familiar to the expat denizens of Bangkok."
—*Art of Living* (Thailand)

"Like a noisy, late-night Thai restaurant, Moore serves up tongue-burning spices that swallow up the literature of Generation X and cyberpsace as if they were merely sticky rice."—*The Daily Yomiuri*

COLD HIT
Sixth in the series
Heaven Lake Press (2004) ISBN 974-920104-1-7

Five foreigners have died in Bangkok. Were they drug overdose victims or victims of a serial killer? Calvino believes the evidence points to a serial killer who stalks tourists in Bangkok. The Thai police, including Calvino's best friend and buddy Colonel Pratt, don't buy his theory.

Calvino teams up with an LAPD officer on a bodyguard assignment. Hidden forces pull them through swank shopping malls, rundown hotels, Klong Toey slum, and the Bangkok bars as they try to keep their man and themselves alive. As Calvino learns more about the bodies being shipped back to America, the secret of the serial killer is revealed.

"The story is plausible and riveting to the end."
—*The Japan Times*

"Tight, intricate plotting, wickedly astute ... *Cold Hit* will have you variously gasping, chuckling, nodding, tut-tutting, ohyesing, and grinding your teeth throughout its 330 pages."—*Guide of Bangkok*

"The plot is equally tricky, brilliantly devised, and clear. One of the best crime fiction in the first half of the year."
—*Ultimo Biedlefeld* (Germany)

"Moore depicts the city from below. He shows its dirt, its inner conflicts, its cruelty, its devotion. Hard, cruel, comical and good."—*Readme.de*

MINOR WIFE
Seventh in the series
Heaven Lake Press (2004) ISBN 974-92126-5-7

A contemporary murder set in Bangkok—a neighbor and friend, a young ex-hooker turned artist, is found dead by an American millionaire's minor wife. Her rich expat husband hires Calvino to investigate. While searching for the killer in exclusive clubs and not-so-exclusive bars of Bangkok, Calvino discovers that a minor wife—*mia noi*—has everything to do with a woman's status. From illegal cock fighting matches to elite Bangkok golf clubs, Calvino finds himself caught in the crossfire as he closes in on the murderer.

"The thriller moves in those convoluted circles within which Thai life and society takes place. Moore's knowledge of these gives insights into many aspects of the cultural mores ... unknown to the expat population. Great writing, great story and a great read."—*Pattaya Mail*

"What distinguishes Christopher G. Moore from other foreign authors setting their stories in the Land of Smiles is how much more he understands its mystique, the psyche of its populace and the futility of its round residents trying to fit into its square holes."—*Bangkok Post*

"Moore pursues in even greater detail in *Minor Wife* the changing social roles of Thai women (changing, but not always quickly or for the better) and their relations among themselves and across class lines and other barriers."
—*Vancouver Sun*

PATTAYA 24/7
Eighth in the series
Heaven Lake Press (2008) ISBN 978-974-8418-41-4

Inside a secluded, lush estate located on the edge of Pattaya, an eccentric Englishman's gardener is found hanged. Calvino has been hired to investigate. He finds himself pulled deep into the shadows of the war against drugs, into the empire of a local warlord with the trail leading to a terrorist who has caused Code Orange alerts to flash across the screen of American intelligence.

In a story packed with twists and turns, Calvino traces the links from the gardener's past to the door of men with power and influence who have everything to lose if the mystery of the gardener's death is solved.

"Original, provocative, and rich with details and insights into the underworld of Thai police, provincial gangsters, hit squads, and terrorists."
—Pieke Bierman, award-wining author of *Violetta*

"Intelligent and articulate, Moore offers a rich, passionate and original take on the private-eye game, fans of the genre should definitely investigate, and fans of foreign intrigue will definitely enjoy."—Kevin Burton Smith, *January Magazine*

"A cast of memorably eccentric figures in an exotic Southeast Asian backdrop."—*The Japan Times*

"The best in the Calvino series ... The story is compelling."
—*Bangkok Post*

THE RISK OF INFIDELITY INDEX
Ninth in the series
Heaven Lake Press (2007) ISBN 974-88168-7-6

Major political demonstrations are rocking Bangkok. Chaos and fear sweep through the Thai and expatriate communities. Calvino steps into the political firestorm as he investigates a drug piracy operation. The piracy is traced to a powerful business interest protected by important political connections.

A nineteen-year-old Thai woman and a middle-age lawyer end up dead on the same evening. Both are connected to Calvino's investigation. The dead lawyer's law firm denies any knowledge of the case. Calvino is left in the cold. Approached by a group of expat housewives—rattled by *The Risk of Infidelity Index* that ranks Bangkok number one for available sexual temptations—to investigate their husbands, Calvino discovers the alliance of forces blocking his effort to disclose the secret pirate drug investigation.

"A hard-boiled, street-smart, often hilarious pursuit of a double murderer."—*San Francisco Chronicle*

"There's plenty of violent action ... Memorable low-life characters ...The real star of the book is Bangkok."
—*Telegraph* (London)

"Taut, spooky, intelligent, and beautifully written."
—T. Jefferson Parker

"A complex, intelligent novel."—*Publishers' Weekly*

"The darkly raffish Bangkok milieu is a treat."
—*Kirkus Review*

PAYING BACK JACK
Tenth in the series
Heaven Lake Press (2009) ISBN 978-974-312-920-9

In *Paying Back Jack*, Calvino agrees to follow the 'minor wife' of a Thai politician and report on her movements. His client is Rick Casey, a shady American whose life has been darkened by the unsolved murder of his idealistic son. It seems to be a simple surveillance job, but soon Calvino is entangled in a dangerous web of political allegiance and a reckless quest for revenge.

And, unknown to our man in Bangkok, in an anonymous tower in the center of the city, a two-man sniper team awaits its shot, a shot that will change everything. *Paying Back Jack* is classic Christopher G. Moore: densely-woven, eye-opening, and riveting.

"Crisp, atmospheric ... Calvino's cynical humour oils the wheels nicely, while the cubist plotting keeps us guessing."
—*The Guardian*

"The best Calvino yet ... There are many wheels within wheels turning in this excellent thriller."
—*The Globe and Mail*

"[*Paying Back Jack*] might be Moore's finest novel yet. A gripping tale of human trafficking, mercenaries, missing interrogation videos, international conspiracies, and revenge, all set against the lovely and sordid backstreets of Bangkok that Moore knows better than anyone."
—Barry Eisler, author of *Fault Line*

"Moore clearly has no fear that his gloriously corrupt Bangkok will ever run dry."—*Kirkus Review*

THE CORRUPTIONIST
Eleventh in the series
Heaven Lake Press (2010) ISBN 978-616-90393-3-4

Set during the recent turbulent times in Thailand, the 11th novel in the Calvino series centers around the street demonstrations and occupations of Government House in Bangkok. Hired by an American businessman, Calvino finds himself caught in the middle of a family conflict over a Chinese corporate takeover. This is no ordinary deal. Calvino and his client are up against powerful forces set to seize much more than a family business.

As the bodies accumulate while he navigates Thailand's business-political landmines, Calvino becomes increasingly entangled in a secret deal made by men who will stop at nothing—and no one—standing in their way but Calvino refuses to step aside. *The Corruptionist* captures with precision the undercurrents enveloping Bangkok, revealing multiple layers of betrayal and deception.

"Politics has a role in the series, more so now than earlier ... Thought-provoking columnists don't do it better."
—*Bangkok Post*

"Moore's understanding of the dynamics of Thai society has always impressed, but considering current events, the timing of his latest [*The Corruptionist*] is absolutely amazing."
—*The Japan Times*

"Entertaining and devilishly informative."
—Tom Plate, *Pacific Perspective*

"Very believable ... A brave book."—*Pattaya Mail*

9 GOLD BULLETS
Twelfth in the series
Heaven Lake Press (2011) ISBN 978-616-90393-7-2

A priceless collection of 9 gold bullet coins issued during the Reign of Rama V has gone missing along with a Thai coin collector. Local police find a link between the missing Thai coins and Calvino's childhood friend, Josh Stein, who happens to be in Bangkok on an errand for his new Russian client. This old friend and his personal and business entanglements with the Russian underworld take Calvino back to New York, along with Pratt.

The gritty, dark vision of *9 Gold Bullets* is tracked through the eyes of a Thai cop operating on a foreign turf, and a private eye expatriated long enough to find himself a stranger in his hometown. As the intrigue behind the missing coins moves between New York and Bangkok, and the levels of deception increase, Calvino discovers the true nature of friendship and where he belongs.

"Moore consistently manages to entertain without having to resort to melodramatics. The most compelling feature of his ongoing Calvino saga, in my view, is the symbiotic relationship between the American protagonist and his Thai friends, who have evolved with the series. The friendships are sometimes strained along cultural stress lines, but they endure, and the Thai characters' supporting roles are very effective in helping keep the narratives interesting and plausible."—*The Japan Times*

"Moore is a master at leading the reader on to what 'should' be the finale, but then you find it isn't...Worth waiting for... However, do not start reading until you have a few hours to spare."—*Pattaya Mail*

Ralf Tooten © 2012

Christopher G. Moore is a Canadian novelist and essayist who lives in Bangkok. He has written 24 novels, including the award-winning Vincent Calvino series and the Land of Smiles Trilogy. The German edition of his third Vincent Calvino novel, *Zero Hour in Phnom Penh*, won the German Critics Award (Deutsche Krimi Preis) for International Crime Fiction in 2004 and the Spanish edition of the same novel won the Premier Special Director's Book Award Semana Negra (Spain) in 2007. The second Calvino novel, *Asia Hand,* won the Shamus Award for Best Original Paperback in 2011.